This Year,
Next Year

This Year, Next Year

Jeanne Whitmee

PIATKUS

First published in Great Britain in 1995 by
Judy Piatkus (Publishers) Ltd of
5 Windmill Street, London W1

**The moral right of the author
has been asserted**

*A catalogue record for this book is available
from the British Library*

ISBN 0–7499–0275–2

Set in 11/12pt Times by
Datix International Limited, Bungay, Suffolk
Printed and bound in Great Britain by
Mackays of Chatham PLC, Chatham, Kent

Part One

Chapter One

Amy knew that the nightmare was about to begin but there was nothing she could do about it. She tried hard to wake up, but it was as if she were frozen – sucked down into a vortex of fear, destined to re-live the terror once again.

She and Mark were walking out onto the pavement when the car stopped a few yards down the road. Before she had time to recognise its occupant it suddenly began to reverse at speed. Alarmed, she snatched Mark up into her arms and jumped back against the hedge to avoid the back wheels as they mounted the pavement.

It was then that she saw him.

Leaving the engine running, Alex leapt from the car and grabbed the child from her arms, pushing him into the back of the car. Then he grasped her roughly by the collar of her coat and bundled her unceremoniously into the front passenger seat. A moment later, they were roaring down the street at speed.

Rigid with terror, Amy hardly dared to look as they careered into the main road without stopping, narrowly avoiding a passing car and tipping a cyclist on to the pavement.

'Alex, for God's sake be careful! What's the matter with you?' Gritting her teeth, she held tightly to the sides of her seat as the car wove perilously in and out of the traffic. 'Why are you here? What's wrong?'

'*What's wrong?*' he mimicked. 'You might well ask.'

She glanced at him, alarmed by his grey-green pallor. There were beads of sweat on his forehead and his lips were drawn back from his teeth in a menacing travesty of a smile. Alone in the back seat, baby Mark was being thrown about like a shuttlecock by Alex's erratic driving. He was wailing loudly with fear and crying out for her. Turning in her seat, Amy tried to comfort him.

'It's all right darling. We'll soon be home.' But the child's wails drowned her soothing. She turned again to Alex. 'Please stop. You've been drinking. You don't know what you're doing . . .'

'I know what I'm doing all right.' He threw her a look of pure hatred, so ferocious that it made her recoil. 'Of course I've been drinking, you bitch – driven to it by you. Why didn't you tell me you'd taken a job? Half the bloody country knew before I did. That must have given you the best laugh of all.'

She bit her lip. So that was it. 'I'm sorry, Alex. I should have told you. I meant to. It was just that . . .'

'That you knew I'd put a stop to it, right?' He turned to glare at her with bloodshot eyes. 'Well, if you want to make a fool of yourself, do it. I don't give a damn any more. You're a selfish little cow and always were. But I won't have you farming my son out to some idiot stranger. I told you what would happen if you ever did that again, and by God I mean to see that it does.'

Panic quickened her already racing heartbeat as she remembered his threats. In this mood he was capable of anything. 'Alex, *don't.* It's not like you think. You can't imagine how lonely I've been – how frustrated, alone in the house with you away all the time. It's wonderful to be working again. And it's not doing Mark any harm . . . *Oh!*' She gasped as he swung the car across the road directly in the path of an oncoming lorry. Its brakes screeched and the driver leaned out of his cab to hurl abuse at Alex. There was a thud, followed by a scream as Mark fell off the back seat onto the floor.

'Alex! For God's sake. You've hurt Mark now.'

But the child's cries only served to anger him more. As the car lurched forward again he rounded on her furiously.

'*I've* hurt him? That's rich. It's *you* who've hurt him. If he's crying it's because of what you've done to him – to Chloe's child. He's all I have left of her, but do you care? Dumping him like a parcel of rubbish anywhere that suits you. You've done it on purpose, haven't you? To get back at me – at us – at me and Chloe. But you shan't have our child. *We won't let you!* Do you hear?'

Cold with terror, Amy stared at him. What was he talking about? His eyes were wild, the pupils dilated. He was completely out of control; living in some fantasy nightmare of his own making in which she was the enemy. How could she reason with him in this state?

They were speeding through the tree-lined streets of the estate now. Children were playing outside after school. A ball rolled into the road in front of them and a little girl ran out from between parked cars to retrieve it. Amy screamed, clenching her fists and closing her eyes as she waited for what seemed inevitable. But the child jumped back in time and the accident was miraculously avoided. Next time – oh God, next time they wouldn't be as lucky.

She turned and pleaded with him, her voice trembling. 'Please, oh *please*, Alex. You must stop and listen to me. We can talk this out quietly at home. I can make you see if only you'll calm down. Please – please stop before you kill someone. If not for me, then for Mark. He's hurt. Can't you hear him?'

They had turned into Willow Drive now and suddenly he stood on the brakes. The tyres shrieked and the car shuddered to a halt, throwing Amy forward so violently that her forehead met the windscreen with a dizzying thud.

'Get out,' he snapped. 'Go on, get out – *now*, before I throw you out.'

Her head still spinning with pain, she opened the door and got out of the car on trembling legs, almost weeping with relief. Thank God he'd listened to reason at last. She reached for the handle of the rear door to get Mark, but before she could open it Alex had slammed the car into gear and revved the engine. With a screech and a grinding of gears the car leapt forward, gathering speed as it roared down the road.

In a blind panic she ran after it, her arms outstretched, oblivious of the blood trickling down her face from the cut on her forehead. In vain she screamed for him to stop. She could see Mark standing on the back seat looking out of the rear window as the car sped away. His little face contorted with terror, he held out his arms to her as the distance between them lengthened. Then the car rounded the corner and disappeared from view.

Amy staggered to a stop. Her legs gave way beneath her and she sank to her knees in the road, tears streaming down her cheeks.

'Mark – Mark, my baby! Oh God – *God* what shall I do?'

Shocked neighbours who had witnessed the harrowing scene from their windows were running out to help, but it was Addie Shaw who was first at her side, enfolding her in motherly arms and murmuring soothing words.

'There, there, luvvie, it'll be all right, you'll see. You come home with me. Jack's already rung the police. They'll catch him, never fear. I'm here now.'

Amy surfaced, dragging herself up from the depths only to find that Addie had turned into her mother. She closed her eyes, then opened them again. She was still there – watching – waiting. *Mum* . . . after all this time.

Chapter Two

It was in 1906 that fourteen-year-old Sam Leigh went to work for Jacob Feldman at his clothing factory in Ox Lane, Hackney. The job had been secured for him at the orphanage where he had grown up. He was hired to run errands and to make himself generally useful until he was older and strong enough to get himself a labouring job. But Jacob's shrewd eyes picked up the boy's potential almost immediately. Slightly built and small for his age, Sam was bright and quick to learn. He was willing and eager to please, too, and seemed to blossom under his employer's attentive eye. Until now he had been a mere face in a crowd. A number with a body attached. A child of no importance. Being noticed and called by his name was a new and heady experience to Sam and he responded to it encouragingly.

The more Jacob saw of the boy the more he liked him. His wife Esther had died giving birth to his only child, a daughter, Rachel, who was the apple of his eye. With the help of a daily woman, nineteen-year-old Rachel had kept house for him since leaving school and, being blessed with a gift for figures, had lately taken over the book-keeping side of the business; something which was a great source of pride to Jacob. She also visited the outworkers once a week to pay them.

Young Sam learned quickly and when he had been with Feldman's Clothing for a year Jacob decided that the boy should become an apprentice. He would teach him all he knew about the clothing trade, just as he himself had learned from his father, and perhaps with luck, by the time he was ready to retire, Sam would be able to manage the business for him.

He decided that he must first remove the boy from the spartan lodgings found for him by the orphanage and take him into his own household. But before doing so, Jacob tried to discover something about his protégé's origins. His enquiries at the orphanage were met with indifference. All that anyone knew about him was that he had been abandoned as a newly born infant on the steps of the workhouse, apparently by some servant girl who had given birth to her illegitimate child in secret, but as time went by Jacob became more and more convinced that the boy had Jewish blood. His dark good looks and his aptitude for business certainly pointed in that direction.

Gradually Sam's pinched, waif-like little face filled out and his body developed bone and muscle. By the time three years had passed and he had reached the age of seventeen he had grown into a tall, handsome young man. His dark hair curled glossily and his brown eyes shone with health and a zest for learning. Jacob felt blessed, happy that his judgement of the boy had proved well-founded. He felt sure that the good Lord had sent him Sam as a substitute for the son he had never had. It was up to him to bring out the boy's full potential.

When he approached Sam on the subject of religion he found him willing and as eager to embrace the Jewish faith as he had been to learn the business. Since living with Jacob and Rachel he had already become accustomed to their food and customs. Why not join them in their acts of worship too?

After approaching the Jewish religious authorities, the Beth Din, Jacob himself undertook Sam's instruction and found him a delight to teach. Once he had been taught something he never forgot it, and to Jacob's delight Sam was finally judged ready to be accepted into Judaism by the Jewish rabbis – the dayanim.

Rachel watched her father's preoccupation with Sam with mixed feelings. All her life she had been first in her father's affections, though she recognised that like all fathers he had always wanted a son. She liked Sam. Who could fail to like the cheerful, good-natured young man who had come into their lives? As he grew to manhood she was far from impervious to his physical attractiveness, too. Although he was five years her junior, he was already as mature as she was, and he was as keen and dedicated to the business as she and her father. On her visits to the factory she had seen him at work. Already he was an expert cutter; the maintenance of the machines gave him no problems at all, so that Jacob had been able to dispense with the services of the repair man. The female machinists loved Sam with his ready wit and cheerful manner. He encouraged them to sing as they worked, leading them with his pleasant baritone voice in all the current popular songs, so that the workshop rang with the sound of singing mingled with the whirr of machinery. With his charm he could twist them around his little finger, effortlessly getting twice the work out of them. A delighted Jacob had already made him workshop foreman.

As Rachel watched and saw how things were progressing, it became clear to her that to fall in with her father's plans and to re-establish her prior entitlement to her father's affection there was only one thing for it. She must marry Sam Leigh and give her father a grandson.

When she went to Jacob and shyly confessed her wish he was overjoyed. He was also relieved. Rachel was twenty-four. Most Jewish girls were married long before this. If her mother had been alive she would have seen to it that her daughter met the right young men. She would have entertained friends with sons of a suitable age, sifting through them until the right one was selected. Jacob had neither the time nor the necessary social skill for this. His life had been dedicated to his business, his home and his child. There had been no time in his busy working schedule for socialising except, of course, at the synagogue. Also, if he were to put aside his natural paternal prejudice he would have been obliged to admit that Rachel was not the prettiest of girls. True she had inherited her mother's fine dark eyes and abundant hair, but working long hours over the ledgers had made her short-sighted, which necessitated the wearing of ugly wire-rimmed spectacles. For the same reason, she had also developed a slight stoop, and truth to tell she was inclined to be a little on the heavy side for current tastes. If her mother were alive she would doubtless have known how to alleviate these problems, Jacob told himself, stroking his beard wistfully. Though he had never yet met a man who had complained of a good build in a wife. Broad child-bearing hips were surely a definite advantage. And she could cook like an angel. Her honey cakes melted in the mouth. Jacob smiled, nodding to himself. Yes, Sam was particularly partial to them, as he was to her other culinary accomplishments.

He broached the subject with Sam one evening as they walked home from the factory together.

'Tell me, Samuel, what do you think of Rachel?'

The young man looked surprised. 'Rachel? I like her, of course. She's a very clever young woman and a good cook.'

Jacob cleared his throat. 'Ah, but – have you ever thought of her in an – er – affectionate way at all?'

Sam considered. 'Since I have lived with you she has been like a sister. She has been very good to me.'

Jacob frowned. Was the boy really so naive or was he deliberately misunderstanding him? He decided to take the bull by the horns. 'I'm asking if you have ever thought that she might make you a suitable wife, Samuel,' he said. 'After all, you'll be needing to marry soon, won't you? A man is not complete without a wife.' He spread his hands. 'And there is my Rachel – needing a husband. What could be better – for either of you?'

Sam's cheeks coloured scarlet. It was totally unexpected. He'd never seen Rachel as anything but Jacob's daughter. Never actually *looked* at her properly. And certainly never thought of her as a potential wife. That Jacob was actually offering his beloved only daughter to him was the most tremendous compliment; he recognised that, and yet ... He tried to speak, but his voice seemed to have deserted him. He slipped a finger inside his collar to loosen it. Jacob smiled indulgently and shook his head.

'Ah, I see I have overwhelmed you. No need to answer now,' he said. 'Just think about it. I can tell you in confidence though that Rachel is very fond of you. And if you were to approach her I know she would not rebuff you. Ask her out to the theatre, why don't you? Buy her a little gift – some flowers or sweetmeats to show her that you admire her. You have my permission – and my blessing,' he added hopefully.

Alone in his room later, Sam weighed the situation and found it heavily loaded on the side of marriage. He was already one of the Feldman family in all but name. He liked his job and the comfortable life he had with the Feldmans. Already he had embraced their religion as his own. He felt happy and established with it, so why not complete the conversion? At the back of his mind the possibility that Feldman's might one day pass into his hands occurred to him fleetingly. But he thrust the thought aside, dismissing it as mercenary and unworthy. He had been so lucky. Jacob Feldman had been like a father to him and he liked and respected Rachel. They were the only family he had ever known, so why not repay them in this way if it was what they both wanted?

On Jacob's advice he invited Rachel to go to the theatre with him. He chose the music hall. Over the past few years it had become more respectable. It had even been rumoured that this year's Royal Command Performance was to include some music hall acts. But Sam had a particular reason for taking his prospective bride there. He wanted to see if she could actually laugh. In all his years in the Feldman household he had seldom seen her smile and had certainly never seen her rather serious face relax into a full-blown laugh. He wasn't at all sure that he could commit himself for life to a woman who never laughed.

They went to the Hackney Empire where Marie Lloyd was on the bill. Sam could see right away that Rachel thought Marie's saucy

7

songs and suggestive manner vulgar, and he was just beginning to feel he'd made a mistake in bringing her when the comedian came on; a little man with a white face and outsized boots in which he performed a fantastic dance. Halfway through the little man's act Sam heard a strange spluttering noise from the seat beside him. He turned to see that Rachel's face was contorted and that she was holding her handkerchief to her mouth. Full of concern, he laid a hand on her arm and asked if she was all right. Lowering the handkerchief, Rachel turned to him, her dark eyes swimming with tears.

'Oh, Sam,' she spluttered. It was only then that he realised that she was not ill but actually convulsed with laughter. 'Oh, *Sam*, I don't know when I've enjoyed myself so much.'

It was a swift courtship. Rachel had already known that she intended to marry Sam, but once they began to spend time in each other's company and she discovered what a fascinating companion he was, she was even more determined to become his wife. To her surprise she found that with Sam she felt relaxed as never before. He brought her a kind of happiness she had never experienced. He made her laugh. With his quick, light-hearted wit he made her see things in a totally different light, so that suddenly people and life were fun. And the first time he kissed her the sudden and explosive revelation that she had actually fallen in love struck her like a bolt from the blue.

Jacob was ecstatic. He had never seen his daughter look so happy. Sam had achieved wonders; he had transformed Rachel from a plain girl into a radiant woman. Her eyes shone (she now wore the ugly spectacles only when she was working), her hair gleamed and she began to take more interest in her appearance. She bought new clothes and held herself in a new, upright, proud way that actually made her look slimmer.

They were married in November 1911, just before the festival of Chanukah, which Jacob felt was most appropriate. God had sent a miracle into his life and he gave thanks for it every day.

The wedding was a quiet affair. Jacob had only one sister, Naomi, who had emigrated to America back in the nineties. When he knew that Rachel was to be married he had written to Naomi, inviting her and her husband Aaron to the wedding. Naomi had replied, saying that they could not afford to make such an expensive journey, but that she longed to see her brother again and if Jacob could pay his passage he would be more than welcome to come to New York and stay with them for a holiday.

At first he dismissed the idea as out of the question. The business was doing well and he could easily afford to go. But in all his years in London he had never taken so much as a day off. Rachel tried to persuade him to accept her Aunt Naomi's offer.

'You've never even taken a day off for illness, Father. You deserve a holiday. Sam and I can easily manage the factory.'

Sam too did his best to persuade his father-in-law to take the trip. Secretly he looked forward to having his new wife the house and the factory to himself for a few weeks. He was eager to prove both to Jacob and to himself that he was competent and to establish himself properly as Rachel's husband. Although Rachel was now married, Jacob could not quite relinquish his hold on his daughter. He still seemed to feel that he and he alone knew what was best for her. It was for this reason that neither of them had told him that Rachel was almost certainly pregnant. If he knew there was a baby on the way nothing on earth would persuade him to leave the country.

At last, between them Sam and Rachel managed to convince Jacob that a trip to America to see his only sister was an opportunity not to be missed. And, once the idea had established itself in his mind, he became quite excited at the prospect and began to look forward to it, making plans to look at new fabrics and machines while he was in America. Because as well as enjoying his stay he meant to make it work for him.

It was on a dull grey February afternoon that he came home in a state of high excitement to tell his daughter and son-in-law that his passage was booked. Taking out his wallet he waved the steamship ticket at them.

'I sail from Southampton on April the tenth. And it's to be on a brand-new ship too,' he told them proudly. 'The one we've been reading about in all the newspapers. It will be her maiden voyage. They say she's a miracle of engineering – impossible to sink. Can you imagine?'

As the boat train pulled out of the harbour, Rachel stifled a sob and Sam put a protective arm around her.

'Don't cry, sweetheart. Your father deserves a good holiday. He's really looking forward to it, and think what a joyful reunion he and your aunt will have. He tells me it's over twenty years since they last set eyes on each other.'

But Rachel was sobbing on his shoulder. 'But it's such a long way, Sam. He's never been away from me before.'

'But you have *me* now, darling,' he reminded her, slightly hurt. 'Please don't upset yourself. You'll harm the child.'

Rachel took a deep breath and put away her handkerchief. 'We

9

should have told him, Sam,' she said. 'If anything were to happen . . .'

He laughed and tipped up her chin with his finger. '*Happen*? My silly girl, what can possibly happen? He couldn't be sailing on a more up-to-date vessel. And think of the lovely surprise we'll have for him when he comes home. Can you imagine his face?'

Rachel smiled, imagining the joy on her father's dear face when they told him he was to be a grandfather. The thought cheered her.

But little did Rachel know that she had said a final goodbye to her father, or that he would never know the joy of holding his grandson in his arms. It was just five days later that he succumbed along with fifteen hundred other passengers when the SS *Titanic* sank in the icy waters of the North Atlantic.

On 20 November 1912 Rachel gave birth to a baby son. It was a painful and protracted birth. The highly qualified midwife Sam had engaged finally admitted after Rachel had suffered three days of agonising pain that she could not deliver the child without the help of a doctor and Jacob's old friend Doctor Epstein was sent for. Thanks to his skilful ministrations the child was safely delivered, but Rachel was severely weakened by her ordeal. The months of grieving for her father and the complicated birth had taken all her strength. Her life hung in the balance for several worrying days and the doctor informed Sam gravely that Rachel would bear no more children.

At first she seemed to have lost the will to live. Even Sam, who sat tirelessly at her bedside, urging her to get better, failed to rally her. But eventually the sound of her child's pitiful cries and the thought of leaving him motherless seemed to give her the necessary strength to revive and she began, slowly, to pull round.

The little boy was named Marcus Jacob in memory of his grandfather. But even after a month had gone by and the time arrived for the boy's redemption ceremony, Rachel was still too weak and ill to leave the house.

When the elderly daily woman who had served the Feldmans since Rachel was a baby announced her retirement, Sam engaged the services of a younger woman to help her in the house. Sarah Brown was a young married woman, one of Feldman's outworkers, whom Rachel had known for some time. Until recently she had been obliged to work at home, bound to the house in nearby Crimea Terrace by her invalid mother-in-law. But now that the old woman had died Sarah was looking for a better paid job. Although she was not Jewish, Sarah was a clean woman of good character who was used to caring for invalids. Rachel had always liked her and Sam felt it would be good for her to have a woman of her own age at hand, someone to talk to as well as to help her during his long hours of absence; for now that Jacob had gone Feldman's was Sam's responsibility alone and he was busy at the factory and in the office all day and often late into the evening.

Jacob had left his entire estate – the business, factory and house – intact to his daughter, Rachel. Sam had tried hard not to show his shock and disappointment when the will was read. His late father-in-law had indicated at the time of their marriage that on his demise the house was to go to Rachel, the business to him. Although of course as husband and wife they would naturally share everything, to have been left nothing in his own right, after all the years of hard work and loyalty, seemed hard and hurtful to Sam.

Rachel, sensing his hurt, had assured him that it was only Jacob's way of looking after her future – that it was only hers on paper, which meant nothing, because she could never manage any of it without his help.

Little by little Rachel grew stronger. Sarah Brown was a strong, competent worker and the two women became good friends. Sarah was good with Marcus, too. He was a beautiful child but strong-willed, like his mother. Sarah could always manage him, however. She seemed to have the knack and the patience that Rachel lacked. Truth to tell, as time went by and she regained her strength and energy, Rachel was bored. She missed her visits to the factory and outworkers, and the satisfaction she had always had from keeping the accounts and balancing the books. She saw so little of Sam, and when he was at home all his time seemed to be devoted to playing with his baby son. If she were to help him in the business, she told herself, he would have more time to spend with her.

By the time Marcus was a year old Rachel decided that she was sufficiently recovered to return to her duties and take an interest in the business once again. Sam was a good manager, but he was clearly struggling on his own. His talent lay in organisation and with managing the workforce. He lacked the business skills that Jacob had, and which Rachel herself had inherited. She decided that she could do much of the work at home, while Sarah took care of Marcus and the housework. But when she put the idea to Sam he was shocked.

'There is no need for you to work, my love. I am your husband, your provider. You are needed here, caring for our home and our son.'

'But I want to help just as I helped Father,' Rachel protested.

11

'Sarah can manage Marcus much better than I, and see to the housework, too. It is our business. Yours and mine.'

Sam frowned moodily. 'It's yours, you mean. You're saying that you can't trust me to manage it properly.'

'No, no, darling,' Rachel soothed him. 'You're better even than father was at getting the best out of the workers. Why not concentrate on that and let me take care of the books and the orders as I did before?' Sidling up to him she rubbed her cheek against his handsome, newly grown beard and slipped her arms around his waist. 'Please let me take my share of the work, sweetheart,' she wheedled. 'I want so much for us to share everything, and I can do most of the work right here at home while Marcus is little. And I shall still cook your meals. You can be sure I shall not neglect either of you.'

As always, Rachel got her way. She was determined to make her rightful contribution to the business again. She was good at it, and although she would die rather than remind Sam of the fact, it was hers. Why should she relinquish it just because she had become a mother?

On 30 June 1914 the newspapers were full of the assassination of the Archduke Ferdinand in Sarajevo. Soon it seemed that all Europe was inflamed and in turmoil. A month later it was reported that Germany had invaded Belgium in contravention of the Treaty of Neutrality, drawn up in 1839. Sam sat over the breakfast table shaking his head over his copy of the *Daily Chronicle*.

'It's beginning to look serious,' he said. 'The Kaiser is riding roughshod over poor Belgium. It says here that he dismisses the Treaty as a mere scrap of paper. I can't see Britain standing for it.'

Rachel put down her teacup. 'You don't mean we might go to war, surely?'

'It could come to it.'

'But what will that mean?'

Sam glanced up at her. 'It needn't worry you my dear. It's a long way off. It won't affect us much, I daresay. Imports and exports might be affected, though. There could be shortages if it lasts long.'

'And men killed.' Rachel shuddered. 'I hate the thought of it.'

'The general opinion seems to be that it'd be over in a few months. The idea is that the French will be able to contain it, but Kitchener doesn't agree.' He pointed to the paper. 'According to this article, he's planning to assemble an army of a hundred thousand volunteers. Can you imagine that?'

Rachel paused, her cup halfway to her lips. 'A hundred thousand

12

men?' she said thoughtfully, trying to visualise the number. 'A new army will need uniforms, Sam. Maybe it's something we should look into.'

By Christmas life for the Leighs and the Browns had changed drastically. When war was first declared, Sam, stirred by patriotism, had longed to volunteer.

'The whole of the Empire's in it now, my love,' he told Rachel, reading to her from the newspaper. 'Australia, New Zealand – even Africa. Look, it says here that Russian soldiers have landed on their way to France.'

But Rachel argued that there was valuable work for him to do at home. Thanks to her quick action and careful costing, Feldman's tender for making uniforms for Kitchener's new army had been accepted. In just a few months the Leighs' income had increased dramatically. Feldman's Clothing had moved to larger premises, acquired new machines and taken on more workers. With so many of the men going off to war there were plenty of women wanting work. Already, far-sighted Rachel was planning to make good use of their new equipment by going in for tailoring once the war was over. Off-the-peg suits, perhaps. And she had her eye on an elegant little Regency villa she had seen for sale on Hackney Road. There was a garden at the back in which little Marcus would be able to play – a place where washing could be hung out to dry in the fresh air instead of dripping from the rack in the dismal basement kitchen as it did now.

For the Browns, life was not so rosy. Sarah's husband Alf was one of the first to respond to Kitchener's jingoistic rallying call. Kissing Sarah, now pregnant with their first child, goodbye he marched off to France full of patriotic euphoria, to be killed within the first weeks, along with many others at the retreat from Mons. He was never to see his baby girl, Maryan, born the following January.

Rachel comforted Sarah as best she could, promising to give her whatever money she needed to pay the rent and keep a roof over their heads until she was fit to return to work. In private Rachel thanked the Lord that she had managed to persuade her own man to stay where he was and work for the country in other ways.

By the time the war ended Crimea Terrace was full of war widows, all struggling to bring up their families on pitifully inadequate incomes. They helped each other, sharing what little they had in good times and bad. While Maryan was a toddler, all Sarah could

13

manage by the way of paid work was the rough work and washing, which Miss Rachel allowed her to do whenever Sarah could get Cissie Jessop next door to look after the baby for her. A widow like Sarah, Cissie eked out a living for herself and her two young sons by assisting at confinements and layings-out. Soon Maryan began school, so that her mother could accept the job of housekeeper that Miss Rachel had offered her, with a substantially increased wage now that they had moved to the smart house in Hackney Road. With Maryan attending school full-time Sarah could put in longer hours. Eight-year-old Tom, Cissie's youngest, could be relied on to make sure she got home safely. He was a good boy, running errands for the neighbours for coppers and looking after the younger kids.

Sarah was deeply grateful to Miss Rachel for her help and compassion through the hard war years. She'd known her ever since they were both girls and Rachel had called weekly to pay her wages for the outwork she'd done. She'd been a good and generous friend to them when times were rough, passing on clothes she had done with, some of them hardly worn. Sarah often thought wistfully that if young Marcus could only have been a girl, Maryan would have been the best dressed kid in the street.

Nowadays Rachel often let Sarah take home the leftovers from the dinner parties she had started to give since Feldman's had become so prosperous. Rachel would never allow anyone else to use her kitchen, insisting on preparing everything herself, however busy she was. But Sarah loved to watch her employer cook, fascinated by the way she prepared her meat and the various taboos and rituals of her religion. Maryan would await her mother's homecoming eagerly, her blue eyes round with anticipation as she waited to see what succulent delicacy there would be for supper that night.

As the years passed life became easier. In spite of the slump, Feldman's Clothing – now renamed Feldman Fashions – flourished. As the twenties dawned Rachel shrewdly foresaw a new demand for cheap copies of couture fashions. The war had brought a lot of changes for women and more were working. Now that they had the vote they were a new breed, energetic and independent. Young working women had more money to spend on clothes and they would want to be wearing something fashionable but affordable. With this in mind, she took herself off to some of the shows given by top fashion houses and made sketches, later simplifying the latest in line and trends and adapting them for everyday wear. With her collection of sketches and made-up samples she approached the buyers at all the big West End department stores and came away with orders that rendered an admiring Sam speechless.

'My wife is a marvel,' he said throwing up his hands. 'A wonder already. What can I do to reward her?' He kissed her. 'What would you like, sweetheart? A ring – a bracelet?'

But practical Rachel shook her head. 'Take on a dozen more machinists,' she said. 'Let's just deliver on time. Give them good value for their money and maybe they'll order more from us.'

They did. And Feldman's went from strength to strength. Over the years that followed the business expanded again and Feldman Fashions grew to be a respected name in the trade.

Rachel refurnished the house and had electric light installed. She revolutionised the kitchen, organising the removal of the old cast-iron cooking range and replacing it with one of the newest gas stoves. She even bought an electric iron and a vacuum cleaner. Sarah viewed the changes with deep mistrust and suspicion. Every time she plugged in one of the appliances she feared electrocution, and the hissing, popping gas rings terrified her. But once she conquered her fear of the modern gadgets she was surprised and delighted by the time they saved and the way they lightened her workload.

Marcus was sent away to an expensive boarding school when he reached the age of eight. This saddened Sarah. He seemed so young to be going away from his home. Rachel too was sad. She confided to Sarah that Sam had insisted on the best education they could afford for the boy. It was a good investment, he said. And boarding school would teach him to stand on his own feet and make his own decisions.

When Maryan was ready to leave school Sarah asked Rachel if Sam would consider giving her a job. In Sarah's eyes the girl could do no better than work for the Leighs, whom she saw as her benefactors and providers. Ever since she could remember they had provided security for her. But when she told Maryan what she had arranged for her, the girl seemed less than grateful.

'I'm not sure that I want to be a machinist,' she said.

Sarah stared at her. 'Then what *do* you want to do, miss?'

'I don't know. Maybe work in a shop – or an office.'

'*Office?*' Sarah looked at her daughter contemptuously. 'What makes you think anyone'd give *you* a job in an office? You need to be able to typewrite and such. That means more schoolin', my gel. We ain't got the money for that kinda high-falutin' nonsense.'

'I could go to night school,' Maryan suggested.

Sarah shook her head. 'Ideas above your station is what you're gettin'. What good would you be for work, sitting in some stuffy classroom half the night?'

'But I want to better myself, Mum,' Maryan wailed. 'I don't want to stay in Crimea Terrace for the rest of my life.'

'Hard work is the only way for the likes of us to better ourselves,' Sarah said. 'Mr Sam is the livin' proof of that. Look at what he's done for 'imself.'

'He married the boss's daughter,' Maryan said under her breath. Mercifully her mother didn't hear the remark.

'That business has more'n doubled in size since old Mr Jacob died. Did I ever tell you that Mr Sam was a poor boy who started life with only the clothes he stood up in?' In actual fact Maryan had heard the story countless times. 'He's not proud neither,' Sarah went on. 'Not Mr Sam – told me that himself, he did. Proud of it. No, you stick with Feldman's, my girl, and you never know, you might end up as rich as what they are some day. In the meantime, we needs the extra money, so just you get yourself round there Monday morning, eight o'clock sharp, and don't let me 'ear no more about no office.'

Maryan had no choice but to accept what her mother said. The work at Feldman's was undemanding and she liked her workmates well enough. She'd grown up with most of them. But she knew instinctively that it would never lead to riches as it had for Mr Sam, whatever her mother said.

As she grew older and observed the lives of those around her, it angered her the way that everyone in Crimea Terrace accepted that they were destined to a life of poverty. They were born to it and would die with it. In between they would make what they could of life, living hand-to-mouth and struggling from one pay day to the next. Why should it be like this? she asked herself. Why should some have so much whilst others, like her and her mother, had next to nothing? She'd seen the inside of the Leighs' house when she occasionally went along to help her mother wash up after a dinner party. Thick, soft carpets and glittering crystal. Fine china and velvet curtains. The first time she saw it her eyes had almost popped out with the sheer luxury of it. She'd heard how her father, along with a good many others, had laid down his lives for his country. What good had it done them? Mr Sam, nice and kind though he was, had not laid down *his* life. Instead he had made a fortune out of making uniforms for men to get killed in. But when she dared to express these views, her mother was furious.

'Don't you ever dare let me hear you say such things again, you wicked girl. We owe everything to Feldman's. The Leighs have been

16

good to us. Many's the night you'd have gone to bed with an empty belly if it hadn't been for Miss Rachel and don't you ever forget it.'

But Maryan turned away sullenly. Her mother was like all the others in Crimea Terrace: content to feel inferior, to take handouts from those better off – people who could shut the door in their faces without a second thought if it suited them. Maryan wanted something better – independence; a better life; never having to grovel and be forever thankful. She often spoke to her friend Tom Jessop about it. He agreed with her, though he didn't see how they could make things any better.

'We don't get the chance to be educated like they do and what can we do without education?' he said. 'Look at that Marcus Leigh. He's eighteen, the same age as me. But is he out looking for work – standing in the dole queue? No, he's at some posh school or other. And when he's done there he'll probably go off to Cambridge University or some other posh college. He'll never know what it is to struggle, will he? He'll just step into his dad's business and start raking it in like they do.'

Maryan was silent. The last time she'd seen Marcus Leigh had been at his Bar Mitzvah celebration five years ago, when she'd gone to help her mother lay the tables and wash up after the celebration party. She'd been surprised on that day to see how tall and handsome he'd become. His hair was dark and curly like his father's and he had the most stunning brown eyes. Ten-year-old Maryan had been quite smitten. She and Sarah had listened to him making his speech from behind the kitchen door. His voice was already deep and strong and he'd looked much older than his thirteen years in his smart new suit. From her place behind the kitchen door Sarah had almost burst with pride in the boy she had known from birth and cared for as a baby.

'A proper young gent,' she'd remarked. 'A credit to his mum and dad, he is. No mistake.'

Reminded of the occasion, Maryan wondered briefly what he was like now.

She picked up the job easily. By the time she had been at Feldman's a year, Sam had declared her a fully fledged machinist and she was allowed to work on their best lines. Talking to older girls, some of whom had worked elsewhere, she realised that she was privileged to work at Feldman's. Some other clothing factories she'd heard of in the East End were nothing more than sweat shops where the owners worked their girls long, gruelling hours for pitifully low wages that were docked for the smallest discrepancy, and where illness meant arbitrary dismissal. The Leighs were fair and considerate employers. As long as you pulled your weight and didn't take advantage of their kindness you could rely on being treated properly; which was why many of their employees had remained loyal workers from leaving school until retirement. Yes, Maryan was happy enough at Feldman's – for the time being. But although she still didn't quite know how, she was determined to better herself someday. She was confident that her chance would come, somehow. And when it did she would seize it with both hands.

It was in July 1930 that Marcus left the school where he had spent the best part of his eighteen years. His parents had discussed his future long and hard. Rachel wanted him to go to university, but Marcus had had enough of full-time education. He wanted to come straight into the business.

Sam was proud of his only son. He felt he was a chip off the old block. The boy seemed to have been blessed with the best attributes of all three of them. He had his father's good looks, his mother's quick, creative brain and his grandfather's shrewdness and good nature. In Sam's opinion he was ideally suited to the business.

Rachel argued that he should go to commerce college. Sam said he could do no better than learn as he worked, just as Sam himself had done – from the bottom upwards.

'It won't harm the boy to know how it feels to be a shop floor worker,' he argued. 'That is how good employers are born.'

Rachel was scandalised. 'You'd have him sweeping *up* and running *errands*?' she squeaked. 'My son? After all that expensive education?'

'And why not?' Sam argued, stubborn for once. 'It was good enough for me.' For once he did not intend to let Rachel override him. 'He might have had a better education than I ever had, but he's still my son.' Finally they decided to compromise and put it to Marcus himself. Rachel was certain that her cultured son would be as appalled as she was, and she was speechless when the boy calmly agreed.

'If I'm to manage the business on my own one day I'll have to know how everything works, Mother,' he said reasonably. 'I think Dad's right.'

And so it was that on a sunny August morning in 1930, just a year and a half after she had begun work at Feldman's herself, Maryan found herself showing Marcus Leigh how to thread up a machine on his first morning at the factory.

Over six feet tall and broad-shouldered, Marcus towered over Maryan, yet he was almost humble in his eagerness to learn. It amused Sam to put his son in her charge. He chuckled to himself as he watched from the window of his office. The slightly built little blonde girl, taking it all so seriously, and his tall, grown-up son with his thick dark hair and laughing eyes. Two such extremes. He was so proud of the way Marcus mixed with the factory workers, acknowledging that in this, their trade, they knew all and he nothing. In spite of his matriculation certificate and his fine intellect he had the right attitude, and when the time came, he would make a fine businessman, Sam told himself with satisfaction.

But Rachel still had misgivings. It offended her to think of her son working in the factory. He would learn coarse language and rough ways. It irked her to think of the attention she had paid to bringing him up to be a gentleman only to have him spend his days with uneducated artisans. To try to make it up to him – and much against Sam's better judgement – she bought him a sports car for his birthday that year. When he came home from the factory with his father that grey November afternoon a shiny red MG Midget was standing at the kerbside outside the house.

'Go on, did they really buy you a car? A brand-new one, all to yourself?' Maryan gazed at Marcus with wide blue eyes. It was the last week that they'd be working together. Marcus was to move on to cutting the following week, working with Jim Harris, Sam's head cutter. He'd be sorry to move. He'd enjoyed working with the girls, his shirtsleeves rolled up, singing all the popular songs along with them as the machines whirred merrily. Maryan had taught him the words of 'Tiptoe Through the Tulips' and 'Stardust' and, much to the delight of all the girls, he'd even attempted harmonising with them in his pleasant baritone voice.

'Yes, they really have, though I don't think it was Dad's idea. I could tell he didn't approve.'

'Why not? You've worked hard. You deserve it,' Maryan said stoutly. Somehow she didn't resent Marcus's good fortune. He didn't lord it over them like some would have, and he was good fun. He'd make a good boss one day just as long as he didn't change.

'I'm going to miss you next week,' Marcus said.

Maryan laughed as she raised the foot of her machine and turned her material deftly. 'Go on with you.'

'No, really. For one thing, Jim isn't as pretty as you are. I won't be able to sing along with him either. Have you heard his voice? He sounds like a cat with its tail shut in the door. A tone deaf one at that.'

Maryan laughed and Marcus watched with pleasure as the dimple in her cheek twinkled and her blue eyes shone. It struck him

19

suddenly that she was a very pretty girl indeed. Before long someone would marry her and she'd turn into a drudge like the others he'd seen, down at heel as they pushed their second-hand prams in Hackney Market on Saturday nights, looking for bargains; harassed and worn out with poverty and childbearing before they were thirty. His heart suddenly full of tender compassion, he reached out his hand to touch her arm. 'Maryan – tell you what, let me take you for a spin this evening?'

Her smile vanished and she stared at him, her eyes round with astonishment. 'Me?'

He laughed. 'Yes, you. Well, I have to have someone to show off to, don't I?'

They arranged to meet at Whitechapel, outside the Underground station. Somehow keeping it secret made it all the more exciting, and the tacit understanding not to mention it to anyone was taken for granted. It would not be popular among the other girls and they both knew without actually voicing the thought that Sarah would disapprove of their meeting outside working hours as much as Rachel. If Sarah assumed that her daughter was with Tom Jessop, as she often was, Maryan was content to let her. After all, it was just this once.

She'd never been in a car before and as she slipped into the passenger seat her heart quickened with excitement at the feel of it. The scent of new leather and hot oil filled her nostrils. It was the smell of adventure. Marcus told her that he had learned to drive from one of the day boys at his school whose father had bought him a car and let him drive it to school. Maryan tried to assimilate this information. Fancy a schoolboy having a car. As Marcus drove off she caught her breath and held on tightly to the sides of the seat. They went so *fast*; faster than she had ever travelled before, even on a bus. And she felt as though everyone was looking at them. It was terrifying and wonderful all at the same time.

But although Maryan had expected to be taken out only once, it turned out to be the first of many outings. As the New Year came in and winter turned to spring, the trips became regular weekly treats. One Saturday afternoon Marcus drove her out into the Kent countryside and for the first time in her life Maryan saw fields full of baby lambs, and fruit trees bowed down with frothy blossom. They passed pretty cottages that had gardens full of daffodils and nodding tulips, children playing in the fields and people out walking dogs on leads. To a wide-eyed Maryan it was a whole new world.

During the drives they got to know one another. Marcus felt he could talk to Maryan as to no one else. He confided to her his secret ambition to be a designer.

'One day I'd like to make Feldman's a proper fashion house,' he said. 'What I really want is to go to Paris and study haute couture.' He glanced at her uncomprehending face. 'That's French for high-class fashion.'

'Can you really speak French?' Maryan asked him in awe.

'Yes. German and Latin too,' he told her. 'But art is what I was always best at. I want to design clothes that will be recognised all over the world. The kind of clothes that film stars and aristocratic women will give their eye-teeth for.'

'I bet you'll do it, too,' Maryan said, catching some of his enthusiasm. 'You can do what you want when your mum and dad are rich,' she added wistfully. 'I'll never get the chance to do the things I want.'

Marcus took her hand and gently squeezed it. 'And what are they?' he asked.

She shrugged. 'Oh, I don't know. I'm not clever enough to get a better job than what I've got now. I thought I'd go to night school once and learn typing and shorthand, but it's too late now, I suppose. I just know I'd like to have a better life. To talk like you do and – you know – *be* someone.' She looked at him, shaking her blonde head, suddenly embarrassed. 'I expect that sounds silly to you.'

'No, it doesn't,' he said gravely. 'It's not surprising you want to get away from a place like Crimea Terrace.'

Immediately Maryan was defensive. 'It's not a *slum* you know,' she told him warmly. 'All the folks who live there are respectable. They've got their pride, same as anyone else. They're clean too, as far as they're able to be.' She saw his indulgent smile and turned away crossly. 'Oh, what's the use of telling the likes of you? You don't know nothing about it. You don't know you're born, Marcus Leigh.'

'Oh yes, I do,' he told her firmly, taking her shoulders and turning her to face him. 'I appreciate all that my parents have done for me, but my dream is as far away as yours. They are so short-sighted. They can't see how I mean to take Feldman's on to better things. They're dead against my going to Paris. Can you imagine how frustrating that is?'

Maryan looked at him. But she wasn't trying to imagine his frustration. She was thinking how grateful she was to the Leighs for keeping Marcus close to home. And to her.

On Whit Monday Marcus took her to Southend. Maryan had

21

never seen the sea before and she gazed in wonder at the vast expanse of water, sparkling in the sunlight. They walked along the promenade and ate ice cream. Marcus even persuaded her to go for a ride along the sands on a donkey. On the way home they bought fish and chips and Marcus parked in a quiet lane so they could eat them.

'What would your mum say if she could see us now?' Maryan asked suddenly as she rolled up the empty paper.

Marcus coloured suddenly. His mother had become curious about his outings in the car lately and he'd had to make up an old schoolfriend who lived in Surrey. Recently she'd begun to give dinner parties for friends with daughters and he was fairly sure she was trying to pair him off with one of them before he could make a doubtful choice. 'Why should she say anything?' he said a little too brightly. 'After all, your mother and mine have known each other for a long time.'

But not as equals, Maryan thought. Mrs Leigh doted on her only son. She had great plans for his future. Plans that obviously would not include the daughter of her charwoman. But she couldn't quite bring herself to voice the thought. Instead she said: 'She'll be hoping for a Jewish girl for you. Soon we'll be hearing of your betrothal.'

Taken aback by her perception, Marcus paused for just a fraction too long. Then he turned to her with the smile that always melted her heart. 'That's not for ages yet. Till then we can have a good time, you and me, can't we?'

Maryan shrugged and looked away, wounded by the implication that he was using her to pass the time. 'I don't know. P'raps we should stop.'

He took her hands. 'Why do you say that?'

'You know why. Because you're upper class and I'm working class.'

He threw back his head and laughed. 'Rubbish. Dad started life in the workhouse. He's always telling me that. He's proud of the fact.'

'It's all right to be proud of it when you've made your fortune.'

'He's worked hard, that's all. My parents are as working class as yours.'

Maryan shook her head. 'You know as well as I do that it's not the same,' she said. 'Besides, you're Jewish and I'm not.'

'Who *cares*?' He drew her into his arms and held her tightly, but she struggled free.

'*They* will, Marcus,' she said, her eyes full of tears. 'Your mum and dad. You know they will.'

He looked down at her for a long time. Her brimming eyes moved him more than words could express. 'All I know is that I love you,

22

Maryan,' he said at last. 'I think you love me too.' He cradled her face between his two hands. 'You do, don't you?'

Maryan swallowed hard. Of course she loved him. She'd die for him if she had to. But she'd been brought up to know that there were things she couldn't have. *No use cryin' for the moon*, her mother was fond of saying. Marcus Leigh might as well have been the moon. 'Even – even if I do, it isn't any use,' she said unhappily. 'We never should've started this, Marcus. I've told lies and I expect you have too. It was bound to end in tears.'

'It *won't*. Trust me. I won't let it,' Marcus said fiercely. 'Oh, Maryan, I want you so much. Don't say we have to end it now.' Before she could reply he pulled her to him and kissed her. For a moment she tried to resist, but his arms, strong around her and his mouth on hers were too much. Her arms crept around his neck and she gave herself up to his rising passion.

'Oh, Marcus. We mustn't – we shouldn't – I . . .' But her muttered words were lost in kisses. Their breath quickened and their passion rose to a fever as desire overcame all reason – all caution.

'I'll speak to them tomorrow. I'll make them see that there'll never be anyone but you in my life.' Marcus sat with Maryan's head on his shoulder. How long they'd been there neither of them could say, except that the moon had risen since they first parked there.

Chapter Three

On the night when she'd given herself to Marcus he had made all kinds of promises. They would be married. He'd make his parents see that they were made for each other. Together they would make the name of Feldman's great. He would design beautiful clothes for her and she would be his model. They would travel and she would be the most glamorous, the most talked-about woman in the world. His wife. Mrs Marcus Leigh.

The following day everything had changed. He didn't come to the factory that morning. When it was time for her lunch break she went outside to eat her sandwiches in the yard at the back of the factory. It was warm and the sun was shining, but already the feeling of foreboding that had been with her since waking that morning was making her heart heavy. Then she saw him coming towards her. At first, when she saw the expression on his face she was relieved. Obviously he had good news. She needn't have worried. It was going to be all right after all. But she could not have guessed what his good news was.

'Maryan, you'll never guess.'

'No – what?'

'I'm going to France.'

The smile that had begun to lift the corners of her mouth froze. 'To *France*? But – I thought your parents were so against it. I thought – you said you'd tell them – about us.'

'I was going to. I was all set to begin.' He took both her hands and held them tightly. 'And I will darling, I promise you I will. In a way this is the beginning of our dream coming true. There I was, you see, with my mouth open ready to begin, when Mother suddenly came out with it. She said she and Dad had been talking and they thought it would be best if I went to France to study design after all. She said I'd proved myself at the factory and they felt I was ready.'

24

He grasped her hands and swung her round. 'Isn't it *wonderful?* Oh, say you're pleased for me.'

'But, Marcus – *France*. You said . . .'

He caught her to him. 'Oh, please don't be sad, sweetheart. Don't you see, when I come home I'll be in a much better position to ask for what I want. We'll be married then, I promise. I'll only be away for a year.'

'A year? A whole *year*.' To Maryan it might as well have been a century. It was over. She knew it as well as if he had told her bluntly. After a year away, the excitement and adventure of living in a foreign land, of doing the thing he so passionately wanted to do, he would have forgotten her. She was beaten and she knew it. *No good cryin' for the moon.* Her mother's voice echoed mockingly in her brain. She should have known that dreams like that would never come true for the likes of her. She swallowed hard. 'When do you go?'

'At the weekend. Mother is booking my passage on the cross channel ferry for me this morning. There is so much to do, getting my passport, packing and so on. That's why I didn't come in this morning. But I made an excuse to come out. I had to tell you.' He raised her hand to his lips and looked earnestly into her eyes. 'You will wait for me, won't you, Maryan? You won't forget me and marry someone else?'

She shook her head, smiling wistfully. 'Of course I'll never forget you. You know that. Especially not after . . .'

'I know darling.' He drew her close. 'We belong to each other for ever now, Maryan. You're my own dear girl and always will be. I'll write. You will write back, won't you?'

She nodded miserably. Once he read her letters he'd know how far apart they truly were. She'd never be able to put on paper what she felt inside. It was hopeless.

By the time Marcus had been gone two months Maryan knew with dreaded certainty that she carried his child. She was frantic. There was no one she could go to. No one she dared confide in. She felt so ill too. In the early morning and at intervals throughout the day she was violently sick. The girls at the factory began to nudge each other and exchange knowing looks as she fled past them on her way to the lavatories.

It was one rainy evening in August when Tom Jessop heard the sound of weeping coming from the outside lavatory the two houses shared. He was on his way home from doing a late shift at the furniture factory. He paused, walked on a little, then returned to tap gently on the door.

'Are you all right in there? Can I do anything? Are you ill?'

The sobbing stopped and a muffled voice that he recognised at once said: 'I'm all right. Go away.'

'Maryan? Is that you?'

The door opened and Maryan emerged, her eyes red and swollen in her chalk-white face. He gasped with shock at her appearance and reached out a hand to grasp hers.

'What's happened? You look like death.'

For a moment she stared at him, then she fell against him, tears pouring down her cheeks. 'Oh Tom – Tom, I don't know what to do.'

He supported her gently. 'Look, come indoors with me. You don't want the neighbours seein' you like this. Mum's out. She's gone to help with a confinement in Rosedale Street. Chances are she'll be gone most of the night, so we can talk – if you feel like it, that is.'

In the Jessops' living kitchen Maryan sat by the range and tried to control her sobs. She'd held them back for so long and now that she'd finally given way to them they wouldn't seem to stop, hiccupping uncontrollably in her throat till her chest hurt. Tom made a pot of tea and pressed a warm mug into her hands.

'Here, drink that. I reckon you'd better tell me about it, eh?'

She shook her head. 'I can't, Tom. Not you.'

'Well, if not me then who *can* you tell?' he asked, pulling his chair up close. 'We've known each other long enough. And one thing's for sure you gotta tell someone or go barmy by the looks of you.'

Maryan swallowed the tea and felt a bit better. Tom was right. She had to tell someone, though she couldn't see that there was anything to be done about it. She looked up at him. Kind Tom who had wiped her nose and dried her tears on her first day at school. Tom, with his earnest grey eyes and his floppy brown hair.

'Oh, Tom, I don't know what you'll think of me,' she said with a shuddering sigh. 'I – I'm having a baby.' It was out. She'd said it. The relief was so enormous that she began to cry again, quietly this time, and with a despair that wrung Tom's heart.

'Oh – poor kid. Poor little Mar,' he said, rocking her gently. 'Who was it? Just you tell me who did this to you. I'll kill the bastard.'

She shook her head. 'No, Tom. It wasn't like that. He doesn't know and he never must.'

'Oh?' He looked questioningly into her eyes. 'And why's that?'

'Don't ask me, please. I'm never going to tell anyone. I couldn't.'

'I see. He's married then?'

'No. But it was all a mistake. It was just the once and it never should've happened. It'd ruin his life.'

26

'Pity 'e didn't think o' that before. And what about *your* life?'

'That's my problem, isn't it?' She looked up at him with wide terrified eyes. 'Don't you dare say nothing to Mum – your mum either.' she grasped his hands. '*Promise* me, Tom.'

''Course I won't. Not if you say so. But I don't see how you're gonna keep a thing like that secret.'

Maryan took a deep breath and clamped her teeth over her lower lip. 'I've heard about this woman. Down by the docks. She knows how to – to sort it out. I thought I'd . . .'

'No.' Tom was on his feet in an instant. Holding her hands tightly, he pulled her to her feet. '*No*, Mar. Them women are dangerous – evil old witches who don't know what they're doing. I've 'eard Mum talk about them. You'll kill yourself. Promise me you won't go an' do nothing like that. *Promise me.*'

'What else can I do?' she wailed. 'I'll lose my job. Mum might even lose hers too if it gets out. I don't know which way to turn.'

He looked deep into her eyes. 'Just tell me one thing, Mar. This bloke – would he marry you if you was to tell 'im?'

She shook her head. 'I told you – I can't tell him.'

'You sure, are you?'

'Certain.'

'Then there's only one thing for it.'

'What?'

'Marry *me*.'

For a moment she stared at him, relief almost overwhelming her. Then guilt and her inborn sense of decency took over and she shook her head. 'I couldn't let you do a thing like that, Tom.'

'Why not? It's what everyone expects anyway. We've always been together, you'n me, ever since we was nippers.'

'I know. It's not that.' She turned away, shaking her head. 'I'm – you know – *spoilt*. When you marry a girl you'll want to be the first. And anyway people will know soon enough that there's a baby coming.'

'So? They'll just think it's mine. And we'll be respectably 'itched by then anyway.'

'I couldn't do it to you, Tom. It's not fair. It'd be living a lie.'

He grasped her by the shoulders and turned her to face him. 'Look. If you say yes, it'll be nobody's business but ours, Mar. Yours and mine. It don't matter what anyone else thinks in the end, does it? What matters is that you're having a baby and you need someone to take care of you. I'm asking you to let it be me.'

'But why? Why should you, Tom?'

'Because I love you. I always 'ave, Mar. You know that. Blimey, if you don't, then you should do by now.' He tipped up her chin to look into her swollen eyes. 'Come on, gel, say yes and be done with it. Let's get things moving before any more time gets wasted.'

'You might be sorry tomorrow, Tom,' she said. 'Let's sleep on it, eh?'

He pulled her into his arms and held her tightly. 'I shan't never be sorry, Mar,' he said huskily. 'I ain't never wanted no other girl but you.'

She hid her face against his chest, tears beginning again. 'I've let you down, Tom. I feel ashamed. Not many men would do what you're doing.'

'Not many blokes got my common sense,' he told her with a grin. 'I know when I'm onto a good thing all right, don't you worry. Listen, you made a mistake, that's all. Everyone makes mistakes. God knows, plenty of blokes makes the same 'un. Difference is, they usually gets away with it.'

'Well – if you're really sure . . .'

'You mean you *will*?'

'All right then, Tom – yes.'

Tom was so happy. The delight shone out of his grey eyes like the sun on a spring morning. He couldn't wait to tell everyone, his mother, his brother and sister-in-law. He wanted to shout it from the rooftops. Maryan's mother was pleased too, when he went to ask formally if he could marry her daughter. She'd already guessed that Maryan might be pregnant, but knowing that it was Tom was a relief. She'd always looked forward to having him for her son-in-law. Such a good, steady lad. She couldn't ask for better than the son of her good friend and neighbour, Cissie.

Deep in his heart, Tom was more than happy, he was grateful. As Maryan had grown up and blossomed from a skinny little girl into a lovely young woman, he'd begun to think she'd grown out of his reach. She'd been clever at school and she was always saying that she wanted something better from life than her mother had been content with. Surely she'd be planning for something better than marrying a carpenter and setting up home in a two-up two-down, shared with her mother in Crimea Terrace. Perhaps it was these very aspirations that had led to her alliance with this mystery man who had betrayed her. Perhaps he was well off and upper class and that was why he couldn't marry her. Although Tom knew that Maryan was fond of him, in his heart of hearts he suspected that she would never have contemplated marriage with him had it not been for her unplanned pregnancy. But he wasn't going to probe too deeply into that theory. Maryan's past was behind them, and that was where it

28

would stay. She had assured him that she wanted to forget it. She was to be his, and that was all he cared about.

The letters that Marcus wrote, telling of the exciting things he was doing and seeing, gradually dwindled and stopped when Maryan failed to respond to them. She continued to work at Feldman's and she and Tom let it become known that they were to marry. The girls clubbed together to give her a little wedding present, a pretty glass jam dish in a chromium-plated holder. Mr and Mrs Leigh also gave her a gift when they heard from Sarah that she was to be married. Mr Sam called her into the office on the Friday before the wedding.

'Mrs Leigh and I would like you to have this, with our best wishes,' he said, passing a prettily wrapped parcel across his desk.

Blushing, Maryan had unwrapped it to find a beautiful little china jug nestling on blue velvet in a shiny black box. 'Oh, it's lovely. Thank you, Mr Leigh,' she said, backing away in embarrassment. 'And please – thank Mrs Leigh too, won't you.'

'I will, my dear. I will. And the best of happiness to you both.' Sam had smiled as she escaped, clutching her present. He'd always liked the girl and he didn't really understand that strange tightening of his wife's mouth and her look of disapproval at the mention of her name. After all, she and the girl's mother had known each other since girlhood, and Sarah had been a loyal servant to them for the past twenty years. But then who really understood women? Rachel had been adamant in her refusal to allow Marcus to study design in France. She wouldn't even discuss the idea. Then suddenly, almost overnight and for no apparent reason she'd changed her mind. He sighed and lifted his shoulders. Such mysterious creatures. But wonderful. Ah, yes, wonderful for all that.

The wedding went off quietly. There was a small celebration at the Prince of Wales pub in the evening. Sarah had made sure of that, pawning her mother-in-law's old sewing machine to pay for the treat. The whole street gathered to drink the health of the young couple in the customary fashion, with much good-natured ragging and jibing. The sing-song was in full swing when Maryan and Tom left, grateful to escape the smoky atmosphere and the ribald remarks and breathe in the comparatively fresh night air.

The month was September, but the season of mists and mellow fruitfulness was much like any other season in Crimea Terrace. It was a short street, one of a warren that made up the friendly community that Tom and Maryan had known from birth. The backs of the houses gave onto the mews housing the horses and wagons used by the brewery and other local traders, and the air was always redolent of dung and sweating horseflesh. When they reached number eight Maryan opened the door and they went inside.

They were to live with Sarah until they were on their feet and could afford a place of their own. In the meantime, they would share Maryan's bedroom over the parlour, which looked out onto the street. Sarah had prepared it specially for them, moving her own double bed into it and making it up with her best sheets, the ones Miss Rachel had given her when she bought new. The large brass bedstead dominated the small room, leaving only just enough room to move round it, but Sarah had baulked at moving out of the room she had shared with her Alf. Although he had been killed almost twenty years ago, she still felt that while she slept within the four walls she had shared with him he was not entirely lost to her.

1931 wasn't the best time to be starting married life. Already there had been bitter riots over the unemployment that was sweeping the country. But at least Tom had his job with the furniture factory at Bow. And Maryan's job at Feldman's would last for as long as she could still fit behind her machine. Sarah's job as housekeeper to the Leighs was secure, too. So with three wages coming in they were a great deal better off than most.

A door in the corner of the kitchen opened onto the steep, narrow staircase, which they ascended in single file. In the front bedroom Maryan opened the window. The singing from the pub reached her on the still night air. They'd got to the sentimental stage now, and she could hear full-throated snatches of 'I Can't Give You Anything But Love – Bay-bee'. She shook her head, wishing her mother hadn't spent her hard-earned money on booze for the neighbours. Heaven only knew there were better things they could have done with it. She turned towards Tom who was removing his specially bought tie and celluloid collar with obvious relief.

'They're well away. Just listen to them.'

He grinned ruefully. 'Just s'long as I don't 'ave to be there, I don't care what they do. Thank God I can take that thing off. Fair chokin' me, it was. Cuttin' right into my neck. Look at that.' He peered into the mirror, rubbing at the red wheals the rigid collar had left on his neck. Seeing her wistful expression he put down the collar and moved to where she stood at the window.

'Not regretin' marryin' me, are you, love?'

Her eyes filled with tears. 'Oh, Tom. How can you ask me that? By rights it should be me asking you. You deserve better than what you're getting.'

He held her at arms' length and looked into her eyes. 'I couldn't never get no one better than you, Mar. You know I've always wanted you. I just – just wondered if you was thinkin' of *him* today. Wishin' it was him standing beside you 'stead of me.'

She shook her head firmly. 'I told you, Tom. That's all over. It was a mistake, and I never want to talk about it again.'

'You're sure you don't want to tell me . . .?'

'No. Better you don't know, Tom. I know you've got every right to ask, but I'd rather we forgot it.' She looked at him in anguish. 'Oh, it isn't fair, is it? Expecting you to father another man's child. I shouldn't have let you . . .' He stopped her words with a kiss.

'Shhh. It'll be *your* child, Mar,' he said softly. 'That's good enough for me. And we've got all the time in the world to 'ave kids of our own. But I'll always love this one just as much as ours. I promise you that.'

Maryan laid her head against his shoulder with relief. No one must ever know the identity of her baby's father. Not even Marcus himself. But as for forgetting him – that was something she would have to learn to come to terms with by herself in secret.

As they lay side by side in the big brass bed Tom asked her: 'Well, how does it feel to be Mrs Jessop?'

'It feels safe, Tom,' she whispered. 'It feels like nothing can ever hurt me again.'

Christmas came, the happiest Maryan had ever known. The Browns and the Jessops gathered together for the occasion: Tom's brother, Bill, his wife, Maggie, and their small son, Johnny; Tom's mother, Cissie, and of course, Sarah. The seven of them squeezed round the table for Christmas dinner at Sarah's and again for tea on Boxing Day at Cissie's. There were crackers and games and everyone was jolly.

For the Leighs the season was less jolly. It was the very first Chanukah since Marcus was born that the three of them had been apart. As they went to the Synagogue to pray; as they lit the candles and put the Chanukah lamp in the window, they thought of their son and missed him sadly, though privately Rachel told herself it was for the best. She had done the right thing in giving in to her son's wish to travel and study. She had never told Sam about the evening she had been visiting a friend in the London Hospital and had seen Marcus pick up Maryan in his car outside the Underground station at Whitechapel. In the radiant smiles the two young people had exchanged Rachel had recognised the danger signals. She had kept the discovery to herself and given a lot of thought to the situation. Finally she came up with what she considered to be the

31

right solution. She did what had to be done, and the pain of missing her beloved son would be a worthwhile sacrifice. As for Sam – better he knew nothing.

Since their wedding Maryan and Tom had saved hard and managed to put away a bit towards their own home. Maryan's health had improved as the months of her pregnancy progressed, and by the end of December she was blooming, despite the awkwardness and discomfort of her widening girth.

At the end of January she was finally forced to give up work. She could no longer sit comfortably at her machine for hours at a time, nor get close enough to work accurately. Sam promised to keep her job open for her for a few weeks at least. Cissie had promised to care for the baby for her so that she could go back and work for a few hours each day. When she was called out to a confinement or a laying out they could come to some arrangement between them, she assured Maryan.

It was on the 9th of February in the small hours of the morning that Tom wakened to find Maryan tossing restlessly beside him. He reached out to touch her arm.

'What's up? Are you all right, love?'

She turned to him. 'It's the pains. I think it's the baby, Tom.'

He was out of bed in an instant and knocking on Sarah's bedroom door. Half an hour later the two of them were in the kitchen, Tom stoking the range whilst Sarah filled her largest saucepan and the kettle, setting them both on to boil. Tom had already fetched Cissie, who was upstairs, examining Maryan. Presently she appeared at the open door to the stairway, rolling down her sleeves.

'She'll be a few hours yet. Go up and talk to her, Tom. Keep her mind off it while Sarah and me get things ready.' She looked round the kitchen. 'Glad to see you've got plenty of water on the boil. Don't want no nasty infection settin' in do we?' she grinned. 'Besides, I reckon we could all do with a cup of tea.'

Dawn was breaking when Cissie turned her son out of the bedroom at last, announcing that it was time for things to start happening.

'There's little enough room in 'ere for me and Sarah,' she grumbled. 'We don't want no clumsy great bloke under our feet, do we, darlin'?' She bent over Maryan and wiped the sweat from her brow. 'Come on, luvvie, we'll soon 'ave that baby 'ere for you,' she said gently. 'Not much longer now.'

But it was almost midday before Maryan was finally released from her suffering. For four long hours she had strained to push her child into the world. Gritting her teeth and pulling on the towel Sarah had tied to the bedrail, she bore down with every ounce of strength she possessed. The two older women had worked tirelessly, encouraging and reassuring, Cissie pressing down on Maryan's abdomen with every pain to aid the passage of the child. She was used to such scenes of suffering. Painful birth was a matter of routine to her, but Sarah had never seen a baby born before and she was terrified. She felt sure she was about to lose her daughter and the child with her. How could such a frail body endure such toil and agony?

'Shall I go for the doctor?' she asked anxiously for the third time.

Cissie shook her head. 'No sense in lettin' yourself in for a bill you can't afford to pay,' she said brusquely. 'Take it from me, Sarah, she's doin' all right – no worse than most and better'n a good many. Couple more pushes and we'll 'ave it born. I c'n see the head already.'

Sarah bit her lip and looked on helplessly at her exhausted daughter.

Cissie shook her head at her. 'Oh come on, gel. Surely you can remember when you 'ad her. Two days an' nights you took. I was with you, remember?'

Reassured, Sarah turned back to Maryan. 'Cissie's right, love,' she said. 'You're doin ever so well. Not long now. Almost over.'

And Cissie proved to be right. Ten minutes later the child was born. Yelling lustily, Maryan's little girl was delivered into Sarah's waiting hands. Cissie worked quickly, tying off and cutting the cord. She made a perfunctory examination of the baby, then bundled her into a towel and handed her to Sarah.

'Well, she's all right, thank Gawd,' she said. 'Everything in its right place and lungs on 'er as'd put a costermonger out o' business.' She turned to Maryan with a smile. 'Right, me luvvie. You got a healthy baby. All over bar the shoutin' now.'

Sarah stood by the window, hugging her tiny granddaughter to her bosom, tears of relief coursing down her cheeks. Thank God it was over and they were both alive.

When the baby was put into Maryan's arms she looked down at her in wonder. So much pain and hard work for something so little. It had been worth it though. Very tenderly she touched the soft head with its covering of dark downy hair. The huge dark blue eyes looked up, unfocused, at her and love coursed through her veins like some powerful drug.

She's mine, Maryan told herself. All mine. My flesh and blood. Her eyes scrutinised every detail of the tiny features, searching for a likeness – to herself. And, if she were honest, to Marcus. In a way she hoped the child would not resemble him. She did not want a daily reminder of her folly. This child belonged to her – and to Tom.

33

It was the least she owed him. But on one thing she was determined. Her daughter would never know that she had been conceived out of wedlock. She would grow up to hold her head up high – to think of herself as someone special. Somehow or other Maryan meant to make sure of it.

'What are you going to call her?' Cissie asked when she looked in next morning.

Too excited to sleep, Maryan had spent most of the night thinking about this. In the early hours when she had wakened to feed the child she had remembered something she had read in a film magazine Tom had bought her. Some months ago an American film actress had married an exiled Russian nobleman among great publicity and fuss. Recently she had given birth to a baby daughter and had named her Amethyst. The name had stuck in Maryan's mind. It had such an exotic sound. Surely no one with a name like that could grow up to be ordinary.

'I'm going to call her Amethyst,' she told her mother-in-law.

Cissie stared at her, her round face a mask of amazement. 'That's a funny old name,' she said bluntly.

'It's a jewel,' Maryan told her. 'It's unusual, isn't it – a bit special?'

'It's *that* all right.' Cissie thought about her son and how proud he had been to announce his daughter's birth to his workmates at the factory. They'd have a good old laugh when he told them her name was to be *Amethyst*. It sounded more like a race horse or a new kind of fruit off a barrow down the market. Besides, Amethyst *Jessop* didn't sound right somehow. Poor little mite. Oh well, never mind. I expect she'll get called Amy anyway, she told herself as she tucked the covers in round the sleeping baby.

From the very first moment he set eyes on her Tom Jessop adored his little daughter. There was no doubt about it. She was his child. He refused even to think of her as anything else. There was nothing he liked better than to nurse her, loving the sweet, wriggly feeling of her little arms and legs inside the shawl as he held her in his arms, and the trusting way she looked up at him with her big blue eyes. When Maryan stopped feeding the child herself he would delight in giving her a bottle; sitting patiently with her until every drop had gone, then putting her against his shoulder as he'd seen Maryan do, to bring up her wind. He even enjoyed changing her nappy, getting enormous satisfaction out of making her all comfy and sweet-smelling again. And, in spite of the amusement and even catcalls he

34

received from other men in the neighbourhood, he was proud to walk her out in her pram on Sunday afternoons while Maryan put her feet up for an hour. The only thing he would not do was to call her Amethyst. To Tom she was Amy from the day of her birth. And nothing Maryan could do or say would induce him to call her anything else.

When she was old enough she would wait at the window each evening, watching for him to turn the corner of the street. Then she would run to the door, calling '*Daddy – Daddy*,' until Maryan or Sarah opened it for her to run out into his arms.

Maryan had gone back to work at Feldman's when Amethyst was two months old. She hated handing her baby over to her mother-in-law each morning, but they needed the money if they were to afford a place of their own. But when Amethyst was a year old Cissie met with an accident. She was stepping down from a tram when she slipped on a patch of ice and fell heavily. At the hospital she was found to have broken her leg in two places. As well as being in plaster from thigh to ankle, she would have to remain in hospital for several weeks.

The family had a hurried conference. If no one else could be found to care for little Amethyst during the day there was nothing for it but for Maryan to give up her job. Everyone looked at Maggie, whose small son Johnny had recently started school. Flushing, she reminded them that she had just started work again herself.

'I'd like to 'elp, honest, but we really need the money,' she said plaintively. 'I ain't worked since Johnny was born and Bill's been put on short time. I was lucky to get this job down the canning factory. If I give it up I'll never get nothin' else.'

Resigned to being reduced to only Tom's wage, Maryan looked at her mother. Sarah was looking tired and pale. The long hours she put in at the Leighs were beginning to tell on her. 'Tell you what, Mum. Could we take it in turns to look after baby?' she asked. 'Do you think Mrs Leigh would let me take on your evening work? After all, there's no cooking. It's only washing up and such. And you could do with working shorter hours.'

Sarah nodded. 'I think that's a very good idea – split the money between us. Long as I earn enough to pay the rent and buy my bit of food I'm quite content. You need it more'n I do. I'll ask Mrs Leigh first thing tomorrow.'

Rachel agreed that Maryan should replace Sarah on two evenings a week when she was entertaining. She did it with some reluctance. She and Sarah were used to each other's ways and when Sarah was there to help everything went without a hitch. True, Maryan had often been along to help at larger dinner parties, and the girl was pleasant and willing enough. A fleeting vision of Maryan getting into Marcus's car returned, but she pushed the thought aside. Marcus looked set to stay in Paris for some time to come. He wrote enthusiastically of all he was learning and how much he loved his life there. There were parties and a gay social life as well as hard work. He would certainly have forgotten his little fling with Maryan by now. And anyway, the girl was married and settled, with a child to support. Surely she would have put impossible girlish dreams behind her now that she had the realities of life to face.

The new arrangement worked out well enough, though with less money coming in Maryan and Tom had to abandon their plans for getting a place of their own. It would only be temporary, they told each other. Once Amethyst was at school Maryan would get a full-time job again. By then the slump would surely be over and things would be looking up for all of them. But they had reckoned without the demise of the furniture factory where Tom worked. The following January it went into liquidation and the fifty-two men employed there found themselves joining the ever lengthening dole queues.

Amy was the one person to be glad her father stayed at home all day. At two years old she was too young to realise the despair of the situation. She had her beloved Dad to play with all day. Wrapping her warmly in her woolly scarf and hat against the winter cold and fog, he would take her down to the docks to watch the big ships or to the mews behind their street to feed the big, gentle drayhorses with carrots. Sometimes they would go to the market last thing Saturday nights to buy leftover veg before the stallholders packed up. But whatever they did, it was always fun. To innocent Amy they were halcyon days, to everyone else they were bleak and desperately worrying, especially when Sarah went down with a severe bout of influenza which left her with a bad chest that stubbornly refused to clear up.

Maryan temporarily took over her mother's job at the Leighs' until the doctor finally diagnosed chronic bronchitis. Sarah's job was far too arduous for her, he warned. Unless she gave it up for something less taxing she would be in serious danger of contracting consumption. The answer was obvious. Maryan would take over her job completely.

Rachel accepted the change with a good grace. Maryan was used to the household routine now. Keeping her on was preferable to training someone new. Besides, Marcus had indicated in his letters that he would be home in a few months' time and she was already planning to entertain extensively for his benefit. Both she and Sam agreed that it was high time he took a wife. And Rachel meant to see to it that he chose wisely and well.

Maryan admired and resented the Leighs' home in equal measure. Rachel's tastes in furnishing and colour were superb. Ever since she had first been inside the house as a young girl she had promised herself that this was the kind of house she would have one day. But as the years passed the possibility grew fainter and fainter. Like Sarah, she watched Rachel cook and picked up tips on how to present food attractively, though the kind of food consumed in the Leigh household was far beyond anything she could ever afford. Rachel, knowing of their enforced poverty, allowed her to take home the leftovers, just as she always had. Some nights they feasted like lords, on chicken and asparagus, while on others they made do with bread and margarine. But at least they got by without having to apply for Public Assistance; a humiliation they all dreaded.

When Cissie first came home from hospital she tried to go back to her old job and even managed to attend the occasional confinement, but her leg was badly crippled. It hadn't healed well and she was in constant pain. Eventually she went to live with Bill and Maggie. Sarah, too, was feeling the effects of her illness. Taking care of the child and managing the housework tired her, although she would rather die than admit it, and Maryan could see the lines of exhaustion on her mother's face at the end of a long day. But there was little she could do about it. She was now the only provider. She worked such long hours herself that she hardly ever saw her child. In the early months it was bearable. There was always the hope that Tom would get work, but as week followed week and nothing materialised for him, he began to sink into depression.

From the good-natured, considerate boy that Maryan had married, he degenerated into a sour, embittered man before her eyes. Grey-faced and round-shouldered with despair, he gave up looking for work. He gave up hope, and with it, his zest for life, until it seemed that the only thing he lived for was his little daughter.

To Maryan, coming home tired after a hard day's work, he appeared ungrateful, lazy and resentful. He blamed her for everything, goading her until she snapped back angrily at him, accusing him of letting her do everything; reminding him that she was the breadwinner. At which he would fling out of the house and stay out till late at night, accepting beer from better off pals who felt sorry for him, and coming home in the small hours the worse for drink.

Lying awake, waiting to hear his stumbling footsteps coming up the stairs, Maryan would weep tears of frustration, angry with the hand life had dealt her. Why should they have to live like this, while people like the Leighs lived in luxury? What had they done to deserve it?

She voiced these thoughts to her mother one day.

'Don't you go bitin' the 'and that feeds you,' Sarah admonished. 'I don't know where we'd be today if it hadn't been for the Leighs. Miss Rachel has been a good friend to us, my girl, and don't you ever forget it.'

'I'm not likely to with you to remind me,' Maryan said waspishly. 'Anyway, it's paid her to be reasonable with us, hasn't it? We've slaved our fingers to the bone for her, specially you. Look at you with your wheezy chest and rheumaticky knees. You're an old woman and you're not even fifty yet. What do you owe your wonderful Miss Rachel when all's said and done?'

'Friendship, that's what,' Sarah said stoutly. 'I'm proud to have been her friend – since your gran was alive – since before you was born. Ever since we was both gels.'

'You've been her *servant*, Mum. Nothing else. Her servant.' Maryan turned away, her lip curling. 'That's how she sees you and always has. If you don't believe me, just ask her. She don't invite *you* to her posh dinner parties, does she?'

'Of course she don't,' Sarah said. 'I wouldn't expect her to.' She took her daughter by the arm and looked into her eyes. 'Listen to me, Maryan. I've lived longer than you and I know what's what. The likes of us is all right so long as we knows our place and keep to our side of the fence. It's when folks starts getting above themselves that all the trouble starts.' She smiled in an attempt at reassurance. 'Things'll get better by 'n by. We was happy before. We'll be happy again. Don't get bitter, there's a good gel. There's no good'll come of it.'

But Maryan wasn't convinced. If she wasn't happy with the way things were there must be others who felt the same, who noticed how some people had made money out of the war, whilst others had died horribly in the trenches, leaving wives and children to manage as best they could. And now there was all this unemployment. The men and women who were rioting, *they* felt as she did – that something should be done to make things fairer, more equal; to bring about the Land Fit For Heroes that they'd been promised. Tom might have given up but she wouldn't. She might not be able to put the world to rights, but if she could do something for herself and her own family, then she would.

*

She was taking off her coat in the Leighs' basement kitchen the following Monday morning when Rachel appeared in the doorway.

'I'd like you to make a start on the downstairs rooms this morning, Maryan,' she said. 'Mr Marcus arrived home in the early hours and he's still asleep.'

At the mention of his name Maryan's heart skipped a beat. 'Just as you say, Mrs Leigh,' she said, trying to make her voice matter-of-fact. 'I didn't know he was due home.'

'He wasn't,' Rachel told her. 'At least, not yet. It was quite unexpected. But he isn't going back. He's had enough of life on the Continent, so I'm afraid we'll have to put up with having him at home again.' The smile on her face belied her words. She was obviously pleased and excited to have her son home again, whatever the reason.

'I've got to go down to the factory this morning,' she went on, putting on her hat and coat, 'but I'll be back around eleven. I want Marcus to have his sleep out so perhaps you could leave upstairs till this afternoon just this once.'

'Of course, Mrs Leigh.' Rachel went about her work, washing up the dinner dishes from the night before, scrubbing the front steps and cleaning the brasses on the street door. She had just carried the ashes from the drawing-room grate out to the dustbin and was about to lay the fire when she heard footsteps on the stairs. Looking out into the hall, she saw Marcus coming down the stairs wearing his dressing gown. When he saw her he stopped in his tracks.

'*Maryan*. What are you doing here?'

'I work here now. Didn't your mother tell you?'

He laughed. 'She's hardly had time to tell me anything yet.'

Acutely aware of her dishevelled appearance, Maryan wiped her hands on the coarse apron she wore and brushed away a stray lock of hair with the back of her hand. 'I see,' she said. 'What brought you home so unexpectedly?'

He sighed and stroked his cheek ruefully. For the first time she noticed a long scar that ran down from his temple to below his left ear. 'It's a long story. Do you think you could make me some breakfast? Then perhaps we can have a little talk.'

'Of course.'

Her hands trembled as she filled the kettle and began to cut bread for toast. It felt so strange – almost dreamlike – to be standing here, making breakfast for Marcus. He was as handsome as ever. A little heavier perhaps. Taller and broader than she remembered, but apart from that life seemed not to have touched him as it had touched her.

39

She wondered about the scar on his cheek, and whether he would tell her about it.

'Mother wrote and told me you were married.'

She looked up, startled. 'Did she? I wonder why.'

'Maybe she thought I'd be interested,' he said, looking at her quizzically. 'Why didn't you write – answer my letters?'

She blushed. 'I – there wasn't anything to say.'

'Really? I'd have thought there was quite a lot.'

There was a moment's silence between them, then he said cheerfully: 'So, what's he like, this husband of yours?'

'Tom? Oh, he's just ordinary, like me,' she said. 'We've known each other since we were kids.' She set the plate of bacon and eggs before him. 'I've – we've got a little girl. She's called Amethyst.'

He stared up at her. 'A child? Well, you don't waste any time, do you? It seems hardly any time at all since you and I . . .'

'It does to me,' she interrupted quickly. 'You've been away a long time – almost three years, isn't it? We were just a couple of silly kids. Better we forget it, eh?'

'If you say so.' She made to leave, to get on with her work, but he put out his hand to stop her. 'Don't run away. Stay and talk to me, Maryan. It's all right. I'll clear it with Mother if you haven't finished your work.'

Reluctantly, she slid into the seat opposite and watched him eat. 'What – happened to your face?' she asked.

Again he touched the livid scar and his mouth hardened. 'I thought I'd like to visit Germany before I came home,' he told her. 'I meant to stay for a few months. But they aren't very partial to Jews in Germany at the moment.'

'You got into a fight?'

'You could call it that, I suppose. A pretty one-sided one, though. I tried to break up what I thought was a brawl. Some youths were beating up an old man. A woman had accused him of trying to steal her purse. She attracted the attention of some drunken thugs.'

'Had he stolen her purse?' Maryan asked. Marcus shook his head.

'No. He was a harmless old Jew on his way to the synagogue. Anyone could see that. And that was the real reason he was getting beaten. If I hadn't intervened they would have killed him. One of them drew a knife on me. That's how I got this. I don't doubt they would have liked to kill me too.'

Maryan gasped. There were certain people who were prejudiced in England, but not to this extent. 'But why?'

'Haven't you heard of Adolf Hitler?'

'I've read about him in the papers. He's the new German President, isn't he?'

'*Fuehrer*, he calls himself. He wants everyone in Germany to be of pure blood. He's telling the people that he's trying to create what he calls a Master Race. He's encouraging the German people to hate gypsies, blacks, anyone who isn't pure German. But Jews in particular, because there are more of them. Do you know that we are banned from public places and dubbed "sub-human"?'

'That's terrible.' Maryan shook her head. 'That's why you came home?'

'Partly. The old man I rescued had had enough. It wasn't the first time he'd been set upon in the street. He wanted to come to England. His son lives here in London. I offered to escort him. I'd seen more than enough myself.' He leaned forward earnestly. 'He has to be stopped, Maryan. Hitler, I mean. If someone doesn't do something about him soon he'll get worse. He's amassing the most enormous fighting force; men, weapons. How our Government can sit back and ignore it . . .'

'What could he do, though?' Maryan asked.

'Invade us. Take us over, Central Europe first, then us. We should be arming too. Hitler is a madman. Hungry for power. Nothing will stop him once he's allowed to get a hold.'

'*Don't.*' Maryan shuddered. 'You're frightening me. It's not long since we had a war with Germany. My dad got killed in it. We beat them that time. Surely they wouldn't start another.'

He looked at her wide, frightened eyes and his mouth softened into a smile. Reaching out he touched her hand reassuringly. 'I'm sorry, Maryan. Of course it won't happen. It's just my over-active imagination.'

She let out her breath on a sigh of relief. Men were always talking about war. She might have known it was all talk. 'Are you going back to work for your father now then?' she asked.

He nodded enthusiastically. 'In a way, yes. I'm hoping to persuade him to let me try out some new ideas. I've learned so much while I've been away, Maryan. I've worked with top designers and couturiers. It's a whole different world over there. You'd love it.'

'I daresay.' She was silent, wistfully remembering the promises – how she would wear his designs and travel with him, be his model. Ridiculous nonsense. The stuff of childish dreams.

Oblivious of her thoughts, Marcus was buttering a piece of toast. 'Tell me about this husband of yours. And the little girl – what did you say she's called?'

'Amethyst.'

41

He smiled. 'Very exotic. Sounds like a model. Is she pretty – like you?'

She blushed, imagining what she must look like, with her hair awry and streaks of soot on her face more than likely. 'She's not like me at all, really. Her hair is dark and curly and she has big blue eyes. More a dark violet really, like pansies.'

'She sounds a real charmer. Does she have your dimple?'

'Two,' she said proudly.

'And her father?'

For a moment she stared at him, then, realising that he suspected nothing, she said quickly: 'Tom lost his job twelve months ago. And Mum's been poorly too with her chest, which is why I'm working here now.'

He looked concerned. 'Poor Maryan. Life must be hard for you.'

She summoned a smile. 'Oh – we manage well enough. Your mum is very good to us,' she added, despising herself for the echo of her mother she could hear in her ingratiating tone.

'She would be. Mother's a good sort.' Marcus wiped his mouth on his napkin and stood up. 'Well, I'd better have a bath and shave and make myself presentable before she gets back. I'll be seeing you a lot from now on, Maryan. Better get used to my clutter around the place. I'm hoping Mother will let me have the boxroom for a studio. I mean to start work on my designs immediately.'

Rachel lost no time in organising a busy social programme for Marcus. He tolerated it with a mixture of amusement and irritation.

'She's matchmaking,' he confided to Maryan. 'She won't rest until I've got a wife and three children. She's set her heart on it and when Mother sets her heart on anything there's no putting her off.'

'And will she get her way this time?' Maryan ventured. They were moving the collection of clutter out of the boxroom. Marcus put down the brass-bound portmanteau he was carrying and looked at her, one eyebrow cocked. 'Between you and me, Maryan, no. But don't breathe a word of it to her. I'm not ready to settle down yet. I want to become established as a designer first. A wife and all that marriage entails would only encumber me.'

Maryan turned away to pick up a stack of old newspapers, relief lightening her heart. Although she would not admit it, even to herself, deep in her heart she still loved him. Her work had been lighter since his homecoming. She actually looked forward to coming to Hackney Road each morning, because he would be there. There was the way he treated her too – as a friend instead of his mother's servant. She looked forward to their easy, relaxed conversations, storing them up to think about later when she was alone. He could never be hers, she acknowledged that, but until he belonged to someone else she still felt free to indulge in a little secret dreaming.

The dinner parties meant she often had to work late. There was extra work to do, too: silver to clean and glasses to polish, extra dusting and cleaning. On the evenings the Leighs entertained she would stay late to help serve the meal and then wash up afterwards. She didn't grumble because Mrs Leigh was generous with extra money, but things were difficult at home. Tom complained constantly and unreasonably that she was hardly ever there.

'I can't be in two places at once,' she told him tetchily. 'And heaven only knows we can do with the extra cash.'

'Oh, that's right. Rub it in,' he shouted. 'Do you think I sit here on my backside all day for the fun of it?'

'No, I don't. So why can't you help Mum a bit more instead of drinking with that bunch of layabouts down the Prince of Wales? You always seem to have the price of a pint, I notice.'

'You'd grudge a bloke the only bit of pleasure he gets, wouldn't you?' he snapped bitterly. 'You used to be a kind-hearted woman, Maryan. Now you're nothing but a bloody nag.'

'A bloody nag, am I?' Stung, Maryan rounded on him, close to tears. 'Ever asked yourself why, Tom Jessop? Sometimes I wonder why we're married, you 'n me.'

He gave a harsh laugh. 'You *wonder*, do you? Only one reason why you ever married me. And we both know what that is, don't we?'

Maryan stopped, her mouth dropping open with shock. She'd known he was bitter about losing his job, but she had no idea he bore a grudge about the reason for their marriage. Chastened, she went to him, her arms outstretched.

'Tom. Oh, Tom, love, don't say that.'

He turned from her. 'It's true though, isn't it? You never really wanted me.'

'No. No, it *isn't* true. You love Amethyst as much as I do. And she adores you. You're her dad.'

'In name, maybe. And what about you?' He turned to look at her and she saw that tears stood in his eyes. 'What about the kids you 'n me was gonna 'ave, Maryan? Seems I can't do nothin' on my own account. Not even be a real father.'

'Tom, you know as well as I do that it's just as well with the way things are. Another baby would put an end to me working, and then where'd we be?'

'Yes – *where*? You're already married to a no-hoper, aren't you?

You've got an invalid mum and a kid to support too. No wonder you take such good care not to have kids.'

She stared at him. 'I don't do anything to stop it, Tom. It just – hasn't happened.'

'No, not likely to either when you've got no time for your husband any more, is it? I might as well be married to a bloody nun.' Before she could stop him he flung out of the house.

Maryan sank into a chair, her heart heavy with despair. She felt torn several ways at once. What was she supposed to do? How many people could she hope to please? And how much more worry could she take?

It was two weeks later that the Weiss family were invited to dinner with the Leighs. They too had a clothing factory and the two firms had been friendly rivals for some years. As usual Maryan worked hard. Rachel had taken special care with the meal. The house was decked with fresh flowers and all day wonderful smells had drifted up the stairs from the kitchen. Maryan's mouth watered as the various aromas tantalised her nostrils. There was roast chicken in a wonderful spicy sauce with a variety of vegetables, and for dessert Rachel had made one of her special strudels, rich with fruit, nuts and cinnamon. Maryan hoped the guests would not be too hungry so that there would be some left over.

While the two families were having drinks she washed and changed into the black dress and lace apron Rachel had provided, then, at the signal from Rachel's little bell, she carried the first course upstairs to the dining room where the Leighs and the Weiss's were seated.

It was a small party tonight. Mr and Mrs Weiss had just the one daughter, Jessica. As Maryan served the soup, she couldn't help looking at the glamorous young lady in the bead-embroidered white evening dress. Jessica was about nineteen, and quite exquisite. She wore her glossy black hair in the latest style with a heavy wave falling forward over her brow and she had the largest, most expressive brown eyes that Maryan had ever seen. She could see that Marcus too was mesmerised by the girl's beauty. As the meal progressed his eyes hardly left her face. Placed side by side, they talked incessantly, totally engrossed in each other's company. At her end of the table Rachel, dressed in regal blue, beamed her approval. Sam looked on benignly, happy that his wife and his business colleagues were happy; and Mr and Mrs Weiss seemed delighted with everything.

Washing up alone in the kitchen later, Maryan pictured the scene upstairs. Mrs Leigh had looked especially handsome this evening. Her thick hair, beginning now to grey, waved in attractive silver wings against her head; her tightly corsetted figure was upright and proudly held in her blue velvet dress; and her white hands were adorned with rings. Maryan compared her to her own mother, picturing the face lined with years of struggle, old before its time; the straggling grey hair, crudely sawn off with the household scissors; and the drooping, shapeless body, rarely clad in anything but a fraying print overall. What had Sarah to show for a lifetime of gruellingly hard work? Was that to be her fate too?

But it wasn't the prospect of that bleak future that dampened Maryan's spirits and dragged at her heart as she carefully put away Rachel's fine china. Far worse was the knowledge that this evening marked the end of her few months of innocent happiness. Jessica Weiss was clearly Rachel Leigh's trump card – her chosen daughter-in-law. If it came off it would be the perfect alliance of family and business. Now she saw why Rachel had gone to such endless pains with this evening's meal. Whether he knew it not, Marcus's bachelor days were rapidly nearing their end.

Chapter Four

Amy's first days at school were traumatic to say the least. To begin with, because of her February birthday she started after the Easter holidays and she seemed to be the only new girl. Everyone else appeared to have been at school for ever. Then Mum had told her she must only answer to her proper name.

'You're a big girl now and you're entitled to be called by your real name. Amethyst is a very special name, so don't forget.'

As she'd always been called Amy she wasn't at all sure that she liked her real name. It felt strange and funny, but she meant to try. After all, it was special. Mum said so. No one else was called Amethyst.

It was Tom who took her along on that first morning and when he kissed her briefly at the school gates and left her with a request to 'be a good girl for Dad' she felt her lower lip tremble. She felt bleak and lonely. Why couldn't she have stayed at home with Dad and Grandma like always? Already she hated this bewildering, unfriendly red brick building filled with noisy, rough children.

When the bell rang she was herded inside with all the others, jostled and pushed into a big cloakroom where a kindly bigger girl took pity on her and showed her where to hang her coat. Then, borne along on the tide, she found herself in a classroom. It had a big blackboard and rows of desks, each with a sloping lid and an inkwell and a little groove where you put your pencils. And it smelled funny: a mixture of socks and chalk and the stuff Grandma put down the drain.

The teacher was tall with grey hair and glasses and a very stern face. Towering over Amy like an avenging angel, she took her by the arm and steered her to a desk in the front row.

'I am Miss Vickers,' she said in her strange, deep voice. Her face was so close to Amy's that she could feel her breath on her forehead.

It smelled of peppermints. 'You are to call me Miss.'

Then she went and sat at a tall thin desk in front of the class and began to call out all the children's names one by one. Everyone said 'here, Miss', but when it came to Amy's turn she said nothing. Miss Vickers peered over the top of her glasses at Amy in the most ferocious way.

'Amy Jessop, you are to say "here, Miss" like the others,' she told her.

'Not till you say my proper name,' Amy said, wagging an admonishing finger and using the tone her grandma used when reminding her to say please.

Miss Vickers' indignant eyebrows shot up. 'You are a very impertinent little girl. Remember your manners and answer properly when you're told.'

Amy's cheeks blazed. She didn't know what "impertinent" meant but she was sure it wasn't nice. 'Mum said I 'adn't got to answer to nothing but my proper name,' she protested, close to tears.

'Which is?' The teacher stared down at her register. The child's father had come to enrol her. Amy Jessop was the name he'd given.

'Amethyst,' the small voice piped up.

There was a moment's silence then some of the children began to giggle.

'*Silence.*' Miss Vickers thundered. 'I will not have levity in my class.' She glared at Amy. 'I think it would be best if we were to call you Amy,' she said. 'Amethyst is a very outlandish and difficult name. The other children will find it awkward. You will be called Amy whilst you are in school. Do you understand?'

Amy's mouth tightened into a stubborn pout. 'No. *Amethyst*. Mum said. It's a special name and you got to call me it.'

'I do not intend to discuss it with you. While you are here, you will be Amy.'

Amy tried again to protest but the teacher ignored her, descending from her lofty perch to give out reading cards and proceeding with the morning's lessons. But the little scene had set a precedent. If the truth were known, Amy would have preferred to be called by her familiar name, but after Miss Vickers' arbitrary put-down her mind was made up. She would be called Amethyst or she would not respond. The battle was on.

Amy's first month at school was spent mainly standing in the corner. She was as determined as Miss Vickers. Either she was called by her proper name like Mum told her, or she would do nothing. She had her legs slapped, she was deprived of her playtime and she was made to stand in the corner for whole lessons, but still she would not answer to Amy.

When she did go out to play she had to suffer the taunts of the other children. They considered that she put on airs and graces, but it wasn't only on account of her name. Amy was by far the best dressed child in the class. Most of the others came from large families and wore garments that had been handed down so many times that they were tattered and worn almost beyond recognition. By contrast Amy's clothes were crisp and new, which to the other children was a source of bitter envy and resentment. In actual fact, Amy's clothes cost nothing. They were lovingly made by Sarah, run up on the ancient sewing machine that had belonged to her mother-in-law out of leftover scraps of material that Feldman's employees were allowed to buy occasionally for a few pence a bundle. But of course Amy's schoolmates were not to know this. Dancing round her they would taunt her with cries of 'swank-pot' and 'show-off'. They also delighted in chanting their own crude, humiliating version of her name: 'Amy-pissed. Amy-pissed.'

Miss Vickers, who in spite of her strictness was a compassionate woman at heart, witnessed Amy's increasing disquiet with some concern and in the end decided to wait by the school gate one afternoon and have a quiet word with the child's father.

When they got home that afternoon Tom questioned Amy about her defiance.

'Miss Vickers is very worried about you. Why are you being so naughty? You could be having a nice time with the other children. You want to learn, don't you?' he said. 'You don't want to grow up a dunce, not able to read and write.' Amy hung her head. 'Well, *do* you?'

'No, Dad.'

'Then why are you behaving like this? You've always been Amy. Don't you like your name no more?'

'Yes, Dad.'

'Then what's it all about?' Tom asked.

'Mum *said*,' Amy muttered, hanging her head. 'Mum said I wasn't to answer to nothing but my proper name. I was on'y doing what she said.'

Exasperated, Tom pulled her into his arms and hugged her tightly. 'Oh, you silly girl, Mum didn't mean you hadn't do the lessons unless . . .' He broke off. 'Look – what do *you* want to be called?'

Amy's lip began to quiver and two fat tears dripped onto her cardigan. 'I want to be like all the others,' she hiccupped. 'I don't want to be kept in and stand in the corner while they all laugh at me. I want to go on being called Amy like always.'

'Then you shall.' He kissed her. 'Just you tell the teacher tomor-row. Tell her your Dad says it's all right, eh? And don't you worry about it no more. All right?'

'Yes, Dad.'

He took out his handkerchief and mopped her face. 'Dry them tears then and off out to play with you.' Under his breath he muttered: 'Wait till she gets 'ome. I'll Amethyst her.'

When Tom took Maryan to task about the incident there was a row. Maryan was tired as usual and inclined to be truculent.

'Fancy puttin' the kid through all that. I always said it was a stupid name to give 'er,' Tom complained. 'She was always bound to get ribbed about it. Why the 'ell did you 'ave to insist on it? It's made the poor little kid's life a misery.'

'I can't see what's wrong with having a nice name. It's unusual, that's all.' Maryan took off her coat and hung it behind the kitchen door. 'I suppose *you'd* like her to have been called Ada or Elsie or something equally common. Why shouldn't she have a classy name?'

'Because she don't belong to that class of people,' Tom argued. 'We're ordinary folks, you an' me, Mar. Yes, all right, *common* if you want to call it that. But you can't make a silk purse out of a sow's ear.'

Maryan rounded on him. 'Oh, that's typical of you, Tom Jessop. No ambition and never have. You never look no higher than the gutter. When she was born I made up my mind she'd 'ave something better than what I've 'ad. Calling her Amethyst was part of it.'

Tom sighed. 'It don't do to try and be somethin' you're not, Mar. We're workin' class and Amy's ours. She'll be like us. What's wrong with that?'

'*You* might be working class, but how do you know what class *she* is, eh?' The moment the words were out of her mouth she regretted them. The hurt in Tom's eyes wounded her and she reached out her hand. 'Tom – Tom, I'm sorry. I didn't mean that the way it sounded . . .' But this time he wouldn't be won over. Her cruel reminder that he was not Amy's father had cut him to the quick.

'You'll throw that in my face once too often,' he muttered as he pushed her aside and barged out through the back door. 'I'm goin' down the Prince. An' don't wait up for me. As if you *would*.' As he went he almost knocked Sarah off balance as she came through the door with a basket of washing. The older woman, who'd overheard the heated exchange from the yard, put down her basket and looked sceptically at her daughter across the kitchen table.

'You'll drive that feller away with your sharp tongue, my gel.'

White-faced and defensive, Maryan shook her head. 'He's so

touchy. And he thinks he's the only one who knows what's best for Amy.'

'He's practically brought her up,' Sarah reminded her, beginning to fold the clothes. 'And how do you expect him to be anything else but touchy, the time's he's been out of work? A man's got 'is pride.' She looked at her daughter sideways. 'What did you mean when you said he didn't know what *class* Amy was?'

Maryan's tightly reined temper exploded. 'Oh, why don't you mind your own bloody business for once, Mum? I slave myself silly for all of you, and what thanks do I get? I've got ideas above my station. I don't treat my husband right. I'm making my kid miserable because of the name I gave her. Seems I'm nothing but the bloody villain round here. Well I'd like to know where the 'ell you'd all be without me, that's all.' She turned and pulled open the door to the stairs. 'There's no bloody privacy in this hole either – always someone with their ear stuck up against the keyhole. I'm *sick* of it.'

Upstairs in the room she shared with Tom she collapsed onto the bed and let the tears flow. She was tired and fed up with the way they were forced to live, but that was only half the reason for her misery. She was used to the inconvenience and discomforts of Crimea Terrace. She was used to being tired too. But she was strong and healthy. A good night's sleep usually put her to rights again. It was mental anguish that took its toll of her spirits and ground her down relentlessly.

Marcus had married Jessica Weiss eighteen months ago. The wedding had been a grand affair. The ceremony had taken place at the synagogue at Golders Green, where the Weiss family lived. It had been for family and Jewish friends only, of course. In contrast to the small Leigh family, there seemed to be hundreds of Weiss's – cousins and aunts and uncles, nieces and nephews by the score all of whom were invited to the ceremony and to the reception afterwards at a smart hotel. But to mark the occasion of their only son's nuptials Sam and Rachel had given a party for the staff at Feldman's a few days before the wedding. Maryan and Sarah had been invited, and Rachel had insisted that Tom and Amy were to come too.

It was to be an evening that Maryan would never forget as long as she lived. The hall that had been hired for the party was decked with coloured streamers and flowers and she watched the happy couple as they circulated among the guests. It was sheer torture for her. They were so happy, so obviously head over heels in love. The way Marcus looked at his bride-to-be tore at Maryan's heart 'till she thought she would die of the pain. When they reached the table at

50

which she sat with her family, Marcus shook hands with Tom, kissed Sarah's cheek, then bent to look at Amy.

'So this is the little angel I've heard so much about,' he said. 'Don't you think she's pretty, Jessie?'

Jessica bent down and took Amy's little face between her hands. 'She's sweet.' She smiled at Maryan. 'You must be so proud of her. I'm hoping for a big family,' she confided. 'I love children. I want at least four. Six if possible.'

Marcus laughed and squeezed his wife's tiny waist. 'I'm marrying a woman with plans, Maryan. She intends to be very busy.' He let his fiancée go and watched with pride as she drifted on to the next table. Bending, he whispered in Maryan's ear, 'What do you think of her dress?'

Maryan had already admired it. Made of rose-pink lace, it had a close-fitting long bodice which ended in petal-like points over the hips. The skirt, made of chiffon in a softer shade of pink, hung in handkerchief points that swirled about Jessica's shapely legs as she walked. 'It's lovely, really beautiful,' she said.

Marcus looked pleased. 'One of my first creations,' he told her, watching appreciatively as the skirt followed Jessica's graceful movements. 'And there couldn't be a more exquisite model for it, could there?'

He couldn't have had the least idea of the hurt his remark inflicted on her. Clearly he remembered nothing of the closeness they had shared, the plans, the promises they'd made to each other.

The two firms were to amalgamate. Weiss's had always made industrial clothing, whilst Feldman's served the fashion industry. The two families formed a board of directors and decided that it would make economic sense to sell the two smaller factories and buy one larger building. Fortunately it was in Hackney that a larger factory was found, which proved a great relief to most of Sam's staff and workers.

Marcus was working hard on the newly formed board to get them to let him try a few of his couture dresses on the market. At first they'd been dubious, but after he'd done the rounds of the West End stores with his samples and persuaded one or two of them to order for their 'model gowns' department, the Leighs and the Weiss's gave in and agreed to give it a trial.

Jessica's father had bought them a pretty little town house in Highgate for a wedding present. The spacious attic had already been converted into a studio with a huge south-facing window, from which, as Marcus told Maryan, he had a view of Hampstead Heath. In spite of his resolve to remain single he was ecstatically happy and deeply in love. And all she could do was to stand by, watching and suffering in silence.

It had been a blessed relief when the wedding was over and the couple had departed for a honeymoon in Venice. When they returned they would move into the little house that lay in readiness for them, to begin their life together, Marcus to his designing career, Jessica to the babies she looked forward to so much.

Occasionally they came to dinner at 124 Hackney Road. Maryan, dressed in her black dress and apron would wait on them, her mouth set in an expression of resigned subservience as she watched the loving glances the couple exchanged. She couldn't help noticing the way their hands met frequently during the meal: it was as though they couldn't resist touching each other. And once, when she dropped her serving napkin and bent to pick it up, she saw Jessica's bare foot secretly caressing Marcus's calf under the table. The sight had given her so much pain that she had left the dining room at the first opportunity, to be physically sick in the downstairs cloakroom. Her love and longing for Marcus was more powerful than ever. It overwhelmed her like an illness, an incurable disease that ate at her heart and soul until she thought it must surely kill her.

Only one thing seemed to mar the young Leighs' perfect marriage. After a year and a half had passed Jessica still had not become pregnant. Maryan knew she should be ashamed of the stab of triumph it gave her. But why should they have everything they wanted? What had they done to deserve to have every one of their wishes granted? It was only fair that they should have some disappointments. It gave her a feeling of secret satisfaction, knowing that, although no one else would ever share her knowledge, she had been able to give Marcus what Jessica had not.

But only this morning that one small bubble of compensation had been burst. Mrs Leigh had come into the kitchen with a broad smile on her face.

'Maryan, I'd like you and Sarah to be among the first to know: Mr Leigh and I are to become grandparents. Isn't it wonderful news?'

Maryan forced a smile. 'Yes – wonderful. Congratulations.'

'I didn't say anything before,' Rachel went on confidentially, 'But poor darling Jessica had two miscarriages last year. Such a bitter disappointment to them. As you know, they want a family so badly.' She clasped her hands together ecstatically. 'But this time the doctor assures them that everything will be all right. He's taking extra special care of her, and of course Marcus is treating her as though she were made of Dresden china.'

'Of course.'

Rachel prattled on. 'Of course the other grandparents are delighted too, but it isn't the first for them. They already have four other grandchildren. For Mr Sam and me it's very special.'

'When is it due?' Maryan made herself ask.

'November. She's booked into a nursing home in Kensington. Very exclusive. Private rooms and a nurse to every patient. Just think – hardly any time at all to wait,' Rachel said happily. 'It's July already, so there are only four more months. They didn't tell us this time, you see. They wanted to be quite sure, though I must say I had my suspicions. We mothers have an instinct for that kind of thing, don't we?'

Four more months. The words echoed in Maryan's ears as she lay on the bed. She shut her eyes, hating herself for the resentment she felt. So they were to have their dearest wish after all. If only she could be happy for them. If only things could have been different. If only . . .

She must have fallen asleep, exhausted by her emotional turmoil, and it was an hour later when Sarah touched her shoulder.

'I've brought you a cup of tea. Come on, love. Sit up and drink it. It's nearly nine o'clock and you've had nothing down you since breakfast.'

Maryan hauled herself into a sitting position and took the cup. 'Thanks, Mum. I did have a bite at the Leighs', dinner time, but like you say, it was a long time ago.'

Sarah sat down on the edge of the bed. 'I had a nice supper ready for you. Neck o'mutton with plenty of veg. You like that. It's still 'ot if you fancy it. I kept it on the hob for you.'

'Thanks, Mum. Where's Amy?'

'In bed and fast asleep in my room, bless 'er.'

'Tom?'

Sarah shrugged. 'I wish you 'n 'im wouldn't get across each other so. He does appreciate what you do, you know. Just as I do. But he don't want 'is nose rubbed in it all the time.'

'Then he shouldn't blame everythin' on me, should he?'

'He don't mean to. He worries me some times, moochin' round with nothin' to do. And he worships you and Amy, you know.'

Maryan bit her lip. 'I know, Mum.'

'Try 'n be nicer to him, eh?' Sarah said.

'Yes, Mum. I will.'

It was late when Tom came home. Maryan wakened as he slipped into bed beside her. She could smell the beer on him, but she knew he wasn't drunk or he would have made more noise on the stairs. As she felt the bed dip she reached out her hand.

'Tom . . .?'

'You still awake?'

'Yes. You all right?'

He moved closer and put his arms round her. 'Better than all right, love. I been offered a job.'

Her heart leapt. 'Tom. That's good news. What kind of job?'

He nuzzled her neck. 'Never mind it now. Tell you in the morning.'

'Tom – I'm sorry. About earlier, I never meant . . .'

'I know, love. You were tired.'

'Yes. I didn't mean what I . . .'

'I know you didn't.' He kissed her gently. 'Are you tired now?'

His hands had begun to caress her and she knew what the question meant. 'No. I'm not tired now.'

'Oh Mar. I love you so much, you know that. Amy too. I'd do anything for you both, you do know that, don't you?'

'Course I do, Tom.'

She submitted to his lovemaking, but inside her head the hateful images of Marcus and Jessica tormented her. Tears squeezed out from under her closed eyelids and soaked into the pillow. Tears for herself and for Tom. He deserved better. He was a good man; a better person than she was. If only this open wound of her love for Marcus would heal so that she could be free of its endless torture. He reached his climax and rolled away to lie still beside her, his breathing steadying.

'It'll be all right for us from now on, love,' he said, stroking her cheek. 'I can feel it in my bones. Just you wait 'n see. When I get back again everything'll be fine.'

'Get back?' Suddenly she was wide awake and alert. 'Back from where? Where is this job then?'

He raised himself on one elbow to look at her. 'Spain.'

'Spain? But that's abroad. What job can there be for you there?'

'They got a war there, love. A civil war. Ain't you read about it in the papers?'

Maryan shook her head. 'But that's got nothin' to do with you – with England. Why would you be going there?'

'Well – there was this bloke in the pub, see. He was talking about what's goin' on there. This new government they all hate so much. It's all about gettin' rid of people like Hitler. Fascists, they're called. Remember what the Leighs' son told you when he came back from Germany?'

'But that wasn't Spain,' Maryan argued. 'And it was to do with the Jews, not Spanish people.'

'No, *no*. I never said it was. Look, it's complicated. I'll explain proper tomorrow. The thing is, this bloke was recruiting for something called the International Brigade. They need all the 'elp they c'n get, from every country who'll join. It's a good cause, love. There's even blokes from universities givin' up their studies to go 'n 'elp, so it *must* be right.'

'You'd have to fight, though. It'd be dangerous.'

'Nah. Nothing to it. This bloke reckons that a lot of it will be mendin' the roads that've been blown up so's the proper soldiers can get their tanks on the go.' When he saw the doubt and anguish in her eyes he grasped her shoulders. 'I want to go, Mar. Don't you see? It's a proper man's job. Something worthwhile. I'll be able to hold my head up again.'

'How long would you be gone?'

'I dunno. This bloke reckons if everyone 'elps, all the other countries, it'll be over in no time. And maybe by then there'll be jobs goin' 'ere again.'

'We'll miss you, Tom.'

'Get on wi' you. Glad to have me out from under your feet, I shouldn't wonder.'

She put her arms around him and held him tightly. 'Oh, *Tom*. I might get onto you sometimes, but I do love you.'

It seemed no time at all before Tom was gone. Maryan had visualised him going off to Spain, smart in some kind of uniform, but he left home in his best suit and cap, carrying a cheap, newly purchased suitcase containing a few essentials. She wanted to go with him to the station to see him off, but he told her that they were all to meet at a rallying point, so she had to be content with going with him to the end of the street, where he kissed her and Amy and set off to catch the tram. Maryan watched him go with a bleak feeling of helplessness. Tears thickened her throat. He looked shabby and vulnerable, yet he carried himself erect, proud to be part of something which would restore his pride. Suddenly her heart was flooded with love and pity and a sadness she could hardly contain.

'Oh, Tom. Come back safe,' she begged inwardly. 'If you only come back safe I'll put all those impossible girlish dreams out of my head and be a good wife to you.' Beside her, Amy wept noisily.

'I want my dad. I don't want him to go away,' she wailed.

Autumn came early that year. By mid-September it was already cold and wet. Each morning they wakened to fog, swirling and clammy, trapping all the city fumes and odours so that it became as noxious and choking as poisonous gas. Sarah's chest was bad. The damp weather always brought on her cough and made her joints painful. Amy seemed to have an almost permanent cold and Maryan put it all down to the rising damp the little house was prone to. If only they had somewhere better to live.

There had been only two short letters from Tom: one to say that he had arrived at a place called Aragon, and another several weeks later to say that they were now bound for Madrid where the worst of the fighting was. The letters told very little. Tom's education had been even sketchier than Maryan's and he was no letter writer. His hastily scribbled notes gave nothing more than the barest facts, but they always ended with the words: *I love you. Kiss Amy for me. Your loving husband, Tom.* Never before had she read the newspapers so avidly. At the Leighs' she searched the pages of *The Times* and the *Daily Express* for news about the Civil War in Spain. Recently she had read something that seriously alarmed her. The British Government had decreed that men who enlisted on either side in the Spanish conflict would be liable to two years' imprisonment on their return. Would Tom return only to disappear inside for two years? It seemed so unfair when he was only trying to help.

She arrived early one morning at 124 Hackney Road and let herself in at the area door with her key. The kitchen felt chilly and it was soon evident that the boiler had gone out. Maryan took off her coat and rolled up her sleeves, setting about the clearing and re-lighting of it. Mr Sam would not be happy if there was no hot water for his bath at eight o'clock. It struck her as odd as she fetched coke from the bunker in the yard. Normally Mr Sam attended to the boiler himself before retiring. He must have forgotten last night.

It wasn't long before she had the fire alight and the kitchen warm again. The kettle boiled and she made the tea, setting the early morning tray and putting on a clean white apron, ready to take it upstairs. But before she had time to fill the pot the door opened and Rachel stood on the threshold in her dressing gown. Maryan took one look at her face and felt the blood chill in her veins. Something was terribly wrong. Mrs Leigh never came downstairs in her dressing gown. She always dressed as soon as she got up. But what Maryan found so alarming was the expression on her employer's face. Since yesterday she seemed to have aged ten years. Her eyes were red and swollen with weeping and her whole face seemed to sag dejectedly. Maryan put down the tray and went to her.

'Mrs Leigh – come and sit down. Whatever is the matter?'

Rachel walked past her into the kitchen and sank heavily into a

56

chair. 'Sit down, Maryan,' she said quietly. 'I'm afraid I've got some very bad news to tell you.'

Maryan did as she was told, her heart quickening with apprehension.

'Last night Jessica went into premature labour,' Rachel said. 'Marcus telephoned his father and I around midnight and asked us to go to the nursing home. He said that he just wanted us to be with him, but we guessed from his voice that there was something seriously wrong.'

'Oh no.' Maryan put out her hand instinctively. 'Not the baby – is it . . .?'

'It was a little boy – stillborn.' Rachel bit her lips in the effort to keep the tears at bay. 'Jessica died an hour later. They're both dead, Maryan. We've lost our daughter-in-law and our grandchild.' As she said the words her control left her and she dissolved into a helpless torrent of weeping.

Rigid with shock, Maryan sat for a moment, longing to help and yet unsure of what to do. She'd never seen her employer lose control like this. She was such a strong woman. It was terrible to see her distress. The older woman's face crumpled and distorted with grief as the passionate sobs seemed to tear her apart. Rising, Maryan went round the table and put her arms awkwardly around Rachel's heaving shoulders.

'Oh, Mrs Leigh – if only there was something I could do,' she said. 'If only I could help you. Oh, please don't cry like that. Don't take on so.' Hastily she poured a cup of the fresh tea she had made and put the cup in front of Rachel. 'Here – drink that,' she urged. 'It'll make you feel a bit better.'

Rachel drank the tea and, with an enormous effort, regained control of herself. 'Th-thank you, dear,' she said hoarsely. 'I'm so sorry. I'll be myself again in a moment.'

'What happened?' Maryan whispered. 'Were there – complications?'

'It was her heart,' Rachel said. 'The doctor told Marcus afterwards that Jessica had a heart condition. The pregnancy had already worsened it and the labour was more than she could stand. He'd told Jessica early in the pregnancy but she refused to let him tell Marcus. It seems now that she'd had the condition from birth. She should never have tried to have children. But no one told Marcus. Can you imagine how he feels?'

Maryan was stunned. 'But – didn't her parents know?'

'Of *course* they did,' Rachel said angrily, her colour returning. 'They knew, but they never told Marcus – never mentioned a word about it to any of us. They let her marry him and try to have children and they knew all the time what it might do to her.'

Maryan shook her head. 'I don't understand. Their own daughter. How *could* they?'

Rachel dabbed at her eyes. 'We went straight to their house last night and faced them with it. I couldn't rest until I'd spoken to them.'

'And what did they say?'

'Apart from being upset at losing Jessica they were quite calm. They'd been expecting it since she was a small child, so unlike us, they were prepared. They said they never told her about her heart. They wanted her to have what happiness she could from life while she lived. They said that she'd had more happiness in the past two years than most people have in a lifetime. And they thanked us. Can you believe that? They actually *thanked* us for giving her our son. My poor Marcus. My poor, poor boy.' Rachel began to weep again, silent, hopeless tears that slipped down her cheeks unchecked. Maryan took both her hands and pressed them warmly, tears filling her own eyes.

'Mrs Leigh, I know how you must feel, but I can see what they meant,' she said gently. 'I expect they only did what they thought was best for their daughter. But they should have considered you too. And poor Mr Marcus.'

'If you could have seen him last night,' Rachel said, shaking her head. 'He's devastated – sick with grief. I don't think he'll ever get over it. All he could say was that he wanted to die too.' Rachel clasped her hand to her mouth. 'My own dear boy – and there's nothing I can do to ease his pain.'

'Look – would you like me to go home and bring Mum?' Maryan said suddenly.

Rachel's face brightened. 'Sarah? Oh, I would like to see her. The Rabbi will be coming later to say the Kaddish with us, but it would mean a lot to me to be able to see Sarah in the meantime.'

'Of course, I'll go at once.' Glad to have something positive to do, Maryan was already putting on her coat.

All the way to Crimea Terrace all she could think about was the way she'd wanted the bright bubble of happiness that Marcus shared with his lovely Jessica to burst. How could she have been so spiteful? Now he'd lost his wife and the child they'd both longed for, and she felt partly responsible, almost as though she had caused the tragedy through the power of her evil jealousy.

When Sarah heard the news she was stunned. 'Oh my dear lord. What a terrible thing to happen. Of course I'll come. My poor Miss

Rachel,' she said, shaking her head. Eager to help, she moved quickly. Changing out of her working clothes, she donned her best coat and hat and hurried back to Hackney Road with Maryan to give what comfort she could to her old friend and employer.

In the dining room Sam ate his breakfast sad-faced and alone, an hour and a half later than was normal. He hardly touched the omelette Maryan made for him, toying only with a piece of toast. As he rose to leave the table Maryan put out her hand.

'Mr Sam. I'm so sorry – about – poor Mr Marcus's wife.'

Sam shook his head slowly from side to side. 'Sometimes when things like this happen it makes us wonder why,' he said. 'If only the child could have lived, he would at least have had something left of her. As it is . . .' he shook his head again. 'It seems so cruel.'

'Is he upstairs in his old room? Can I do anything for him?' Maryan asked. 'Take him something to eat – a drink?'

Sam shook his head. 'Oh no, my dear. He isn't here. He will remain with dear little Jessica until she is laid to rest.' He smiled gently at her shocked expression. 'That is our custom, Maryan. It's usual. There is something you can do for me though, if you will?'

'Of course. Anything.'

'Go to the factory for me and tell them what has happened. I shall not return for a week. Jim Harris will understand. Tell him I want him to take charge for me.'

The weeks of mourning that followed were bleak, but gradually the Leighs returned to normal, at least on the surface. The two familes spent much of the mourning month of shloshim together. After much talking they came to terms with Jessica's death and her parents made the Leighs understand, at least in part, the motives for their deceit. They had loved their daughter, wanted so much for her to be happy for what little time she had. She had been so in love with Marcus that they were afraid to tell him in case he was daunted by the thought of her illness. They had hoped against hope for some miracle to come out of that love.

For Maryan it was a depressing time. No more letters came from Tom and although she knew he was no letter writer she began to grow anxious. She thought of him in October when she read of the men who marched all the way from Jarrow to London with their petition. Tom would certainly have taken part had he still been here. When would all the trouble and hardship end?

Marcus was rarely seen. Unable to face the house in Highgate without Jessica, he had returned to his parents' home permanently, but he spent most of his time either at the factory or locked in his old studio at the top of the house, sometimes even taking his meals there. On the occasions when Maryan did see him she hardly recognised the gaunt, hollow-cheeked man as the carefree, debonair Marcus Leigh she had once known, and she wondered how she could have thought that the better off were immune to suffering. Tragedy could strike anywhere, on rich and poor alike, she told herself.

Amy still missed her dad. But life at school was better. Once the controversy over her name had died down she began to enjoy her lessons and Miss Vickers soon discovered that she had a quick and able pupil in Amy Jessop. At first the endless questions from the little girl with the bright blue enquiring eyes and soft dark curls, sitting at the desk directly beneath her, caused her irritation. She could barely get out half a sentence before the child was asking the whys and wherefores of the subject, but soon the two grew used to each other and learned to come to a compromise.

'If you will only wait until I have finished speaking, Amy, you will probably find there is no need to ask your question,' she said patiently. 'But if there is when I have finished, I will answer it for you.'

So Amy would wait with barely concealed impatience until Miss Vickers had finished speaking; during which time she would store up, not one question, but half a dozen.

That Christmas they put on a play. It was based on Cinderella and, to her great delight, Amy was given the part of the fairy. Sarah made her a spangled costume and every night either Sarah or Maryan would hear the lines for her before she went to bed. She was so proud and excited.

'Will Dad be home in time to come and see me in the play?' she asked repeatedly. But Maryan could not say.

It was now almost five months since she had heard from Tom and although she said nothing to her mother, the worry of it was eating at her constantly. Searching through the discarded newspapers for news of the Spanish conflict at the Leighs', she read about the bombing and the fierce fighting that was raging there. Tom had made it sound like a mere skirmish, yet it seemed to her like a dangerous, full-scale war. The papers spoke frighteningly of many casualties and some even had pictures of wounded and bandaged men. It was all very worrying.

But in early December something happened that took everyone's mind off their immediate problems. The new, uncrowned king abdicated in order to marry a divorced woman.

Everywhere people were talking about it. Mrs Leigh let Maryan come up to the drawing room to hear the abdication speech on the wireless. By the time it was over Maryan was in tears and Rachel's eyes were suspiciously moist. Sarah had been tight-lipped and uncompromising in her view; she was adamant that he shouldn't do it. He was letting his family down, deserting the destiny he was born to, neglecting his duty. But as Maryan listened to the young king's speech, so clearly painful for him to make, she thought she understood. He could not go on – could not face the duties of being king without the woman he loved at his side. Poor man. Poor, lonely man. It was true, sadness was not the prerogative of the poor and lowly.

The school play was a great success. Cinderella and her 'Prince Charming' sang the hit song of the year – 'Just the Way You Look Tonight' – with Miss Vickers at the piano and brought the house down. And Amy looked so dainty in her spangled frock as the fairy, remembering to wave her wand at exactly the right moment and not forgetting her lines once. Maryan was so proud of her. After the play was over she and Sarah helped her change out of her costume and brought her home, tired out but still chattering excitedly. After a cup of cocoa she was packed off to bed and Maryan and Sarah sat down to drink a last cup of tea before going to bed themselves.

The sudden knocking on the street door startled them both. Sarah looked at her daughter.

'Who can that be, this time o' night?'

Maryan stood up. 'I'll go, Mum. I expect it's one of the neighbours.'

But when she opened the door she found a man standing outside. He wore a raincoat and cap and he was leaning heavily on a stick.

'Mrs Jessop?' he enquired. 'Mrs Maryan Jessop?'

'That's right.' Maryan was mystified. Not only was the man a total stranger but he had a strange accent too. He wasn't even a Londoner. Yet he knew her name.

'I wonder – could I p'raps come in a minute?' The man said, swaying a little. 'I came round earlier, you see, and you weren't in. I got a bad leg injury in Spain and . . .'

At the word *Spain* Maryan instantly felt a stab of alarm. She held the door open. 'Of course, come in, Mr . . .'

'Bell,' the man said. 'Frank Bell.'

In the kitchen Maryan introduced her mother. 'This is my mother, Mrs Brown. Mum, this is Mr Bell. He's been in Spain.' She looked at the man. 'There's tea in the pot. Would you like a cup?'

He removed his cap. 'Thank you. That'd be right welcome.' He sat on the chair Maryan pulled out for him, shuffling his feet a little and staring into the fire.

When Maryan went through to the scullery to refill the kettle, Sarah said quickly: 'Is it 'er Tom? Has something happened to 'im?'

The man looked up at her. Biting his lip, he nodded briefly.

'Then tell her quickly,' Sarah said. 'Don't keep 'er hangin' on.'

'Where are you from, Mr Bell?' Maryan asked as she came back.

'Yorkshire. A little place called Bedale.'

'And you came all this way to see us? To – to see – me ...' Maryan looked from Sarah to Frank Bell and back again. She'd known instinctively the moment she opened the door that the man was the bearer of bad news. Now she couldn't put off the dreaded moment any longer. She put down the teapot and sat down at the table. 'What is it, Mr Bell? Is it Tom?'

Frank Bell stood up, folding and refolding his cap nervously. 'Tom was a mate of mine,' he said. 'We were together all through the fighting. He were a good mate. A fine chap.'

'You say, *was*? Are you trying to tell me he's . . .?'

'I'm sorry, Mrs Jessop. It were at Madrid, about two months since. I came to find you as soon as they sent me home. We both promised each other we'd do that, you see – if anything 'appened like.' He moistened his lips, looking anxiously from one to the other. 'It were right quick, Missis. He must've died instant-like. A shell, it were. I got me leg smashed and Tom . . .' He broke off as Maryan crumpled before his eyes, sinking into a chair with a groan. Sarah rose quickly and saw him to the door.

'Thank you for coming, Mr Bell. It was good of you. But for you God knows when we'd have heard. It can't have been a nice thing for you to 'ave to do.'

In the kitchen she gathered Maryan to her and rocked her gently. 'There, there, luvvie. I know how it feels, believe me. He did what he felt he had to do, just like your dad. He died fightin' bravely for something he believed in. One day, when you feel better, you'll be proud of 'im. You'll be glad he gave his life tryin' to 'elp folks.'

On the dark stairs behind the closed door Amy shivered in her thin nightdress. Alone upstairs in the little truckle bed in the room she shared with Grandma she'd been unable to sleep. The words she'd had to say in the play were still going round and round in her head and every time she shut her eyes she could see the sparkle of the lights on her pretty frock and hear the music Miss Vickers played on the piano. It had all been so exciting, the applause and the laughter, the gasps of delight when she made her entrance in the sparkly dress with real wings at the back and waved her magic wand. She wished they could do it all again tomorrow. Perhaps if she went downstairs again Mum and Grandma wouldn't be too cross, just this once. Maybe they'd let her talk about it all some more – maybe even make her another cup of cocoa.

She'd been halfway down when she heard the man's voice and stopped, deciding to wait till he'd gone. Sitting down on the stairs she pulled her nightie down over her knees till it reached her ankles, to keep her legs warm. It was cold here on the stairs but it'd be warm in the kitchen. She pictured it: the range fire, glowing red under the high mantel with the china dogs; the red chenille cloth on the table with its fringe of bobbles that she loved to play with; Grandma's chair with the squashy round crocheted cushion on it. Then suddenly her attention was caught by something the man was saying. *Tom was a mate of mine – a good mate – a fine chap. He must've died instant-like.*

So – Dad wasn't coming home after all. He was dead. Very slowly she got up and crept back up the cold oilcloth-covered stairs and into bed. Slipping under the covers and shivering in the darkness, she tried to absorb what she'd heard the man say. *He must've died instant-like.* She didn't know what 'instant-like' meant, but Kenny Jackson's dad had died in hospital last summer so she knew what that meant. She'd asked Grandma at the time and she'd said it meant he'd gone to live with Jesus in heaven and wasn't ever coming home no more. Suddenly she felt afraid and small and lonely. 'I want my dad,' she whimpered plaintively into the darkness as the tears ran down her cheeks and into her mouth. It was Mum's fault, she decided. Mum had made him go away. Amy had heard their quarrels even if they thought she hadn't; all those times when they thought she was asleep or not listening or didn't understand. She was sure Dad only went because he hadn't got a job and Mum made him feel bad about it. And now he was dead and never coming home – and they'd never, *never* see him again. And it hurt so much that she didn't know how to bear it.

Chapter Five

'There, is that better? Can you see now?' Marcus hoisted Amy up onto his shoulders.

'Oooh, yes. I can see lovely now.'

With her head high above the crowd, Amy could see clear along the Mall all the way to the Palace. 'And they're coming – they're *coming*,' she squealed delightedly'. Marcus pushed Maryan in front of him so that she too could see the coronation procession as it passed. Everyone cheered as the golden coach carrying the new King George and his pretty queen drew nearer. Amy waved the little Union Jack that Marcus had bought her from the man selling them at Hyde Park Corner. Her eyes were round as she watched the scarlet-clad Yeomen of the Guard who flanked the coach and the splendidly liveried postilians. Then came the Guards in their plumed helmets, riding on proudly stepping horses, the light flashing on their polished golden breastplates and their spurs jingling. As the coach itself passed she leaned forward to get a better view of the figures inside. She glimpsed crimson and purple velvet robes, trimmed with snowy ermine; she caught the flash of a diamond tiara and, very briefly, glimpsed the profile of the King himself, his thin face sober and dignified.

'I saw them, Mum. I *saw* them!' she yelled, jumping up and down with excitement.

'Steady on, you'll have me over,' Marcus laughed as he swung her down to the ground again. 'There – that's all for now.' He looked at Maryan. 'It'll be a couple of hours before they're back from the Abbey. Do you want to stay here and keep your place, or would you like to go to the park?'

Maryan shook her head. 'I think Amy has had enough for the time being. Maybe we should go and have something to eat. It's been a long time since breakfast.'

The three of them had been up since dawn, travelling up to Buckingham Palace from Hackney in Marcus's car. He had left it at a friend's house in Knightsbridge and they'd walked the rest of the way to get a good position from which to watch the procession. But even at that early hour the pavements had already been crowded. Some people had been there all night, camping out to get a better view. Whole families were there, frying breakfast on camping stoves, passing round mugs of tea, singing and joking merrily. All of them were oblivious to the cool weather and determined to make the most of the historic occasion. And now, after their long wait, they had finally been rewarded. The splendour, the pomp and ceremony had thrilled everyone. But for now there was a lull and people were moving off – some to take up new positions; some, like Maryan, Marcus and Amy, to find a place where they could snatch an hour's respite.

They walked across into St James's Park and found a bench under the trees. There, Maryan unpacked the picnic they had brought with them. Mrs Leigh had insisted on providing the lunch, but it had been Maryan who had made the sandwiches, filled the flasks and packed everything into the specially equipped hamper Rachel had lent. Amy's eyes were round as she accepted a chicken sandwich and a ripe tomato and glimpsed the other delicacies awaiting them in the basket.

'It's very good of you to bring us like this,' Maryan said, passing the sandwiches to Marcus.

He smiled. 'Not at all. We couldn't let Amy miss seeing a piece of history in the making, could we?'

Maryan took a bite of her sandwich and chewed thoughtfully. 'I couldn't help feeling sorry for them. They never wanted to be king and queen, did they? I mean, it was Edward who was brought up for it. They do say that King George is very shy and has difficulty with his speech, poor man.'

Marcus shrugged. 'We none of us know what's in store for us, do we?' he said ruefully. 'We just have to get on with life and play the hand it deals us the best we can. I daresay he'll do his best just as we all have to.'

Maryan stole a sideways glance at him. It was eight months now since Jessica's death. For the first four he had hardly spoken to anyone, remaining in his room and working long hours, often far into the night. When they passed on the stairs or in the hallway he would nod to her as though she were a stranger. She longed to help him, but this cold, gaunt stranger seemed so distant, so remote that she didn't dare to approach him. Mrs Leigh had been at her wits'

65

end, fearing for his health. But in the early spring of this year he had launched his first fashion collection. It had been a great success and now the orders were rolling in. His success had cheered him and he'd begun to look more like his old self. Gradually he'd become more approachable. He'd even begun to smile occasionally. And then he had astonished Maryan one morning a few weeks ago by offering to take her and Amy to see the coronation.

She'd been working on the top floor one morning when he suddenly emerged from his studio, making her jump.

'Oh – Mr Marcus. I thought you were out this morning.'

He laughed. '*Mr* Marcus? For heaven's sake, Maryan, don't call me that. It makes me feel like an old man, and it makes *you* sound like a faithful old retainer. We're still friends, I hope.'

She'd blushed. 'Of course. It's just . . .'

'That my mother employs you? Well, as if that makes any differ-ence.' He took a step closer and touched her arm, his eyes serious. 'Maryan, I want to apologise for not speaking to you before. I've been meaning to for months; to say how very sorry I was to hear about your husband.'

She averted her eyes. 'Oh, thank you, Mr – er – thank you, Marcus.'

'Believe me, I know all too well how you must be feeling. Losing the person you love is the very worst thing that can happen to you. And when it's your husband – and you have his child to bring up alone . . .'

'*Don't*.' She stopped him with a shake of her head. Not, as he thought, because it was too painful for her to speak of, but because talking about it in this way still made her feel guilty. She'd been fond of Tom, of course. She had grieved over his death, and it was certainly true that she missed him. But Amy wasn't Tom's child, and Tom wasn't, and never had been, the man she loved. Not in the same way that Marcus had loved Jessica. Nothing, not even his death, could alter that. Talking about their respective bereavements in the same breath seemed wrong somehow. It made her uncomfortable.

'I'm sorry, Maryan,' he said. 'I understand how difficult it is to talk about it. I just wanted you to know that I do feel for you.'

'I know. Thank you.' She made herself look at him. 'It's good to see you looking better.' He *did* look better. Leaner and older, perhaps. He had grown a moustache, too, which gave him a more mature appearance, but the light was back in his eyes again. He had, as his relieved mother had put it, 'come back to them'.

'I've been thinking,' he went on. 'How would Amy like to go and see the coronation?'

She stared at him in surprise. 'Well – I'm sure she'd love it. I was trying to think of some way we could get there.'

'Then think no more. I'll take you. We can go up in the car, early in the morning before the crowds get too thick. Perhaps we could take a picnic. Make a day of it.'

'I'm sure she'd love that. It would be a real treat. But are you sure you won't have better things to do – other people to spend the day with?'

'Who better than you and Amy?' He laughed. 'To tell you the truth it's a good excuse for me to go and see it myself. I'm just a big kid at heart.' He sighed. 'And I seem to have lost touch with most of my friends these past months. So – if *you've* nothing better to do on May the twelfth?'

So here they were. At first Maryan had had doubts about whether she should have accepted his offer. What would Mrs Leigh think about it? Would she feel it was beneath her son to take his mother's servant and her child out for the day? But Rachel had seemed as pleased as Marcus at her acceptance, even offering to provide a picnic lunch for them all.

'It's so good to see him taking an interest in something again,' she said as they made a list of what to buy for the picnic. 'And it's so like him to think of those less fortunate than himself. Did you know he'd become interested in underprivileged children lately?' Somewhat deflated, Maryan admitted that she didn't.

'Oh yes,' Mrs Leigh went on. 'He's become very interested in charity. He was saying only yesterday that he might organise a fashion show and give the proceeds to Jewish refugee children. There are so many fleeing from Hitler's tyrany in Germany.' She smiled at Maryan. 'And they do say, don't they, that charity begins at home?'

It was only then that Maryan realised that far from viewing her as a contender for Marcus's heart, Mrs Leigh saw her son's gesture as purely altruistic.

When they had finished their lunch and Amy had fed her crusts to the clamouring ducks, the clouds that had been gathering all morning suddenly fulfilled their promise of rain. As Maryan took out the Mackintosh cape she had brought with her Amy began to whine.

'I don't want that on. It makes me feel all hot and sticky.'

Maryan shook her gently. 'Don't be awkward. You're showing us up in front of Mr Leigh – when he's been so kind to us too.'

Seeing that the child looked tired, Marcus said: 'What do you say we collect the car and go for a run in the country? I think perhaps we've all had enough of crowds for one day.'

Amy brightened. 'Oh, yes, please. Can we, Mum? I want to see some cows and horses.'

So Maryan gave in. Driving out into the green of the countryside brought back poignant memories. It seemed strange to her, sitting beside Marcus as he drove, unaware that the child in the back seat was his own flesh and blood. She shut the thought out quickly. She had promised herself when she married Tom that no one else should ever know. It could do no good now that he was dead. All the same, she couldn't help fantasising a little as they drove along; imagining what it might have been like, had things turned out differently; if they could have been a proper family.

'Where are we going?' Amy asked.

'I'm going to show you something.' Marcus turned to Maryan. 'I don't suppose my parents have told you that they're building a house in the country?'

'No.' She shook her head, a little alarmed. 'They're thinking of moving then?'

'Not yet. It's for their retirement really. And perhaps weekends and holidays in the meantime.' He glanced at her and lowered his voice. 'And of course if there's a war they'll be safer out of London.'

She felt a chill run through her veins. War was something she refused even to let herself think about. 'There won't be, though, will there? Surely, after last time . . .'

He shook his head. 'I'm afraid it looks more and more as though Hitler will have to be taught a lesson by someone. I can't think why the Government are so complacent over it. We should be arming – showing him our might instead of trying to placate him.' He sighed. 'But let's not talk of war today of all days. Look, this is the place I've brought you to see. It's called Hazelfield.'

They were driving into a pretty village. It nestled in a green hollow in the leafy Essex countryside. In the centre was a large pond surrounded by emerald grass. Cottages were ranged above it on all sides, some with thatched roofs. On the hill on the farthest side a little church perched, its tower just visible above the tall trees of chestnut, elm and oak that were bursting into new green leaf.

'Oh, isn't it pretty?' Maryan exclaimed. 'Amy, isn't this a nice place?''

'Look – more ducks,' Amy said delightedly. 'Can I go and feed them? There are still some crusts left in the basket.'

When the ducks had had their fill Marcus took them to see the Leighs' partly built house. It was on the fringe of the village, not far from the church, which Marcus told them was called St Peter and St Paul. Built in the fashionable mock-Tudor style, the house was almost finished; only the interior had yet to be completed. They walked about in the empty shell and Amy enjoyed herself by trying to guess what the unplastered rooms would be.

'There are to be five bedrooms and a housekeeper's flat over the garage,' Marcus told them. 'They decided on five so that Jessica and I could have a permanent nursery here, with room for a nursemaid too.'

'I see.' Maryan glanced at him apprehensively. She had carefully avoided mentioning Jessica to him, but he spoke her name almost casually.

'But there, I always say you can't have too many bedrooms,' he went on brightly. 'You never know who you might want to invite. Everyone loves a country house party.'

'When are they thinking of retiring?' Maryan asked. 'I'd have thought your father had plenty of time yet.'

Marcus smiled. 'Not for ages, I daresay. Dad likes to be in charge at the factory, as you know. I daresay he'll keep on for as long as he's able. But they couldn't resist buying this plot of land when it came on the market. If there's a war building will probably stop, so they thought they'd better build their dream house while they still could.' He looked at her, one eyebrow raised. 'If you're worried about your job, don't be.' He laughed. 'Anyway, you'll have married again long before then.'

'Marry again? Oh no.' Maryan shook her head. 'I'm not sure I'd want to.'

He nodded. 'Nor me.'

'Anyway, who'd have me?'

'Anyone who wasn't blind, I'd say,' Marcus said, his eyes twinkling. 'You're pretty and still young – what, twenty-one?'

'Twenty-three now.' Maryan was silent as they walked back to the car. She had enjoyed the day, but in a way she wished it had never happened. When Marcus had invited them to the coronation her hopes had foolishly risen again. Perhaps he had asked her because . . . Maybe it might still be possible . . . She had quickly squashed the hope, admonishing herself – telling herself it was out of the question. Marcus would never look at another woman, let alone her. What they had shared six years ago had been a mere childish fling – nothing more. Certainly nothing to compare with the love he had had for Jessica.

Amy was quiet on the drive back to London and, turning to look at her, Maryan found she had fallen fast asleep on the back seat.

'Tuck the rug round her,' Marcus said. 'We don't want her to catch cold after such a perfect day, do we?'

Maryan did as he suggested. 'Thank you for everything, Marcus,' she said. 'Today has meant a lot to Amy. It'll be something she'll never forget. I daresay I wouldn't have managed to take her on my own.'

'Not a bit of it. I've enjoyed myself tremendously. And, like you, I wouldn't have come on my own, so you've done me a favour.' For a moment he was silent, his eyes on the road ahead, then he said: 'Maryan, can I tell you something?'

'Of course.'

'In confidence, I mean.' He glanced at her. 'I'm not even telling my parents.'

She shifted anxiously in her seat. What disclosure was he about to make? 'Are you sure you want to tell me?'

'Yes. I need to tell someone, just in case . . .' He glanced at her. 'I'm going to Germany again in a couple of weeks' time. Ostensibly it's a trip to Paris for the summer collections. But afterwards I'm going on into Germany.'

Remembering his experiences there three years before Maryan felt her blood run cold. 'But – what for?'

'My brother-in-law, Harry Weiss, is going with me. The Weiss's have relatives over there. They're trying to help them get out before they're interned. At the moment they're still free to leave, but they aren't allowed to take their money or valuables out of the country.' He glanced at her. 'So we're going to smuggle out what we can for them.'

She turned to look at him. 'But how will you do that?'

'There is a friend who is a dealer in precious gems. He will convert the money into diamonds for them. Harry and I will arrange it and bring the stones back with us. We'll sell them over here and bank the money ready for when they get away.'

'But – won't it be dangerous?'

Marcus shrugged. 'Frankly, Maryan, I don't much care one way or the other.'

Shocked, she touched his arm. 'Please – don't say that.'

He sighed. 'Everything I lived for is gone. I might as well use what's left of my life helping others.'

'If your mother heard you say that . . .'

'You mustn't tell her. You promised.'

'Of course I won't. But you must think of them, Marcus. They love you. You're all they have. If anything happened to you . . .'

He shook his head. 'There are so many desperate people in danger over there. Others are risking their lives every day to help their

70

friends. I've been so lucky all my life. I've had so much happiness, Maryan. Maybe my time has already run out, who knows? But what's my one meaningless life when there are so many at risk?'

Later that night, lying in bed with Amy sleeping soundly beside her, Maryan thought about their day together. And of the secret Marcus had confided to her on the way home. In some ways she wished he hadn't. He could have no idea how much the prospect of what he was about to do worried her. The weight of it lay heavy on her mind. What he proposed to do was madness. If he were caught ... She shuddered at the prospect. One read in the papers about how Hitler's cruel regime was persecuting Jewish people. It seemed one needed only the remotest blood tie to be labelled Jew and made to wear the star of David on one's clothing and be jeered at in the streets. She had read even the mothers of little babies were made to display the star on their prams. Closing her eyes she whispered a prayer that he might be kept safe, wishing that there were more that she could do.

I saw the King and Queen in their golden coach. I went in a big car, all the way there an' back, and we went for a drive in the country after and we 'ad a picnic an' fed some ducks on a pond.'

'You never. You're makin' it up again. You're a great big liar, Amy Jessop.'

Amy stood in the playground surrounded by her disbelieving schoolmates.

'No I ain't then.' She stood firm, her hands on her hips and her chin thrust forward. 'I *did* go, s'there.'

'Whose car did you go in then?'

'Mr Leigh's. It's big, with lovely soft seats and it c'n go ever so fast.'

'Don't b'lieve yer. Why'd Mr Leigh take *you* to see the coronation?'

''Cause – 'cause ...' Amy cast around in her mind for a really watertight reason. ''Cause he's gonna marry my mum,' she said with a sudden burst of inspiration.

This revelation silenced her tormenters, apart from a girl called Lily Smith, a little older and more streetwise than the rest. She elbowed her way to the front of the group and stood challengingly in front of Amy.

'Bet 'e ain't,' she said scathingly. 'Bet yer tellin' whoppers again, Amy Jessop. Anyway – you ain't so clever. You missed the street party. We had a lovely time. We 'ad jelly an' cake and we all got a mug with a piksher of the King's 'ead on it.'

'Mr Leigh bought me a flag. *We* 'ad chicken sandwiches an' salmon ones an' cream cakes an' lemonade an' *pop*,' Amy retaliated.

'You *never*.'

'We *did*. Ask my mum.'

'You're a show-off, Amy Jessop. I '*ates* show-offs.'

Amy took a step towards her accuser, her hand reaching for one of Lily's scrawny pigtails, but before the two girls could resort to fisticuffs the bell went for the end of playtime and they all trooped back into school. Behind the lid of her desk Amy put out her tongue at Lily Smith, a gesture to which Lily responded with her best grimace, carefully perfected after long hours of practice at the mirror. It consisted of pushing up the tip of her nose whilst pulling down her lower eyelids with the fingers of the other hand. It made her look like a bulldog. Amy treated it with the contempt it deserved, tossing her head disdainfully and wrinkling her nose.

After Tom's death Amy had become what her grandmother called 'disagreeable'. She seemed to bear a grudge against her mother and she became uncommunicative, clamming up and refusing to talk. Sarah said they should ignore it. She was sure that Amy's truculence would pass, but as the weeks went on and the situation worsened, Maryan grew anxious. Why did Amy treat her as though she'd done something wrong? Her patience gradually wore thin and finally, after one of Amy's worst attacks of awkwardness she lost her temper and became downright angry. It was almost as though the child deliberately tried to goad her into anger.

'What's the matter with you, Amy?' she demanded, shaking her by the arm. 'Your Grandma and I do everything we can for you. Why are you so naughty all the time?' When Amy turned away with a toss of her head and refused to answer, Maryan's temper snapped and she lashed out, grabbing Amy and slapping her legs.

'You naughty girl. You don't know how lucky you are,' she shouted. 'You're a horrid, ungrateful little girl.'

'I'm not. *You're* horrid.' The angry tears sprang from Amy's eyes and her face grew red as she said: '*You* sent my dad away. You didn't love him and you don't love me. You never take me out like he did. You never play with me. Nothing's nice no more. I – I *hate* you.' The tears grew into noisy sobs and she flung herself face downwards onto the floor.

The outburst frightened Maryan. She'd always known that Amy was fond of Tom, and she knew she missed him, but she'd had no idea that she actually held her to blame for his going away. Sinking to her knees beside the sobbing child she touched her gently.

72

'Amy – Amy love. Don't take on like that. I did love Dad. And I love you too. It hurts me when you behave like you do.'

Amy stopped crying and looked up at her, her huge blue eyes swimming with pain and bewilderment. 'You – you were always nagging him. I heard him say so. You wanted 'im to go away. I want Dad to come 'ome again. I – I want my Dad,' she whimpered.

Moved to tears herself, Maryan gathered the child to her and held her close. 'Amy – don't cry like that. You're too little to understand. Grown-up people don't always mean what they say. It wasn't like you think. Dad went away because he wanted to do something good. To help people. But he can't come home again, love. You know that. And we've got to try to get used to it as best we can.' She took out her handkerchief and wiped Amy's tears away. 'I do love you, Amy. Now that Dad's gone you're all I've got. You're the most important person in my life. But I need you to help me. I get sad too.' She sat in her mother's chair close to the range and pulled Amy onto her lap. 'Look, I'll spend more time with you from now on. We'll do all the things you like together. How's that?'

Amy nodded, still hiccupping a little. 'Can – can we go down the market, Sat'day nights?'

'Yes, if you like.'

'An' – an' feed the 'orses round the mews? Take 'em sugar and carrots?'

'Course – anything you like.'

'An' – an' will you stop at 'ome with me all day like Dad did?'

Maryan sighed. 'I can't do that, love. I have to go to work at Mrs Leigh's to earn some money for us all. To buy us food and pay the rent.' She gave Amy a hug. 'Listen, I'll make you a promise. One day it'll all be different. We'll go and live somewhere really nice and have nice clothes to wear.'

'When, Mum – when?' Amy looked at her with round eyes. 'How will we do that?'

'I don't know when or how. It might not be very soon. But I just know that one day we will. You're special, Amy. You've always been special to me since the day you were born. That's why I called you Amethyst.'

Amy frowned. 'I don't wanna be called Amethyst.'

'Not now, maybe. But one day you will,' Maryan prophesied. 'One day – when our ship comes in.'

Amy hadn't the least idea what her mother meant by their ship coming in. But she looked into her eyes and knew that whatever it meant it would certainly happen. Mum was determined that it should. Later she had asked Grandma, who had explained that it meant that something lucky would happen. And now it had begun. Marcus Leigh had taken them out for the day. He was rich. He must be to have such a posh car. They had seen the palace and the coronation. She, Amy Jessop, had seen the new King and Queen. And afterwards they had been for a drive to the country. *Anything* could happen now. Her remark about Mr Leigh marrying her mother had been made on impulse, to shut up that rotten Lily Smith, but the more she thought about it, the more it seemed possible. They liked each other, didn't they? Maybe that was what Mum had meant when she said they'd go and live in a nice house and have smart clothes to wear. Wouldn't it be lovely to be able to ride in that car every day, whenever you liked? Yes – all she had to do was wait. Wait for the ship to come in.

At playtime Lily Smith was back with her taunts and jibes. She cornered Amy in the playground.

'Go on then – when's the weddin'? You gonna be bridesmaid, are yer? In a big frilly frock.'

'I'm not tellin' *you*, Lily Smith.'

'No – 'cause it ain't true,' Lily sneered.

'*Tis* true then. Jus' you wait 'n see.'

'I s'pose you know there's rumours going round about you?' Sarah asked Maryan one evening a week later, after Amy had gone to bed.

Maryan looked up from the pile of darning she was helping her mother with. Sarah had started to take in mending lately. Turning shirt collars and cuffs was easy enough for her on her old sewing machine, but the darning tried her failing eyesight so much that Maryan had taken to helping her with it in the evenings.

'No. What rumours?' she asked.

'It's going round that you're engaged to Mr Marcus, that's what,' said a scandalised Sarah. 'I always said nothing good'd come of him taking you up west on coronation day.'

Maryan let the sock she was darning drop into her lap as she stared at her mother. '*Engaged* – to Marcus? Where did you hear that?'

'That Elsie Smith at number twenty-eight. She said her Lily come 'ome from school with the tale.' Her mouth tightened. 'Seems Amy's been puttin' it about. You want to speak to that young madam.'

'Little devil. I'll have a word with her in the morning.'

Sarah looked at her daughter thoughtfully. 'There ain't no truth in it, is there? Ain't nothin' going on between you an' 'im, I 'ope.'

'Good heavens, Mum, 'course there isn't. You know how shook

up he was over his wife dying. He'll never look at another woman – least of all me.'

But Sarah was shaking her head. 'You be careful, my gel. A man's a man. He might not think of marryin' again, but he'll be needin' a woman for you-know-what. They all do. They're not like us, you know, content to keep ourselves to ourselves.'

'*Mum*!' Maryan flushed. 'I'm sure I don't know what you mean.'

'Oh yes you do.' Sarah bent her head over the sewing machine again. 'I'm on'y thinkin' of you. I don't want you losin' your 'ead, gel. Don't want to see you get used – and hurt.'

'You're being unfair,' Maryan said sharply. 'He was kind enough to take us out, Amy and me. That's all. He's a perfect gentleman.'

'They're all perfect gentlemen till they think they c'n get what they wants.'

'I *told* you, Mum. There's no need for you to worry.'

'All right, if you say so.' Sarah's mouth tightened. 'Just s'long as you both remembers it. Meantime, you better scotch them rumours 'fore they gets back to Miss Rachel and Mr Sam. I wouldn't 'ave them upset for the world.'

Maryan bit back her resentment. Apparently even her own mother felt the Leighs would be appalled at the idea of their son contemplating marriage with the likes of her. Nevertheless, she went hot and cold at the thought of the groundless rumour spreading further. If it reached Marcus's ears she'd die of shame. The following morning before school she spoke to Amy about it.

'Have you been saying anything to that Lily Smith about me and Mr Marcus?'

Amy's cheeks turned very pink. 'On'y that he took us to see the King and Queen getting crowned.'

'Nothing else?'

Amy shuffled her feet. 'No – not much.'

'Because Grandma heard a silly tale about him and me getting married. It's supposed to be you that said it. I'm sure that can't be true.'

'No, Mum.'

'So if you hear anyone spreading stories like that, I want you to tell them it isn't true. Do you understand?'

Amy nodded, swallowing hard. 'Yes, Mum.'

All the way to school she puzzled over how she would wriggle out of her boast without losing face. But by the time she came face to face with Lily Smith her face was beaming. She had thought of the perfect compromise.

'My mum's not going to marry Mr Leigh now,' she said, her

tip-tilted nose in the air. 'Instead me 'n Mum are goin' to go and live with 'im in a lovely big 'ouse in the country.'

Marcus came back safely from his visit to the Paris summer collections. Nothing was said, but once, when he came into the sitting room while Maryan was cleaning, she asked him if his trip had been successful. He winked conspiratorially and held up his thumb.

'Everything went according to plan,' he whispered. 'Not a word, eh?'

Since then he had been abroad twice more. Maryan had no way of knowing if he'd embarked on any more risky exploits, but she strongly suspected that he had.

Christmas loomed closer and, true to her word, Maryan took Amy to the market after work. Amy loved the market best in winter time when the evenings were dark and the hissing naphta flares lit the faces of the traders and threw exciting shadows. She loved to be out when it was dark and frosty; to hear the stallholders' cheerful shouts as they advertised their wares; smell the mingled scents of oranges and evergreens and chrysanthemums, and hear the happy heart-lifting music of the barrel organ. Sometimes Mum would give her a penny to buy chestnuts from the man with the glowing brazier. The hot nuts would warm her chilled fingers and the smell and taste of the roasted nuts would set her mouth watering in anticipation. Of course it wasn't the same without Dad, but the constant pain of missing him had left her now. Sometimes recently she'd had to remind herself of what it was like when he was here, and the thought made her sad. She couldn't be forgetting him, could she? She'd never do that, because nothing would ever be quite as much fun without him. But Mum did her best. And they were friends again now.

In the year that followed Maryan saw Marcus rarely. When he wasn't working away in his studio or out on business, he was abroad on one of his mysterious trips. If she'd harboured any hopes about their friendship blossoming again they were to be dashed. Her mother certainly needn't have worried.

She searched the papers avidly and worried about what she read. Franco was winning the war in Spain. Had Tom's sacrifice been for nothing? She refused to let herself think about that. Some schools were carrying out experimental gas drills and there were pictures of small children wearing the hideous gas masks. It made her shudder. She read about German children being taught to ignore Jewish children. In the schools they were not allowed to speak to, or play with them. It all seemed so senseless and cruel, teaching innocent children to hate. And even Mussolini was following Hitler's lead,

76

expelling Jews from Italy. It all began to look as though Marcus had been right. Someone should teach Hitler a lesson. If only it could be someone else and not poor old England, she mused wistfully.

In August came the terrifying Czechoslovakian crisis. Maryan was sure, like many others, that war would erupt at any moment. But the Prime Minister saved the day, flying home from Munich with the new peace accord he had struck with Herr Hitler and Mussolini. Desperately wanting to believe the best, the British public let out its collective breath again.

It was early one afternoon in mid-November that Marcus arrived home unexpectedly. Both Leighs were at the factory and Maryan met him in the hall. She was shocked by his appearance. He looked pale and haggard and almost dropping with exhaustion.

'There's a fire in the sitting room,' she told him. 'If you go in there I'll bring you some tea. You look chilled through.'

When she took him the tea and some hot buttered toast she had made for him he turned to her with a smile.

'Thank you, Maryan. You're very good to me.'

'Are you all right?' She poured him a cup of tea. 'You look so tired.'

He sighed and leaned forward in his chair, holding his hands out to the blaze. The firelight on his face highlighted the new sharpness and deepened the hollows beneath his cheekbones. As she turned to go he looked up.

'Don't go, Maryan,' he said softly. 'Stay with me. Bring another cup and share the tea. I need someone to talk to.'

Slowly she lowered herself into a chair. 'What's wrong?' she whispered. 'Tell me.'

He was silent for a moment, then he stood up and began to pace the room restlessly. 'I've been in hell, Maryan. I was in Berlin the night before last. I saw things that will haunt me for the rest of my life.' He went on to tell her of the horrors he had seen – of the marauding storm troopers; of well-dressed women, screaming for blood; of a thousand shattered shop windows and broken bodies. 'It's the end of civilisation,' he said, turning gaunt eyes on her. 'And here people believe that blind fool when he comes home waving his piece of paper and talking of peace.'

'Please. You mustn't go again.' She got to her feet. 'It's too dangerous. Anything might have happened to you. You might have been killed too. Please – you must stop now, Marcus. Say you will.'

He stopped to look at her in surprise. 'Don't you see, Maryan – we can't turn our backs on those people. What will the Nazis do next? Someone must *do* something.'

'Of course, but you can't. What good is one man against that?'

He threw up his hands in frustration. 'That's what everyone is saying. In the meantime the madness grows and gathers momentum.'

She looked at his haggard face and love and pity for him overwhelmed her. Throwing caution to the winds she followed her instincts and went to him, putting her arms around him. 'Marcus – please, don't. You're making yourself ill. You helped your brother-in-law get his relatives out. You made sure their money was here for them. You've risked so much, done so much already. Please stop now.'

He leaned against her heavily, seeming to relax for the first time. 'Maryan. What would I do without you? Thank God I have you to talk to.' His arms closed round her and they stood together for a moment.

'You're so tired,' she said at last. 'Finish your tea and toast. I'll go and put a hot water bottle in your bed. What you need is a good long sleep.' She smiled at him. 'Things'll look better then.'

He smiled down at her sadly. 'They'll never look better, Maryan. I've got a terrible feeling deep inside that they're going to get a whole lot worse.' He gave her a little hug. 'But I'll do as you say. You're right. I do need some sleep.' As she made to move away from him he caught her to him and kissed her gently. 'My sweet little Maryan,' he said. 'You re so good to me. Bless you.'

As she prepared his bed for him his words warmed her through and through. He might never love her as she loved him, but she was his confidante. He trusted and depended on her. He told her things he wouldn't even tell his mother. That was worth so much to her.

Summer in Crimea Terrace was never pleasant. The heat seemed to bring out all its worst aspects. The antique drains gave off their noxious odours, dust and flies abounded and the heat in the narrow little streets and alleyways was oppressive and exhausting. Close all the doors and windows and the heat became unbearable; open them and you were obliged to put up with the smells, the dust and flies. The options brought little comfort. And in the summer of 1939 it was worse than ever. The powers that be had decided that precautions must be taken against the possibility of war and air attacks. The sand-bag blast walls that had been built outside the street doors seemed to seal in the heat and keep out the air. It had been suggested that strips of sticky paper be pasted criss-cross on windows, which was supposed to prevent flying glass, and buckets of sand and water were to be kept replenished at back doors in case of incendiary bombs. To most people the precautions were just an irritating nuisance. It was only when gas masks were issued and talk of evacuating the children began to circulate that the prospect of war began to look less like a bad joke and more like a serious possibility.

The previous winter the Leighs had made the decision to take a summer holiday abroad. Rachel had always wanted to go to Norway and, to surprise her, Sam had booked a cruise. Maryan envied them. She had seen the pictures of Norway in the brochures Mr Sam brought home: tall snow-capped mountains, vast blue fjords, cool and serene, reflecting blue skies; forests of beautiful tall trees – a far cry from London's East End, especially in summer. But as the months advanced, the Civil Defence precautions were stepped up and the news grew daily more grave, Sam began to have serious doubts about the wisdom of the holiday he had planned. It seemed mad to risk going abroad unless one had to. Suppose war were to break out while they were away? They might find it difficult to get back into the country. Rachel insisted that he was being pessimistic, but Sam could not agree. War now seemed inevitable. He worried constantly about Marcus. The boy seemed to spend so much of his time in France, almost making it his second home. It was true that Hitler seemed more interested in the countries on Germany's eastern flank, but who knew where he might strike? And if, as was feared, he had his eye on Great Britain, France would be standing in his way. Sam cancelled the holiday and booked one in Scotland instead. He wrote to Marcus asking him to come home and take over the factory for him as a special favour. In fact he wanted his son back in England and in comparative safety, but he knew better than to say so. To Sam's disappointment and frustration, Marcus replied that he had urgent business to attend to and could not return at the moment. So, for the very first time, Sam was obliged to leave the factory in someone else's hands. Harry Weiss, his partner's son, would be taking charge with the able assistance of Jim Harris, his head cutter. It would be the first holiday Sam had ever had. He and Rachel left for Inverness on 26 August.

On 1 September Hitler invaded Poland.

'You're not tellin' me you're lettin' 'er *go*?' Sarah stared at her daughter, aghast. 'You must be mad. 'Eaven knows where them poor little mites'll end up. You might never see 'er again. Besides, it's Poland that 'itler's invaded, not England.'

'Oh, Mum, do leave *off*.' Maryan was at the end of her tether. Whilst they were away Rachel had left her in charge at 124 Hackney Road and she felt the responsibility keenly. For the past month she had lain awake every night, worrying about Marcus. He had left for France almost a month ago, saying that he would be home in a week. Since his departure there had been rumours by the dozen about what was happening on the other side of the Channel. And where was he? It was quite likely that he wasn't in France at all, but back in Germany again. Surely there was nothing more he could do to help Jewish families. She had read in the papers as long ago as last December that Hitler had seized all Jewish property and possessions. Whatever good Marcus had managed to do had been done in the nick of time. There would be little or nothing he could do from now on. And being Jewish himself he was in constant danger, even with his British passport. If only he would come home. And now she was faced with her mother's opposition to the evacuation scheme. Did she let the child go somewhere where she would be safe, or remain here to face God only knew what? The dilemma was almost more than she could cope with.

'You've already lost a father and an 'usband to war. Ain't that enough for you? Do you want to lose your child as well?'

'I won't be losing her, Mum. They'll be taking her where she'll be safe. Why can't you understand that?'

Sarah shook her head obstinately. 'It's splittin' families. It can't be right,' she argued. 'What'll become of 'er if something 'appens to us – tell me that? She'll be left an orphan. I say we should all stick together.'

Maryan turned on her mother. 'Do you think I haven't thought about all that? I've been half out of my mind with worrying about it, day and night. I've had no sleep since I don't know when. All I do know is that I want her to be safe. So I'm letting her go, Mum, and that's that.'

Maryan had tried to explain to Amy as best she could why she was sending her away.

'It'll be a kind of adventure,' she said. 'Something to look forward to. And when you're settled I'll come and see you as often as I can.'

'Will we live in a big house?' Amy asked, round-eyed. 'Is it because the ship's coming in?'

Maryan smiled to hide the hurt inside her. 'Maybe,' she said, wishing she didn't have to lie to the child. 'Who knows what might happen if you're good?'

Amy hugged the exciting idea to herself. Maybe they *would* end up living in a big house with Mr Marcus just like she'd told Lily Smith. Maybe it would come true. Maybe – as Mum said – if she was very good.

The evacuation was well organised and orderly. The children

gathered in the school playground with their little cases and paper bags, name labels carefully tied to their coats. Maryan went along with the other mothers to see them off at Euston station. In spite of her initial eagerness, Amy was tense and silent when the train pulled alongside the platform, clinging to her mother's hand until the very last minute, so that Maryan almost snatched her back and held onto her tightly. It was Miss Vickers who gently prised them apart and said with a gentle smile, 'As soon as she gets there she'll write you a postcard so that you can come and visit. Don't worry, Mrs Jessop, we'll take very good care of them.'

As the train began to move dozens of scared little faces pressed against its windows. Small hands waved frantically and Maryan swallowed a feeling of near panic. Oh God, how could she have let her child go, just like that, to an unknown destination? If Mum was right and they never saw her again it would be all her fault. 'What will become of us all?' she muttered as, blinded by tears, she hurried out into the street again. Would anything or anyone ever be the same again?

To Maryan's relief the Leighs arrived home on Saturday the second, a week earlier than planned, and there was plenty to take her mind off her parting with Amy. Immediately she got to work helping Rachel to make blackout linings for all the curtains and trying to make sure that they'd followed the Civil Defence instructions to the letter. Meantime, Sam was doing the same at the factory. When on Sunday morning war was officially declared and Marcus still had not arrived home, Rachel was distraught. Almost hysterical with worry, she implored Sam to do something. He did his best to calm her, telling her that the boy would not be stupid enough to take any risks. He would surely be on his way home and would arrive any day now. There would be a telephone call – a letter from him by the next post. But no letter came.

Maryan saw and heard their anxiety with an increasing feeling of guilt. When each successive post brought no word from Marcus she became convinced that she should speak. Although Marcus had sworn her to secrecy, the circumstances had changed. He would surely not want his parents to worry so. At last she decided to have a quiet word with Sam when he was alone.

She saw her opportunity on Monday morning, stopping Sam in the hall as he was on his way out of the house to the factory.

'Mr Leigh. There's something I need to talk to you about,' she said. 'Can I speak to you now?'

He pulled out his pocket watch and glanced at it briefly. 'Of course, my dear. I expect you're going to ask my advice about

81

joining little Amy in the country. Why don't you speak to Mrs Leigh about it?'

'No. It's not that. I must speak to you alone. It's about Mr Marcus.'

His expression changed. Taking her arm he drew her into the small room at the front of the house which he used as a study. 'Come in here for a moment,' he said. 'We shan't be disturbed. Rachel is still dressing.'

He walked to the fireplace, then turned to face her. 'You know something?' he said. 'Something he hasn't told his mother and me?'

She nodded. 'He's been making trips into Germany for some time. The first time he went with Mr Weiss – Mr Harry Weiss. They went to try to help get some relatives out of the country. He was very upset by what he saw there and he's been back many times more – times when he was supposed to be in Paris. He was there on the terrible night they called Crystal Night. He's been trying to do what he could to help.' She took a deep breath and clasped her hands nervously before going on: 'I – I've been worrying in case he might have been caught there when war broke out.'

Sam closed his eyes and drew a long breath. Passing a hand over his brow he pulled out a chair and sank into it. 'I had an idea there was something like this going on,' he said. 'But I can't believe that he would be such a fool as to remain in Germany for longer than necessary, not at such a time as this.'

'I'm sorry, Mr Leigh,' Maryan said. 'I've been feeling so guilty knowing about this when you didn't. I couldn't keep it to myself any longer, even though I promised not to say anything.'

He rose and came to her, patting her arm. 'Don't worry, my dear. You kept quiet out of loyalty to Marcus. I understand that. And there was little we could have done anyway.' He sighed. 'I shall say nothing of this to his mother for the moment. All we can do is hope and pray that he's safe.' He looked at her stricken face. 'Marcus must hold you in very high regard to confide in you.'

She bit her lip. 'I – I'm sure he would have told you. It was just that he didn't want to worry you. I think he told me because he needed someone to talk to.'

Sam nodded. 'And he knew of course that we would have done all in our power to stop him if we'd known what he was doing.' He smiled his gentle smile. 'I'm just glad he had someone sympathetic who he felt he could trust.' He took both her hands in his and pressed them reassuringly. 'You did right to tell me, my dear. And I appreciate it. But it shall be our secret for the time being.'

It was just two weeks later that the letter came. It bore a London postmark. Maryan recognised the handwriting as soon as she picked up the post that morning and put the letter in her apron pocket until Sam was alone in his study. He glanced at it and then at her.

'Stay with me while I read it.' She stood by the door and waited while he slit open the envelope and read the single sheet of paper inside. After a moment he gave a sigh and passed it to her. 'Read it for yourself,' he said. 'There is a message for you at the end.'

With trembling fingers she took the letter from him, noticing as she did so that it was dated almost three weeks before. It read:

My dearest Mother and Father,

I don't know when you will get this letter. I'm giving it to a friend who is leaving France today. He will post it for me when he arrives in London, but I'm sure that by the time you read it England will be at war with Germany.

I may not be seeing you for some time. I have made some good friends here in France and have decided to remain with them and help for as long as they need me. There is much I can do to help our people, work that I am sure you would want me to do. Please forgive me for not getting in touch before, and please try not to worry.
Your loving son, Marcus.

P.S. Please give my regards and my sincere thanks to Maryan for all she has done.

She looked up at Sam. 'What does it mean?'

He was shaking his head. 'I suspect that he's joined some kind of resistance movement.'

'But surely – if he wanted to fight he could have come home and joined up.'

Sam smiled at her ruefully. 'It's my guess that Marcus is fighting a much more personal war,' he said with a sigh. 'The thing is, how am I to tell his mother?'

Rachel took the news badly. She railed so bitterly over what Marcus had done that she made herself ill and had to take to her bed with a severe migraine. Lying in a darkened room, she refused to eat and wept incessantly until finally, two days later, Sam sent for the doctor, who gave her a sedative and prescribed some calming medicine.

Downstairs in the kitchen Maryan remembered Marcus's last words to her. *I've got a terrible feeling deep inside that things will get a lot worse.* Bleakly she wondered just how much worse.

Part Two

Chapter Six

1943

Amy stood on the platform of Rhensham Halt waiting for her mother's train.

It was over six months since they had seen each other and she was looking forward with mixed feelings to the coming Easter. Maryan had written to say that she had arranged to take a week off to be with Amy for the Easter holiday. Since her evacuation to Rhensham, her mother's visits – even at Christmas – had been brief, snatched affairs. This was the first time Maryan had been able to get away for more than a day to stay with her daughter in the Suffolk village.

Amy had been with the Taylors at Mitcham Lodge ever since that afternoon in September '39 when, along with a couple of dozen other tired and bewildered children from her school, she had arrived at the village hall in Rhensham. Almost immediately the tall, dark-haired lady with the gentle smile, whom she later learned to call Auntie Marjorie, had picked out Amy and two other little girls to stay with her at her home.

'I can easily take three,' she generously told the billeting officer. 'There's just my son and me in that great house, and with my husband away in the army there's nothing much else I can do to help the war effort.'

But Amy's two companions had stayed only a few weeks. When the devastating bombardment of all major cities that everyone had feared failed to materialise, their mothers had thankfully whisked them home again. At the time Amy had expected her mother to come and take her home too, but Maryan had written to say that she was busy helping the Leighs to prepare their new house in Hazelfield for occupation. She had assured Amy that it would be best for her to stay where she was for a little longer. The

84

'little longer' had stretched to ten months, after which Maryan decided that Amy might as well stay in Suffolk for the summer holidays and get the benefit of the country air. The Leighs were spending every weekend at Hazelfield and needed her to go with them. And as Amy had settled so well in Rhensham, surely she would be happier there, in the company of her new friends. There would be nothing for her to do in London anyway. Maryan concluded the disappointing letter with a half promise: *Perhaps if things are still quiet and you're still homesick you could come home for good when the new school term begins.*

But in September 1940 the blitz had taken them all unawares, coming as it did with the ferocity and unpredictability of a summer storm. When the London raids became a regular nightly occurrence it clearly became unthinkable for Amy to return home. The Leighs moved out of London altogether and took up residence at Whitegates. Maryan and her mother went with them and were installed in the little flat.

Although Amy was homesick for the first few months she had taken to Rhensham, and especially to Mitcham Lodge the moment she had seen it. Her first sight of the house had been late that September afternoon. The setting sun bathed the white walls with a soft, warm glow that made them look as though they were made of gold. To Amy's eyes it had looked just like the gingerbread house in the fairy story and she could hardly believe that she was actually going to live in it. When her two companions had gone home she had felt abandoned, but kind, motherly Mrs Taylor had soon made her feel wanted. Her son Michael, however, had been quite another matter. An only child, he had deeply resented Amy at first and made no secret of the fact that he would have preferred her to have gone back to London with the others. Three years older than Amy, he lorded it over her, boasting about his army officer father and laughing at her accent and her manners. Her fear of farm animals, and her ineptitude with a football drew the most scathing remarks of all from him.

'Why couldn't they have sent us a *boy*, for heaven's sake?' he was always asking exasperatedly, grey eyes raised to the ceiling. 'Girls are useless. They're no good at *anything*.'

Amy had burned with humiliation. She wasn't useless and she was determined to show him that she was good at things. It was just a question of finding out what.

On the brief occasions when Michael's father, Captain Philip Taylor, came home on leave Amy had felt shy and left out. He was a tall, handsome man and although he was kind to Amy she was slightly in awe of him. It was so long since she had known what it was to share a house with a grown-up male. Having him around made her remember Tom and she began to miss him anew, especially when Michael and his father went off together, unthinkingly excluding her from their expeditions. But on these occasions Marjorie would involve her in helping with the horses or in the kitchen, something they both enjoyed.

The year after war had started Michael passed his scholarship examination and moved on to the Grammar School in Ipswich. For the first few weeks he was quite unbearably conceited and there were times when Amy would have positively disliked him – if she hadn't already become his devoted (but secret) admirer. But as the term progressed and the work became harder his air of brash confidence gradually diminished. For hours on end each evening he struggled manfully with his homework, flatly refusing to let his mother help him. He would not admit that he was finding the work harder than he had envisaged, and his attitude towards Amy grew more amenable as a result.

In September '42 Amy too passed her scholarship and moved to the Girls' High School. She travelled in with Michael on the train each morning and home again at night. Now she had her own homework and, after tea and 'Children's Hour' on the wireless, she and Michael would work companionably together till bedtime. Gradually their relationship mellowed from squabbling rivalry into one of tolerant comradeship.

But Amy knew that the question of where she and her mother would live after the war was over must inevitably arise sooner or later. There was constant talk of a 'second front' which, so everyone said, would turn the tide. The prospect of leaving Rhensham and the Taylors; her new school and the lifestyle she had grown so accustomed to, filled her with foreboding.

The sound of a distant whistle made Amy look up hopefully. A plume of smoke appeared at the bend in the line and a moment later the locomotive chugged into view. In spite of her apprehension, Amy could not help the tingle of excitement in the pit of her stomach. It was so long since she had spent any time with her mother. It was almost as if they were strangers. She stepped back as, with a screech of brakes and a hiss of steam, the train came to a stop alongside the platform. Doors began to swing open and crowds of people streamed out: shoppers laden with parcels; Easter weekend visitors with suitcases; servicemen coming home on leave, heaving bulging kit bags onto their shoulders. She stood on tiptoe, her eyes raking the sea of faces. Then at last there was Maryan, looking so smart in a new black costume with a crisp white blouse, a perky little hat with a spotted half-veil perched on her blonde shoulder-length hair. She spotted Amy and her face lit up in the familiar smile. She put down her suitcase to hold out her arms.

'Amy, love. Heavens, how you've grown. You're quite the young lady.' She hugged her daughter, who was now almost as tall as her. Amy seemed to have grown at least six inches since she saw her last.

'I like your new costume,' Amy said admiringly. 'How's Grandma?'

Maryan laughed. 'Gone back to Hackney. She never did take to it at Hazelfield and everyone reckons the bombing's stopped for good now.'

'But Crimea Terrace was bombed,' Amy said.

Maryan nodded. 'Not directly, though. Our old house is still standing – just about. It can't be very comfortable, but it's where she wanted to be, Amy. There was nothing I could say to change her mind. Mr Leigh says they'll pull the rest of the terrace down when the war's finished. What she'll have to say about that, I don't know.'

Amy took her mother's hand and pulled her towards the barrier. 'Come on, Auntie Marjorie's got a special tea waiting for you.'

When they were seated on top of the bus Amy asked about the Leighs. 'Has Mr Marcus been home on leave?'

Maryan sighed. 'No. It's over three years now since he went away. Sometimes they get word from him to say he's safe, mostly through other people who've seen him.'

'Is he still in France?'

'We think so, but we don't really know, not for sure.' Maryan was silent, thinking about Rachel and the anguish she had suffered since Marcus had left. It was fairly certain from what information they had managed to piece together that he was fighting with the Resistance in occupied France and everyone knew how dangerous that was. It was heartbreaking to see her health deteriorate as she anxiously waited for every post, refusing to believe Sam when he kept telling her that no letter would get through. Daily she prayed to have him home again. But still no word came.

'People are saying that the war won't last much longer,' Amy was saying. 'What will we do then, Mum?'

'Mrs Leigh seems to want to stay on at Whitegates,' Maryan said. 'And my job is with them, so I suppose I'll stay too.'

Amy frowned. 'I'd hate to leave my new school.'

'We'll find you another school, just as nice as this one. You'll see.' She tucked her arm through Amy's. 'We'll make a new life together. We've got so much to catch up with.'

'What about Grandma? Couldn't we go back to London too?'

'The papers say that the Government are to build a lot of nice new houses for people who've been bombed out,' Maryan said. 'Maybe she'll get one of those, or perhaps a little flat. She'll be all right. Anyway, you like the country, don't you?'

Amy's heart sank. She felt confused. It was true that she loved Rhensham, but if she had to leave here she'd rather go back to London than move to Hazelfield. But she could see that nothing would ever be the same as it was before the war.

On her one disastrous visit to Whitegates she had been dismayed and disappointed by the size of the flat, after the build-up Maryan had given it. It felt so small and cramped after the spaciousness of Mitcham Lodge. And the house seemed to be full of sick old people who must not be disturbed. Mrs Leigh had a permanent headache and Grandma had one of her 'chests'. She was told to play quietly and there were parts of the garden where she wasn't allowed. She hated the thought of living there permanently after the freedom she enjoyed at Rhensham.

'I wish you could come and live here, Mum,' she said wistfully.

Maryan took her daughter's hand and drew it through her arm. 'My job is with the Leighs, love. You'll like it all right when you get used to it. Just as you got used to it here.'

As they walked down the drive at Mitcham Lodge, Maryan looked at the house and understood her daughter's reluctance to leave it. The L-shaped house with its white painted walls stood in four acres of land. There was a walled kitchen garden and a paddock with two horses, which Marjorie Taylor stabled for a friend who owned the local riding school.

Marjorie worked hard, tending the garden and growing vegetables; caring for the horses. As they neared the house she came to meet them, a tall, slim figure, her dark hair pulled back into a chignon. She wore jodhpurs and a yellow polo-necked sweater.

'Hello. How nice to see you.' She rubbed one hand on the seat of her jodhpurs and held it out to Maryan. 'Heavens, you look so smart, you quite put me to shame. I can't remember when I last dressed up in town clothes. There's never time any more. And there's so much to do out here at this time of year.'

Maryan shook the slim hand and was surprised to find it work-roughened. 'I hope you get Amy to help you,' she said.

'Oh, I do. She and Michael do their share,' Marjorie said. 'Amy's

88

a little marvel with the horses. She tells me she used to like to visit the ones that were stabled behind your house in London.'

'That's right. Always a great one for the horses, she was. Even as a little kiddie.' Maryan looked at the tall eleven-year-old beside her and felt a pang of regret for the years she had missed. It seemed no time at all since Tom had taken her to the mews to feed the big, gentle drayhorses with carrots. She had a sudden nostalgic vision of Amy, wrapped up warmly against the cold, big blue eyes shining and her little nose like a frozen cherry, holding Tom's hand as she trotted up the street beside him. But Tom was gone. And Amy was a child no longer. Suddenly Maryan realised how little she knew her. Not only was Amy more grown-up than when she last saw her, she was different in a dozen new subtle little ways. Since she had lived with the Taylors she had all but lost her London accent. Now she spoke like they did – not *posh* exactly, but in a more defined, precise way, carefully sounding her G's and aitches and effortlessly getting all the grammar right. It made Maryan proud, yet slightly uncomfortable, though she couldn't have explained why.

'I've got the kettle on. I'm sure you're dying for a cup of tea,' Marjorie was saying, leading the way indoors. 'Amy, why don't you show your mother her room, then you can go and help Michael finish off the horses while we have a cosy chat.'

In the long sitting room with its low beamed ceiling and stone fireplace Marjorie had tea laid out on a trolley drawn up in front of a crackling log fire. The room was pleasantly furnished with a comfortable settee and chairs covered in faded chintz; the parquet floor was strewn with Indian rugs patterned in pastel colours; and there were pictures on the ivory-coloured walls – pretty watercolours of local landscapes, which, Maryan learned later, had been painted by Marjorie's husband, Philip. The room had a lived-in, welcoming look that made visitors feel instantly at home and relaxed.

Maryan looked at the spread on the trolley: home-made bread and scones and two kinds of cake. Her eyes widened. 'Did you make all this?'

Marjorie laughed. 'I like baking – all cooking, in fact. It's no chore to me. And here in the country food is a little easier. But then you live in the country too. I keep forgetting. You must have found that too.'

Maryan nodded, wondering if the remark held a hint of reproach that she hadn't taken Amy back to live with her. 'Food is certainly easier than in London. A lot of people have taken to keeping chickens and pigs, which helps out the rations a treat.' She accepted a cup of tea and a scone. 'I'd like to thank you – for all you've done for Amy. She's been so lucky.'

Marjorie looked surprised. 'Nonsense. I've loved having her. She's a delightful child.'

Maryan sipped her tea. 'You must have wondered why I didn't have her with me when I moved to a safe zone with my employers when the blitz began.'

'Not at all. Amy told me how little room there was there, with your mother being with you.' She smiled. 'To tell you the truth, I was quite relieved. Michael and I would have missed her terribly if she'd left.'

'She's growing up so fast,' Maryan said. 'Quite the young woman. I couldn't get over how tall she'd grown when she met me at the station.' She cleared her throat. 'I suppose I should really have a little talk with her while I'm here this weekend.'

'If you mean a talk about the so-called facts of life, we've already had one,' Marjorie said. 'I hope you don't mind, but she had her first period a couple of months ago, so I really had no choice.'

'Oh? No, of course not. I'm sure it was very good of you.' Maryan swallowed the small stab of resentment she felt. So she wouldn't even be allowed to share this precious-intimate milestone with her daughter. She said quickly: 'This is a lovely place. When you hear of the places some children were sent to . . .'

'I know.' Marjorie nodded. 'And we've been so safe. One would hardly know there was a war on. It makes me feel quite guilty sometimes.' She smiled. 'I'm lucky to have Mitcham Lodge. My parents left it to me, you know. My father bought the house and land quite cheaply in the early twenties. It was badly run down and he restored it. He planned to make it a hobby for his retirement.' She refilled Maryan's cup. 'Being able to grow our own vegetables and stable the horses has helped enormously.' She smiled. 'It's nice to have time to talk, isn't it? We've never had a chance to get to know each other properly before. I don't know Hazelfield, but Amy tells me it's very pleasant.'

Maryan was silent for a moment, remembering the one disastrous visit Amy had made to Whitegates. Mrs Leigh had been ill with a severe migraine that weekend and Sarah, who had left blitz-torn London with great reluctance, had grumbled throughout the entire weekend too, insisting that in spite of the modern conveniences at the flat, she still preferred having her own back yard and taking her bath in front of the range of a Friday night. When Maryan had seen Amy onto the train on Sunday evening she'd felt depressed and exhausted; torn three ways between loyalty to her mother, her daughter and her employers. She was all too aware of how short-tempered she'd been all weekend. It was hardly surprising that the child was eager to leave.

'I hear that your employers moved their business out of London,' Marjorie was saying.

Maryan looked up. 'Yes. The factory was bombed. The building was damaged beyond repair. Mr Leigh and his partner salvaged what they could of the equipment and machinery and found suitable premises in Essex. They've been working on a Government contract – making uniforms. They did it in the first war too.'

'I see. How interesting.' Marjorie pushed the trolley nearer Maryan. 'Do help yourself to more cake. We don't stand on ceremony here. You didn't consider taking up war work then?'

Maryan took a slice of cake and broke a piece off thoughtfully. 'I was tempted. Munition work is very well paid. But Mrs Leigh, my employer, hasn't been at all well since the war began. As she gave me a job when I badly needed one, I felt I couldn't desert her when she needed me. Domestic staff are very hard to replace once you lose someone.'

Marjorie smiled. 'Don't I know it. Before the war we used to employ a full-time gardener and a daily woman here. Now I've had to learn to do everything myself. But you know, I've found to my surprise that I absolutely love it.' She looked at Maryan. 'It's very loyal of you to stay on, though. A good many women would have seized the opportunity to earn more.' She sipped her tea, continuing to look thoughtfully at Maryan over the rim of the cup. 'Amy tells me that her father was killed in Spain – the civil war?'

'That's right.'

'You must miss him dreadfully.' Marjorie shook her head. 'My own husband is in Burma just now. I try to keep myself as busy as possible so as not to worry, but it's always there, at the back of your mind, isn't it?'

'Yes.'

Marjorie looked up with a smile. 'But you're sure to marry again. You're still young.'

Maryan shook her head.

Marjorie nodded. 'Well, I know how you feel. I don't think I could marry again either if Philip – if the worst happened. We keep hearing rumours about this so-called second front they're supposed to be planning. If only it could be soon.' She pushed the tea trolley aside and stood up. 'Well, I must go and have a bath and make myself presentable. Why don't you find Amy and get her to take you for a walk before dinner? The village is looking lovely just now.'

Maryan found Amy at the back of the house in the stable yard, where she was helping a tall, good-looking boy whom she barely recognised as Michael Taylor to muck out. He too had grown since she saw him last. Standing there, watching them, Maryan was struck again by the change in her daughter. She looked so *at home* here; as though she'd been born to this kind of life. As she watched, the boy turned and caught sight of her.

'Oh, hello, Mrs Jessop,' he said politely in his new deep voice. He smiled at her. 'It's nice to see you. I hope you had a pleasant journey.'

'Thank you, Michael. Your mother has suggested Amy might take me for a walk round the village. I hope you can spare her.'

Michael glanced at Amy. ''Course. Glad to get her out of the way for five minutes.' He waved a dismissive hand. 'Off you go, kid.'

Amy pulled a face at him and, leaning her pitchfork against the wall, she crossed the yard to join her mother. 'Right, where would you like to go first?' She'd changed out of the cotton dress she had worn, into jodhpurs and boots, and tied back her dark curls with a length of black ribbon.

'Where did you get those breeches?' Maryan asked as they walked down the drive.

Amy looked down. 'These? Oh they're some that Mike had grown out of.' As they walked down the road and past the church she voiced the thought that was uppermost in her mind. 'Mum – now that Grandma has gone back to London are you here to persuade me to come back to Hazelfield with you?'

By her tone it was clearly the thing she most dreaded and Maryan felt a sharp pang of hurt.

'Not if you don't want to,' she said. 'But you are only an evacuee here, love. When the war is over you'll have to leave. We'll have to start trying to get back to normal sometime,' She glanced at Amy's glum expression. 'Is coming back to live with your mum such a horrible thought?'

Sensing her mother's hurt, Amy slipped a hand through her arm. 'Of course it isn't. I'd just rather not live at Hazelfield though. Do you think the Leighs will go back to London when the war ends?'

Maryan shrugged. 'Who knows, love? Mrs Leigh is getting on in years now. And she hasn't been very well either. It's all the worry over Marcus. I think she'll probably prefer to stay in the quiet of the country.'

'But *you* don't have to stay there too, do you, Mum? Couldn't you get another job?'

Maryan sighed. 'We'll see. The war is far from over yet. And anyway, there's no way of telling what'll happen afterwards. Better wait and see.'

'But until it does – I can stay here?'

Maryan looked at the eager blue eyes, looking so hopefully into hers, and gave in. 'All right. I expect it would be better for you to stay on at this school for the moment. If Mrs Taylor doesn't mind, that is. But it would be nice if you were to come and stay with me for a few days. I think you'd find it better now that Grandma has gone back home. I admit it was a bit crowded before.' She looked at Amy. 'Why not come in the summer holidays? I could get some time off and we could go for days out. We could go up to Town and spend a day with Grandma. She'd love to see you. And we could even slip over and see Auntie Maggie and Granny Jessop too.'

Her mother was clearly trying so hard to make it all sound attractive that Amy felt obliged to agree. 'Okay then,' she said. It was odd, sometimes she felt as though her mother was the child and she the parent.

Later, lying awake in the pretty blue and white bedroom, Maryan thought back over the evening. The dinner Marjorie had prepared had been laid on specially: roast chicken with home-grown vegetables, and sherry trifle to follow, with cream bartered from one of the local dairy farmers in exchange for some of her home-grown broccoli. The table had been exquisitely laid with fine china and a lace cloth. There'd even been candles and serviettes too. Marjorie had changed into a soft wool dress of dark blue, which, although starkly plain, looked sophisticated and expensive, worn with a string of pearls and matching earrings. Maryan, in a frilly white blouse and red skirt, felt common and over-dressed by contrast.

This house, the whole set-up had the ambience of a comfortable middle-class lifestyle that Maryan knew she could never aspire to. To the Taylors, being 'poor' meant having to do without a car, a gardener and a daily cleaning woman. It had nothing at all to do with going hungry or not being able to pay the rent. Maryan could not imagine how Amy would settle down to their old life again. The answer was that she shouldn't have to. Hadn't she always promised something better for them? Of course they had the flat at Whitegates, which was far more comfortable and convenient than anything they had known before the war, but if Maryan had taken the opportunity to go into munitions she could have put enough money aside for something better; perhaps a place of their own. Even Sarah had taken her to task over it during one of the frequent arguments they'd had when they were sharing the flat at Hazelfield.

'I thought you were all for betterin' yourself,' she'd said accusingly.

'I happen to think that this is an improvement on Crimea Terrace,' Maryan said.

Sarah sniffed. 'I seem to remember you tellin' me I was nothing but a servant, yet *you* don't seem to mind bein' one nowadays. This flat might have all mod cons but it ain't yours, is it? If the Leighs chucked you out tomorrer you'd be 'omeless.

'Well, they're not *going* to chuck me out, are they, Mum? Not today or tomorrow or ever, as far as I can see,' Maryan told her firmly. 'Mrs Leigh needs me. Surely you wouldn't want me to desert her? You've always been the one to point out that she was your *friend*, after all.'

Sarah shrugged non-committally. 'That's as may be. It's true that Miss Rachel an' me was always good friends. But she never took advantage of me like what she's doing to you. She's got you at her beck and call twenty-four hours a day, what with 'er 'eadaches and everything.'

'She can't help it. It's because of Marcus, Mum,' Maryan said. 'Surely you can understand that. He's her only child and the poor woman is worried half out of her mind about him.'

'So's a good many others,' Sarah said. 'After all, from what I c'n make out he didn't *'ave* to go an' put 'is life at risk. He wouldn't never 'ave been called up like all the rest. He'd've been in a reserved occupation, makin' uniforms an' that. There's women losin' their menfolk all up 'n down the country – strugglin' on with kids to bring up and work to do; 'omes to keep together on next to nothin'.' She gave another of her explosive, disapproving sniffs. 'Seems to me Miss Rachel don't know she's born. Wouldn't 'urt 'er to get out and do somethin' to 'elp, 'stead of moping her life away down 'ere in this 'ole at the back of beyond.'

Maryan had been surprised at her mother's vehemence against the employer she had always defended so strongly. It was almost as though their roles were reversed. She put it down to her mother's dislike of the country. The place had seemed to sour her whole outlook. Ever since she'd first arrived she'd done nothing but grumble and find fault. She refused to see that Maryan's relationship with Mrs Leigh had developed beyond that of servant and mistress. Sometimes even felt that what they had was more like a daughter and mother situation. Mrs Leigh depended on her support, as a friend and helper – as a nurse too at times. And, mainly because of Marcus, Maryan was happy to remain at Whitegates and do all she could to support Rachel through this stressful time in her life.

94

Always – right at the back of her mind and barely acknowledged – was the hope that one day, when the war was over, Marcus would come back and he would finally turn to her again. She dismissed her mother's criticism as jealousy, and when Sarah had announced her intention to return to Hackney she'd felt guilty. But on the whole she considered it to be for the best. Sarah was a Cockney, born and bred. She'd never settle in the country.

Before Maryan's weekend was up it had been arranged thay Amy should visit Hazelfield the last week in August. Amy and Michael were involved in a carnival the combined villages were organising. It was to take place in July for the 'Holidays at Home' project. All the schools and organisations were taking part. There was to be a pageant, a picnic, a garden fête with sideshows and competitions, and a flower and produce show, in which Marjorie hoped to exhibit. Everyone was looking forward to it enormously.

But a month before it was due to begin, the excitement was eclipsed by the news of the allied invasion of Normandy. The great push forward that everyone had been longing for had finally come at last. Surely now it could only be a matter of time before the war was won. Michael pinned a map up on the kitchen wall and he and Amy made little flags which they moved every day to check the progress of the invasion: red ones for the British; blue for the Allies.

Then in the midst of all the euphoria came the shocking news of the first of the V-1 bombs falling on London. Hitler was making a last desperate attempt at destruction with this new and deadly weapon. Terrifying robot planes that fell indiscriminately at any hour of the day or night had engulfed a war-weary London in a new blitz. A new flood of evacuees descended on all the 'safe' areas and Marjorie took in the young wife of a naval officer and her twin babies, converting her two spare rooms into a flat for them.

It was while they were having breakfast one morning in July that the telephone rang. Marjorie went to answer it and came back with a worried look on her face.

'That was your mother, Amy,' she said. 'She'd like you to go over to Hazelfield today.'

Amy looked up in dismay. 'But why? I'm going in a few weeks' time anyway.'

'She's worried about your grandmother staying in London now that these V-1s have started. She feels that you should both go up and persuade her to come back.'

'Can't she go?'

'She seems to think your grandma would listen to you.'

Amy was silent. It was because Grandma and Mum fell out badly when they were living at the flat together that Mum wanted her to go too. Grandma could be really stubborn when she dug her heels in. She looked at Marjorie. 'Did you say I could go?'

Marjorie smiled wryly. 'It isn't for me to say, Amy. If your mother needs you, I think you must go.' She began to clear the breakfast table. 'I've looked up the trains and there's one in an hour. I told her I'd put you on it, so you'd better hurry upstairs and pack a few things.'

'You can't go. You'll miss the carnival,' Michael said bluntly.

Amy looked at him. 'I know. Maybe Grandma will agree quickly. Maybe I'll be back by tomorrow.'

Michael opened his mouth to protest further, but a look from his mother stopped him. He stared down at his plate moodily It would all be spoilt if Amy wasn't here to share the fun. He really didn't see why she had to go. He told her so later as she packed her small case for the journey.

'I don't see why your mother can't cope with it,' he said, staring gloomily out of the window.

'Because they haven't been getting on too well,' Amy told him. 'When Grandma went to live at Hazelfield before, they were always quarrelling.'

'So – what does she think you can do about it?'

'I don't know, but I have to try and do something. I love Grandma. I don't want anything to happen to her.'

'They'll want you to stay for the rest of the hols,' he said.

Amy shrugged. 'No they won't. But I suppose I'd have to if they did.'

Michael watched her in silence for a moment, then: 'I suppose you know that nothing's going to be any fun with you not there.'

Amy looked at him in surprise. '*Me?* But you've lots of friends of your own.'

Michael went pink and kicked at the carpet. 'It's not the same,' he mumbled.

She snapped her case shut, trying to hide the little smile that pulled at the corners of her mouth. 'I'll probably be back in no time.' She looked up at him. 'Coming to the station with me, Mike?'

'No. I hate stations.' He pulled something out of his pocket and tossed it onto the bed. 'Look, you might as well have this,' he said casually.

Amy picked up the bar of chocolate, looking at him in surprise. 'Thanks, Mike – but, your sweet ration . . .?'

96

He shrugged off her thanks. 'It was all they had at the village shop,' he said. 'And it's the kind I don't like.'

When the train pulled in at Hazelfield Maryan was waiting. 'I thought we'd go up to Town tomorrow and try and get your Grandma to come back with us,' she said. 'She'll probably argue, but we'll have to persuade her somehow. Those buzz bombs are getting more and more frequent – horrible things. I don't like to think of her there in the thick of it.'

'I know, but did you really need me to come too, Mum?' Amy asked. 'We're ever so busy at Rhensham getting the carnival ready. Will I have to stay long, do you think?'

Maryan stared at her daughter. 'Don't you care about your Grandma?' she asked tetchily. 'I don't know about you, Amy, really I don't. Sometimes I think you've got really selfish, living over there in Suffolk, away from it all. People have suffered terribly in this war, you know. You're old enough to realise that there's a bit more at stake than a carnival.'

Amy coloured, slightly ashamed. 'Okay – sorry, Mum.'

They were having lunch together in the kitchen of the flat at Whitegates when Amy looked out of the window and saw Sam Leigh coming up the drive. 'Here's Mr Sam, Mum,' she said. 'Does he usually come home at this time of day?'

Maryan joined her at the window, a puzzled frown on her face. 'No, he doesn't. He must be ill.' She leaned forward to get a better view. 'I think he must be. He looks terrible. I'd better go down.'

But as she turned away Amy said. 'No need. He's coming up here.'

A quick look from Maryan confirmed that Sam had started to climb the staircase that led up to the flat. She turned to Amy. 'I think perhaps you'd better go in the bedroom,' she said. 'He might want to see me privately about something. Better if you're not here.'

Amy went reluctantly. One minute she was wanted, the next she was being pushed out of sight like a bundle of dirty washing.

As the bedroom door closed behind her Maryan took a deep breath and then opened the door to find Sam waiting, white-faced, outside.

'Mr Leigh, whatever is it? You look done in.' She put out her hand to help him inside.

Inside the closed door he stared dazedly at her. 'Oh, Maryan, I've had some terrible news,' he said brokenly. 'I don't know how to tell Rachel – how to face her. Will you come with me – be with me when I tell her?'

'Of course.' She led him gently to a chair, her heart thumping with apprehension. It was Marcus. It had to be. Nothing else could affect him like this. She forced herself to be calm. 'Sit down,' she said. 'Take your time. Let me get you a nip of brandy. I think you'd better tell me about it first.'

Sam accepted the brandy gratefully and as he sipped it a little of the colour gradually came back into his cheeks. At last he began to speak, slowly and painfully, his voice husky with emotion: 'This morning I had a visitor. An English airman who had been shot down over France. He'd been taken in and hidden by a farmer and his family after his crash and when he was well enough a small group of Resistance workers were going to try to get him and a group of Jews across the border into Switzerland.' His voice faltered and stopped as he stared into his empty glass.

'And – he had news – of Marcus?' Maryan prompted.

'Yes, Marcus was one of them.' Sam looked up at her, his dark eyes huge and full of pain. 'Maryan – Marcus is dead,' he said, his voice almost a whisper. 'This man couldn't tell me everything because he didn't know. Perhaps no one will ever discover the truth of it. But it seems that someone must have betrayed them. They were meant to hand them over to another group close to the border, but when they arrived it was the Germans who were waiting. They scattered, but it was no use. The airman and one other man escaped, but the rest were caught and – and executed on the spot.' The words caught in his throat and he slumped forward, his head in his hands. 'Oh, my God. My boy – my son – Marcus, *Marcus.*'

Tears streaming down her cheeks, Maryan sank to her knees and put her arms round Sam's heaving shoulders. Putting her own desolation aside she asked: 'And this airman – he knew Marcus well?'

Sam shook his head. 'Not well, but it seems that Marcus had asked him to come and see us if he got home to England safely. He was supposed to tell us that Marcus was safe and – and well . . .' Once more his words were lost in grief. Maryan took both his hands in hers.

'Mr Leigh, Marcus was very brave. He went into it with his eyes open. He'd seen the terrible things that were happening on his visits to Germany before the war. He told me about them. They disturbed him deeply. He did what he felt he had to do. I believe that. And we – you should be very proud of him.' She pressed the cold hands, warming them with hers. 'After Jessica and the baby died I don't think he felt that his life mattered any more. This would have been the way he wanted it. He'd want you to see it that way too. I know he would.'

Sam gathered himself together and raised his head to look into her eyes. 'You're right.' His fingers closed around hers, returning the comforting pressure. 'And I am proud of him. Very proud.' He looked into her eyes. 'You knew him well, didn't you, Maryan? You understood him.' He leant forward to kiss her forehead. 'You've been a good girl to Rachel and me all this time. Don't ever think we don't appreciate the sacrifices you've made for us.' He closed his eyes. 'But I wish – oh God, how I *wish* he could have come back safely to us.'

'I know.' She swallowed a sob. 'I wish he could have too.'

'And my Rachel. How shall I face my Rachel?' Sam asked plaintively. 'You'll have to help me tell her, Maryan. I can't do it alone.'

'Of course I'll help. We must try to be strong – for her.'

'Yes, yes.' He heaved himself to his feet. 'We had better go now. Get it over with.'

When Rachel heard Sam's key in the front door she came out into the hall to meet him. Maryan saw at once the wariness in her eyes. It was almost as though she already knew. She even took a step backwards, one hand held up protectively before her, as though to ward off what she read on their faces.

'Samuel? What is it? Are you ill?'

He took a hurried step towards her. 'Rachel, come into the sitting room, dearest. Maryan and I – have something to tell . . .'

'It's not Marcus?' Rachel was shaking her head. 'Not my Marcus? You're not – going to tell me . . . She saw from the look in Sam's eyes that it was as she feared. She clapped her hands over her ears. 'No. *Don't*. I won't listen. It's not true. No, no, I can't bear it.'

Sam grasped her by the shoulders, steered her into the sitting room and pressed her rigid body into a sofa. 'Rachel. Please don't make this harder for me. You're right. It is Marcus and you must try to be brave. It's bad news, my dear. The worst, I'm afraid. The very worst.'

Rachel looked from her husband to Maryan and then back again, all the while shaking her head slowly from side to side, her eyes wide and disbelieving. 'He's not – not, dead?' she whispered. 'No, he can't be. No – no – *No!*' she last syllable came from her throat in an agonised howl as she threw herself full length on the sofa.

Maryan ran to her side. 'Oh, Mrs Leigh, please don't take on like that. I'm here. Let me get you something.'

But Rachel would not be comforted. Hysterical with grief she sobbed inconsolably, rolling back and forth and plucking heedlessly at the sofa cushions. Sam stood by, looking helplessly at Maryan.

'I think we should call the doctor,' Maryan said. 'Perhaps he could give her something to calm her down.'

She sat with the distraught Rachel while Sam telephoned the doctor. By the time he had arrived Maryan had managed to get her upstairs to her room. She felt icy cold and her teeth were chattering. The doctor gave her an injection and within minutes she was asleep.

Downstairs in the hall Sam explained. 'We heard today that our only son has been killed,' he said.

The elderly doctor nodded sadly. 'Sometimes I think that this war is especially hard on mothers,' he said. 'I'm sure she will be calmer when she wakes, once the shock has diminished. But don't hesitate to call me if she isn't.'

Back in the flat Maryan explained to Amy what had happened. 'I can't leave them in this state,' she said. 'It may be a couple of days before we can go to London now. You don't mind, love, do you?'

Amy shook her head. The news about Marcus had shocked her too. She remembered him very well, even though it was five years since she'd last seen him. She had never forgotten the day he took them to see the coronation and what fun it had been. It was awful to think that he was dead.

'Mrs Leigh might ask to see your grandma,' Maryan was saying, half to herself. 'She was the one person she wanted when her daughter-in-law died. In fact, this might be the one sure way we'll get Grandma to leave London.'

But Rachel made no requests of any kind. She did not leave her bed at all that day. That night Sam gave her the tablet the doctor had left and she slept soundly till morning. But when she wakened to the horror of reality her agony returned. She turned her face to the wall, refusing to get up, to eat or to see anyone, not even the Rabbi, summoned to the house by a distraught Sam, himself almost sick with grief and worry.

'She says that we have nothing left,' he told Maryan. 'First her poor father perished on the *Titanic*, then there was our dear Jessica and the little one; now we've lost Marcus. She seems to think there is some kind of curse on us; that we are doomed to lose everyone we love because of some unspeakable wrong we must have committed. I've tried to reassure her but it's no use. She won't listen.'

Rachel remained in her room, refusing food or comfort of any kind. On the third day, when Maryan was preparing a lunch tray for her in the kitchen, she looked up to see Amy watching her.

'When are we going to London to get Grandma?' Amy asked. 'It's really boring here, Mum. There's nothing to do.'

'I can't go while Mrs Leigh is in this state,' Maryan said.

100

'You said she might want to see Grandma.'

Maryan sighed. 'I know, but I haven't had the chance to ask her. She doesn t seem to want anyone at the moment.'

'Shall *I* ask her?' Maryan looked up in surprise. Amy nodded towards the tray. 'I'll take that up if you like,' she suggested. 'Then I can ask her while I'm there.'

After a moment's hesitation Maryan lifted the tray and held it out to her. 'Well – all right. You might as well have a try at getting her to eat, I suppose. But don't say anything,' she warned. 'Not unless she speaks to you. We don't want her upset again.'

On the landing Amy knocked on the door. There was no reply, so she opened it and went in. Rachel was sitting up in bed, propped against a pile of pillows, as limp as a rag doll. She stared unseeingly out of the window at the blue sky, apparently unaware that anyone had entered the room.

Amy cleared her throat. 'Mrs Leigh, I've brought you some lunch. It's only an omelette, but Mum says it's very light and it'll do you good.'

Rachel turned her head and looked slightly surprised to see the young girl standing at the foot of her bed. 'Who are you, child?'

Amy moved closer and set the tray across Rachel's legs. 'I'm Amy.'

'Maryan's daughter?'

'Yes.'

Rachel looked without interest at the food on the tray. 'Take this away, child. Tell your mother I'm not hungry. I can't eat it.'

'Oh, please try,' Amy said. 'It's nice and hot and there's home-made bread to go with it, look. And the coffee's freshly made. We're not supposed to waste food, are we? Not with the war on. And Mum's gone to a lot of trouble to make it look nice for you.'

Rachel looked again at the tray with its crisp white embroidered cloth and matching napkin. A small glass vase held two pink roses from the garden. The wisp of steam that rose from the spout of the coffee pot was fragrant and appetising. Rachel looked up at the slim, dark-haired schoolgirl standing by her bed. 'How old are you now, Amy?'

'Twelve and three-quarters.'

'Are you really? You're tall for your age, just like Marcus was at thirteen.'

'I'm sorry about Mr Marcus being killed,' Amy said. 'Mum wondered if you'd like to see Grandma. She's known him since he was a little boy, hasn't she?'

Rachel looked at her. The child was the first person to speak of what had happened openly and frankly. It brought her a strange relief. The shadow of a smile lifted the corners of her mouth. 'Sarah?' she said. 'Oh yes. That would be nice.'

'We thought we might go up to London and fetch her.'

'Would you really?'

'Yes. But only if you eat your lunch,' Amy said daringly. She picked up a fork and held it out. 'Go on, why don't you try a little bit? I bet you'll like it. Mum put herbs and things in it.'

Rachel paused, smiling at the child's naivety, then she obliged by forking up a piece of the omelette.

Amy nodded her encouragement, unselfconsciously sitting down on the edge of the bed. 'That's right. Nice, isn't it? Mum makes lovely omelettes. It isn't made of dried egg either. Go on, have a bit more.'

Rachel ate another forkful – and suddenly her stomach, tantalised by its first nourishment in days, reminded her of how hungry she was. She ate on until, to her own surprise, the plate was empty. When she had put down the fork and dabbed her mouth with the napkin, she smiled at Amy. 'You're a good girl, Amy. You can pour me a cup of coffee now. I do believe I could drink one.'

Downstairs in the kitchen Maryan was amazed and delighted by Amy's success, and when later she went up to Rachel's room she found her employer much brighter. She seemed pleased with the idea of a visit from Sarah, and she was obviously taken with Amy and impressed by way she had persuaded her to eat.

Unable to unleash her own private feelings, Maryan had saved her grieving for when she was alone. Night after night she lay awake far into the small hours, her heart aching for the brief, sweet love whose promise would never be fulfilled. She agonised about Marcus's death. Had he suffered at the hands of the Nazis? Had they hurt him? Had he ever, in those dark and terrible days, thought of her? She searched the corners of her mind for every little scrap of detail about him, carefully storing the few precious times they had shared, pressing them into her memory like flowers between the pages of a book. Maybe one day she would tell Amy about him. Surely she too should share the shining joy that had brought about her very being. As she grew up Amy was getting so much like him. She had his dark curly hair and classic features, and as her body grew and developed it was becoming clear that she would have his tall, supple figure. Her clear blue eyes were all she had inherited from Maryan.

It was almost a week after Sam had brought home his dreadful news that Rachel decided to get up and dress for the first time. She sat in the conservatory at the back of the house, looking out over the garden, ablaze with summer colour. Maryan took her coffee and biscuits to her there and asked again if she would like to have Sarah to visit.

'If you would be kind enough to fetch her for me.'

'Amy and I could go up the day after tomorrow if that's all right.'

'Perfectly.' Rachel looked up. 'I wonder – could you spare me your daughter for a little while this morning?' she asked.

'Of course. I'm sure she'd love to come and sit with you.'

Amy took a draught board with her and she and Rachel played draughts all morning, Amy chattering and laughing uninhibitedly, drawing the grief-stricken woman out until she too was smiling in spite of herself.

The idea came to Maryan in the small hours of the following morning. The more she thought about it, the more she felt that it would be the answer to everything. Amy was the Leighs' grandchild after all. Surely they should know it, especially now that Marcus was gone. Rachel seemed so taken with her. It would be something new for her to live for. And Amy's future would be secure, too; secure in a way that Maryan could never hope for. Of course it meant that her mother would have to know as well, but that couldn't be helped. It was a problem Maryan would meet when she came to it.

She chose the following evening, after dinner. It was the first time Rachel had joined Sam downstairs in the dining room for their evening meal. When Maryan took them their coffee she stood by the door.

'May I speak to you?' she asked, her heart drumming.

Sam looked up at her in surprise. 'Of course. Is something wrong, Maryan?'

'No.' She cleared her throat. Her legs were shaking so much that she longed to ask if she might sit down, but she took a deep breath and went on: 'I have something to tell you. It – it's bound to come as a shock. But – but not a nasty one, I hope.'

Rachel turned to look at her, a slight frown on her face. 'I'm not sure that I want any more shocks just at present. Whatever it is I think you had better tell us quickly, Maryan. I do hope you're not thinking of leaving?'

'Oh no. It's – er . . .' The words died in her throat. It was proving much harder than she'd imagined.

Sam smiled at her kindly. 'Come and sit down, Maryan. Would you like a cup of coffee?'

'Thank you.' Maryan sat down at the table, grateful for the small respite and to take the weight off her trembling legs. She accepted the cup of coffee that Sam poured for her, and it was only then that she noticed that there was no jug of hot milk on the tray. 'Oh – I've forgotten the milk . . .' She made to jump up but Sam put out a restraining hand.

'Never mind the milk, it doesn't matter. Stay where you are. Rachel and I prefer our coffee black anyway. Now, won't you get this thing that's worrying you off your chest?'

'It's not exactly worrying me.' Maryan took a sip of the hot black coffee. 'It's about – about Amy.' She looked up to find the faces of her employers looking expectantly at her.

'You'd like to have her here to live with you permanently?' Sam prompted.

Maryan shook her head. 'Not that, no – although . . .'

'What then?' Rachel asked sharply.

Maryan moistened her dry lips and looked at Rachel. 'Mrs Leigh – this will come as a surprise to you, but Amy – Amy is your granddaughter.' There was a shocked pause as Maryan swallowed and went on: 'Marcus was her father. It – it was long before he met Jessica. And he never knew. I never told him.' She lowered her eyes. 'I – I loved him very much.'

Having actually got the words out filled her with relief, but this was to be short-lived. She looked up at the two faces staring at her on either side. Sam's expression was incredulous and confused. But Rachel's was dark with suppressed anger. Clutching the edge of the table, she rose unsteadily to her feet to glare down at Maryan.

'How – *dare* you?' she hissed. 'How dare you come to us with this outrageous lie? To think that you are asking me to believe that my son would seduce a *servant* girl – would father her child. It's disgusting – *obscene*.'

Horrified at Rachel's reaction, Maryan rose to face her. 'But – it's *true*. And it wasn't sordid. We were very young and – and in love. Marcus did once ask me to marry him. He was going to speak to you – and then . . .'

'*Be quiet!*' Rachel waved her hands at Maryan as though trying to rid herself of some horrific delirium. 'You are a wicked woman to put us through this. My son is dead and you are trying to blacken his character; to spoil our memory of him. Making him out as some kind of promiscuous philanderer. I know for certain that he would never have dreamed of touching a . . . someone not of his faith. I don't know who the unfortunate father of your child was, but I do know that it was *not – my – son*.' She banged her clenched fist on the table to emphasise the words, then, exhausted by her emotional outburst, she collapsed into her chair, gasping and clutching at her chest. Sam sprang up and poured her a glass of water.

'Rachel, Rachel, my love – don't upset yourself like this.' He glanced round at Maryan, his face white and shocked. 'Perhaps it would be best if you were to leave us now,' he said quietly. As Maryan made a move towards the distressed Rachel he held up his hand. 'I'll see to her. Leave her to me.'

Outside the door a white-faced Amy stood clutching the jug of hot milk that her mother had left on the kitchen table. Hoping to be helpful, she had taken it along to the dining room and overheard every word of the exchange that had taken place behind the door, from her mother's halting revelation to Rachel's hysterical reaction. Turning, she made her way back to the kitchen, placed the jug on the table, then let herself quietly out of the side door to make her way across the yard to the flat.

Sitting there in the dusky light of evening she felt cold and numb with shock. So – the man she had called 'Dad'; the sweet, kind man she still missed so much, was not her father after all. How could her mother have deceived all of them for so many years? Why had she not told her? Surely everyone should know who their father was. Tom Jessop must surely have believed he was her father. He had loved her so much, cared for her like the tenderest of fathers right from babyhood. He had spent so much of his time with her. She remembered the overheard rows between her parents – their angry voices. Harsh words like 'boozing' and 'nagging'. A sentence here and there that she had puzzled over. *'We both know why you married me.' 'You might be working class but how do you know what class she is?'* She'd never forgotten them or the bitterness with which they were voiced. Now it all slipped into place. A hateful suspicion occurred to her: had her mother sent him away on purpose – because she loved Marcus Leigh? Had she perhaps hoped that Marcus would marry her if Tom were out of the way? Was that the basis for all the vague promises about the ship coming in and the lovely life they'd have when it did? Or was it all lies? Either way it seemed that her mother really was a wicked woman just as Mrs Leigh said.

She got up and ran into her room, slamming the door; sobbing as she undressed and climbed into bed. If her mother came to her she would pretend to be asleep. She couldn't see or speak to her, not tonight. Tomorrow she would go back to Rhensham. But much as she needed to talk to someone, she couldn't even tell Auntie Marjorie about this. It was too bad – too shaming.

Lying in the darkness she tried to sort out the confused, tangled thoughts that chased round and round inside her head. It was no use asking her mother for the truth. She had lied to her and to everyone else for almost thirteen years, so how could she believe her now? But there was one thing she had to know: if it were true and Marcus Leigh was her father, *who did that make her*? Was she still Amy Jessop, or should her name be Brown, like Mum's before she was married? Or was her real name Leigh? And if it was, was she half Jewish? If only there were someone who knew for sure; someone she could trust to be honest, to tell her the real truth.

Grandma. Amy opened her eyes. Grandma must surely know. She wouldn't keep the truth from her. Not if she asked. Somehow she would go up to London and ask her. But she would have to go alone. No one else must know this terrible, shameful secret her mother had imposed on her.

Chapter Seven

Sam reached out his hand for his watch, lying on the bedside table. Peering at its face he could just make out the time: 4.30. He sighed and turned towards his wife, who lay with her back towards him, body hunched.

'Rachel. Are you awake, dear?'

After a pause she sighed and turned onto her back. 'Awake? I haven't closed my eyes once all night. I'm sorry if I've been restless and disturbed you.'

'You haven't. I haven't slept much either.' He sat up and looked at her. 'Shall I get up and make you some tea?'

She shook her head. 'No. At least try to get some rest. You'll be so tired at work all day.'

Sam slid down the bed again with a sigh. There was little hope of relaxing in the same bed as Rachel. He could feel her tension, taut as a tightly coiled spring as she lay stiffly beside him. He dreaded bringing up the subject that he knew they must talk about and searched his mind for something placating to say, but Rachel forestalled him.

'She'll have to go, Samuel,' she said quietly.

He winced. Her use of his full name was ominous. 'Oh, surely not. She's been very good to us, you know. And think how hard life would be without her here to run the house for you.'

'How can you even suggest that she should stay?' Her voice tightened. 'After last night – the vile accusation she made against Marcus.'

'It wasn't an accusation, my love. She was just telling us a fact.'

'A fact?' She turned to stare at him, her dark eyes glittering like jet. 'You're not trying to tell me that you actually *believe* her?' She was sitting up now, staring down at her husband with an expression of horror. 'How *can* you, Samuel? Our son. Our own Marcus . . .' Her

107

shoulders began to shake with emotion and Sam sat up hurriedly and put his arms around her.

'Rachel, dearest, please don't upset yourself again.' He held her until her trembling ceased, then gently pressed her back against her pillow again. 'Listen, dear. Our boy was a wonderful son, that's true, of course, and nothing he could ever do would change that. He was a loving and devoted husband to dear Jessica and I don't doubt that he would have been a fine father too, if God had willed it. But he was once a very young man, and prone to the follies of all young men. I believe that it is quite possible that Maryan was telling us the truth. And doing it with the best of motives, because she thought we would welcome her telling of it.'

'How could she have imagined that we would *welcome* it?' Rachel said bitterly.

'Because – because of our loss. Because we have no one now.' When she was silent he went on: 'Think, Rachel. Have you ever known Maryan to do anything to hurt us?'

'No. But we have been good employers to her. Why should she?'

'And have you ever known her to tell us a lie?'

'No. But then she has had no reason to – till now.'

'And what reason had she to lie to us now? Now of all times? Tell me that.'

'You are so naive at times, Samuel. She saw her chance, that's why. Saw a chance to gain – for herself and for the child.'

Sam shook his head. 'You think she schemed up the story as some kind of – of blackmail – seizing the death of our son as a chance to gain for herself? Rachel, you shock me. You can't believe that Maryan could even think of such a cruel thing. I don't . . .'

'*I want her out.*' The words squeezed themselves past Rachel's rigid lips and, looking into her face, Sam knew that she would not relent. Nevertheless, he tried once more.

'My dear – please.'

'Can't you see what she is doing to us? Putting us against each other. Driving a wedge between us. And you're letting it work – letting it happen.'

'Won't you wait a few days? Let your anger cool and examine your feelings again. I'm sure you will agree that . . .'

'She has to *go*.' She was really angry now. 'I won't be treated like a fool, Samuel. I won't have that woman under my roof an hour longer than I have to. She must leave as soon as possible. And *you* must tell her this morning. I don't want to see or speak to her again.'

Sam groaned inwardly as he climbed out of bed. How was he to dismiss the young woman they had grown so fond of, who had worked for them so devotedly all these years? And if what she said was true and her child really was their granddaughter, were they driving away their own flesh and blood? Rachel seemed to have closed her mind to the possibility. With a heavy heart he made his way to the bathroom. The sooner he got it over with, the better, he supposed.

Maryan got up as soon as it was light. She was glad to leave her bed where she had tossed and turned restlessly all night. She was in the kitchen making herself a pot of tea when a soft tap came on the door. She opened it and found to her dismay that Sam stood outside.

'Mr Leigh. Come in, I'm afraid I'm not dressed yet.' She pulled her dressing gown around her and tied the belt.

'Forgive me for disturbing you so early, my dear.' Sam stepped inside the door. 'I felt I must come and see you before Rachel gets up.'

'Of course. I'm just making tea. I expect you'd like a cup.' She pushed her uncombed hair back from her forehead. 'I'm afraid I must look terrible. I didn't sleep very well.'

'It's not surprising.' He reached out to touch her arm. 'Neither did we, if it's any consolation. Though Rachel has dropped off now.' He looked at her. 'Maryan – about – last night . . .'

'Please . . .' Maryan turned away. 'I can guess why you're here. Let's forget it. Telling you like that was a terrible mistake. It's better if we don't talk about it any more.' As he opened his mouth to speak, she held up her hand. 'And there's no need for you to dismiss me. I realise that I must leave now. I'll stay on until you find a replacement – if you want me to, that is. But I think we both know that it would be best all round if I went.'

Sam sighed, trying hard not to show his relief. He had dreaded having to give her notice. With a soft groan he sat down at the kitchen table. 'My dear – if only you had waited a little while.'

'Would it really have made any difference?' Mary poured two cups of tea and pushed one towards him. 'I think we both realise now that Mrs Leigh would never accept Amy as her own flesh and blood. She was obviously horrified. Outraged at the very idea.'

'No, no. It was just the shock,' Sam protested. 'Coming so quickly after . . .'

'*More* bad news, you mean?' Maryan shook her head. 'I made a mistake – a bad one. I thought she was fond of Amy. I was stupid enough to think it might be a happy surprise for her. I was wrong.'

'Maybe – maybe in time . . .' Sam said without conviction. 'She's had such a bad time since the war began. He meant everything to her – the world. You know that. I don't think she will ever get over losing him.'

And from now on Amy and I would be an uncomfortable reminder that he was a human being and not a saint. Maryan stopped herself from saying the bitter words that filled her mind. 'One thing's certain. She won't want to have me around from now on,' she said instead.

Sam drew a long brown envelope from his pocket. 'This is a reference, my dear. It's the very least I can do for you.' He looked at her, his kind brown eyes infinitely sad. 'Maryan. If there's any-thing I can do – anything at all, you will let me know, won't you?'

'Of course. I'll go into Colchester to the Labour Exchange this morning,' she told him. 'I won't leave without making sure you've got a replacement.'

'It's very good of you to take it so well.' Sam shook his head unhappily. 'I hate seeing you go like this. If only it could have been different. My dear – where will you go?'

'Go? Home, of course. Back to London.'

'And – the child – Amy?'

'She'll stay where she is for the moment. It'll be safer in Suffolk.'

'Then you must let me give you some money. Make you an allowance of some sort.'

'No.'

'But – for Amy's needs. After all . . .'

Amy had wakened to the sound of voices. Slipping out of bed, she went to the bedroom door and opened it. Her mother was talking to someone in the kitchen. She recognised the other voice as Mr Leigh's. The kitchen door was ajar and their voices reached her easily across the narrow hallway.

'After all, you'll need money to bring the child up properly and provide . . .'

'No,' Maryan said sharply, cutting him off in mid-sentence. 'I hope you don't think that I was trying to get money from you when I . . .'

'No, no, my dear, of course I don't. Nevertheless . . .'

'Please. Don't let's talk about it any more. I'll be all right.' Maryan paused. 'I'll get Amy out of the way this morning as soon as I can; put her on the train for Rhensham this morning. Mrs Leigh needn't see her again. As for me – I'll do my best to keep out of the way as far as possible.'

'Don't say that, Maryan. You've been so good to Rachel. No daughter could have done more.'

'But I'm *not* her daughter, Mr Leigh,' Maryan said. 'I'm her maid. A servant, that's all I've ever been.' *And now I'm leaving as a disgraced one*, she added to herself.

Amy crept back to her room and began to dress. It sickened her to hear her mother demeaning them both like that. *I'll get Amy out of the way as soon as I can. Mrs Leigh needn't see her again.* As though she was unclean, or some kind of freak, not fit to be seen.

But freak or not, they wanted her out of the way. All of them, even her mother. Now that the secret was out she was an embarrassment to everybody; a mistake, something to be ashamed of – pushed hastily out of sight in case she should cause offence.

She dressed hurriedly and packed her things neatly into her suitcase. Thank goodness Auntie Marjorie and Mike didn't know. They at least would be pleased to see her.

In the kitchen Maryan was busy laying the breakfast table. Mr Leigh had gone. Amy sat in her place, saying nothing. Maryan smiled a little too brightly as she passed her the cereal packet and milk jug.

'I've been thinking, Amy. You might as well go back to Rhensham today. It doesn't look as though we'll get up to see Grandma after all. It isn't fair to keep you here any longer. You'll be wanting to help out with that carnival thing, won't you?'

'Yes. Okay.' Amy poured milk onto her cornflakes, watching her mother out of the corner of her eye. She looked haggard and pale, her eyes red and puffy, as though she'd been crying. But try as she would, Amy couldn't feel sorry for her. Her mother didn't know that Amy had overheard last night's revelation and what followed. It was clear that she had no intention of telling her about it either. Or of telling her the truth about who her father really was. So far she hadn't even said anything about going back to London to live. Did she think that she, Amy, was deaf or stupid – or both? Or was she just so unimportant that her feelings didn't matter? Well, she wouldn't say anything either – wouldn't admit that she'd overheard, or force her mother to confess to her, even though a dozen urgent questions burned to be answered.

After breakfast she put on her coat and they walked to the station together in silence. Maryan was so preoccupied that her daughter's unusual silence went unnoticed. When the train pulled in she kissed Amy, saw her safely into the carriage and handed up her suitcase.

'Don't forget to write,' she called as the train drew out. 'And be a good girl for Auntie Marjorie.'

Be a good girl. Just as though nothing had happened. As though she were still a little girl. Maybe yesterday she had been. Today, weighed down by this shameful secret that questioned her identity – her right to exist at all – she knew she had left her childhood behind for ever.

Amy sat in her corner seat all the way to Rhensham, trying to sort out in her mind who she was and where she was going. Grandma had told her once that Mr Leigh had been a foundling, brought up in an orphanage because he had no parents. Well, now she knew what that felt like. She might as well be an orphan herself. At least orphans knew where they stood. They were at least free to start life with a clean slate and make what they might of themselves. Two days ago Mrs Leigh had seemed fond of her. She'd even asked for her company; chatted and laughed with her. Now she hated her so much that she couldn't even bear to have her in the same house. And all because she had been told that Amy was her own flesh and blood. The thought hurt so much that she wanted to curl up into a little ball and hide herself away from the world.

When she arrived at Mitcham Lodge she was relieved to find that Marjorie Taylor was out. Only Michael was at home. He was upstairs in his room, making posters for the carnival. He saw her pass through his open door and called to her.

'Hello. So you're back at last. About time too, there's heaps to do. I was thinking of going over to Snape tomorrow, to put up some of these posters. Want to come?'

She stood in the doorway. 'I can't. I've got to go up to London, Mike; to see my Grandma.'

He looked up with a frown. 'But – I thought you'd been. Thought that was why you went to Hazelfield in the first place?'

'Yes, but we never got there. The Leighs heard that their son had been killed in France. Mrs Leigh was ill and Mum wouldn't leave her.'

'I see. What rotten luck. So you have to go up?' Amy nodded. He paused in his work to look at her. 'On your own? Are you sure that's what your mother wants you to do?'

Amy walked across to the table and sat down opposite him. 'Mum doesn't know I'm going.' She picked up a paintbrush and dipped it abstractedly into a pot of red paint. 'I – I have to see Grandma, you see – about something – something secret.' While she was speaking she made swirling patterns on a piece of plain paper.

'Hey!' Michael reached out and snatched the brush out of her hand. 'Don't do that, stupid,' he snapped. 'There's a shortage of paper. Don't you know there's a war on?' The phrase was borrowed

112

from the village butcher. It was a running joke with the Taylor family; something the three of them had laughed about many times. Michael was shocked to see Amy's eyes suddenly brim with tears. She fled from the room and crossed the landing to her own room, Michael following. He stared bemusedly at the closed bedroom door through which he could hear her muffled sobs.

'Amy – what's up?' he called. 'Don't be daft. I didn't mean anything. You know that.'

He couldn't know that for Amy his thoughtless rebuke had felt like a cruel slap in the face. It had been the last straw. She was an outcast, she told herself miserably; a misfit whom nobody wanted. This wasn't her home. She had no home. She didn't belong anywhere – or to anyone.

'Amy – Amy, look, can I come in? I didn't mean to shout at you. He opened the door and stood hesitantly in the doorway, his eyes troubled. 'Look, come on, cheer up before Mum comes home and sees you or you'll get me into a row.'

Amy stopped crying and sat up, fumbling in her sleeve for a handkerchief. Michael crossed the room to stand in front of her.

'Come on, what's up? Did you have a rotten time with your mum?'

Amy nodded, swallowing her tears. 'Sorry, Mike. I didn't mean to be feeble. It's just – something that happened yesterday.'

'And is that why you want to go and see your Grandmother?'

She nodded. 'Don't ask me what it is, Mike. I can't tell you. I can't tell anyone, not till I've talked to Grandma about it. It's too – too awful.'

'Oh, come on. It can't be that bad.'

'It *is*,' she said despairingly. She looked up at him. 'I'll go tomorrow. I think I've got enough money saved up to pay the fare. I can say I'm going to Snape with you.'

Michael looked doubtful. 'I wish you'd ask Mum first. It's dangerous with these buzz bomb things though, isn't it? I can't just let you go like that, on your own. Mum'd kill me if anything happened and she found out I knew.'

But Amy shook her head adamantly. 'I *have* to go, Mike. It's terribly important. You'll just have to pretend you don't know about it. It'll be all right. And if Auntie finds out I shan't tell her you knew.'

'That's not the point, though.' He was silent for a moment, then his face lit up. 'Tell you what,' he said. 'I'll come with you. I've still got some of my birthday money left.'

*

113

It was the first time Amy had been back to London since that day just before the outbreak of war when she had left with all the other children. Euston station looked much as she remembered it. As she and Michael stepped down from the train a small spiral of excitement stirred in the pit of her stomach. It was a bit like an adventure; scary as well as exciting. There was guilt too – that they'd deceived Auntie Marjorie. But that had been necessary. She would never have let them come if she'd known. Michael looked at her enquiringly.

'Right – what do we do now?'

'We get the Underground,' Amy told him decisively.

'Do you know where to go? Which train to get on?' he asked.

Amy took his hand. 'Come on, we'll ask.'

When they emerged from Liverpool Street Underground station Amy looked around her in dismay. Nothing here was as she remembered it at all. They might as well have been on another planet. Where previously buildings had stood there were now open spaces, rubble-strewn battle scars with blades of dusty grass already pushing their way up between broken walls. Some of the older bomb sites had been cleared, whilst on other, more recent ones, precariously leaning walls still stood, with here and there small reminders of human occupancy: a shred of patterned wallpaper, a broken fireplace. Amy looked away, ashamed of staring. It was a bit like reading someone's private letters, or catching them in their underwear. Where were those people? she asked herself. With a shudder, she realised that they had probably been killed by the bomb that wrecked their homes.

'It's awful, isn't it?' Michael was looking at her. 'I've seen the pictures in the newspapers but I never thought it'd be as bad as this. Where do we go now?'

She pulled herself together, looking at the people, bustling about their daily lives as though nothing had changed. 'Over there,' She pointed to a bus stop. 'We get the bus to Hackney.' At least the bus would still know the way, she reflected.

Even when they got off the bus Amy had trouble finding Crimea Terrace. As at Liverpool Street, nothing looked as she remembered it. In the end she asked a policeman who was passing.

'Crimea Terrace? Yes, love.' He looked at her doubtfully. 'Not that there's much of it left, mind.'

They followed his directions and when they stood at the corner of the street Amy stopped. The warden was right. Most of the street had gone. The space where the Prince of Wales public house had once stood was flattened; and the mews at the back where Amy had spent so much time with the horses was gone too. The maze of

114

streets, lanes and alleys that had been so familiar to her was changed beyond all recognition. Just two houses and the corner shop were left in Crimea Terrace. Some of the windows were boarded up and the end walls were shored up with strong girders, but the shop was open for business, its familiar trays of vegetables stacked outside for customers to inspect. And at the remaining windows of number ten Amy recognised Grandma's curtains. Her heart lifted a little. They were the first reassuring, familiar sight she had had since getting off the train.

'There it is,' she said, pointing excitedly. 'That's our house.'

'What – that?' Michael quickly tried to hide his initial reaction of shock and dismay. 'Look, I'll go for a walk.' He looked at his watch. 'I'll come back for you in about an hour. That long enough?'

'Plenty. Thanks, Mike.' She watched him till he got to the corner, then knocked on the door. Sarah was so long answering that she thought for one crestfallen moment that she'd made the journey in vain, then suddenly there was the scrape of a bolt being drawn on the other side and the door opened a crack. Sarah's astonished face looked out.

'*Amy*? My Gawd, what brings you 'ere?' She pushed her face a little further out to look up and down the street. 'Is your mother with you?'

'No, Grandma. I'm on my own. Can I come in?'

Sarah shook her head. 'Not this way you can't, love. You'll have to come round the back. Street door won't open properly since the bombing. Something to do with the foundations shiftin', so they say. Come round an I'll let you in the back door.'

The back, where all the yards had once given onto a narrow passage was now an open space. All that was left of the yard was the remains of one wall and the outside lavatory. Sarah already had the back door open and stood, arms held wide to receive her granddaughter. Her hug was warm and welcoming.

'Gawd, gel, you've grown,' she said, holding Amy at arms' length. 'Proper little woman you are an' no mistake. But what brings you up to see your old Grandma? What's that Mrs Taylor thinkin' about, lettin' you come up alone?'

'I'm not alone, Grandma. Michael came with me. He's gone for a walk so that you and me can have a talk.'

'Oh, yes?' Sarah drew her into the kitchen and pulled a chair out from the table. 'What's up? There's somethin'. I c'n see that. Come on gel. Better spit it out and be done with it.'

Amy bit her lip. 'Grandma – I've been staying with Mum at

115

Hazelfield and – er – Mr Marcus has been killed. A man came to tell Mr and Mrs Leigh.'

'Oh my dear Lord.' Sarah grasped the back of a chair and eased herself into it. 'Poor Miss Rachel. She'll've taken it badly if I know anythin'. The apple of her eye, he was.' She shook her head. 'And to think there was no need for 'im to have gone in the first place. What a waste.' She looked at Amy. 'But your Mum will've written to tell me. There's sure to be a letter in the post. No need for you to come all this way to tell me, love.'

'No, Grandma. That's not why I'm here. There's something else; something I have to know – to ask you.'

Sarah looked at her curiously. 'Come on then. What's this all about?' When Amy remained apparently tongue-tied she made an impatient little gesture with her hands. 'Well? You gonna make me sit 'ere an' guess then, are you?'

'No. It's this, Grandma. I heard Mum telling Mr and Mrs Leigh something the night before last. I didn't mean to listen. Mum had forgotten the milk for their coffee, you see, and I . . .'

'Oh do get *on* with it,' Sarah said impatiently. 'You'll 'ave that Michael back again any minute. What *is* this thing you 'eard?'

Amy swallowed hard. 'I heard her – Mum – telling the Leighs that I was their grandchild. That Mr Marcus was my real father.' She studied her grandmother's face carefully, looking for signs of anything – surprise; shock; acknowledgement. She saw none of them. Sarah stared at her blankly for a moment, then she got up and began to fill the kettle at the sink.

'Well?' Amy pressed. 'Is it true, Grandma? That's why I'm here. That's what I've come to find out. I have to know, you see.'

Sarah turned to her. 'What's she want to go tellin' 'em that for?' She peered into Amy's face. 'And anyway, what does a kid your age know about them sort of things?'

'I'm not a kid, Grandma. I'm almost thirteen. And I do know – about babies and all those grown-up things. Auntie Marjorie told me.'

Sarah looked scandalised. 'Then she'd no call to. Things like that's private, between a gel an' 'er mother.'

'But Mum wasn't there and . . .'

'When I was a gel them things was kept from us till we got married,' Sarah said. 'That's time enough to know if you ask me.'

'But is it *true*, Grandma? About Mr Marcus and Mum?'

Sarah wiped her hands on a teatowel and sank into her chair again. So many things were clear to her now. If she were truly honest with herself she'd known all along that those two were more than just sweet on each other. If Maryan had come right out with it like that, then it must be true. She'd never have said so otherwise. But why in God's name had she chosen a moment like that to tell the Leighs?

'Grandma . . .?'

She pulled herself up straight. 'If it's true then she never told me,' she said truthfully. 'Far as I know, Tom Jessop was your dad. An' a better one you could never 'ave 'ad. An' if I was you, gel, I'd leave it at that an' be grateful.'

'But I have to *know*, Grandma,' Amy persisted. 'If I don't know who my real father was I'm not – not a real person, am I?'

'Not *real*? What kinda talk is that?' Sarah demanded. But her own mind was travelling along a different track entirely. 'What did the Leighs say?' she asked.

Amy shook her head. 'It was awful. Mrs Leigh was angry – really angry. She said Mum was lying – trying to blacken Mr Marcus's name. Mum's leaving. I think she's coming home. I heard her telling Mr Leigh so this morning.'

'Silly cat,' Sarah muttered under her breath. 'After all these years, to go and lose her job just for the sake of . . .' She looked up at Amy. 'Don't you worry about it no more, luvvie. It'll all come right in the end, you'll see.' Seeing the girl's distressed look she reached across the table and took her hands. 'Why didn't you ask your mum about it there an' then? Why come all the way up 'ere to me?'

'She didn't know I'd heard. She still doesn't. I don't want to talk to her about it, Grandma. And I don't want you to tell her I've been here – that I know. Promise you won't tell – please?'

'I won't say nothin', love. Not if you don't want me to.'

Amy sighed. 'If it really is true why didn't she tell *me* first?'

'I don't know that, love. My Maryan's always been a close one when it come to feelin's. P'raps she was ashamed. Mothers always want their kids to look up to 'em, y'know. That's on'y natural. Then there was Tom to think about. She must've had good reason to keep it to 'erself all these years.'

Amy looked at her. 'Grandma – if it's true, am I half Jewish? Am I really a Leigh?'

Sarah sighed, racking her brain for the right answers. 'You can't be *half* Jewish, love,' she said, frowning. 'Either you are or you ain't. And you can't be Jewish if you ain't been brought up Jewish,' she added slowly. 'It's a religion, see. Like the Catholics an' Methodists, on'y different. An' the name on your birth certificate is Jessop. No doubt about that.'

It wasn't exactly what Amy meant. But then she didn't really know what she meant, so the questions were impossible to pursue any further. Anyway it was at that moment that they both heard the knocking on the street door. 'That'll be Michael,' Amy said, jumping up. 'I'll go round and get him, shall I?'

'I'll make you both a cuppa and a sandwich and then you'd better be on your way,' Sarah said. 'Them doodlebugs comes over any time o' the day or night. Sooner you're out of here the happier I'll be.'

It was only when she and Michael were eating their sandwiches that Amy realised how badly damaged the house was. Looking round she saw that large pieces of plaster had fallen off the kitchen walls, leaving the brickwork exposed. In some places the ceiling was showing bare wooden laths and the kitchen range smoked badly through a crack in the chimney. Sarah saw her looking round and said: 'They sent the builders round after the last lot – to make sure it was still safe. No chance of gettin' nothing permanent done till after the war.'

'Do you go to the shelter when there's a raid?' Michael asked.

Sarah shook her head. 'With these doodlebugs you don't always get any warnin', love. Anyway, I'd rather stay 'ere. I get under me old table.' She patted the chenille-covered table affectionately. 'Oak, that is. Strong as a rock; belonged to my old mother-in-law.'

'It can't be very comfortable for you living here like this, Mrs Brown,' Michael remarked.

For a moment Sarah looked as though she was about to make a resentful reply to the boy's remark, then she smiled ruefully. 'Beggars can't be choosers, love. I was lucky to be allowed back at all. They on'y let me come back 'cause the lav was still working.' She laughed. 'Marvellous, ain't it? Still, can't be long now 'fore old 'itler chucks in the towel, can it? These doodlebugs is just is last kick, so they reckon. P'raps when the war's over they'll build me a nice new 'ouse with a bathroom an a real front garden with geraniums an' everythin'. Never knows your luck, eh?'

Amy was quiet as they walked back to the bus stop together. Michael peered into her closed face once or twice, then he ventured: 'Well – get everything sorted out, did you?'

'Not really.'

'Has it been a waste of time then?'

She turned to look at him. 'Of course it wasn't a waste of time. It was lovely seeing Grandma again.' They'd stopped now at the bus stop and she looked him in the eye. 'You didn't think much of our house, Mike, did you?'

He blushed. 'No one can help the bomb damage.'

118

'Why don't you say what you're thinking? I expect *you'd* call it a slum.'

'Of course I wouldn't. I . . .'

'Grandma always used to have the whitest doorstep in the street,' she interrupted. 'And the shiniest brasses. The curtains were washed and starched regularly and there used to be nice wallpaper and a sofa in the front room.'

'All right, all *right*. I believe you.' Michael kicked at the kerb with the toe of his shoe. 'No need to go on about it. Anyway, I haven't said a word, have I?'

'No, but you've looked and thought a lot,' she said waspishly. 'Grandma doesn't talk like *you*, does she? I expect you think she's common. Well, *I* used to talk like that and maybe I will again when I come back here to live. You won't want to know me then, will you, stuck-up snobby Michael Taylor?'

'*Amy*. What's the matter with you? Why are you being so nasty? As a matter of fact I think your grandma is very brave. She . . .' He stopped speaking to stare up into the sky, his attention taken by the strange droning sound of an aircraft overhead. They'd been so engrossed in their quarrel that he hadn't noticed it before. Looking up he could clearly see it silhouetted against the sky and flying quite low; a strangely shaped craft with a red flame shooting from its tail.

There was a sudden cry of: '*Buzzbomb. Take cover!*' and at the same moment Michael saw the flame vanish and heard the splutter of the engine as it cut out.

Grabbing Amy by the arm he dragged her into a nearby doorway where they crouched together as passers-by scattered, running past them in all directions for the nearest cover. Traffic stopped. Everything came to a halt. The sudden empty silence of a city street brought abruptly to a frozen standstill was eerie and terrifying. There was a tense wait that seemed interminable, then came a deafening explosion that shook the ground beneath them and almost seemed to batter the breath from their bodies. To Michael it seemed almost on top of them, but he learned later that the flying bomb had fallen several streets away. Amy gave a shrill, startled scream as shattered glass and bits of masonry rained into the street. He put his arms protectively round her, pulling her close and shielding her head with his own as he bent over her. For a moment he felt her heart thumping frantically in time with his and in that moment he wondered how city people had stood this – and worse than this – for so long. He had seen the newspaper photographs and newsreel film of the devastation, but they came nowhere near the reality of it. The

119

raids on the east coast had been bad enough; even Ipswich had had its share, but what he had seen today had shocked him to the heart.

'Hello – you kids all right then?' A man wearing a steel helmet, with a big 'W' painted on it, bent and held out a hand to them.

'Yes, thank you, we're okay.' Michael got unsteadily to his feet, pulling Amy up with him and brushing the dust from his trousers.

Amy's eyes were round with fear. 'Grandma,' she said. 'Do you think Grandma's all right?'

'Where does your gran live, duckie?' the man asked kindly.

'Crimea Terrace. We've just come from there.'

'Oh no, you're all right. This one landed further up, towards Hoxton.' He pointed in the opposite direction.

'Do you want to go back and see?' Michael asked, looking doubtfully at Amy.

'Where do you live?' the warden asked.

'Rhensham – in Suffolk. We've come up for the day.'

'Well, I'd cut off home sharpish on the first train I could get if I were you. Never know when these blighters will turn up. Daresay your mum'll be worryin' about you.'

'Yes, sir. We will.' Michael took Amy's hand. 'Come on. Look, the buses have started again.'

As they sat side by side in the bus on the way to the station Amy's hand reached out for his.

'Thanks, Mike.'

'What for?'

'You saved my life.'

He flushed a dark red. 'Don't be daft, course I didn't. That thing was nowhere near us. We weren't in any danger really.'

'It felt like it to me.' She looked at him sideways. 'If you hadn't pulled me into that doorway – all that glass and stuff – we'd have been hurt . . .' She broke off, biting her lip. 'You didn't have to come with me, Mike. I'm sorry I said those rotten things to you. I sounded just like Lily Smith.'

'Good job I did come,' Michael said gruffly. 'Heaven knows what kind of a mess you'd have got into on your own.'

'I'd've been all right,' she began sharply, then she smiled. 'Still, I'm glad you were there.' She squeezed his hand. 'Were you scared?'

He shrugged. 'Not really. All I was worried about was what on earth I'd say to Mum if anything'd happened to you.'

She smiled, unimpressed by his bravado. 'Well I was,' she whispered. 'I'll be glad when we're home. I'm really looking forward to the carnival next week, aren't you?'

'Yes – yes, I am.' He was sharing Amy's euphoric feeling of

thankfulness at being alive and safe. Suddenly he realised that they were still holding hands. It embarrassed him a bit, but he found to his surprise that he didn't want to pull away. Being in danger together had forged a kind of bond between them and whether he admitted it or not, he too was in need of comfort at that moment. He looked at her enquiringly. 'Amy?'

'Yes?'

'Who's Lily Smith?'

'You don't seem very surprised to see me.' Maryan stood surrounded by her luggage in the kitchen at Crimea Terrace.

'When you gets to be my age and you've lived through two wars there's nothin' much surprises you no more,' Sarah said with a sniff. 'This just a visit then?' She asked ironically as she eyed the two suitcases, holdall and various parcels at Maryan's feet.

'No, Mum. I'm home for good.' Maryan began to take off her coat. 'I've given up my job with the Leighs.'

As Sarah had predicted, Maryan had written to her mother to tell her of Marcus's death. It had been a brief letter, giving only the barest details. The rest – her revelation and the Leighs' reaction – had been impossible to put into a letter and she had finally decided that it would be better to break the rest of her news when they were face to face.

'Given up – just when they need you most?' Sarah challenged. 'How could you do that after all the years you've been with them?'

Maryan sighed and sank into her mother's chair by the range. 'Things change, Mum. I felt I needed a break. I'm not getting any younger. I was sick of being buried in the country.'

'I see. Lookin' for a new 'usband, are you?'

'Of course not. A new job. Something different. I'd like to make a new life for Amy and me when the war's over. She hated Hazelfield anyway.'

'Oh, so it's for Amy you're doing this – letting the Leighs down?'

'If you like, yes.'

Sarah stood in front of her daughter, forcing her to look her in the eye. 'There's more to this than meets the eye, my gel. Are you gonna tell me the truth, or aren't you?'

'Mum – I'm a grown woman, not a kid. I've told you all you need to know.'

Sarah turned away, making a great clatter over putting the kettle on and laying the table. 'I don't suppose you're too old to want your tea,' she muttered. 'And if you won't tell me p'raps Miss Rachel will.'

Maryan looked up sharply. 'What do you mean?'

'What I say. I'll write and ask 'er why you've left if you won't tell me. There's gotta be more reason than what you've given me.'

'You'll do nothing of the sort, Mum. I won't let you.'

'Won't let me, eh?' Sarah stood on the hearthrug, hand on hips. 'I'd like to know how you think you're gonna stop me?'

Maryan sighed. 'It's not a good idea, Mum. Let it rest.'

Sarah made the tea and set the pot on the hob to brew. 'They give you the push, didn't they?'

'No.'

'But they would've done, if you'd given 'em the chance. That's it, ain't it? Come on, what 'appened, Maryan? Out with it, gel. You know I won't rest till you've told me the truth.'

'We – had a disagreement. Maybe I'd been there too long.'

'A disagreement over what?'

Maryan could see that she would have no peace till she'd told her mother everything. And perhaps she owed her the truth anyway. 'I – told them something, Mum. Told them with the best of motives. It misfired. It was a bad mistake. They didn't want to know.'

'Yes – you told 'em – what?'

'That Marcus was Amy's father.' She glanced up at her mother's stony face. 'I thought they'd be happy, Mum. Mrs Leigh seemed fond of Amy. She was the one person who seemed to comfort her after she heard about Marcus being killed. I thought she and Mr Sam'd be glad to think they had a grandchild.'

'Then you hadn't thought about it enough,' Sarah said bluntly. 'Couldn't you see that everything was against it: their class, their – their culture or whatever it is they calls it? You should've seen all that. How could you expect them to be pleased? Anyway . . .' She eyed her daughter enquiringly. 'Is it true?'

Maryan stared at her. 'Of *course* it's true. I wouldn't lie about a thing like that.'

'Seems to me you lied enough about it in the past.'

'Tom knew,' Maryan said. 'He knew right from the start. I never deceived him, though he never knew who Amy's real father was. I've never told anyone but the Leighs themselves till now. Even Marcus didn't know. And now . . .' Her voice broke. 'Now – he never will.' She began to cry, leaning forward to hide her face in her hands as tears overwhelmed her. 'I loved him, Mum,' she sobbed. 'I loved him so much – all those years. I never stopped loving him, not even when I knew he'd stopped loving me. I never stopped hoping that some day . . . And – and now there can be no more hope – ever.'

Swallowing her compassion and blinking back her own tears,

Sarah took the teapot from the hob and poured two strong cups. Adding milk and two spoons of sugar to Maryan's, she passed it to her. 'Here, drink this, gel.' She watched as a red-eyed Maryan sipped at the tea. 'So – what're you gonna do now? London still ain't much of a place to be makin' a new start in.'

Maryan looked at her mother. Sarah was close to sixty now, but she looked at least ten years older. She glanced round her. Living in this place couldn't be doing her any good. 'I haven't asked you how you are yet, Mum,' she said. 'The house is a mess. Can't they rehouse you?'

'I'm all right where I am,' Sarah said stoically. 'Everything still works – after a fashion, anyway. I got me wireless. I've still got Vera Lynn and 'Music While You Work' to cheer me up. I'm all right.'

'What about when the winter comes, though? This place won't be fit to live in then. The draughts must be terrible.'

'If you've on'y come 'ome to find fault then maybe you should'a stayed where you were.'

Maryan stood up and took her mother's hands. 'I'm going to look after you, Mum,' she said gently. 'Like you looked after me and Amy and Tom all those years. Time you had things a bit easier. You're not going to argue with that, are you?'

Sarah shrugged. 'Well, we'll see,' she said. But she responded to Maryan's embrace warmly enough. It was true she'd been lonely. It had been a struggle what with the buzzbombs and everything. And she had to admit that the prospect of the coming winter with its inevitable crop of chest colds had worried her too. Yes, it was good to have her daughter back again.

Major Armstrong, who owned Rhensham Manor, had given the Holidays At Home committee the use of his twenty-acre meadow for Rhensham's part in the festivities. It was to take place on the bank holiday Monday and Marjorie Taylor was helping her friend Jane Frencham at the riding school with pony rides. Amy and Michael were helping too. They spent the whole of the Sunday helping to set up their pitch, erecting a coloured awning to keep the sun off the ponies and staking out the rides round the meadow's perimeter.

They were looking forward to the festivities. There were to be sideshows and competitions, a baby show and a dog show, bowling for the pig and other entertainments. Amy and Mike had planned to take it in turns to work and play.

Since the onslaught of V-1 bombings, more London evacuees had arrived in Rhensham. The village school was full to overflowing once again just as it had been in '39 and '41. Amy had already seen many new faces in the village, but they didn't affect Mike and her so much now that they had moved on to the grammar schools in Ipswich. As they staked out the rides on Sunday afternoon Michael mentioned their visit to London.

'I don't think I'd like to live there.' He looked at her. 'Will you really go back there to live when the war's over?'

She shrugged. 'I don't suppose I'll have any choice.'

'You could always stay here. You have to admit, it's nicer.'

'London looks awful now, but it won't when they've built it up again,' Amy said loyally.

'But that could take years.' Michael drove in another stake, hitting it with the mallet. 'You and your mother hardly know each other now. You're not homesick any more, are you? I bet she wouldn't mind if you stayed on with us,' he said. 'At least until you've finished at school. Why don't you ask her?'

'Take a lot for granted, don't you, Mike Taylor?' Amy said. 'What makes you think I want to stay on here with you?' Immediately she could see that she'd hurt him. His face turned a dull red and he turned away quickly so that she wouldn't see.

'Okay. I was only trying to help. I'll be glad to see the back of you if you want to know.' He gave the stake an almighty whack with his mallet. 'It'll be nice to have the place to myself again. You're just a boring little nuisance most of the time. Anyway, I'll be going to college once I've got my Matric, so it's no skin off my nose.'

She looked at him in surprise. '*Mike*. I was only joking.'

'Humph. Funny joke,' he retorted. 'Pardon me while I kill myself laughing.'

Amy giggled and gave him a playful push. 'Don't be such a twerp. Come on, bossy-boots.'

Their quarrel was soon forgotten, but later Amy thought about what he had said. She wondered if her mother would let her stay on at Mitcham Lodge till she'd finished school. If she were honest, it had been a shock, seeing what the war had done to the London she knew. But the war apart, the house in Crimea Terrace had made her think. Had she really lived there – called a place like that home? And could she ever really be happy there again? Would Maryan expect to pick up the threads and make a home again in that *hovel*, or some place like it? Everyone said that after the war hundreds of bright new houses would be built to replace the bombed ones. Some were of the opinion that it was the slum clearance London had always wanted. But as Mike had said, it would surely take an awfully long time? She had her education to finish. Surely Mum wouldn't expect her to leave before it was completed?

The day of the Rhensham Carnival dawned fine and bright. From early in the morning it promised to be a hot day. When the Taylors and Amy arrived at Armstrong's Meadow the sky was a hazy azure blue and a fine heat haze hovered on the horizon. They tethered the ponies and set out the saddles on a bench. There were folding chairs to sit on and a camping table for the tickets and money. Mike went off to fill the buckets with water for the ponies, then they sat down to await their first customer.

By ten o'clock the meadow was full of people and Amy and Mike were kept fully occupied. Pony rides were in great demand, especially among the younger evacuees. Amy was halfway round a ride, leading a nervous little girl on Cobby, the smallest Shetland pony, when a shrill voice hailed her.

'Well, if it ain't Miss High and Mighty Jessop. Wotcher, toffee-nose.'

The voice was unmistakable and Amy could hardly believe her ears. Looking up, she saw a group of children standing watching. Most of them were strangers to Amy, but the one who had called out to her was her old adversary, Lily Smith. Even though she had grown taller in the intervening years, her voice and manner hadn't changed. If anything, she was even more shrewish-looking than before, with her long, pink-tipped nose and small close-set eyes. She was dressed as usual in an ill-fitting dress a size too small for her and she was clearly spoiling for a fight. Unwilling to oblige, Amy continued as though she had neither seen nor heard her – a gesture guaranteed to infuriate Lily.

''Ere, who the 'ell do you think you are?' she yelled. 'Look at 'er,' she addressed the group of younger children. 'Never think she come from the worst slum in 'ackney, would yer? All rigged out like Lady bleedin' Muck.'

Michael caught up with them, leading another child on a pony. 'What do you want?' he asked Lily haughtily. 'If you want a pony ride you pay back there. If not, kindly stop shouting.'

Lily laughed raucously. '*Kaindly stop showtin*',' she mimicked. 'Oh, Gawd blimey. Listen to Lord flipping Snooty. 'E your feller then is 'e, Jessop? Goes for the posh ones, do you? Like your mum and that Marcus Leigh.'

Amy felt her cheeks turn hot as she rounded furiously on Lily. 'Go away, Lily Smith. Mind your own business.'

'Mind yer business, is it? All lies, weren't it – when you said they was gettin' married. Lying little cow.'

'If you don't go away I'll get someone to throw you out,' Amy shouted.

125

Lily's face turned scarlet and her eyes glittered spitefully in the ominous way that Amy remembered all too well. 'Right. I'll get you fer that, Amy-pissed Jessop. You can't play Lady Muck with me. I *knows* you, remember. Always did think you was better than anybody else. We'll see what you looks like when I'm done wi' you, s'there.' She turned on her heel. 'Come on, kids, let's go. It stinks o' snobs 'ere.'

Michael looked at her. 'What an awful girl. Don't tell me that was *the* Lily Smith?'

Amy gave him a wry grin. 'It certainly was.'

'Really? No kidding. Why does she hate you so much?'

'I don't know. Mum used to say she was jealous.'

'What was all that about your mother and Marcus Leigh?'

Amy blushed and turned away. 'I don't know. Rubbish.'

Mike looked to where Lily stood some way off, whispering to the other children and throwing occasional spiteful glances at them over her shoulder. 'She's a nasty piece of work.' He grinned. 'What was that name she called you?'

Amy's colour heightened. 'You heard her. I'm not repeating it.'

'But why did she call you that?'

'At my old school I used to get teased about my real name. It's Amethyst.'

'*Amethyst*? Wow, I never knew that before. Does Mum know?'

''Course. It's on my ration book for the whole world to see.'

Seething with resentment, Amy watched him walk away, chuckling to himself. At that moment something inside her hardened. The encounter with Lily Smith had made her mind up. She wasn't going back to London and her old life any more. She wasn't Amy Jessop anyway, but someone bewilderingly different. She'd stay here some-how and find out who that new person was. But one thing was certain. The new Amy would be someone special; maybe she'd even be famous one day, that'd show them all. She'd be a person to be respected and envied, not teased and jeered at for being raised in an East End back street. Crimea Terrace where she was born had gone for ever. Well, so had the old Amy Jessop.

Chapter Eight

Maryan found settling back into life at home in Hackney much more difficult than she'd envisaged. To begin with, the house in Crimea Terrace felt cramped and inconvenient after Whitegates, and try as she would, she could not get used to the constant threat of the buzzbombs. Sarah seemed to take it all in her stride, diving for cover under the kitchen table whenever there was a warning, thanking God vociferously when a loud explosion and a few more bits of fallen plaster were the only result. But Maryan, used to the peace and quiet of the Essex countryside, found the constant tension made her jumpy and short-tempered.

Finding a job was harder than she'd foreseen, too. It was true there was plenty of domestic work, but she'd made up her mind to make a new start and try for something completely different. She'd done with being at the beck and call of some other woman, she told herself. She'd always thought her mother's job demeaning – always wanted to better herself. And if she'd deceived herself into believing that she was something more to the Leighs than a mere housekeeper, their reaction to her revelation had put her straight on that count. Obviously her years of loyal service meant nothing to them. They despised her for having the effrontery to love their son and bear his child. Mrs Leigh had even called her a liar. Well, now she was free of any obligation she had felt towards them. Marcus was dead. She had come to the end of a chapter. The wasted years of girlish dreaming were buried with him, once and for all; at least, so she told herself. But on 25 August, when she and her mother listened to the news of the liberation of Paris on the wireless, Maryan shed silent tears. If he could only have been spared another few months all might have turned out so very differently.

Yet hard though it was proving to make that new start, Maryan was determined to survive and make a new and better life for herself and eventually for Amy. Even though she had no qualifications and no experience in anything but domestic skills and machine sewing, she felt sure that somehow something would turn up.

Her dole money and Sarah's tiny widow's pension didn't go very far. By the time the rent was paid and food bought there was very little left over. Maryan had managed to put a little money by while she lived rent-free at Whitegates, but it wasn't very much. She'd sent her mother some each week, knowing how tight money was for her. She was hoping not to touch what was left in her Post Office account, saving it for when she had Amy back again and they would start to build a new home together.

Every day she went hopefully along to the Labour Exchange. She was offered jobs, but there was never anything she fancied and she became increasingly aware that she would soon be obliged to accept one of the positions offered her or lose her dole. Eventually she reluctantly went along for an interview with a greengrocer who had a shop in Whitechapel Road. His wife had gone into hospital for an operation and he was looking for a woman to take over his daily stall in the market.

'It's on'y temp'r'y, mind,' he told her when she applied. 'Till about Christmas I should think. Soon's the missis is fit to take over again she will.' The man pushed his cap to the back of his bald head. 'Mind you,' he said, his eyes sweeping lustfully over the slim figure and blonde hair, 'play yer cards rights, gel, an' I might find some other little jobs you c'n do for me, if yer know what I mean.' He winked at her suggestively.

Maryan swallowed her revulsion and took the job. It wasn't what she would have liked but she badly needed the money. Besides, as the man said, it was only temporary, and truth to tell she was glad of the opportunity to get out of the house for a few hours each day. She and her mother were beginning to get under each other's feet in the confined space at Crimea Terrace, where only two of the rooms were strictly habitable. She wouldn't trust her new employer any further than she could throw him, but she told herself that as long as he was in his shop and she was running the market stall she'd be safe enough.

Running the stall was hard work. Summer had given way to autumn now and there was a chill nip in the early morning air. She had to be at the shop at six to help Arthur Pratt, or Artie, as he insisted on being called, to load up the produce. Then he would run her down to the market and help her set out the stall before going back to open up the shop for the day. On the short drive to Hackney in his draughty, overloaded van he always contrived to touch her knee at least twice whilst changing gear, and as they set out the produce together he was always finding excuses to squeeze past her in the confined space behind the stall, usually leering at her and making some suggestive remark as he did so. Maryan loathed it. It made her flesh creep, but she kept reminding herself that he would soon be gone. She didn't have to spend too much time with him and at least she was earning again.

As autumn turned to winter it grew bitterly cold and Maryan was chilled to the bone standing still behind the stall in the open all day long. Sarah knitted her some long woollen stockings and mittens, made from an old sweater of Tom's which she had unravelled, but in spite of the layers of clothing Maryan wore, the cold and damp seemed to penetrate right through to her skin. The Pratts' pitch was close to a pub which served tea and coffee as well as alcoholic drinks. Once she had paid a boy to mind the stall while she slipped inside for a cup of tea, but to the pub regulars an unfamiliar woman alone was an object for speculation. Acutely uncomfortable with the experience, she hadn't tried it again.

For the most part the stallholders were a friendly, good-natured bunch, but Maryan found their earthy language and ribald humour embarrassing and off-putting. She was no prude, but she had a natural reserve. Sarah had brought her up to believe that nice women didn't swear or shriek with laughter at coarse jokes, and she found the way that some of the women talked embarrassing. She took sandwiches along each day for her lunch and managed with a bottle of cold tea for drink until she got home at night.

The customers at the market were shrewd and discerning. They demanded value for money and were always on the watch for any kind of sharp practice. One morning she had just been harangued for putting a split potato onto the scales when a man's voice addressed her.

'I think some of them would like you to weigh the bag first.'

She looked up to see the young man from the junk stall opposite smiling at her. He wore an ex-navy duffle coat and a striped scarf wound round his neck. Whenever she had the time she loved to browse through the fascinating articles on his stall, and they'd often exchanged a friendly greeting as they set up opposite each other.

She smiled back at him. 'You're right there. I think some of them'd bring their own scales if they could.'

He walked across to her. 'Look, someone is coming to stand in for me in a minute while I go for a drink. Will you join me?'

Maryan smiled wistfully. 'I'd love to, but I've no one to mind the stall,' she told him.

'Doesn't your employer send anyone to relieve you?' he asked. 'You're entitled to a break, you know.'

'He hasn't got anyone to send. It's all right. I don't mind really. I bring sandwiches – eat them when I've got a minute.'

He looked doubtfully at her chapped fingers, soiled from serving potatoes. 'Can't be very satisfactory. Can I bring you a hot drink when I come back?'

She smiled gratefully. 'Oh, I'd love a nice cup of tea – if you could manage it.'

'Of course I will. I'm Colin, by the way.' He held out his hand. 'Colin Freer.'

Maryan shook his hand. 'I'm Maryan Jessop.'

'Right, Maryan. See you later.'

She watched as he went off whistling in the direction of the pub. He looked about twenty-four and she wondered why he wasn't in one of the services and what an obviously well-educated young man like him was doing serving on a junk stall in Hackney Market. His voice and manner suggested that he was used to something better.

He was as good as his word, arriving with the tea in a thick mug about twenty minutes later. He had thoughtfully placed a beer mat over the top to keep it hot and Maryan took it from him gratefully, wrapping her chilled fingers round the mug and drinking it thirstily.

After that day Colin Freer would wander across to talk to her whenever he wasn't too busy. She learned that he'd been invalided out of the Navy eight months ago after his ship had been torpedoed. He'd suffered severe burns and exposure after being in the water for several hours and had spent long painful months in hospital having skin grafts to his legs and back. Now he was waiting for a government grant to come through so that he could take up the place at university he'd won just before war broke out.

Maryan looked wistful. 'I'd have loved the chance of a proper education,' she said. 'It opens up a whole new world to you, doesn't it? My daughter won a scholarship to high school,' she told him proudly. 'It's more than I ever did.'

'You have a daughter at high school?' Colin looked surprised and Maryan laughed delightedly.

'Yes. She's almost thirteen. I was very young when she was born. She's in Suffolk – evacuated there at the beginning of the war.'

'You must miss her.'

'I do. I'm hoping to have her back soon. With a bit of luck I'll have a better job than this by then. This is only temporary.' She laughed. 'Can't say I'll be sorry when it comes to an end either, even if I do need work.'

130

He looked thoughtful. 'Have you always been in this line – fruit and veg?'

'Heavens, no,' she told him. 'I started as a machinist in a clothing factory, then I took over my mother's job as housekeeper to the factory owner and his wife. I only took this job because I badly needed to earn some money. I'd really like to learn something new and interesting if only I could get the chance.'

He nodded. 'I see. This is temporary for me too. I'm helping my uncle out. He'll be needing someone else when I leave.' He looked at her thoughtfully, but Maryan changed the subject. She didn't really see serving on a junk stall as an improvement to what she was doing now.

It was at the end of that week that Maryan first met Vincent Donlan. She had seen the tall man in the dark overcoat talking to Colin once or twice before, usually late in the afternoon when he came to help Colin pack up. But on this particular day he arrived in the morning. They left a boy in charge of the stall and went off to the pub together at lunch time. When they came back Colin brought the man across to her.

'Maryan, this is my Uncle Vinnie. I've been telling him about you needing a permanent job.'

The man held out his hand to her and when he spoke she detected a slight Irish accent. 'Hello – Maryan, isn't it? I'm Vincent Donlan. Glad to know you.' He looked at the produce on the stall. 'Colin tells me this isn't really your line.'

She smiled. 'That's right. It's only temporary – till I can get something better.'

'I see. What sort of work are you looking for?'

Maryan served a customer and then turned back to him. She was grateful for the diversion. It had given her time to think. Better put the man straight before they began. 'To tell you the truth, Mr Donlan, I'm fed up with standing on the market all day; specially now that the winter's set in. I don't think I'm cut out for it, whatever line it's in.'

He laughed, the relaxed expression lighting up his rather craggy features. 'Well, that's honest at least. As a matter of fact I wasn't planning to keep the stall on after Christmas anyway. I don't know whether Colin has told you, but I have an antique shop. It's in Chelsea. The stuff I sell here is some of the dross I get landed with when I buy job lots at auctions.' He took a card from his wallet and gave it to her. 'Why not come along and see me on your day off?'

Maryan looked at the card. It was embossed in black italic lettering: '*Vincente*', *24 Simons Mews, Chelsea*. In one corner:

Antiques and objets d'art bought and sold. In the other: *Proprietor V. Donlan.* She was impressed. Judging by the things for sale on the stall, she'd imagined Colin's uncle as the kind of dealer who went around clearing homes. 'I don't know the first thing about antiques, Mr Donlan,' she told him doubtfully.

He gave her his warm smile again. 'Ah, you'd soon learn. And in the meantime there are plenty of other things you could do.' Maryan had a brief recollection of Artie Pratt's leering innuendoes and she must have registered suspicion because Vincent added quickly: 'Young Colin there will vouch for my respectability if that's what's worrying you.'

Maryan blushed. 'Oh – it wasn't that. I just . . . The trouble is, Mr Donlan, I don't really get a day off, except Sunday, that is.' She handed the card back to him, but he waved it away.

'Put it in your pocket. Make it next Sunday if you like. I live above the shop. If you decide to come I'll be there anyway. Just ring the bell at the side door. I think you'd be interested to see the shop, even if you decide you don't want to come and work for me.'

Maryan found Simons Mews without too much trouble. She hadn't told Sarah where she was going. Better not to raise her hopes in case the job didn't materialise. She wasn't even sure that it would suit her. It was more curiosity that had driven her to brave visiting a man alone in his flat. But she reckoned that Colin was her insurance. He was such a thoroughly nice young man, and if he said his uncle was a respectable businessman she felt sure he was right.

The shop itself turned out to be converted from the original stables, the double doors having been replaced by a Georgian-style bow window. It appeared to be disappointingly empty, but Maryan's ring at the side-door bell was quickly answered by Vincent himself. He looked less formal this afternoon without his long dark overcoat, wearing instead a casual cream sweater over an open-necked shirt. She noticed that his dark hair was on the long side and slightly tousled. Today he had a distinctly raffish, arty look.

'Come in, come in,' he said welcomingly, holding the door open wide.

The flat, reached by a narrow flight of stairs, was surprisingly spacious, and in the comfortable living room Maryan saw that a trolley was laid with delicate bone china cups and a plate of scones and chocolate biscuits. She stopped in the doorway.

'Oh – you're expecting company?'

'I am,' Vincent agreed. 'Isn't it yourself?'

132

Maryan laughed with him. 'You didn't know for sure that I was coming.'

'Ah . . .' He grinned at her. 'Haven't I the sixth sense for these things? I felt it in me bones as my old mother used to say.'

Maryan looked at the chocolate biscuits and her mouth watered. 'You really shouldn't have gone to so much trouble, though. Look at those biscuits. Your precious points coupons. I know how many they take.'

'Ah, to hell with the points coupons, pesky bits of paper, that's all they are. Just sit down and tuck in,' he invited. 'There's only me to eat the bit of food they let us buy so don't you be worrying your head about it. I eat out most of the time, having no one to look after my creature needs as it were.'

Maryan took off her coat and sat down. As she accepted a cup of tea and a scone she looked around her. The flat was exquisitely furnished. There were beautiful pictures on the walls and carpets of soft pastel colours. 'It's a lovely flat,' she said shyly.

'Thank you. When you've had your tea I'll take you downstairs to see the stock. Since the war I've kept everything of value down in the cellar. It's a good thing I have. I've been bombed twice, though not badly enough to have to move out, thanks be to God.'

As they ate he told her that he'd come over to England with his family as a baby at the turn of the century.

'Irish father, Italian mother.' He grinned. 'That's where the 'Vincente' comes in. It's what I was christened, though I knocked off the last 'e' as a kid. It sounded classy when I took over the business, so I put it back on again.' He also explained that he had one sister, Roisan, who was Colin's mother. 'Father sent both of us kids to art school to help us learn the trade, but Roisan met her husband there and married him, so she never actually came into the business at all.'

He told how his father had built up the business by buying and selling, learning as he went, from a second-hand furniture stall in the Portobello Road through a series of small shops to the present thriving antiques shop in a fashionable area. Colin's mother had settled down to bring up her son, so when their parents died it had fallen to Vincent to take over the business.

'It's been a devil of a struggle to keep the business going through the war, I can tell you,' he told her as he refilled her cup. 'There's not been much call for antiques since '39. Who wants to put their money into things that might get blown to bits? I put in a spell in the army till I was discharged, unfit.' He grinned at her ruefully, 'Flat feet, wouldn't you know. Not as romantic as a consumptive chest, but more practical. Ah, but I haven't wasted the time. I've been buying, investing all I could afford in new stock for after the war. I've been making my living restoring paintings for the big galleries, and in my spare time I've been attending every auction sale I could; buying things at knock-down prices from houses that have been bombed, and restoring them down in my workshop.'

'So you'll soon be able to open the shop again?' Maryan asked, stirred by the man's infectious enthusiasm.

'More than just that. I'm planning to go in for interior design and decorating along with my sister Roisan. We reckon there'll be a big demand when folks start rebuilding their battered homes again.' He reached out and took the cup and saucer from her hand. 'Come on. I'll take you downstairs and show you the stock and the workshop.'

Below the spacious, almost empty showroom was a cellar, reached by a wooden stairway. It was like Aladdin's cave. In it was every kind of antique and curio Maryan could imagine, from the tiniest carved ivory and delicate porcelain figurine to the largest, most exquisite pieces of furniture she'd had ever seen.

'I had the whole place reinforced with steel girders when the war started,' Vincent told her. 'Well, I had to protect my investment, didn't I? I even used to sleep down here when the raids were bad.'

Maryan looked at it all, wide-eyed with wonder at so many beautiful things under one roof. She went from one thing to another, eagerly asking questions till suddenly she stopped, looking at him self-consciously. 'Oh dear, I'm sorry. I'm being nosey.'

Vincent smiled. 'Not a bit of it. You're interested and you're obviously eager to learn. You're just the kind of person I'm looking for. Just as I guessed you'd be.'

In the workshop she saw half-finished pieces in various stages of restoration and the tools of Vincent's trade methodically laid out: finely honed chisels and saws; pots of glue and stain; waxes and varnishes; sheets of veneer.

'Roisan does the soft furnishing side, the upholstery and curtains,' he explained. 'She has a fine hand with the needle and a wonderful eye for colour and fabrics.' He looked around him with satisfaction. 'All we're waiting for is for the hostilities to cease, then there'll be no holding the pair of us.'

Maryan was wondering just where she fitted into his scheme of things, but she didn't like to ask.

'Roisan is a widow,' he told her. 'Her husband died before the war. She and Colin share a nice little house in Notting Hill, but when Colin has gone off to university I'll be moving in with her. She hates the thought of living alone again and I like her cooking, so it suits us both. Besides, if we're going into business together it'll be more convenient – save time on business meetings. We can have those over our meals.' He smiled at her. 'And that's where you come in, as I daresay you've been wondering. Once the shop is up and running again I'll be needing someone to look after it while I'm working. I'm expecting to be out a lot of the time, at sales and touting for business. I'll be needing someone who'll live here too. I'd feel happier knowing that someone was on the premises.'

'Oh, but I told you, I know nothing about antiques,' Maryan reminded him.

'And *I* told *you* that you'd soon learn.' He smiled. 'Until the peace is declared there won't be much to do up there. You'd just be looking after the flat and keeping the place clean and tidy. But in your spare time you could be learning – coming to sales with me; reading the books I'll lend you and generally getting to know the business.' He patted her shoulder. 'Ah, a bright girl like yourself will pick it up in no time at all. Everything in the shop will be priced and I'll be calling in every day to make sure you're all right. So – what have you to say to it?'

Maryan was sorely tempted. It promised to be the most interesting and challenging job she'd ever had. And with a beautiful home thrown in she could hardly believe her luck. She'd be a fool not to snap the chance up. But there was more than just herself to consider.

'Well, it sounds lovely, but there are a couple of snags. I'm not alone, you see. There's my mother. She hasn't been too well and I wouldn't be happy leaving her alone. Then I have a daughter, Amy. She's thirteen and she's living in Suffolk at the moment, evacuated. But when the war is over . . .'

'You're welcome to bring your family with you,' Vincent said generously. 'Bring them both with you. There's plenty of room, and they'll be keeping the beds aired.'

'Thanks. It's very generous of you, Mr Donlan.' She paused. 'But – there's the question of references.' She took the envelope containing Sam's reference from her handbag and handed it to him. 'This is from my previous employer. I was with him since leaving school.'

He read it carefully, then handed it back with a smile. 'I'd love to have you working for me, Maryan, but I'm looking for someone permanent – someone I can train to my own ways. Come on a couple of months' trial if you like. Then we'll both be sure it's right for you. Now, as to wages . . .'

As Maryan rode back to Hackney on the bus she thought over all she had seen and heard. The wage Mr Donlan had offered her was generous, especially as she'd be living rent free. And to think that they'd be able to move out of Crimea Terrace with all its draughts and inconveniences, into the comparative luxury of the flat – it was like the answer to all her prayers.

Unfortunately Sarah didn't see it that way. 'You go if you must. I ain't moving from here.' She stood in front of the kitchen range, her arms folded and her mouth set in the stubborn line that Maryan knew all too well.

'But Mum, if you only *saw* the place. It's warm and so comfy. There'd be a bedroom each and a nice cosy bathroom and lav. No going outside for anything. You know how bad your chest has been since the winter set in.'

'My bronicals ain't gonna change just 'cause I move into some posh flat Up West.'

'But they *will*, Mum. It's the damp that makes you bad. The draughts and the damp and going from one temperature to the other. The doctor said so last time you . . .'

'I ain't going and you can't say nothing as'll make me.'

Frustration made Maryan want to shake her mother. Seeing her standing there stubbornly refusing the chance to spend her life in comfort was maddening. 'You wouldn't have to do anything, Mum. It's the chance of a lifetime.'

'I'd be bored silly in half a day,' Sarah said.

'All right then, you can help keep the place clean while I work down in the shop, and you can do the cooking,' Maryan said. 'We can share the work if that's the way you want it. But do say you'll come.'

'No. I'm sorry, gel. I know you mean well, but this is my ome and I'm stayin' 'ere.'

'Mum – they'll pull it down anyway when the war's over.'

'Then they'll re'ouse me. If I move out of me own accord I'll lose me place on the 'ousin' list. Suppose we move into this feller's flat and you don't suit? What then?'

'I *will* suit. He said so,' Maryan insisted, though she had to admit secretly that her mother did have a point. Mr Donlan had mentioned a month's trial. Suppose she didn't suit him? Maybe it would be as well for Sarah to hang onto her own home – just until she was sure the job was right for her.

Seeing her indecision, Sarah jumped in: 'See what I mean? Better safe than sorry. But you go. I mean it. Don't miss the chance just cause o' me,' she said. 'I reckon you ought to get Amy back soon too. Wouldn't be fair to bring 'er back here. She'll like this new place, no doubt about that. But me – I'm too old a dog to learn new tricks.'

'But once I'm settled – you'll come then?'

136

'I dunno. We'll see.'

Maryan shook her head. 'I hate leaving you, Mum. I promised I'd look after you. How can I do that if I'm in Chelsea and you're here? And paying out good money for this old place when you could live in comfort seems downright stupid.'

But Sarah's independence meant far more to her than the few shillings she paid each week for the rent.

Although everyone knew that it was likely to be the last Christmas of the war, it seemed to Maryan that no one was in the mood for festivities. She had given in her notice to Arthur Pratt with the promise to work on until after the Christmas rush. On the Sunday after she had formally accepted the job at Vincente Antiques and the final arrangements had been made she took the train to Suffolk for the day to see Amy. She found the girl silent and unresponsive. She showed little interest in her mother's new job and clearly lacked enthusiasm for returning to London. Even the prospect of living in a nice flat in Chelsea failed to arouse her interest.

'I thought I could put your name down at one of the local schools. You could start after Christmas,' Maryan said. 'There are bound to be some nice ones round there. Oh, Amy, just wait till you see the flat. It's ever so smart and really comfy. And I've already started studying the books Mr Donlan has lent me. It's so interesting, reading about the different kinds of antiques. There's so much to learn.'

'Can't I stay on a bit longer?' Amy said. 'There's the school play at the end of next term. I'd like to be in it.'

Trying to hide her disappointment, Maryan agreed that Amy could stay for one more term, but she was deflated by the girl's indifferent response to her good fortune. Later, after Amy and Mike had gone off to feed the horses, she spoke to Marjorie about it.

'She's so grown-up. She's changed so much – even since the summer holidays. I feel I hardly know her any more. I never realised what an uphill job it'd be, making a new life together. I was so looking forward to it, too.'

'Give her time,' Marjorie said. 'I've told her she can come back and see us whenever she wants to. Mike will miss her dreadfully and so will I, but I've already started to prepare them both for the inevitable parting.'

Maryan sighed. Marjorie made it sound as though she was splitting up a family instead of trying to reunite her own. What with Mum and now Amy . . . 'What about Christmas?' she asked aloud.

'You must ask her,' Marjorie said. 'She knows she's welcome to stay with us. But I've told Amy that she should really spend it with you and your mother in London. In the end she must make her own choice. She's old enough to know her own mind now, isn't she?'

Sadly, Maryan had to agree. The days when she could expect Amy to do as she was told were clearly long gone. But she couldn't help feeling that Marjorie made it sound as though spending Christmas with her own family was Amy's duty rather than a pleasure. And when the girl begged with a disconcerting fervour to stay at Mitcham Lodge with the Taylors she felt obliged to say yes. After all, she would be working at the market until late on Christmas Eve now that the blackout had been relaxed, and there would be very little to attract a young girl at Crimea Terrace, especially since all her friends were here. Insisting that she came home would only create more resentment in the girl, and that was the last thing she wanted.

Although it was barely three o'clock the light was already failing as Rachel let herself into number 124 Hackney Road. She hadn't told Sam she was coming, but she'd been planning it for weeks, steeling herself for the visit she knew she must make – and make alone.

There was no electricity and the house smelled damp and musty as she removed her key and closed the front door behind her. The windows had been shuttered both inside and out when they had moved to Hazelfield. Everything of value had been packed away or removed from the house and the remaining furniture was shrouded in dust sheets. She could just make out the ghostly shapes in the winter afternoon gloom.

She'd come prepared. Opening her handbag, she took out a candle and matches. Shielding the flame with her hand, she lit it, then, securing it in a candlestick taken from the dining room, she made her way slowly up to the top of the house, the candle flame throwing large leaping shadows before her as she went.

On the top floor Marcus's studio was just as he had left it. Apart from some powdered plaster on the carpet from blast damage, everything was exactly as she remembered it, the desk behind the door; his drawing board set up under the skylight; the bookcase and the old armchair that had been his grandfather's. She could almost have found her way around it without the aid of a light. She set her candlestick down on the desk and looked around her. The room seemed to breathe his very essence. It was uncanny – as though he might walk in at any moment. She stood quite still, her head on one side as though she were listening for his footsteps on the stairs. She imagined him, whistling a tune as he took the steps two at a time –

138

calling out cheerily to ask if dinner was ready and what she had made. Today would have been his birthday. She'd always made a special meal on his birthday, with all his favourite dishes. They had always made a point of eating together, the three of them. But today there was no sound in the empty house except the faint creaking of the floorboards. Nothing lived – nothing moved – there was only the sound of her own heart beating dully.

On the desk was a picture of Jessica taken on the night of their engagement, radiant in the rose-pink dress he had designed specially for her. She picked it up and looked into the lovely face of the happy, carefree girl, unaware of the tragic future that awaited her.

'You're together now,' she whispered. 'Be happy, my children, my darlings.' She slipped the photograph into her bag and began systematically on her sad task, going through the desk drawers, collecting everything that had belonged to him. For weeks now it had bothered her. It wasn't right, leaving his personal effects here for some stranger to find. She couldn't bear the thought that if anything were to happen to her and Sam some uncaring, faceless official would go through them – see his work, read his letters and his diaries. No. She would take everything home.

Without looking at anything, she piled the letters, folders and papers into the holdall she had brought. Later, when she felt strong enough to deal with it, she would go through them all and deal with anything that was necessary and burn the rest.

She cleared the desk drawers and looked around her, then she spotted a portfolio tucked away at the back of his bookcase. Taking it down she opened it and turned the pages. Her eyes widened and she gasped at the beautifully coloured sketches inside. Design after design, all of them dedicated to Jessica. Her name was written on every page in Marcus's flowing – artist's handwriting. There were day dresses and smart town suits, elegant evening dresses, cocktail and ball gowns, winter coats and fresh casual summer clothes. An entire wardrobe, designed with a beautiful woman in mind. He must have intended to have them made up for her as a surprise after the baby was born. After her death he must have hidden them away, unable to bear to look at them again.

Rachel sat down slowly and turned back to the beginning to go through them again. The designs were outstanding, the style and lines wonderfully and impressively different – like nothing the fashion world had ever seen before. They were quite brilliant; inspired, as they obviously had been, by his love for his beautiful young wife. She stared at them until the lines and colours blurred before her eyes, aware that she must certainly be the first person ever to see them. She devoured them with her eyes; her beloved son's last and most inspired work. Just for a brief moment it was almost like having him back. She could almost feel his presence here in the studio with her as she turned the pages.

Then suddenly in a flash it was all crystal clear to her. She jumped to her feet, her heart quickening. Of course. *This* was the reason she'd been unable to rest all these weeks. He *meant* her to come here – to find these designs. Marcus had spoken to her across the invisible barrier that divided them. Now she understood. She knew what it was he wanted her to do. Hurriedly she wrapped the portfolio in a sheet of drawing paper and tucked it under her arm. Taking up the candle, she made her way downstairs again, picking her way with special care. She must look after herself now. She mustn't fall. Until now she hadn't cared what happened to her – hadn't cared whether she lived or died, but now it was different. Now she had work to do – a reason to live, for him, for Marcus. In the hallway she took a last look round.

'Don't worry, I'll see to it, my darling,' she whispered into the flickering darkness. 'You're free now. Goodnight, my dearest son. Sleep well.'

Sam was frantic. He'd arrived home early that afternoon with the idea that he'd take Rachel out to dinner. Today would have been Marcus's birthday and he knew she would be feeling especially sad. At breakfast she'd been even more preoccupied than usual. He'd scarcely been able to get two words out of her. So when he'd returned early and found the house empty apart from the daily woman from the village who had taken Maryan's place, he'd felt the first twinge of unease. Going to the kitchen he'd asked the woman where Rachel was.

She shrugged. 'I don't know, sir. She went out just after twelve – didn't say where she was going.'

Sam turned away. Maryan would have known. She'd have made it her business to know. She would never have let Rachel go off alone in her depressed state on a cheerless winter afternoon. If she'd been unable to stop her she would have telephoned him at the factory. This new woman did her job reasonably well and took her money. But she would never be what Maryan had been to them. He looked at his watch. It was almost five o'clock. If Rachel left home at twelve she'd been gone five hours. The day was gloomy. Already it was quite dark and a thick mist was rising. Maybe he should telephone the Weiss's. She may have gone there.

When his call drew a blank he began to be seriously alarmed.

140

Perhaps he should notify the police. Anything could have happened to Rachel, the way she'd been since Marcus was killed. He lifted the receiver again and had just begun to dial when he heard the scrape of a key in the front door. His heart leapt with relief as he ran to the door and pulled it open. She stood there on the steps, struggling with her handbag, a heavy holdall and a large, flat parcel wrapped in paper.

'*Rachel* – where have you been? I've been worried out of my mind.' He drew her inside and took her hands. 'My darling, you're frozen. Your hands are like ice.' For the first time he looked into her face. She looked strange. Her cheeks were flushed and her eyes were feverishly bright. He'd been right. She *was* ill. It was some kind of breakdown. He'd been half expecting it. Alarmed, he asked: 'What is it, my love? You're ill?'

'No. I've never felt better.' She threw her arms around his neck and hugged him. 'Oh, Sam – wait till you see what I've got.'

He held her at arm's length, shaking his head in puzzlement. 'You've been *shopping*? Why didn't you tell me you wanted to go Christmas shopping? I'd have come with you. Where have you been – Colchester?'

'No, to London. To Hackney Road – our old house.'

He stared at her. 'Oh, Rachel, no. You really shouldn't have gone alone.'

She waved away his protests. 'Never mind all that. Come into the sitting room and see what I found. It's Marcus's birthday today and he sent me there. I'm convinced of it. He meant me to find this and I know – I just *know* what he wants me to do with it.' She held up the portfolio. The paper was already slipping off it. Pulling off her coat as she went, she hurried into the sitting room, dropping her bag and gloves heedlessly in her haste.

Mystified, Sam followed, picking up her belongings as he went. What in the world could have happened to put her into this strange, excited frame of mind? And what did she mean about Marcus *sending her to Hackney*? He didn't like the sound of it at all.

But when Rachel excitedly opened up the portfolio and showed him the designs he began to understand her excitement. She was right. They certainly were quite special. He studied them all carefully, then looked at her transformed face. She looked twenty years younger.

'They are certainly very good,' he said. 'But what do you plan to do with them?'

'*Do* with them? Why, have them made up, of course,' she told him.

'Listen, Sam, remember all those luxury fabrics we stored away at the beginning of the war when we went over to uniforms? They're just what we'll need – and all without coupons.'

Sam remembered, visualising the stock they had bought in and never used. She was right. There were brocades, silks and chiffons; tweeds and cotton prints.

'We'll have Marcus's designs made up and we'll put on a fashion show,' she hurried on, unfolding the plan she had made coming home on the train. 'It shall be in aid of Jewish refugees, just as he would have wanted. And we'll invite all the buyers from the West End stores. Soon, when the war is over, women will be hungry for glamorous new fashions to wear, just as they were last time, only more so because so many of them have been in uniform for years.' She looked at him, her eyes shining like jet. 'Don't you remember how well it worked last time, darling?'

He kissed her. His heart filled with joy at having the Rachel he remembered back again. 'I remember how proud I was of my talented wife,' he told her.

'Well, this time it will be our talented son we'll be proud of,' she said. 'Oh, Sam, don't you see? This is the one way we can keep his memory fresh – keep him alive.'

Christmas at Mitcham Lodge was a happy one. Amy and the Taylors were aware that it could well be the last Christmas of the war, and therefore their last together, which gave the season a slightly nostalgic as well as a festive feel.

At the start of the new term the school play went into serious rehearsal. It was to be a combined effort: girls from the High School and boys from the Grammar. They were putting on Shakespeare's *Twelfth Night*. Amy hadn't been particularly keen to take part at first. Although English had always been her favourite subject, she hadn't really taken to Shakespeare, thinking the language difficult and the plays over-long and boring. But at the beginning of the winter term they had read and analysed *Twelfth Night* in class, and with the aid of Miss Frazer, their dedicated English mistress, Amy had slowly begun to appreciate the poetry and lyricism of the words and the wit and humour in the comedy scenes. She had been fascinated by the story of the girl Viola, searching for her lost brother and having to take on the identity of a boy for her own protection; falling in love with the man she served, the Count Orsino, yet being obliged to carry his ardent messages to the woman who scorned his love. She identified strongly with poor Viola on a personal level – having a secret she couldn't tell and getting so

142

confused about her own identity. When it came to casting the play, she read the part with such conviction that she drew a round of applause from the casting committee. Two days later, to her great delight, she learned that she had been cast in the coveted role of Viola.

Amy threw herself wholeheartedly into rehearsing for the play. Mike, who had grown tall and broadened out over the last few months, had been given the part of Orsino, so the two were able to rehearse their scenes together at home. Mitcham Lodge rang to the Bard's renowned speeches till Marjorie told herself wryly that she could have put on a one-woman performance of the play herself.

One evening she asked Amy if she would be inviting her mother to come to the performance.

'She'll be too busy, I daresay,' Amy said dismissively.

'Oh, surely not. It's going to be on a Saturday and she can stay here overnight afterwards. Surely you'd like her to see you after all the hard work you've put in.'

Amy shrugged. 'I don't think Shakespeare's quite Mum's cup of tea.'

'Nevertheless, I think I'll write and invite her.' Marjorie looked at her curiously. 'Amy – there's nothing wrong between your mother and you, is there?'

'No.'

'I only ask because you were rather cool with her when she came last time.'

Amy looked at the floor. 'I was afraid she'd ask me to go and live with her again.'

'But surely you want to, don't you?'

'With the play coming up? I don't want to miss that.'

'Look, Amy, I know it will be an upheaval for you, changing schools, settling down in London again. But it will mean a lot to your mother, having you home again,' Marjorie said gently. 'She's looking forward to it so much. I think she was rather hurt when she felt you didn't want to go.'

Amy was silent. How could she explain why she felt as she did? No one must ever know how Maryan had deceived her – her own daughter. It was too shameful; the kind of thing that didn't happen to people like the Taylors. If they knew about it they certainly wouldn't want anything more to do with her. It looked as though they wanted her to move out anyway. Auntie Marjorie was just trying to soften the blow.

'I suppose that when Mr – er – Captain Taylor comes home for good you'll want to be on your own again,' she said hesitantly.

Marjorie smiled. 'Oh, Amy, it isn't that, darling. Mike and I have loved having you here. You've been like my own daughter, a sister for Mike, and we both love you. But your mother and grandmother love you too. They've missed most of your childhood and that's very sad. You belong with them, dear, and they'd be desperately hurt if they thought you didn't want to go home to them.'

Amy sighed. 'I suppose so.' Deep inside she felt that things would never be the same again, for her or for anyone. The little boy the Captain had left behind had grown up now. Mike was almost a man. The war had stolen a huge chunk out of all their lives. Time had moved on somehow while they weren't looking. She could see that it would be hard enough for the Taylor family to settle down without a stranger sharing their home. The time had come to stop pretending. She must go home. She must try to come to terms with the rift between her mother and herself. But the prospect scared her so much that she still tried to pretend it didn't exist. She engrossed herself in the preparations for the play. Just for a few precious weeks she could conceal herself inside Viola's skin and pretend – like Viola – to be someone else. When it was over – time enough then to face the future.

The spring of 1945 had been one of excitement and turbulence; triumph and despair. First there was the Rhine crossing with its heavy loss of lives, then the storming of Berlin and the fall of the Reich, and finally the capture and execution of Mussolini and the suicide of Hitler himself. Sometimes Maryan felt that compassion was dead. It was as though all the pity, all the tears in the world had been shed. And certainly no one grieved for two such brutal and merciless dictators. When Maryan received Marjorie's letter she went immediately to ask Vincent for the Saturday afternoon off so that she could travel to Rhensham. To think that Amy had the leading part in a Shakespeare play! She couldn't wait to see it. It was so kind of Marjorie to invite her for the weekend. Since moving into the Simons Mews flat and taking up her new job she had been busy and preoccupied. Amy's play would make a happy diversion.

Vincent agreed at once that she should go.

'You've worked so hard. You deserve a break,' he said. 'I can easily take over the shop for that Saturday afternoon. And will you be bringing the little lady herself back with you when you come?'

Maryan shook her head. 'I think the play marks half-term,' she said. 'I'm not sure whether she'll want to come till the end.'

'Well, bring her if you can,' Vincent said with a smile. 'I know you'll be happier and more settled when you've got her back.'

As Maryan lay in bed on the Friday night, her case packed and ready, she thought about the visit she'd had a few weeks before from Sam Leigh. His arrival at the shop had been a complete surprise to her. Apparently he'd gone first to Crimea Terrace, where Sarah had given him the Chelsea address. Sitting in the living room over coffee he explained the reason for his visit.

'My conscience has been troubling me,' he said. 'I feel I should do something for Amy.' He held up his hand at the protest he saw in her eyes. 'No. Don't say anything, my dear. I felt so bad, letting you go like that. But Rachel was making herself ill. The shock of losing Marcus was still too great. I couldn't risk making her ill.'

'I know. Please don't blame yourself,' Maryan begged him. 'I should never have spoken. It was all my fault.'

Sam smiled gently. 'I felt bad because I never told you that I believed you, Maryan,' he said. 'I should have given you that comfort at least.'

She looked at him. 'You do?'

'My dear, I know you well enough to know that you'd never lie about something so important. I know that you had the best of motives too. But sadly Rachel doesn't see it that way.' He smiled. 'It was good to see Sarah again. We talked, she and I. She told me that she too only recently learned about Marcus and you.'

'I never told anyone,' Maryan said softly. 'Even Marcus never knew that he was Amy's father.'

'And I'm sure that if he had known he would have made some provision for her,' Sam said. 'Which is why I am here. I want to contribute towards her education. Sarah tells me that she is bright. I would like to have the honour of encouraging that brightness.'

'Mr Leigh – I couldn't . . .'

'For Marcus's sake,' he added. 'Please, my dear, I don't want you to think I'm just trying to salve my conscience. We owe it to his memory – both of us.'

He had even gone to the trouble of applying to several schools in the area and now he opened his briefcase and took out a bundle of prospectuses. He pulled out two and spread them out on the table for her to see.

'I feel these have the most to offer,' he said. 'But the final choice must be yours, of course. Amy could stay on for as long as she needs to. And if she wants to go to university I'll be only too happy . . .'

Maryan waved her hand in protest. 'Please, Mr Leigh. Let's take it a step at a time. I'm sure I could get Amy into a good state school. Now that we have this new education act there are more opportunities and . . .'

'I want her to have the best,' he interrupted firmly. 'This new act – it's still in its infancy. We'll take no chances with Amy's future.' He leaned forward to take Maryan's hands in his, pleading with his gentle brown eyes. 'Give me the pleasure of doing this one small thing for Marcus's daughter, my dear. It saddens me so much that Amy and I can't know one another – can't enjoy the relationship that we should. Please?'

She could do no other than give in gracefully.

It was six a.m. when the telephone wakened her. Hurrying into the living room, she lifted the receiver and muttered drowsily: 'Vincente Antiques, Mrs Jessop speaking.'

'Mrs Jessop, this is Whitechapel Police Station,' said a crisp voice at the other end. 'I'm sorry to tell you that your mother, Mrs Sarah Brown, has been admitted to the London Hospital with severe double pneumonia.'

Maryan was wide awake at one. 'Right. I'll come at once. Thank you for letting me know.' She put down the receiver, her hands trembling. That tumbledown old house. *Why* had she clung to it so stubbornly? Sarah had caught a bad cold just after Christmas. It had gone straight to her chest and refused to clear up. And she hadn't been there to look after her. As she pulled on her clothes, Maryan blamed herself. She should have insisted on her mother moving out, or she should have stayed on at the market, working for Artie Pratt. If she had been stronger this would never have happened. If Sarah died, it would be her fault.

As the curtain came down on the combined schools' production of *Twelfth Night* the applause was tumultuous. The line-up of young actors stepped forward to take their final bow and Mike took Amy by the hand and led her forward to a renewed outburst of clapping. The production had been faultless and Marjorie, sitting in her second-row seat, could have burst with pride. If only Amy's mother could have been here to see it. She had hoped all evening, but the seat beside her, booked for Maryan, had remained empty.

Once again, Marjorie twisted in her seat to look towards the back of the auditorium. If the train had been delayed, if Maryan had arrived late, even after the interval, she would probably have stood at the back, unwilling to disturb people. But there was no one standing there. And now it was too late.

She'd meant to keep Maryan's visit as a surprise for Amy, but unfortunately she'd been too delighted to keep the news to herself. Now she had the unenviable task of breaking the news to the child that her mother had missed her triumph after all.

Chapter Nine

When Maryan arrived at the hospital the night shift was just going off and the morning changeover routine was in full swing. Behind screens in the bed nearest the doors Sarah lay in a deep coma. Propped up on the pillows and minus her dentures, she looked frail and shrivelled, her face grey against the white of the pillows behind her. Her breathing was laboured and stertorous. Racked with guilt and compassion, Maryan stared down at her.

'Will she – is there anything more that can be done?' she asked the ward sister who stood at the end of the bed.

Sister shook her head. 'She hasn't responded to any of the usual medication. Even oxygen isn't helping any more. Her heart is very weak. If only she'd been admitted earlier there might have been a chance.' She looked at Maryan. 'I'm very sorry, my dear. I'm afraid it's only a matter of time.'

Maryan looked helplessly down at her mother. 'Did she send for the doctor herself?'

'No. A neighbour found her. She hadn't been seen for several days. Apparently someone broke in and found her unable to get out of bed.'

'But why didn't she send for me? I didn't even know she was poorly.' Maryan sank onto the chair at the side of the bed and took one of the hot dry hands that lay limp on the counterpane. 'How long?' she asked.

'It's impossible to say. It could be an hour – a day. Even two.'

'I was wondering if there would be time to send for my daughter. She's in Suffolk.'

'How old is she?'

'Thirteen.'

'Don't you think it would be better to let the child remember her grandmother the way she was?'

147

Maryan sighed. 'I daresay you're right.'

'I'll bring you a cup of tea,' the sister said kindly. 'I don't suppose you had time to get yourself anything.'

Maryan drank her tea gratefully and waited, watching for any change, any movement or sign of life. If only Sarah would regain consciousness. There was so much she wanted to say to her. An hour passed and still her mother remained unconscious. After another hour Maryan suddenly caught sight of the ward clock over the top of the screens. It was almost nine o'clock; time she should be opening the shop. She must let Vincent know where she was. Slipping out into the corridor, she went in search of a telephone.

Vincent was sympathetic. 'Don't worry about a thing, my dear. I'll slip round and open up myself. Is there anything I can do to help you?'

'No, thank you. I don't know how long I'll be. I'll be back as soon as I can.'

'Stay as long as you need. Never mind the shop.'

It was only after she had replaced the receiver that she remembered her visit to Rhensham. She could have asked Vincent to telephone Marjorie Taylor for her. Never mind. She would do it later.

As she returned to the ward to resume her vigil she saw through a gap in the screens that the ward sister and a doctor were already by Sarah's bedside. As she entered the doctor straightened up, taking his stethoscope from his ears. He and the sister looked at her.

'My dear, I'm so sorry,' Sister said. 'She just slipped away quietly while I was checking her just now. I sent for Doctor Morris at once, but there was nothing more we could do.'

The young doctor patted her shoulder and withdrew and Sister looked at her. 'It was quite peaceful. I'll leave you with her. Stay as long as you wish. I'll be in my office when you want me.' She withdrew silently, leaving Maryan alone.

Sinking to her knees beside the bed, her tears flowing, Maryan whispered: 'Oh, Mum, why didn't you do as I wanted? I shouldn't have left you there on your own. I'm sorry – so sorry.' But even in her grief she knew deep inside that Sarah would never have moved. She'd hated it at Whitegates. Her roots were in Hackney and it was where she wanted to be, bombs or no bombs. Crimea Terrace was the only home she'd ever known. But she had never reproached her, never wanted her to turn down a good job either. Her characteristic acceptance of life was an essential part of her. It was all as she had willed it.

It was much later that afternoon when she had gone through the traumatic business of visiting the registrar and making the funeral arrangements that Maryan returned to the flat in Simons Mews. Walking from the bus stop she felt desolate and lonely among the bustling Saturday afternoon crowds. There was a euphoric air about the people in the streets now. It was spring, the sun was shining and everyone knew that the war was all but over. There was so much to look forward to, so many lives to be rebuilt. But today Maryan could not share the optimism. She dreaded the moment when she would shut the door behind her and be completely alone. Now they were all gone: Tom, Marcus, and now Sarah. As soon as she could she must get Amy back so that they could start to map out a new life together. Amy was all she had now. In her the best of the past and future were invested. She must do all she could to make that future as good as she could, for both of them.

But the moment she closed the door and began to mount the stairs she sensed that the flat was not empty. Looking up, she saw Vincent standing at the top of the stairs, waiting for her, his craggy face gentle with compassion.

'So there you are. Forgive me for letting myself in, my dear, but I couldn't let you come home to an empty flat. What's the news?'

'She's gone,' Maryan said wearily. 'Mum died just after I telephoned you.'

'Oh dear. I'm so sorry.'

As she reached the top stair her legs buckled beneath her and he put out his arms to steady her. 'There, hold up now. Come and sit down and I'll get you something. When did you last have anything to eat?'

Maryan shook her head. She hadn't even thought of food over the past hours. 'I'm not hungry,' she said. 'Just tired and so ...' Her voice faltered and to her embarrassment the tears began to flow. Her hand over her mouth, she tried desperately to stifle them. 'I'm – sorry. I don't usually make an exhibition of myself like this.'

'Just you have a good cry. Never mind me. I daresay you've been holding it back all day.' He drew her head down onto his shoulder and led her towards the settee. 'Look, hungry or not, I think you should eat something. I'm going to make you a sandwich. It's about all my culinary skills will run to. And I'm not going anywhere till I'm quite sure you're feeling better.' He leaned forward to peer into her face. 'All right?'

'All right.' His quiet words had a soothing effect on Maryan. She stopped trying to hold back her tears and unleashed her emotions, sobbing into his shoulder until finally she felt the pattern of her breathing return to normal and all the tension that had been tying her into tight knots relax.

'She was such a good woman,' she said, wiping away the tears with the large clean handkerchief he pressed into her hand. 'So good and strong and – and wise. She didn't even let me know she wasn't well. I didn't get there in time to say goodbye. I just wish I could have done more for her. I'm going to miss her so much.'

'I know. I remember losing my own mum,' Vincent said. 'No matter how much you've done, you always feel you should have done more.' He smiled. 'You know, there's a little bit of us that dies with our mothers. Call it the final cutting of the cord. Don't they know us the way no one else ever can? We can never be *quite* the same person with anyone else.'

She looked up at him in surprise. He had put into a nutshell just what she had been feeling all day. 'That's it exactly,' she said. 'You've put your finger right on it.'

He smiled. 'Ah, you're looking better now. There's colour in your cheeks again. I'll make us a snack and a hot drink and then I think you should try to get some rest.'

'So – now that your situation has changed, do you think you'll be staying on?' Vincent looked at her across the remains of the snack meal. 'I mean, I think four months is long enough for both of us to see how the arrangement works. I'm more than happy. Are you?'

'Oh yes. I'm learning so much,' Maryan assured him. She found to her surprise that she'd completely forgotten about the two months' trial arrangement. 'I'm really looking forward to the business starting up again. It's the most interesting job I've ever had.'

'I'm relieved that you feel that way, Maryan.' He looked at her thoughtfully. 'As a matter of fact I was going to talk to you about something else I had in mind. But maybe this is hardly the time to be talking business.'

'Oh, please – I've got to think of the future now more than ever. And I'd be grateful for something to take my mind off things.'

'Well – if you're quite sure. I have a little proposition to put to you. I'll not be needing an answer right away, but will you give it some thought?'

'Of course – if I can.'

'What would you say to taking some lessons in typing and book-keeping? I really need someone who'll help me with the administration side of things, you see. Estimates, costing out, accounts, that kind of thing.' He looked at her doubtful expression. 'As soon as the business gets off the ground I'll employ a full-time secretary. There

150

isn't much to do either in the office or the shop as yet, so until I can afford a full staff it's a question of all of us mucking in. I'd pay you a bit extra for the overtime you'd put in, Maryan. I'm not trying to take advantage of your good nature.'

'Oh, it isn't that.' She frowned. 'To be honest, I'm just not sure if I'm capable.'

'Well, I am,' he said positively. 'If I wasn't I wouldn't ask you. You're a lot brighter than you give yourself credit for, Mrs Maryan Jessop.'

Maryan sipped her tea and thought about it. She'd always wanted to be able to type. And she'd always liked arithmetic at school. Figures gave her no problems at all. Maybe he was right. Maybe she *could* do it. 'Where would I learn?' she asked.

'At evening classes. A woman I know runs a little business school. I'm sure you'd pick it up in no time. And you could be working as you learn.' He grinned at her. 'Nothing like jumping in at the deep end. And I can always turn a blind eye to a few typing mistakes.'

'Well, I'll do my best. And I'd better learn quickly. I'm hoping to have Amy back in July.'

He smiled. 'That's great news. It's just what you need.' Suddenly he frowned. 'You were supposed to be visiting her this weekend, weren't you?'

'Yes.' Maryan leapt up. 'I must ring her. I meant to do it as soon as I got in. She doesn't know about her grandma and she'll think I've let her down, missing her school play.' She shook her head. 'They were close. She's going to be so upset.'

He stood up. 'I'll go. You'll want to speak to her in private.'

She reached out and touched his sleeve. 'Thanks, Mr Donlan.'

He turned to look at her. 'Vincent, please. Or, better still, Vinnie. It's what my friends call me.'

'Thanks anyway. I was dreading coming back here alone. You've helped me so much.'

'Ah, it was nothing – nothing at all.' He patted her shoulder, awkward in his embarrassment at her gratitude. 'Just take care of yourself. And I tell you what – I'll come round and pick you up tomorrow. It's time you tasted Roisan's Sunday roast. Her Yorkshire pudding is as light as the mountain mist. Twelve o'clock all right for you?'

'Well – yes, but . . .'

He was already halfway down the stairs. 'High time you and Roisan met. Hasn't she been nagging me for weeks to bring you round?' As he carried on down the stairs he called over his shoulder:

151

'See you tomorrow Maryan. Have yourself a good lie-in in the morning.'

As the door closed behind him Maryan walked back into the room and lifted the receiver, but her heart plummeted as she listened to the Taylors' telephone ringing out at the other end. They must have left home already. She'd left it too late. Now there was no way she could let them know that she wouldn't be coming.

Marjorie had arranged a party for the cast of *Twelfth Night* back at Mitcham Lodge. Everyone came, teachers and parents too. It would have been a happy occasion, but for Amy it was all spoilt before it began. She'd felt so bitterly let down by her mother's failure to be there to witness her triumph. After about half an hour she slipped away from the happy throng downstairs and shut herself in her room. Everyone else's parents had made the effort to be there, she told herself, slumping despondently on her bed. Surely her mother could at least have taken the trouble to telephone. It was just like it had been at the beginning of the war. She obviously thought more of that new job of hers than she did of coming to see the play. No doubt she thought it all some childish nonsense like the time she was the fairy in the school panto in Hackney.

Downstairs Marjorie was answering the telephone, her hand pressed tightly against the other ear as she tried to hear what was being said above the din of thirty excited young people enjoying themselves.

'Who is it? Oh, *Maryan*. My dear, we were so worried when you didn't arrive. The play was such a success. Amy was brilliant. But she was desperately disappointed. Is everything all right?' She listened gravely, her brow creasing into a frown as Maryan explained what had happened.

'Oh, my dear, I'm so sorry to hear that.'

'If Amy is there I'd like to speak to her,' Maryan said.

'Unfortunately there's a party going on here at the moment. You can hardly hear yourself think as you can probably hear for yourself,' Marjorie told her. 'Perhaps it would be better if I broke the news to her myself – upstairs, quietly. I'll get her to ring you later when they've all gone.'

Having got Maryan's permission she rang off and looked around. Seeing Mike passing with a tray of sandwiches, she asked him if he knew where Amy was.

He shrugged. 'I saw her going upstairs a while ago,' he said. 'She's been a bit of a misery all evening since she found out that her mum had missed the play.'

'Didn't you go after her?'

'No. I thought I'd better leave her to it.'

Marjorie took his arm and drew him into the kitchen. 'That was her mother on the phone. It seems that Amy's grandmother died this morning. That's why she couldn't come. I couldn't let her break the news over the phone, especially with this noise going on, so I've got to break it to her now.'

Mike bit his lip. 'Oh, no. Poor Amy. She thought a lot of her gran. Do you want me to come with you?'

'No. I'll go. If she wants you I'll come and get you. In the meantime don't say anything to anyone. Just keep the ball rolling down here.'

On the landing Marjorie tapped on Amy's door. 'Amy – can I come in, dear?'

'Okay,' came the muffled reply.

Marjorie pushed open the door. Amy sat on her bed looking sorry for herself. 'Amy, your mother has just telephoned,' she said. 'I'm afraid she had some very bad news.' She went and sat beside Amy on the bed and took her hand. 'I know you were disappointed and felt let down because she didn't come today. But there was a very good reason. Darling, I'm afraid your grandma was taken ill yesterday. The hospital sent for your mother early this morning.'

Amy's eyes widened as she turned to Marjorie. 'Grandma? What happened? Is she all right?'

Marjorie took a deep breath. 'Amy, dear, I'm afraid your grandma died this morning. I'm so sorry.' Amy burst into tears and she held her close. 'She caught a bad cold that went to her chest. It turned to pneumonia. Your mother said she didn't suffer. It was very peaceful. She was with her at the hospital, that's why she couldn't come.' She tipped up Amy's chin to look into her eyes. 'Amy – your mum is going to need you now. Now that there are just the two of you you'll have to look after each other.'

Amy swallowed her tears. She felt such a bewildering mixture of emotions. Common sense told her that it wasn't Mum's fault that Grandma had died, yet something in her wanted – almost *needed* – to blame her. Her mother had robbed her of *two* fathers. Now Grandma had gone too – all because Mum had gone off to this new job and left her. Why should I go and look after her? she asked herself – a mother who'd done nothing but lie to her all her life, who had always put her job and others first. She didn't deserve it. But, knowing that such bitter resentment would be considered unworthy of her, she swallowed and asked: 'Where's Mike?'

'He's downstairs. Would you like me to send him up?'

Amy nodded. 'Yes please.'

Mike found Amy sitting on the bed, her recent tears drying on her cheeks. He stood by the door, looking hesitantly at her. If she cried again he wouldn't know what to do or say. He wasn't at all sure of how to handle the situation anyway.

'Hello,' he said. 'Mum told me about your gran. I'm really sorry. She was a nice old lady.'

'Thanks.'

She didn't look at him – didn't respond. It was a bit like talking to the wall. What should he do now? Should he go, or try to say something else? What? He stepped towards her. 'Mum says you can telephone your mum later, when the party's over.'

'I'm not going to.'

He frowned. 'Why not? I expect she's pretty upset.'

'If she hadn't taken that job and left Grandma alone it wouldn't have happened.'

He stood uncertainly in front of her. This was a reaction he hadn't bargained for. 'But – you'll be going to London for the funeral, won't you? I mean – you'll need to ring her to know where and when – everything.'

'I'm not going.' For the first time she looked up at him. 'It's her fault, so she can go on her own. I can't help Grandma now. She won't know whether I'm there or not. I'm never going home any more. I hate Mum.'

There was a shocked pause as Mike looked at her. He'd expected it to be difficult, but not this difficult. Her eyes were dark with anguish. He could feel the hurt emanating from her like the vapour from dry ice. What he didn't understand was why. Slowly he sat down beside her on the bed.

'Why do you hate your mum, Amy? It can't really be her fault, your gran dying. And I really think you should go to the funeral.' She was silent and he sensed that she was struggling to hold tears at bay once more. Remembering the day they'd been caught in the buzzbomb raid and the comfort holding hands had given him, he reached out to curl his fingers round hers. After all, she was still only a kid really. 'Come on, Amy,' he said. 'Don't be too hard on your mother. Old people do die, you know – all the time. It's no one's fault and it doesn't help, looking for someone to blame.'

She turned to look at him, her effort not to cry twisting her mouth so that her words were distorted. 'Oh, you – you don't understand. How would you know how it feels?'

'I might find out if you were to tell me.'

For a moment she hesitated. The weight of what she had dragged

154

around with her since last July sometimes seemed as though it would crush her. It would be such a relief to unburden herself. 'Look, Mike,' she said haltingly. 'If I tell you something, will you promise not to say a word to anyone – not even Auntie Marjorie?'

'Of course.'

'Say you promise?'

'Oh, come off it.' He frowned. 'Promises are for kids. If I say I won't tell, then I *won't*. A man is as good as his word, Dad always says.'

'All right then.' She paused, biting her lip. 'Remember that time I went to stay at Hazelfield last summer holidays?'

'Yes.'

'Well, I overheard something the night before I came home. It was something really awful. That was why I wanted to go up to London to see Grandma afterwards. I had to ask her if it was true.'

'I knew there was something. You came back in such a mood. What was it, Amy? What did you hear?'

'I heard Mum telling the Leighs that I was their grandchild,' she said. 'Marcus Leigh, their son – the one who was killed in France – was my real father.'

Mike's eyes opened wide. 'You mean that he and your Mum . . .? Crumbs.' For once he was lost for words. 'But – if this Marcus Leigh person and your mum were – well, you know – *in love*, why didn't she marry him?'

Amy sighed. 'Lots of reasons. Because he was rich and Mum was poor. Because he was Jewish and she wasn't. Anyway, they both married someone else. When Mum told the Leighs they were really mad. She felt she had to leave, after working for them ever since she left school too.'

Mike frowned. 'Just because she loved their son – and had you?'

'No – because they didn't believe her,' Amy told him bitterly. 'They didn't want to believe that their son would mix with someone as common as Mum. She had to get me out of the house quickly so that they didn't have to look at me any more. I heard her telling Mr Leigh she would the next morning. It made me feel like – like something the cat had sicked up.'

Mike looked at her for a long moment. 'But you did *have* a good father,' he said. 'You've often told me. I mean the one you *thought* was . . .'

'That's the awful part. I thought he was but he wasn't. He was just Mum's husband.'

'So – it *was* true then? Your Gran explained what happened – that day?'

'No.' Amy sighed. 'She was as shocked as I was. She said that Mum never told her either. She said I was to forget about it. To think of myself as a Jessop, like it says on my birth certificate. And I've tried, Mike. I've tried and *tried*, but it doesn't work.' She turned to look at him. 'All these years; all these years she's been living a lie – *me*. I've been a lie all my life. I'm not who I thought I was. Can you imagine how that feels? How would you feel if you found out that your dad, the man you feel closest to in all the world, was nothing but a stranger – no relation to you at all?'

Mike couldn't meet the harrowing look in her eyes. 'I can't imagine,' he said, staring at the floor. 'But I know it must feel pretty gruesome.'

'So now can you see why I hate her?'

'But you can't go on hating her for ever, can you?'

'I don't think I'll ever stop,' she said passionately.

'Does she know – that *you* know, I mean?'

'No. I made Grandma promise not to tell and – well, she won't be able to now, will she? Now I've lost her too.' She turned away with a shake of her head. 'I'll never tell Mum that I heard what she told the Leighs that night. I couldn't.'

He looked at her. 'You didn't mean it when you said you wouldn't go to your gran's funeral, did you?'

'Yes. I meant it.'

'Amy?' Maryan was so relieved to hear her daughter's voice at the other end of the line. 'I thought you'd like to know that the funeral went off quite well, love. Granny Jessop, Auntie Maggie and Uncle Bill send their love.' Maryan paused, holding the receiver close to her ear. Honestly, these trunk calls weren't worth the money half the time. The line was awful. She could barely hear Amy's voice. When there was no reply she went on, raising her voice a little: 'Uncle Bill was invalided out of the Army last year – chest trouble. But he's getting on nicely. I wish you could have seen your cousin Johnny. He's so tall, going on seventeen now and quite the young man. He's already in the Air Training Corps. Hoping to join the RAF as soon as he's eighteen.' After another pause she said: 'It was just as well you didn't come, love. Since VE Day the trains have been so crowded. Amy – are you still there?'

'Yes.'

'Did you do anything to celebrate the victory, down there?'

'Not much. There was a bonfire in Armstrong's Meadow with a few fireworks. And they burned a guy, got up to look like Hitler, and there was a bit of dancing.'

'That must have been fun. Mrs Taylor told me how good you were in the play. I wish I could have seen you.'

'Do you?'

'And she sent me the cutting out of the local paper too. It said you were "captivating as Viola". Wasn't that smashing?'

'I s'pose so.'

'I'll keep it always. I've put it in the photo album with all your snaps.'

'Oh.'

'Maybe you'll be in another play.'

'Maybe.'

'I expect you and Mike enjoyed it.'

'It was all right.'

'Amy, I'd like you to come up to Town next weekend,' Maryan went on. 'I've got so much to tell you about my new job. The flat's lovely. I've got your room all ready. I can't wait for you to see it. And I've got a surprise, too.'

'Oh. Have you?'

Maryan felt a twinge of anxiety. 'Amy, love – are you all right? Not feeling poorly or anything, are you? Not upset about Grandma?'

'No. I'm all right, Mum.'

'Good. She wouldn't have wanted you to be upset you know. You always meant a lot to her.' Again there was no reply. 'So you will come, will you – next weekend? I've already spoken to Mrs Taylor about it. I'll meet you off the four-thirty at Euston. That all right?'

'I suppose it's got to be if you've all arranged it between you.'

'Yes – well – I'd better ring off now, love. See you next weekend.' Maryan felt upset and a little put-out at Amy's laconic response, but she told herself that her daughter was a teenager now. Moodiness was all part of growing up, as she remembered from her own adolescence. She would have to employ all her tact and understanding if they were to reestablish their relationship successfully.

As Amy replaced the receiver she caught sight of herself in the hall mirror. Would her eye have returned to normal by the weekend? she wondered. She hated the curious glances she had attracted over the past few days. It would be horrible going up to London on the train, and even worse trying to explain to Mum how it had happened.

Leaning forward she peered more closely at the eye. It had turned from dark red to black and blue at first. Now it was a horrible shade of greenish yellow. Very gingerly she touched the discoloured, still puffy skin and winced at the memory of Lily Smith's well-aimed straight left, consoling herself with the satisfaction that this time she

157

had given back as good as she received. Maybe Lily would stop trying to pick fights with her now.

Ever since that day last summer at the carnival Lily had made a point of making Amy's life a misery whenever their paths crossed. And the news that Mrs Smith had moved the rest of her family to Rhensham permanently after they'd been bombed out had filled Amy with dismay. The large, shiftless family now lived on the council estate on the fringe of the village and Lily, who had left school last Christmas soon after her fourteenth birthday, now worked behind the counter of the village Co-op. But although she now considered herself an adult, she never missed a chance to cat-call and draw attention to Amy whenever she saw her, taking great delight in causing her the maximum of embarrassment and humiliation.

Lily's mousy hair was now bleached and permed to within an inch of its life. She wore bright orange lipstick and short skirts and her jaws permanently rotated on a wad of chewing gum. She was often to be found hanging around the bus stop near the church in the hope of attracting the American servicemen from the nearby camp who sometimes stopped off for a pint of the local ale at the village pub.

As ever, she attracted a string of miscellaneous hangers-on, girls less adventurous than herself who admired her strident outspokenness and her capacity for trouble-making. Lily didn't give a damn. When she was around there was always a bit of fun, usually at someone else's expense; because you were either with Lily or against her. There were no half measures.

On the day in question it was half-day closing and Amy spotted Lily hanging around the bus stop with her usual motley crowd as she stood waiting for the bus to stop. She decided to ignore her. Maybe she'd leave her alone today. And even if she didn't, there wasn't much the girl could do if she refused to take any notice of her. Besides, she was probably waiting for the bus. But Lily wasn't waiting for the bus. She wasn't even waiting to wheedle chewing gum or cigarettes from some hapless American soldier. Today she was waiting for Amy.

She stepped forward eagerly the moment she saw her intended victim get off the bus, the gleefully malicious look on her face that Amy had learned to dread. Her followers gathered round, expressions of smug anticipation on their faces as they waited for the entertainment to begin.

'Well, *well*, if it ain't the great actress 'erself,' Lily sneered. 'Seen 'er name in the paper, did yer? *Captivatin'*, it said she was.' She gave Amy a vicious push and snatched off her school hat, throwing it

158

over the wall. ''Ow much did yer 'ave to pay to get 'em to write that then?' She advanced on Amy, who stepped backwards until she could feel the cold stone of the wall pressing against her back. 'Go on, Amy–pissed. Give us a free show then. I reckon us poor sods deserve a treat, don't you? Act us the bit where you was makin' out to be a bloke, like wot it said in the paper.' She turned to the others. 'Reckon it must've been a queer old play, don't you?' she jeered. They tittered and nudged each other. Encouraged by their approval, Lily made a grab for Amy's hair, her eyes glinting dangerously. 'Think you're someone, don't you, *Jessop*? Lookin' down yer snotty nose an' queenin' it over the rest of us in yer poxy school uniform.'

'I don't queen it. I don't even want to talk to you,' Amy said, wincing with pain as the other girl wound a lock of her hair tightly round her fingers and pulled mercilessly.

'Oh, don't wanna *talk* to me, don't yer? Well, pardon me for livin', I'm sure. I s'pose you think you're all set now that your mum's got herself a new feller.'

Amy's eyes opened wide. 'I – don't know what you mean.'

'No? Well, I wouldn't boast about it if it was me neither. Don't think 'cause I don't live in London no more I don't get to 'ear what's 'appenin'. Me Gran still lives there, y'know, an' there ain't much as *she* misses. She says your mum's living with some bloke in his posh gaff Up West,' she announced triumphantly. 'Some Irish geezer she met when she was working down the market.' She pushed her face close to Amy's. 'My mum says she was always a wrong'un. An now that Marcus Leigh's a gonner I s'pose she's latched onto some other poor bleeder.'

Feeling sick with disgust, Amy kicked out at Lily's shin. The other girl shrieked out in anger.

'Oooh, you little bitch. You've laddered me nylons. New on, they was.'

'I don't care about your nylons, Lily Smith.' Amy's temper was fully aroused now. 'Your skinny legs look stupid in them anyway. Don't you dare say things about my mum. I'll . . .'

Lily gave her no time to complete the sentence. She hit Amy hard in the face with the back of her hand, her knuckles catching her in the eye with a blinding pain. Amy heard the others giggling excitedly and egging Lily on, and suddenly it was as though a red mist of fury rose before her, making her forget every lesson in ladylike manners she'd ever been taught. Wrapping the strap of her heavily loaded school satchel round her hand, she swung it hard at Lily, knocking the other girl off balance and causing her to stagger forward, banging her face against the wall. As Amy seized her chance to

159

escape she heard Lily screech and clutch at her nose, from which a trickle of blood had started to emerge. She didn't wait to see what would happen next. As Lily's shocked admirers gathered round her, enjoying the drama, she ran off along the road and didn't stop until she reached the gates of Mitcham Lodge.

Going round to the back she let herself in at the kitchen door, standing a moment to regain her breath. With luck she would get upstairs to her room before anyone saw her. She felt hot and shaky and close to tears. She just wanted to be by herself to calm down and get over the unpleasant encounter. Lily was jealous as usual, this time it was over the play. But what had she meant about her mother living with a man she met at the market? It was a lie. *Or was it*? Just what kind of woman was her mother? She was beginning to feel she had never really known her. And would she really expect her to go there and live with her and this – this *Irish geezer*? Everything – all of what she had suffered since last summer, including Lily's taunting – had been Mum's fault.

She hurried through the kitchen as silently as she could, but in the hall she came face to face with Marjorie, who was on her way downstairs.

Marjorie stopped in her tracks, her eyes wide with shock. 'Amy. Heavens above, child, what on earth has happened to you?'

Seeing Marjorie's alarmed expression Amy stole a sideways glance at herself in the hall mirror. She was shocked by what she saw. No wonder Marjorie looked as she did. The eye Lily Smith had hit was swollen and already the skin around it was darkening. There was even a small cut where Lily's cheap ring had caught her cheekbone. Her hair was standing on end, too, and she suddenly remembered with dismay that she'd left her school hat where Lily had thrown it, over the churchyard wall. A huge lump rose in her throat and she knew that if Marjorie uttered just one sympathetic word she was in danger of bursting into babyish tears.

'Darling, your poor face?' Marjorie's face was full of concern as she reached out to touch Amy's cheek.

It was too much. A strangled sob escaped Amy's throat as she dropped her satchel on the floor and covered her face with her hands.

'It's all right, darling. Don't cry.' Marjorie put an arm around her. 'Who did this to you? You must tell me.'

'It was – a girl I know,' Amy hiccupped, despising herself for her own weakness. 'She was waiting for me at the bus stop. She's always picking on me for something.'

Marjorie was shocked. 'You mean another girl did it? She actually *attacked* you? Who is this girl? We really should report this, you know.'

Amy swallowed hard. 'It's nothing unusual. She's someone who used to live near us in London and she's always hated me. Trouble is, she lives here now. Her mother moved them all here for good when they were bombed out.'

'Well, first things first. Come upstairs and let me attend to that eye,' Marjorie said.

As she bathed the eye in the bathroom and applied antiseptic to the cut Amy looked at her. 'You won't tell anyone I've been in a fight, will you, Auntie Marjorie?'

Marjorie smiled. 'Of course I won't. Anyway, it was hardly a fight, was it? More of an assault.'

Amy said nothing, but inwardly she felt a small thrill of satisfaction that this time she'd given Lily as good as she'd got. She'd have a fat nose tomorrow. She'd have a job to wheedle any nylons or chewing gum out of her precious 'Yanks' looking like that. Maybe she would think twice before picking on her another time. But although she'd had the satisfaction of getting even with Lily, the remark about her mother still rankled, echoing like a tolling bell at the back of her mind. It was just another of Lily's malicious lies, of course. It had to be; at best an exaggeration. All the same, there was no smoke without fire, so they said. And it wasn't nice to have to listen to people like Lily Smith saying rotten things about your mother, especially when you were in no position to deny them.

Mike went with her to the station on Friday afternoon. They stood together on the platform, Mike making most of the conversation. Amy was in one of her quiet moods again.

'I bet you're looking forward to seeing your new home,' he said brightly.

'Not really.'

'At least your eye is better. It looks normal again now.'

'Yes.' Amy had slipped out of school in the lunch hour the day before and surreptitiously bought a box of face powder at Woolworth's. A dusting of it, applied with cotton wool hid the faint discolouration left by the black eye, much to her relief.

'It'll be nice, though,' Mike was saying. 'Going back to London now all the bombing's finished.'

'It still won't be like it used to be. That'll take years.'

'Maybe just as well, though, eh? I mean all those . . .'

'Slums? Like where we used to live, you mean?'

161

'I was going to say places that needed pulling down anyway.'

'Same thing.'

He looked at her gloomy face. 'Oh cheer up, misery-guts. The war's over and you're going to see your new home. You might try and look a bit more cheerful about it.'

'It's all right for you. You haven't got to leave all the things and people you like to go and live somewhere you don't want to,' she burst out accusingly. 'Besides – I told you what Lily Smith said about Mum.'

'But you don't believe it – do you?'

Amy shrugged sullenly. 'I don't know what I believe any more.' He was silent and she glanced at him, suddenly feeling insecure and a little afraid. Mike was her best friend and she'd been horrid to him lately. If he lost patience with her who would she turn to? 'What are you going to do this weekend?' she asked in a lighter tone. 'Bet you won't miss me.'

'Don't know what we'll do. It depends what Dad feels like when he . . .'

'Dad?' She interrupted, staring at him. 'Your dad, you mean? You didn't tell me he was coming home.'

'Oh – didn't I?' He shuffled his feet, his ears turning red. *Blast*, he'd promised his mother he wouldn't say anything in case Amy thought they were trying to get rid of her. She'd been so touchy lately.

'You *know* you didn't,' she said. 'Is he coming home for keeps then?'

'No, only for the weekend. This'll probably be his last leave before his demob, though.'

'I see. You definitely won't be missing me then.'

The train signal changed with a clang and Mike looked up with some relief. 'Oh look, your train's coming.' He glanced at her. 'Dad's getting his old job back with the paper. He's going to see them this weekend. Did you know he was a journalist?'

'No.' She shook her head, too preoccupied to notice his clumsy attempt at changing the subject. 'No, I didn't.'

'That's what I want to be too. Have you decided what you want to do when you leave school?'

'No.' Amy picked up her small weekend case as the train squealed to a stop alongside the platform. 'Have a nice time with your dad this weekend, Mike,' she said, moving away. 'The three of you will be by yourselves now. It'll be just like old times. You'll like that.'

She climbed into the train and found a corner seat where she sat looking straight ahead of her. The train had begun to move when there was a frantic tapping on the carriage window. Mike was signalling to her to open it. She stood up and pushed it down. 'What do you want?'

Running alongside the moving train, he pushed a bar of chocolate at her through the window. 'Here – for the journey. See you Sunday evening. Bye, Amy. Have a nice time.'

She took the chocolate, torn between shame at her own churlish behaviour and annoyance with him for making her feel guilty. 'Thanks, Mike,' she called as the train reached the end of the platform and he stood back, waving. She waved till he was out of sight, then closed the window and sat down again, her throat tight with tears. She swallowed angrily. She was always wrestling with tears nowadays. What was the matter with her?

She couldn't bring herself to eat the chocolate, knowing that Mike had sacrificed his precious sweet coupons to give her a consolation prize she didn't deserve. If only she hadn't been so beastly to him. She gave it to two small children who got on at the next station with their mother, enjoying her own martyrdom as she watched them eat it.

Sitting back in her corner seat she agonised over what she saw as the Taylors' deception. Marjorie must have conspired with her mother to get her out of the way so that they could have their family reunion. Hurt inflated itself inside her like a balloon until everything ached with the pressure. Was there anyone left in the world who really wanted her? Would she ever fit in anywhere?

Maryan met Amy at the station and brought her back to Simons Mews in a state of suppressed excitement. They made the journey to Chelsea by bus so that she could show Amy the bomb damage and how much had already been done to clear the sites. 'They tell us they're hoping to have London back to normal in five years,' she said.

Standing in the little cobbled mews outside Vincente Antiques, Maryan proudly pointed to the window display she had created herself: a pretty little French secretaire and a Regency sofa table, behind which was a graceful drape of crimson and gold striped satin.

'Roisan gave me the drape,' she said. 'She's Vincent – Mr Donlan's sister and she will be doing all the soft furnishing for the business. She's ever so nice and really clever.' Maryan got out her key. 'Vincent is standing in for me at the shop this afternoon so that I can meet you. You'll meet him later. This really is the most interesting job, Amy. There's so *much* to learn: furniture, porcelain and pottery, silver and enamels and glass. Mr Donlan has taken me

163

along to a couple of sales, but I can't imagine ever buying at one myself. You daren't blink without they think you're bidding.' She laughed a little too brightly, aware that she was talking too much. Amy's silence was making her nervous. She had looked forward so much to this weekend and she refused to believe that she couldn't make Amy enjoy it.

'I've even started taking evening classes in office work,' she went on. 'You know, I was really lucky, meeting Mr Donlan's nephew like that at the market. Getting a job with a lovely home that went with it was a real piece of good luck for us – for you and me.'

'It's a pity Grandma couldn't have come too,' Amy said.

Maryan's smile dissolved and she gave a sad little sigh. 'I know. If only she'd agreed to come with me. I did try, Amy, but she wouldn't budge from that awful old place. You should have seen the state it was in since the bombing.'

'I know – I mean, it must have been.'

Maryan looked at her enquiringly. 'Well – shall we go in? I can't wait for you to see the flat.'

To Maryan's relief Amy seemed quietly impressed by the flat, especially the pretty bedroom that was to be hers. For the first time her expression relaxed and something that was almost a smile flitted across her face.

'I made the curtains and bedspread myself,' Maryan told her. 'I thought you'd like the flowered pattern – to remind you of the countryside.'

'Yes. It's very nice, Mum.'

Maryan looked at her daughter, now almost as tall as she was. She was blossoming into a very attractive young girl. Her thin child's body was filling out, her dark hair shone and she positively glowed with health and vitality. And from her reports she was doing really well at school. She had every reason to be happy and confident. Why then was she so quiet and withdrawn? However, encouraged by Amy's obvious approval of her bedroom, she said: 'Why don't you make yourself at home – take off your coat and freshen up? You can unpack later.'

Amy looked at her. 'You said you had a surprise,' she said warily.

'That's right. But I was saving that for later. Tell you what, I'll show you while we're having tea. It's all ready.'

After the meal of cold meat and salad Maryan got up and went to the sideboard, where she took out a folder. She opened it, spreading the contents on the table. 'This is the prospectus of your new school. It's only a short bus ride away from here and it's called St Hildred's. It's actually a convent and the teachers are all nuns, but it's very

164

modern and forward-thinking. And look . . .' Maryan turned the page. 'They specialise in the arts: music and drama, dancing and singing. I know you're going to love it.'

Amy stared down at the photographs in the prospectus. 'It looks very posh,' she said.

'It is. The facilities are wonderful. Just fancy getting a sports field that size in the middle of London,' Maryan said. 'The girls wear these really smart uniforms. Brown and yellow with lovely straw boaters in the summer and felt Bretons in winter. I've put your name down for next year. You start in September.'

Amy had turned now to the last page where the school fees were printed. She looked up at her mother. 'But it's a private school,' she said in surprise. 'It costs an awful lot, doesn't it?'

Maryan blushed. She'd meant to take that page out before Amy could see it. 'That's all right. I mean – you passed your scholarship, didn't you?'

'But that was for the High School in Suffolk.'

'It's all right though,' Maryan blundered on. 'It just has to be transferred.'

'Are you sure?' Amy looked at her with clear blue eyes that Maryan couldn't quite meet. She couldn't tell Amy that Sam Leigh was paying her school fees so she was obliged to bend the truth a little.

'Of course I am.'

They were washing up together when Vincent arrived. He came in unannounced, entering by the back stairs entrance which led directly up from the shop. Maryan heard his step on the stairs and hurriedly dried her hands.

'This will be Mr Donlan,' she told Amy, her cheeks pink. He appeared smiling in the doorway and she went straight into the introductions: 'Amy, this is Mr Donlan, my new boss and our landlord.'

Vincent raised an eyebrow. 'That sounds very formal. You'll be frightening the girl into thinking I'm the wicked squire.' He held out his hand. 'Hello, Amy. Take no notice of your mother. I'm really quite human when you get to know me. I've heard so much about you, I feel I already know you. Welcome to Simons Mews. I hope you're going to be happy here.'

'Thank you, Mr Donlan.' Amy shook his hand, and he bent a little to look at her.

'My nephew calls me Uncle Vinnie. Maybe you'd like to call me that too.' She said nothing and he went on: 'Have you seen the new school yet?'

'Yes.'

'Only the prospectus so far,' Maryan put in, 'but the Mother Superior has promised to show her round in the summer holidays. It's no problem with the nuns living on the premises.'

'Your mother has chosen well. I know you're going to love it there,' Vincent said. 'My sister Roisan went there until she moved on to art college. You'll have the whale of a time at St Hildreds.'

'Mmm.' Amy looked from one to the other of them, then she said: 'Well – I think I'll just go and unpack now, Mum.'

'When you've finished perhaps you might like to come down and see the shop,' Vincent called out to her as she went. 'Maybe we can find a little something for you, a keepsake.'

When Amy had gone, closing the door quietly behind her Maryan let out her breath on a sigh. Vincent smiled.

'Is it heavy going?'

'A bit,' Maryan admitted. 'She's so grown-up. And so – I don't know – reserved is the word, I suppose. It's so hard to know what she's thinking.'

'Did she like her room?'

'Yes. I think so. She seemed to, anyway.'

'I should hope so,' Vincent said. 'The time and trouble you put into it.'

'She's rising fourteen,' Maryan said thoughtfully. 'A difficult age, I suppose.'

'As I remember it, I was never *allowed* to be difficult as you call it. At fourteen or any other age.' He looked at her, his head on one side. 'Tell me, what were *you* doing at fourteen?'

Maryan laughed. 'Working – as an apprentice machinist.'

'See what I mean? I don't suppose there was much scope for being difficult there.'

'No, there wasn't.'

'So – will she settle, do you think? God knows you've done your best.'

Maryan sighed. 'I hope so, Vinnie. I do hope so. It isn't going to be easy, for either of us. Sometimes I feel I've lost her. Five years is such a big chunk out of your child's life. When the war began she was a little girl, now she's a teenager – almost an adult – brought up by another woman too.' She sighed. 'I only hope we can bridge the gap. There's so much I want to make up to her.'

He slipped an arm around her shoulders. 'You'll be fine, Maryan. She's lucky to have such a mother as you, and I'm sure she knows it.'

But Maryan wasn't so sure. There was a lot Vincent didn't know

166

about her; a lot Amy didn't know too. She'd made so many mistakes. Her loyalties had been so appallingly misplaced all these years. And she was horribly afraid that it might already be too late to redress the balance.

Chapter Ten

Rachel sat at her desk in the office she had created for herself at Whitegates. Since the daily woman from the village had taken Maryan's place she had turned the housekeeper's flat over the garage into her own workplace. It now consisted of an office, a studio and a large workroom. Ever since she had found Marcus's designs she had been working feverishly on a collection to be launched later that summer. Once peace was established she predicted that there would be a boom in the fashion world just as there had been after the last war. Feldman's, and more specifically The Marcus Leigh Collection, could begin to make its mark once again.

She herself was working on the business side and the preparation of the show that would launch the new designs, whilst in the workroom a team of meticulously hand-picked cutters and seamstresses were working on the garments. The project had given Rachel a new lease of life. She had begun to take an interest in her own clothes and her appearance once again. After Marcus's death she had lost weight and begun to look every day of her fifty–eight years, but now, with her thick hair well cut and groomed, and the black mourning dresses she was reluctant to set aside relieved by touches of colour, she was beginning to look herself again.

Marcus's designs were being made individually to fit the models Rachel had already chosen. 'They were all girls at the outset of their careers; young and eager; as fresh and as pretty as Marcus's designs demanded and deserved. She had appointed a designer too, to complete the details of some of the sketchier designs and to create further styles; because Rachel was convinced that once the glamour–starved women of Britain had seen the innovative lines and styles Marcus had created there would be a demand for clothes with the distinctive blue and silver *Marcus Leigh* label. She was determined that it would be one of the most sought-after names in the fashion

168

world and she worked tirelessly towards that end.

Eager to encourage young talent, she had invited submissions from art colleges and had finally chosen a talented young woman from an Essex college. Gina Stern was newly qualified and highly recommended by her tutors. At twenty she was fiercely ambitious and determined to get on and make her mark. She admired Marcus's designs and her portfolio revealed a flair and style that were almost uncannily similar and compatible with his. Rachel was well pleased with her choice. Everything was going to plan and life held some meaning for her again.

Outside the window every tree and hedge row was heavy with the bounty of spring. Today Rachel felt its restlessness stirring inside her, making concentration difficult. The venue for the show, a smart Kensington hotel, was booked and the guest list was complete. The invitations were at the printer's and the menu for the buffet luncheon to be served before the commencement of the show was already selected and ordered.

In the workroom next door the hum of machines and the quiet conversation of the seamstresses told of their steady industry. Rachel had no wish to disturb them. They knew their jobs and she knew she could trust them. In a couple of weeks' time things would begin to heat up and she would be busy again. For now there was very little for her to do – except . . .

She got up and opened the window – then closed it again. The singing of the birds and the evocative honey-and-spice scents of springtime made her jumpy and nervous. Her eyes were constantly drawn to the drawer at the bottom of the filing cabinet. Since that day when she had visited 124 Hackney Road and cleared out Marcus's studio she had done nothing about the package of personal papers she had collected from his desk, pushing it into that empty drawer and conveniently forgetting it. Her project for the new collection to be launched in his name had taken up all her time and energy. But she had known all along that she must go through the papers at some stage. Sam, aware of her reluctance, kept begging her to let him take on the task himself.

'We really should do something about it,' he urged. 'There could be something important there, even bills to be settled.'

Rachel had shrugged this off. 'You know that Marcus never got into debt,' she chided him. 'And if he owed anyone money they would have surely asked for it before this.'

But although she knew in her heart that she must do this one last thing for him she shied away from it with a sick feeling in the pit of her stomach. They had not been allowed to bury their son or go

169

through the proper grieving ritual. At the back of her mind there was always the vain hope that he might, by some miraculous turn of fate, not have been killed after all. Even though they had now received his personal belongings and a letter of commendation from the French Government, his death still seemed unreal to Rachel. Going through his letters and papers would make it real; would force her to face the fact that he had gone for ever. And for this reason she allowed the weeks to pass, and the package of personal papers to remain in the drawer.

But today, with everything under control and no other job demanding her attention, she knew that she could put off the task no longer. With a sigh she got up and went across to the filing cabinet. Sinking to her knees she pulled out the drawer and took out the packet, tipping the contents onto the floor. As she had assured Sam, there seemed nothing of any urgency among the pile. Spreading the papers out she could see at a glance that they consisted largely of letters from friends, receipts, invoices, hurried sketches on the backs of scraps of paper, theatre and concert programmes. There were some letters from Jessica. Rachel caught her breath as she recognised the small, neat handwriting on the scented blue envelopes. She destroyed them, tearing them into tiny pieces and dropping them into her waste-paper basket. Her darlings deserved to keep their privacy.

The pile was diminishing nicely and Rachel felt a wave of relief. The job was almost over. And it hadn't taken as long, or been nearly as traumatic as she had feared. Then she saw it.

The large sealed envelope had stuck inside the packet, too thick to fall out with the rest of the loose papers. As she drew it out she saw printed in large capitals: TO BE OPENED IN THE EVENT OF MY DEATH. Her blood chilled and for a moment she turned it over in her hands, weighing it speculatively – trying to guess what it might contain, half afraid to open it. At last, with trembling fingers, she tore it open. Inside were three smaller envelopes, one addressed to her and Sam; another with the address of his bank written on it. But she was surprised to see that the third envelope was addressed to Mrs Maryan Jessop.

Tearing open her own envelope she read quickly.

Dearest Mother and Father,

If you are reading this you will already know that my life is over and that, sadly, we shall not meet again. I want you to know how much I love you both and that I have always been so very grateful for the happiness, the care and the love you have given me all my life. If I gave you pain by joining the Resistance, please forgive me and try to understand that I could not have lived with myself had I not done what I knew I must do.

I do not have very much to leave behind in the material sense, but there is something that I wish you to put right for me, if I am to be denied the opportunity of doing it myself.

A long time ago I did something foolish that had serious consequences and I believe I hurt someone who did not deserve to be hurt. I have good reason to believe that I am the father of Maryan Jessop's child. By the time I returned home she had married another man and seemed unwilling to acknowledge this. I therefore felt it wiser to remain silent, especially when I met and fell in love with Jessica. I now feel that it was very selfish and wrong of me not to face up to my responsibility. Therefore I have instructed the bank in the letter enclosed to invest any money I might leave and hold it in trust for Amy until her coming of age. I know that you and Father do not need it and as Amy is my only living issue I feel it only right that I should provide for her in some small way.

Please try to understand and forgive me for falling short of your high standards and your expectations of me.

God bless and keep you both,
Your loving son, Marcus

Rachel knelt on the floor, reading the letter through again and again, her face wet with tears. How could he be so misguided? If the child had been his Maryan would surely have told him. He was wrong – *wrong*.

But even as she tried to convince herself she knew deep in her heart that he was not wrong. If she were truthful with herself she had known it all along. With her own eyes she had seen the strong attraction between the two young people. She had even witnessed their secret meeting that evening in Whitechapel. And there was no denying that the child, Amy, resembled Marcus. After his death she had subconsciously gained comfort from the fact, feeling a need to have the girl close to her when Marcus's loss was causing her so much pain. The passion she had seen flowering between the two young people had been the very reason why she had persuaded Sam to allow Marcus to study in France. And now she was faced with the fact that if he had not gone to France he would probably be with them, alive and well today. Had she herself set in motion the chain of events that had led to his death?

A sob tore at her throat and she covered her mouth with her hands. *No.* It was unthinkable. It wasn't her – it was Maryan. If it had

171

not been for that girl she and Sam would still have their lovely son. They had employed Maryan, treated her more like a daughter than an employee, and all the time she had betrayed them. She should not benefit from her betrayal.

She looked at the other two letters that lay on the floor in front of her, one addressed to Maryan herself. *No.* She should *not* have it. She picked up the envelope and began to tear it. Then she stopped, biting her lip in anguish. She couldn't do it. Couldn't destroy a letter that Marcus had entrusted to her. But what of the letter to the bank? She struggled with her conscience. These were his last wishes. How could she not obey them? And yet . . .

An hour later she was still sitting at her desk, the three envelopes before her, wrestling with her conscience, wondering what to do. Kitty, the little junior from the workroom, came in with a cup of tea.

'Four o'clock, Mrs Leigh,' she said, setting the cup down. 'Miss Gina said to tell you she's finished the sketches for the white ball gown if you'd like to come and have a look.'

The white fairy-tale ball gown with its sequin-encrusted bodice and bouffant skirt was to be the show's *pièce de résistance*, the climax of the collection. Rachel looked up at her. 'What? – Oh, right. Tell her I'll be through when I've had my tea.'

When the girl had gone she made up her mind. She would not go against Marcus's wishes. She would simply do – nothing. She opened a drawer and took out another large envelope. Into it she put her own letter and the two unopened ones. She sealed the envelope and wrote on it in large clear capitals: ONLY TO BE OPENED IN THE EVENT OF MY DEATH and signed it, Rachel Leigh. Then she stowed it once again at the back of the bottom drawer of the filing cabinet.

Vincent had invited Maryan and Amy to join him and Roisan for Sunday lunch, and the moment they arrived at the little house in Notting Hill Roisan took Amy under her wing. She had always wanted a daughter and was enchanted by Maryan's, whom she thought pretty and intelligent. Amy, for her part, liked Roisan on sight. Plump and homely, she was the epitome of what a real mother should be, bustling round the big untidy kitchen in a flowered pinny with her grey-streaked auburn hair coming down and her face pink and shiny as she put the finishing touches to the meal.

'Come and give me a hand,' she invited the moment the formal introductions were done with. 'There's no better way of getting to know someone than over a kitchen stove. We'll leave these two to sit and drink sherry like the gentry.'

She hustled Amy downstairs into the semi-basement kitchen and invited her to lay the table while she took a large apple pie out of the oven. Showing her where to find cloth and cutlery she smiled encouragingly.

'I'm sure I don't have to tell you how to do it. You look a very domesticated kind of a girl to me.' As she returned to her cooking she said: 'Vinnie tells me you're going to St Hildred's in September. You'll love it there. I always say it's the best school a girl could go to. If I'd had a daughter myself that's where she'd have gone, so it is.'

Amy soon found she was enjoying herself. She loved Roisan's attractive Irish accent, and the wonderful aromas that filled the kitchen made her mouth water. She had felt instantly at home in the cosy, cluttered little house from the moment she entered it. Upstairs it was all well-worn carpets, their colours mellowed to delicate pastels, and squashy, chintz-covered chairs. But the big living-kitchen was a delight; warm and full of evocative smells. There was a big old-fashioned dresser full of willow-pattern dishes and a huge round Victorian table with Windsor chairs. In a tiled recess stood the Aga stove that Roisan declared she couldn't live without and the floor was covered by an assortment of home-made rugs, each with a history of its own. From the window over the sink there was a fascinating view of people's legs as they passed by in the street above. After half an hour there Amy recognised it, as many had before her, as a haven, the perfect place to escape, to.

'So – have you had a nice weekend with your mammy?' Roisan asked as she took the roast out of the oven.

'Oh yes, thank you.'

'Ah, you must have missed each other with you being evacuated all this time.' Roisan shook her head. 'War's a cruel thing, so it is, splitting up families. I know I missed my Colin. But I was lucky enough to get him back whole, thanks be to God.' She looked up with a smile. 'I hear you went to the theatre last night. Did you enjoy it?'

Amy nodded eagerly. 'It was lovely; a play called *Blithe Spirit*. It was all about a ghost.'

Roisan pulled a face. 'Ugh. I don't care for creepy things myself.'

'Oh no, it was funny,' Amy told her. 'This man married again after his wife died, you see. And his first wife came back to haunt them because she was jealous. There was this funny old lady in it who was a medium. She caused it all to happen when they had a seance.'

173

'Well, it sounds a bit of a pickle to me. But I'm glad you enjoyed it.'

'Oh, I did.' Amy looked up suddenly. 'I want to be an actress myself when I leave school.'

'Is that a fact?' Roisan straightened her shoulders and looked at Amy. 'Well, you've the looks for it, anyway.'

In actual fact Amy had surprised herself by the announcement that she wanted to be an actress. The notion had been there ever since the school play but she hadn't realised quite how strong the feeling was until last night. The moment she had walked into the theatre's foyer with her mother and Vincent Donlan the exotic atmosphere had hit her. The sense of anticipation conjured by the mingled scents of coffee and cigar smoke had made a deep impression on her and when the curtain rose, sending out its exciting aroma of dust and size and revealing the glamorous drawing-room stage set for the play, she had been completely bowled over. The atmosphere in the theatre, steeped in glamour and tradition, had far surpassed that of the hall where they had performed the school play and as the evening progressed Amy had found herself yearning to be part of it. Back at Simons Mews, alone in her room, she had stood for a long time in front of the mirror, re-enacting some of Elvira's best scenes and thinking how much she would love to play the part of the naughty, wayward ghost. She was sure she could do it. She pictured herself floating across the stage in a dress of filmy grey, delicate and ethereal.

'And what makes you fancy a life on the boards?' Roisan was asking as she stirred the gravy.

Amy came out of her daydream and asked herself the same question. What *was* it? She frowned. It was hard to say. It would be lovely to be applauded and complimented; to have people love and admire you, not for who or what you were but for what you could do. Most of all, though, it would be wonderful to pretend to be someone else for a while. To slip out of your skin, and into another's. But not knowing how to put all this into words, all she said was: 'I don't really know.' She looked up at Roisan. 'I played Viola in *Twelfth Night* at school last term. I think I knew then that it was what I wanted to do.'

'Well, St Hildred's put on some grand plays when I was there,' Roisan said. 'I was never in any of them of course.' She chuckled. 'Put me on a stage and suddenly my hands and feet turn into shovels. My voice goes too. I sound like a squeaking mouse. And as for remembering lines . . .' She raised her eyes to the ceiling. 'My mind goes as blank as a stone wall. Ah, but you, now . . .' She

174

smiled. 'That won't happen to you. I can tell already. Don't you look every inch the little actress? You'll be a great success.' She took a tureen of steaming vegetables out of the warming oven and carried it to the table, which she scanned with a practiced eye. 'Right now. I think that's everything. Will you go and get your mammy and that brother of mine to come and eat this food before it's stone cold.'

Later Vincent went with Maryan to see Amy onto the train for Suffolk. As they waved her off Maryan let out a sigh and Vincent looked at her.

'Don't be sad. It won't be long before she's back for good.'

She shook her head. 'It's not that.'

'What then? The weekend was a success, wasn't it? She seemed to enjoy the play last night. And she and Roisan got along like a house on fire.'

'Yes, so I noticed,' Maryan said ruefully. 'She opened up to your sister far more than to me.'

Vincent slipped an arm around her shoulders. 'You're worrying for nothing. I'm sure you are. It's bound to take time for you both to adjust. You said so yourself. Once you're together, sharing your life again, it'll all come right. I know it will.' He smiled at her. 'Tell you what, let's go and have a cup of tea somewhere. It'll help you relax.'

'No. I've got a better idea. Come back to the flat and let me make you one,' she said. 'It's the least I can do after the way you've helped me entertain Amy this weekend. If I'd been left on my own with her I'd have been at a loss. And that's partly what worries me. We don't seem to have a lot in common any more.'

At the flat Maryan put the kettle on and arranged cups on a tray. Vincent stood in the doorway watching her thoughtfully.

'You've never said much about your husband, Maryan. It must be difficult for Amy, losing her grandmother when her father died at such an early age.'

'Tom was killed in the Spanish Civil War.' Maryan said. 'Amy was only little. They were very close.'

'That's sad. Children can't unburden themselves like us and I think they often bottle things like that up for years.' He paused momentarily. 'Did I ever tell you that I had a wife once?'

She turned to look at him. It was odd but it had never occurred to her that he might have been married. 'What happened?' she asked. 'An accident? Did you lose her?'

'I lost her all right, but it wasn't an accident that took her,' he said. 'Fay left me after just two years. We met and married very

175

quickly. It was just before I was called up in 1940. We hadn't much money but we didn't care. At least I didn't. I thought we'd work together after the war to build up the business and make a home. Fay obviously hadn't seen it that way. I'd no inkling of how dissatisfied she was until I came home on leave. For a while she put up a front of being glad to see me, but then it all came out: she'd met someone better looking and better off than me, and our marriage had been a ghastly mistake. And with that, off she went.'

'Oh, Vinnie, I'm so sorry. So you're divorced?'

He shook his head. 'Roisan and I were brought up strict Catholics.' He shrugged. 'Oh, we're not as devout as we were when our parents were alive, but there are certain rules ingrained into you that you just can't bring yourselves to break. Our church doesn't recognise divorce. Marriage is for life.'

'So you're still married to her?'

'Yes.' He took the tray from her and carried it through to the living room. When they were seated he went on: 'Not that my refusal to give her a divorce stopped Fay from going off to live with her wealthy businessman.'

'I see. Do you ever see or hear from her?'

'Only indirectly. He's in some kind of wholesale racket. I hear he's made a fortune out of the war. Black market – everything from cooking fat to petrol. He wangled his way out of being called up – don't ask me how – they've lived their war in luxury on the fat of the land in some baronial hall in Virginia Water.'

'If you loved her I understand how bitter you must feel.' Maryan poured the tea and passed him a cup. 'But if you're still married and she ever wanted to come back to you . . .?' She was stopped by the look on his face.

'I wouldn't have her back if she came crawling to me on her bended knees,' he said vehemently.

Privately Maryan wondered what the point was of staying married if he felt so strongly, but she kept her opinion to herself. It seemed that this was turning out to be an evening for confessions, and maybe it was time she told Vinnie something more of her own past. 'There's something I'd like to tell you too, Vinnie.' She glanced up at him. 'And maybe when I do you'll see me in a different light.'

He smiled gently. 'Away with you. What could you possibly have done that would make me feel like that? You're not going to tell me you've a criminal record, are you?'

'No. I had Amy out of wedlock,' she said. 'At least, I was married, but not to her father. Tom knew when he married me that I was expecting another man's child. We'd known each other all our lives

176

and he wanted to look after me. He was a good man. He and Amy were devoted to each other.'

Vincent reached out and took her hand. 'And – the other man? Amy's father?'

'He died in the war, fighting with the French Resistance. He was Jewish – Marcus Leigh, the son of my employers. There was never any way we could have been married. But I loved him very much, Vinnie. I always will.'

'Oh, my dear.' His face was gentle with compassion as he looked at her. 'And Amy?' he asked. 'Does she know about this?'

Maryan shook her head. 'Oh, no. She adored Tom. He was the only father she ever knew. There is no way I would ever spoil her memory of him. Even my mother never knew.'

He frowned. 'I'm not sure that's right, Maryan. Amy's not a little girl any longer. Don't you feel she has a right to know who she really is?'

'Tom was a good man. Any girl would have been lucky to have had him for a father,' Maryan said loyally. 'No. I'd rather leave things as they are.'

'And no one knows about this? I'm the only person you've told?'

She hesitated. 'I – did tell someone else. It was a terrible mistake. I told Mr and Mrs Leigh. It was after Marcus was killed. I thought they'd be happy to know that Amy was his – that part of him still lived on in her.'

He squeezed her hand. 'And – they weren't?'

'No. Mrs Leigh was horrified. In fact she refused to believe me – couldn't wait to get me out of the house. Mr Leigh was kinder. He found out where I was and came here later, offering to pay Amy's school fees. I think it was to salve his conscience.'

'Well, at least that's something. I hope you accepted.'

'I did. I couldn't have afforded St Hildred's fees otherwise. I thought about it and I felt Amy deserved a good education at least. But I can't tell her Mr Leigh is paying without explaining everything else to her.'

'So you've already had to lie to her?' Vincent sighed. 'Maryan – you're digging a hole for yourself. A hole that's going to get deeper. Don't you feel it would be better to make a complete clean breast of it? You want to make a new start with her after all, don't you?'

'Yes, but she'd never forgive me if I told her about Marcus. She'd despise me. I know she would.'

'Well, it's none of my business, really. It's up to you.' He lifted her hand to his lips and kissed her fingers lightly. 'All I know is that I was lucky to find you. You've fitted into the job and with Roisan

177

and me so well that I feel you've always been with us, and I'd hate anything to happen to spoil that. Between the three of us I know we're going to make a great success of the business.' He raised her chin with one finger to look into her eyes. 'So, if there's ever anything worrying you that I can help with, I want you to promise you'll come to me.'

She smiled. 'I will, I promise, Vinnie.'

On 15 July the lights in the West End were ceremonially switched on again. Vincent, Roisan and Maryan went up to Piccadilly to witness the occasion. But they were celebrating more than the official end to the blackout. Just that day Vincent had had the firm's first whole house refurbishment confirmed. He'd come leaping up the stairs of the flat above the shop that morning while Maryan was making herself some breakfast, waving the letter excitedly.

'I never thought we'd get it,' he said, his eyes alight with success. 'They're a business couple. Their house overlooking Regent's Park was badly bomb-damaged and it's been closed up since 1943. Roisan and I went round it with them over six weeks ago and I'd just about given up on it. Their letter came by the first post.' He spread the letter out before her on the kitchen table. 'Look, they like the ideas and colour schemes we submitted and they want us to start as soon as possible. The builders have already started on the structural repairs.'

Catching some of his excitement, Maryan flushed with pleasure as she scanned the letter. 'Oh, Vinnie, I'm so pleased for you both.'

'For *us*, Maryan – all three of us. This will concern you too. When I get started on this job you will be in complete charge here, you know. My right-hand woman, in fact. In charge of the shop and the office. I'll be relying on you more than ever. In fact, if we do well we might soon have to take on an assistant for you.'

'I hope I can live up to your expectations. I'd hate to let you down,' Maryan said diffidently.

'Let me down? Never.' He laughed. 'Don't sell yourself short, Mrs Jessop. I've never known anyone pick up the business as quickly as you. You'll be just fine. Oh, I almost forgot.' He pulled another piece of paper out of his pocket. 'Roisan has a job to do next week. It's some kind of mannequin parade at the Royal Hamilton in Kensington. They want to hire a few pieces of antique furniture, just to set the atmosphere, and they've asked Roisan to dress the stage. I'll be sending a couple of men round with a van. They're to take that ormolu and marble console, the royal-blue velvet chaiselongue and the big Chinese vase.' He smiled. 'As a matter of fact Roisan wondered if you'd like to go along after the shop closes and give her a hand.'

'Of course I'll go,' Maryan said eagerly. 'I'd love to.'

Maryan was waiting outside the Royal Hamilton Hotel when Roisan arrived in a taxi, laden with bolts of material and various boxes and bags containing other things necessary for her work. She paid the driver and turned to Maryan, her face pink with exertion.

'I keep telling Vinnie, we'll have to get a van of our own now that the bookings are beginning to come in.' She handed a large cardboard box to Maryan. 'Carry that for me, will you, dear? I'll get a porter to fetch the rest of the stuff. It's so good of you to come.'

The hotel's Duchesse Ballroom had been hired for the occasion. It was an elegant room, decorated in white and silver. Maryan watched, fascinated, as Roisan unpacked the material she had brought and, with the help of two men lent by the hotel, arranged it in graceful drapes and loops to frame the platform at one end. Looking closely Maryan could see that it was only butter muslin, dotted with sequins, but, when it was lit it looked marvelously glamorous.

'You're a genius,' she told Roisan.

Vincent's sister shrugged off the compliment modestly. 'I've got a good supply of fabrics that are obtainable without coupons. And I know a theatrical costumier in Wardour Street that lets me have odds and ends cheap. It's surprising what you can do with a few bits and pieces. Heaven only knows I've had enough practice.' She sighed. 'Roll on de-rationing. What I couldn't do if I had access to limitless fabrics.'

But Maryan was stunned with admiration. 'I can't believe you could do better than this,' she said, standing back to look at the results.

The furniture had already been delivered and between them they had arranged the console at the back of the stage with the Chinese vase on top, filled with an assortment of tall gilded grasses that Roisan had brought with her. The chaiselongue stood to one side of the stage with one of the gauzy drapes as a background. A catwalk had been erected and Roisan decorated its sides with more swags of her spangled muslin, caught up with blue satin.'

'These are their colours,' she told Maryan. 'Blue and silver. I understand it's a new designer they're launching – some wonderfully elegant gowns by all accounts. Just what most women are longing for after all the austerity.' She pulled a face. 'All those skimpy skirts and horrid military styles. Ugh.'

'I'd love to see it,' Maryan said. 'I used to work for a clothing

179

firm – Feldman Fashions. And I agree with you about the styles. A bit of glamour would be nice for a change.'

Roisan laughed and tugged at her baggy slacks and well-washed jumper. 'Not really my thing, fashion. As if you hadn't guessed. But if you'd really like to come I've got a couple of complimentary tickets. If you can get Vinnie to stand in for you for an hour why don't you slip down and have a gander?' She opened her bulging handbag and rummaged about in it. 'Now where are they? I know I had them this morning. I must have – no, here they are.' Triumphantly, she produced the two blue and silver deckle-edged cards and handed them to Maryan. 'Here you are. Bring a friend if you want to. I understand all the buyers from the big shops will be here; a few film stars and actresses too, I shouldn't wonder. It might be fun just seeing who you can spot.'

But Maryan regretfully passed back the tickets. 'It's very good of you, Roisan, but I really can't take any time off. Vinnie is going to a sale tomorrow. There are some pieces he badly wants for the Grahams' house. I'll be on my own at the shop all day.'

'Oh, what a pity. Oh well, never mind. Can't be helped. Perhaps I'll find someone else to give them to. Seems a shame to waste them.' Roisan pushed the tickets back into her bag and stood back to look at her finished work, her head on one side. 'The florists are coming first thing in the morning,' she said. 'Flowers will make all the difference. Still, I think it could do with something else – a finishing touch.' She chewed her lip thoughtfully. 'I know. There's a little Victorian wine table at the shop; a walnut one – remember?' Maryan nodded. 'It could stand at the end of the chaise with a posy bowl on it. Just the right touch, don't you think? Give the whole thing a lift.'

'Yes. I think you could be right.'

Roisan looked at her. 'Do you think you could bring it round in a taxi first thing in the morning, Maryan?' she asked, smiling sweetly. 'Charge Vinnie up for overtime. Tell him I said so.'

Maryan was up early next morning. She went down to the shop and brought out the wine table, then rang for a taxi. While she was waiting she snatched a quick breakfast and was waiting by the door, the delicate little table shrouded in a soft baize cloth, when the cab turned into the mews. At the Royal Hamilton the driver looked at her enquiringly.

'Don't you want me to wait, miss?' She shook her head.

'I want to see the table safely in place. I've plenty of time. I can get a bus back.'

In the ballroom the florists were already at work. Small gilt chairs had been laid out around the catwalk and the buffet table at the back was already spread with a snowy cloth ready to take the delicacies the caterers would bring later. Maryan unwrapped the little walnut table and put it in place at the side of the stage, then went to tell one of the florists what Roisan wanted, warning them that the table was valuable and to be extra careful not to spill any water on the surface. Finally, looking at her watch and seeing that it was a quarter to nine, she hurried out into the foyer.

A uniformed commissionaire was setting up a board in the entrance lobby, close to the revolving door. As Maryan stepped in and began to push the door she caught sight of the blue and silver poster advertising the fashion show and the breath caught in her throat. The name that had caught her eye. She must have been mistaken. It couldn't possibly have said what she thought it did. Instead of stepping out into the street she followed the door round and stepped out once more into the entrance lobby to stare at the words on the board.

THE MARCUS LEIGH COLLECTION
12.3O in The Grand Duchess Ballroom
Launching an exciting collection of haute couture
by a brilliant new designer
Proceeds to go to Jewish orphans and victims of war

The name seemed to spring out at her. She had *not* been mistaken after all. For a moment the words on the board swam together and she put out a hand to steady herself against the wall. The doorman took her arm.

'Are you all right, madam? Can I get you anything?'

She looked at the man and shook her head. 'No – no thank you. I felt a little dizzy but I'm all right now.'

'Can I call you a cab?'

'No – well, yes. Perhaps I will. Just this once.'

As she sped back to Simons Mews in the back of the taxi Maryan's mind began to stop reeling with the shock of what she had seen and the one vitally important fact emerged. Marcus. Marcus was *alive*. The man who had brought news of his death must have been mistaken. It must have been someone else who had been caught and executed. She had heard of other cases of mistaken identity. It happened often in wartime. Her heart was overwhelmed with joy and relief. To think that this very afternoon Marcus would be no more than a short bus-ride away from her. She must see him. Somehow she must find the time to go back to the hotel. Vinnie would understand. Oh, to think that in a few hours she would see him again. Marcus – the only man she had ever loved. Alive and free. Perhaps their time had come. At last fate was going to allow them to be together.

At the end of the mews she paid the driver and hurried along the cobbled road to the shop. Vincent was just arriving; letting himself in with his key. He looked at her and saw at once that something had happened.

'Maryan?' His eyes looked into hers enquiringly. 'My dear girl, what is it?'

'Can we go inside?' she asked breathlessly. 'I've got something to tell you – and to ask. A very big favour.'

'Well, of course.'

Inside the shop Vincent put away his keys and looked at her. 'Will this do, or would you like to go into the office?'

'Oh, Vinnie. I've just had such a shock,' she burst out. 'I don't know how to begin. It's – it's a *miracle*.'

He smiled wryly and locked the shop door again. 'In that case I think it'd better be the office,' he said. 'And I've a feeling we're both going to have need of my medicinal brandy.'

He closed the office door and took the bottle of brandy and two glasses out of the filing cabinet. Right,' he said, pouring two measures. 'Fire away.'

Maryan eased herself into a chair. 'The fashion show I helped Roisan prepare for . . .'

'Yes?' He pushed the glass towards her across the desk.

'This morning I took that walnut wine table along. Roisan said it would look nice with . . .'

'Never mind the wine table. What happened?'

She swallowed hard and caught her lower lip between her teeth as she looked at him, her eyes wide and luminous with wonder. 'My *God*, Vinnie. I still can't believe it. When I was coming out of the hotel I saw the poster, advertising the show in the foyer. The new designer they're launching is – is *Marcus*. Marcus Leigh.'

He stopped, his glass halfway to his lips. 'Isn't that the man who . . .?'

'Yes – *yes*, Vinnie. The man I loved – love. Amy's father. I thought he was dead. Do you see what it means?'

'I do indeed. So why are you here, girl? What are you doing, sitting here telling me about it?'

'I don't know.' She shook her head and laughed shakily. 'What shall I do, Vinnie?'

'Get yourself back there, girl. Go and grab him. And this time don't let anything happen to get in your way – no matter what.' He got up from behind the desk. 'I'll hold the fort here. Go and make yourself look marvellous. Not that you need it.' He smiled at her. 'I only wish I could put a look like that in some girl's eyes. But put on your glad rags anyway and get yourself over there.'

At the door she paused. 'The sale. What about the sale you wanted to go to?'

He waved an impatient hand at her. 'I'll go to the sale, don't you worry about it. Roisan will come and look after the shop for a few hours. Leave all that to me.'

When Maryan came down from the flat Vincent already had a taxi waiting at the door. As he handed her into the back and gave the driver the name of the hotel he put his head in at the open window.

'Good luck,' he said softly. 'I'll be thinking about you.'

'Goodbye, Vinnie. And thanks,' she said.

In the foyer of the Royal Hamilton Hotel Maryan sat reading a magazine and looking up every time anyone passed through. By the time midday came guests were beginning to assemble and at twenty past they began to make their way through to the Duchesse Ballroom. Maryan got up and followed them, wishing she had taken Roisan up on her offer of tickets. At the door the liveried attendant looked at her enquiringly and with an assurance she hadn't known she possessed, she said: 'I'm with the staff.'

The man smiled and waved her through.

Now that the room was finished it looked magnificent. There were floral decorations everywhere, echoing the theme of blue and silver: tall delphiniums and love-in-a-mist, white roses and lilac, set off by silver-grey and dark green foliage. The food on the buffet table looked delicious and waiters in immaculate white jackets stood waiting with trays of champagne. It was all very grand. Maryan stood at the back and tried to make herself as inconspicuous as possible. There was no sign of Marcus, or of any other member of the Leigh family. But then they had probably come into the hotel by a rear entrance and were busy attending to the last-minute details, she told herself.

She waited while the guests mingled, ate and chattered. As Roisan had suggested she might, she glimpsed one or two well–known faces. A waiter approached her with a tray of canapés and she took one, more to occupy her hands than to eat.

At last the guests were invited to take their seats. The stage at the far end of the ballroom was subtly lit, making Roisan's spangled drapes glitter like star–sprinkled cobwebs. Soft romantic music began

183

to play. Then onto the stage stepped a woman. She wore a long gown of blue velvet trimmed with silver sequins. Maryan took a step forward, peering at her. It was Rachel. But a very different Rachel from the one she had last seen at Hazelfield last year. This Rachel looked slimmer and carried herself proudly. The dark hair, always previously worn in a heavy plaited coil on the nape of her neck, was cut in a short, fashionable style, the white streak at the front caught back with a diamanté clip. She wore discreet and becoming make-up: her cheeks delicately rouged and her lips enhanced by a rosy lipstick. Maryan realised with surprise that if she had passed her in the street she would not have known her.

Rachel began to speak: 'Ladies and gentlemen, I can't tell you what enormous pleasure it gives me to be here this afternoon, and to introduce with great pride the Marcus Leigh Collection which I sincerely hope you will all like. As some of you will know, Marcus was my son – my only son – who died bravely fighting with the French Resistance movement shortly before the war ended. What you are about to see was his inspired vision for the post-war fashion world, which I am proud to have been able to complete and present to you today. The proceeds of this show are to go to the cause that was so very close to his heart: Jewish children, orphaned by the war. The clothes you are about to see were designed exclusively by him and dedicated to his beloved late wife, Jessica. And so, I will now hand you over to your commère, a lovely lady who needs no introduction from me; actress and singer, Madeleine Clare.'

Rachel stepped aside as a curtain swung back to reveal the glamorously dressed actress. 'Ladies and gentlemen. I give you – the Marcus Leigh Collection.'

Madeleine Clare introduced the first model who paused, turned and then began to parade forward down the catwalk. She wore a stunning suit in garnet-red velvet, which was unlike anything the audience had seen before. The skirt swirled around the models's shapely calves and the jacket was nipped in to the tiny waist with a flared peplum. With it she wore a wide-brimmed hat, tipped saucily over one eye and decorated with a huge black silk rose. Gasps of approval were followed by a flutter of applause and journalists at the back of the hall began to scribble furiously in their notebooks.

But Maryan hardly saw any of it. Crushing disappointment and despair floored her like a blow from a pole-axe. How could she have persuaded herself that Marcus was alive? She should have known that Rachel might do something of this sort in her son's memory. To think that she had prepared so excitedly to come here, expecting to

184

see him – all the time savouring the notion that he was no more than a couple of miles away.

Her heart thudding in her chest, blinded by tears, she stumbled out of the ballroom and through the hotel foyer, oblivious to the curious looks that followed her. Out in the street she stood for a moment, taking deep draughts of the fresh air until her heartbeat steadied and the feeling of suffocation that had threatened to overwhelm her gradually began to ease. Then she began to walk slowly back in the direction of Chelsea. At Simons Mews she let herself into the flat quietly by the side door and climbed the stairs with feet that felt like lead. Without taking off her outdoor things she sat in the living room staring at the wall. When Marcus died she had been unable to show her grief. Then, after a while it was as though a skin had formed over an unhealed wound. Today at the hotel that skin had been ripped away, leaving the raw wound to bleed and agonise afresh. The tears she had suppressed all those months before began to flow like a river. It was like being torn apart by a pain so terrible she thought – *wished* she might die of it. Unheeded, the afternoon and evening wore on and the light began to fade. Maryan, her tears drying on her swollen face, sat staring unseeingly at the patterns on the carpet. Overcome by an apathy that drained every ounce of strength from her, she sat on, too weary to get up and change – too stiff with misery and weak with grief to move.

When the door slammed and Vincent called from the bottom of the stairs she didn't even hear him. It was as though she was no longer part of her surroundings – strangely detached – oblivious. When he burst into the room and shouted her name she gave a shuddering start, her eyes opening wide as she looked up into his startled face through the gathering gloom.

'*Maryan.* Good God, girl, what's wrong?' He was at her side. 'Roisan came home and said you hadn't come back. I had a feeling. I was worried so I thought . . .' He had touched one of her hands and found it icy cold. 'Christ almighty, girl, you're like an iceberg.' He began to chafe her hands between his own. 'What in the world is the matter with you?'

Her dry lips began to move stiffly and she heard her voice as though from a long way off. She found it impossible to keep her teeth from chattering so that speech was difficult and disjointed. 'I – was wrong. He's not . . . Marcus was dead all the time. It – his mother's show. He . . . should have known he wasn't . . .' She looked at him and he winced at the pain he saw in her eyes. 'I've been such a fool. I thought – I really *believed* that Marcus was alive – thought I

185

was going to see him. I – I . . .' Her voice broke and helpless tears began to slip down her cheeks again.

Swallowing hard at the lump in his own throat, Vincent caught her to him and held her close.

'Oh, my dear. My dear girl. How long have you been sitting here like this, all alone, going through this agony?' He held her away from him and looked into her tearstained face. 'All afternoon, by the look of you. Why didn't you go down and talk to Roisan?'

She shook her head. 'I couldn't – couldn't tell anyone. Didn't want to see anyone.'

'Never mind. I'm here now. Will you come back to Roisan's with me? Let us take care of you?'

'No. Leave me. I'll be all right.'

'Then I'll stay here. You're in no state to be by yourself. Now . . .' He pulled her to her feet and began to pull her towards the door. 'I'll get you something to eat while you get out of those clothes and have a warm bath. You're frozen stiff. It's the shock, I daresay.'

He ran the bath for her and put a hot water bottle in her bed, chivvying her like a mother hen. Her white face and hollow-eyed appearance had frightened him. When she was in bed and he'd managed to get her to drink some hot tea and eat a piece of buttered toast he was relieved to see that she began to look a little better. He took the cup and saucer from her. 'Have you got any sleeping tablets?' She shook her head and he looked down at her apprehensively. 'Maybe I should call a doctor. You need a sedative of some sort.'

'I told you, Vinnie. I'll be all right.'

'Do you think you can sleep?'

'I feel I'll never sleep again. And yet I feel so weary.' She looked up at him. 'It's as though I'm losing them all over again – Tom, Mum, Marcus. As though I'm being punished. I'm so afraid of the future. What if Amy . . .'

He sat down on the bed and took her in his arms. 'You still have Amy,' he said. 'You and she will be all right. You'll see. And for what it's worth, Maryan, you still have me. Maybe you haven't realised it yet, and maybe this isn't exactly the right time to be telling you, but you mean a great deal to me, my dear. A very great deal.' He looked into her face with a mixture of love and apprehension and to his relief he saw that she was smiling.

'Oh, Vinnie, you're so good to me. Without you I might have . . .'

'No.' He shook his head at her. 'No. You're far too strong and far too sensible for that. I'm grateful that I found you, Maryan. And

186

that I was able to be here when you needed me. But you're a born survivor.'

She reached up her arms and put them round his neck, and when he kissed her she felt a sense of peace. The deep ache of her hurt seemed to soften and begin to melt as she returned his kiss. 'Stay with me,' she whispered, her cheek against his. 'I don't want to be alone. Stay with me, Vinnie. Just hold me. Don't let me think.'

'You're sure? Really sure?'

'I'm sure.'

Without a word he undressed and slipped into bed beside her, holding her warm and close in his arms, stroking her soft hair and caressing her trembling body. When she pressed closer to him and he felt desire harden him he drew away and looked apologetically into her eyes.

'Maryan – I'd better not stay. If I do . . .'

'I know,' she whispered. 'And it's all right – really.'

He made love to her slowly and gently, as though she were made of something infinitely fragile. He felt a mixture of guilt and wistfulness. Earlier today he'd thought he'd lost her – that he would never have the chance or the right to tell her how he felt. And to his everlasting shame his heart had actually lifted when he had first learned that she'd been mistaken about Marcus Leigh. And now – was he taking advantage of her vulnerability, or helping her to shut out what was too painful to think about? Either way he wished it could have been different. In his secret dreams he had imagined how it would be, making love to her for the first time. It had not been like this. In his dream she had been all his – wanting and needing no one but him. It had been *his* name she had called out at the height of their lovemaking instead of the name of another. In his dream love for him had made her eyes sparkle and glow like fire. But when his passion was spent and he looked lovingly into them now he saw only the brightness of bitter unshed tears.

Chapter Eleven

Amy had been packing to leave Rhensham when the news broke that atom bombs had been dropped on Nagasaki and Hiroshima. Almost immediately the Japanese had surrendered and everyone breathed a sigh of relief. At last the war was well and truly over. The enormity of the devastation caused by the bombs or the implications for future peace escaped most of the war-weary public, to whom the end of the war meant only one thing. Life could return to normal – but not so for Amy. To her, normality was about to be shattered. She must leave behind her beloved Rhensham, her school and all her friends to return to live in London for good. In spite of the euphoria all around her, her spirits failed to rise to the occasion.

Four months later, with her first term at St Hildred's coming to a close, she still hadn't become used to the changes in her life. School was perhaps the most acceptable part. At first she'd found it strange. The whole atmosphere was so very different from her previous school. To begin with she'd felt slightly in awe of the nuns, walking on silent feet with heads bowed like medieval saints. Their soft-voiced sternness had unnerved her to begin with. But she soon found that they were kind and fair, and exerted their very positive authority only where it was needed. She found them gifted and interesting teachers, too, and enjoyed her lessons very much.

It was making friends that she found difficult. Whether it was intentional or not she had no way of knowing, but the other girls seemed to her to shut her out. They had their own little cliques, none of which she was invited to join, and because of this she'd been desperately lonely until half term when a new girl arrived at St Hildred's and changed everything.

The new arrival, who was placed in Amy's form, was called Celia Frazer and Amy took to her on sight. She had long blonde plaits, mischievous blue eyes and a wide, expressive mouth. Finding themselves seated at the same desk and each being in need of an ally, the two girls struck up an instant friendship.

Over lunch on their first day together Celia told Amy that her parents had recently parted and were planning to be divorced. She explained that she and her mother had come to London, leaving her father in the Midlands where he worked as stage manager at a repertory theatre.

'When Dad came out of the army he and Mum used to row all the time,' Celia said dispassionately. 'It was horrible. They just couldn't seem to hit it off at all. Mum and I had such a nice time on our own while the war was on. Once Dad came home for good it was awful, rows all the time. He was a staff sergeant and Mum used to say he thought he was still in the army and he could boss us about like he did the soldiers.'

'Did you mind them breaking up?' Amy asked.

Celia sighed. 'I miss him – actually. It used to be such fun when he came home on leave. I always thought it would be lovely, having him home again for good. It's nice to have some peace again, though. I hated it when they kept shouting at each other.'

'You weren't evacuated while the war was on then?'

'Oh no.' Celia took a bite of her sandwich. 'We were able to stay in Northmere. Hardly any bombing there. Quite boring really. But Mum comes from London, so when she and Dad parted she wanted to come back.'

'I was evacuated to Suffolk,' Amy told her. 'So I hardly saw anything of my mother.'

'It must be nice to be together again.'

'Not really. We didn't see each other very often during the war and it's hard getting to know each other again.'

'Is it?' Celia looked at her. 'What about your dad then? He in the army too, was he?'

'He was killed before it started,' Amy said, fighting down the urge to say that he was killed fighting with the French Resistance. 'Mum works for a man who has an antique shop in Chelsea. She practically runs it for him. I don't really see much of her even now, even though we live in the flat above it.'

Celia nodded. 'My mum's got a job too. She's a secretary. She works in Southampton Street for a magazine called *London's Pride*. Perhaps you've heard of it.'

Amy had. She told Celia that Decor Vincente had recently placed an advertisement in it. It seemed to give the two girls yet another thing in common.

'Your mum got a boyfriend?' Celia asked conversationally. 'Mine

189

has this old chap who's always coming round. His name is Reg Thornton. Mum doesn't really like him much. We often have a laugh about him. But he owns one of those toffee-nosed grocery shops and he brings us lovely things to eat, chocolate biscuits and ham and jars of crystallised ginger, stuff like that – off points, of course.' She grinned. 'So we put up with him.'

'How old is he?' Amy asked.

'Oooh . . .' Celia considered, pulling her mouth into a speculative pout. '*Ever* so old – at least forty. He's even got a bald patch.' She giggled. 'He was a lieutenant in the army – catering corps, and his father kept the shop going till he came out. It's in Fulham.'

Encouraged by her new friend's easy openness, Amy said: 'My mum is quite friendly with her boss.'

Celia took a bite out of her apple and looked up. 'Is that this whatshisname, Vincente bloke?'

'Yes. His name is Vincent Donlan, but Mum calls him Vinnie.'

'Is he nice – handsome and all that?'

Amy shrugged. 'Not what *I'd* call handsome. Quite old too, like yours. He tried to get me to call him Uncle Vinnie, but I won't.' She gave an effective shudder. 'Sometimes I wonder if they might get married.'

'Really?' Celia paused and looked at her enquiringly. 'How would you feel about that?'

Amy pulled a face. She didn't know Celia quite well enough yet to confide her very real misgivings on the subject. 'Don't know really,' she said.

In truth Amy was quite disturbed by the idea. Since she had been at Simons Mews she and her mother had grown even more like strangers than before, seeing little of each other as they went their separate ways each day to school and work. They ate together in the evenings and then separated once again, Amy to her homework, Maryan to her book-keeping or some household job.

It was partly Amy's fault, she acknowledged unrepentantly and with a certain amount of satisfaction. Maryan was always trying to draw her out, but she stubbornly refused to respond, blocking Maryan's every attempt to find a point of contact. Deep inside she was still paying her back for not telling her that Marcus Leigh was her father.

Sometimes she was tempted to give in, to unfreeze a little and be more friendly, knowing that life would be infinitely more comfortable if she did. But somehow, having started her campaign of unyielding silence, her pride wouldn't let her stop.

When she first rejoined her mother she had considered the options.

190

Either she confessed that she had overheard her mother's dramatic revelation to the Leighs, or she kept quiet in the hope that Maryan would one day volunteer the information herself. In fact neither had happened. The secret stood between them like a barrier, unspoken and unresolved, driving an ever deepening wedge between them with each day that passed.

Amy was still bitterly resentful. There was so much she wanted to know about her father. She felt cheated. Having been unaware that he was her father until after his death, she felt that the least her mother could have done was to talk to her about him. But Maryan remained silent on the subject. It seemed she had once again made herself a new and absorbing life here at Simons Mews. She ran the antique shop and the office, doing things Amy had no idea she was capable of. And when Vincent came around they would be closeted together for hours on end, obviously close, sharing jokes that Amy couldn't join in and talking about things of which she knew nothing. Sometimes Vincent took them out, to a film or the theatre. But lately Amy had refused to go, convinced that they would rather be alone anyway. She had a *feeling* about them. It was as though they shared something of which she had no part. She felt in the way.

Some evenings Maryan brought the books and the typewriter upstairs to the flat and worked through the evening in a vain attempt at companionship. Tapping away or totting up figures, she was totally unaware of how excluded Amy felt, sitting at her corner of the table with her homework. Separated by only a couple of feet of carpet, they were as far apart as it was possible to be.

Often in the early weeks there were times when Amy felt achingly homesick for Rhensham and the easy, relaxed relationship she had shared with the Taylors, especially Mike. But she knew that those days were gone and would never come again. On the day she had left, Marjorie had assured her that she would always be welcome at Mitcham Lodge. But Mike would be going away to college next year, where he would no doubt make new friends. Captain Taylor was home now and they were doing their best to pick up the pieces of family life as near as possible to where they had left off. Wallowing in self-pity, Amy felt that, like the war, she was a closed chapter. The one thing that everyone wanted to forget. She belonged to a segment of their lives that they were all trying to put behind them.

Mike wrote to her every week to begin with, but as the months went by his letters grew shorter and the time between them lengthened. She felt like an outsider, abandoned and unwanted. At least, she had until she met Celia.

From that first day their friendship grew. As Christmas drew near excitement mounted at St Hildred's. There was to be a play and a concert, but much to their disgust neither of them was invited to take part in either. Only the fifth and sixth forms were allowed to be in the Christmas entertainment. But they were both selected to sing in the junior choir for the carol service. It was to take place on the last day of term in the school chapel and the parents were invited. Amy and Celia commiserated with each other when they both learned that their respective mothers would be working and unable to attend. To make up for it they threw themselves wholeheartedly into the rehearsals, gaining praise and appreciation from Sister Josephine, the music mistress.

Then, one morning just a week before the end of term, Celia arrived at school with a long face.

'You'll never guess what,' she said gloomily. 'My mum wants me to go and stay with Dad for Christmas.'

'Whatever for?' Amy asked.

'Dad's met this new woman and he's planning to marry her when the divorce comes through. Her name's *Candice*,' she said scathingly. 'Did you ever *hear* anything so pathetic? Mum says he wants me to go and meet her. But I happen to know that's not the real reason,' she added darkly.

'So – what is?'

'It's 'cause rotten old Reggie-boy has asked Mum to go to Scotland with him, *that's* why. I heard her talking to him about it on the phone last night. They've got it all planned. They're going to stay in an hotel.'

'It sounds lovely. Couldn't you go too?'

'Haven't been asked, have I?' Celia said. 'They want to get rid of me so that they can be by themselves. I expect they want to sleep together.'

'Oh, surely not. They're not married,' Amy said naively.

Celia gave her a pitying look. 'Oh, *be* your age, Amy. What about your mum and this Vinnie bloke? I bet they do.'

Amy coloured. 'Of course they don't. I'd know, wouldn't I? I live there.'

'Not all the time, you don't. It doesn't have to be at night, you know. They can do it any time. Sometimes I think grown-ups are *vile*.' She kicked savagely at the cloakroom skirting board. 'Mum and I were happy till he came poking his nose in,' she said, her lower lip thrust out to prevent it from trembling. 'I don't know how she can – imagine doing it with someone with a *bald* patch. If you ask me, lousy rotten *men* ruin everything.'

Amy looked thoughtful. 'You've probably got it all wrong. Look,

192

if you don't want to go to your dad's I daresay you could come to us. It'll probably be boring, but at least we could make our own fun.'

Celia looked brighter for a moment, then her jaw dropped again. 'Dad did write to invite me, so I suppose I've got to go. Anyway, I would *quite* like to see him. And if I don't he'll blame Mum.' For a moment the two girls looked glumly at each other, then Celia said: 'Hey, *I* know – shall I ask if you can come too?'

Amy looked doubtful. 'Oh, but wouldn't that be a bit of a cheek?'

'I don't see why,' Celia said defiantly. 'After all, Dad will have this ghastly *Candice* person, so why shouldn't I have someone too?'

'Well – I won't ask Mum till you've asked yours,' Amy said cautiously. 'Just in case.'

But the following morning Celia arrived at school wreathed in smiles. 'It's okay,' she announced. 'Mum thought it was a marvellous idea. She phoned Dad and asked him and he's happy too. He'll be busy at the theatre with the Christmas show, so he'll be pleased for me to have a friend for company.'

Amy felt a little thrill of excitement. 'I'll ask Mum tonight.'

'No need.' Celia grinned. 'My mum is ringing her this morning. She can be very persuasive, can Mum. It'll be all right, you just see.' She grasped Amy's arm. 'We're to go up to Northmere by train on the twenty-second. That's on Saturday – so you'd better start packing tonight.'

But Maryan had reservations about letting her daughter go to Northmere for Christmas. When Amy arrived home from school, bubbling with excitement and wanting to know if Mrs Frazer had telephoned, she found her mother looking anxious and doubtful.

'I know you want to be with your new friend,' Maryan said. 'But we don't really know these people at all, do we?'

Amy scowled with resentment. 'We didn't know the Taylors when I went to Rhensham, did we?'

'That was different, Amy. The war was on. We didn't have any choice.'

'Yes, it *was* different,' Amy pointed out. 'I was there with them for over five years and I'm only going to Celia's dad's for a week.'

'It's quite a long way too,' Maryan persisted, ignoring the argument.

'Only an hour and a half on the train – about the same as Suffolk.'

Maryan sighed. 'It's the first Christmas we've been together for such a long time, Amy,' she said. 'I thought you would be looking forward to it as much as I am. We've been invited to go to Roisan's.'

193

Amy felt slightly relieved. 'Oh, well – there you are then. You won't be on your own, will you?'

'Would it have worried you if I had been? Anyway, that's not really the point.' Maryan looked directly at her and Amy coloured and turned away. 'Amy – what's wrong?' Maryan reached out to touch the girl's shoulder. 'It's nearly five months now since you came home and we haven't really settled down together at all, have we?'

'Haven't we?' Amy shrugged.

'You know we haven't. We don't even talk to each other properly, do we?'

'What would we talk about?' Amy asked sullenly, shrugging off her mother's hand. 'There's nothing to say, is there?'

'Of course there is,' Maryan protested. 'I'm interested in what you're doing at school. I thought you might be interested in what I'm doing too. You seemed to be interested in the shop when Vinnie showed you round that time.'

'It's all right,' Amy said laconically. She turned and looked at her mother. 'Are you saying I can't go to Celia's dad's then, or what?'

Maryan sighed. 'All I'm saying is . . .'

'He's a stage manager at the Theatre Royal in Northmere,' Amy interrupted. 'Celia says he'll take us behind the scenes and everything. And we'll have free seats for the Christmas show. They're doing *The Sleeping Beauty*. Oh, *please* let me go, Mum.'

Maryan looked at Amy's shining eyes and pleading expression. If she were to say yes, would it improve the sadly impaired relationship between them? She sometimes felt she'd do anything to get closer to this strangely aloof young person who was her daughter. She had hoped that Christmas might bring them closer. The special present she'd chosen with such care; a visit to a West End pantomime; Christmas Day at Roisan's. Amy had taken to Vinnie's sister. She was always at her best when they went there. She'd planned it all so carefully. But it seemed that all Amy wanted was to spend the holiday in some sooty little industrial town in the Midlands with people she hardly knew. Well – if it meant so much to her . . .

'All right then,' she said. 'But if you . . .' Amy didn't wait to hear the rest of the sentence. With a yelp of delight she was already on her way to her bedroom to begin packing.

The Frazers' home was a rambling Regency villa in the centre of the town. It was one of three such villas which stood at the end of the town's best shopping street. It wasn't at all what Amy had imagined and she wondered why they had lived in such a large house.

'It was my gran's house,' Celia explained as the girls unpacked. 'When she got too old to manage it and moved to a smaller house Mum and Dad moved in here. Gran used to take in lodgers; mostly actors from the theatre, and Mum did that too when we lived here.

Celia's father, a stout, rather harassed looking man with a thatch of sandy hair and the same blue eyes as Celia, had met them at the station, brought them home to Arncliffe House and left again in a hurry, explaining that he was due at the theatre for a matinée. Celia took Amy upstairs to her old room, which they were to share. It was a large room on the second floor. From the dormer window there was a wonderful view over the rooftops to the park and the river beyond. There were two single beds, pushed under the sloping ceiling; between them were shelves on which sat several rather battered dolls and teddies as well as a dozen or more books. Kneeling on the floor, Amy looked at the titles – *Winnie The Pooh*; *Just William*; *Alice in Wonderland* – all of them well remembered favourites.

'Didn't you want to take any of these with you?' she asked. Celia shrugged. 'Mum said there wasn't room. Anyway, they're a bit babyish, aren't they? I'm reading *Forever Amber* at the moment. I'll lend it to you when I've finished it if you like.' She finished her unpacking and held out her hand. 'Come on, I'll show you the rest of the house.'

Amy was impressed. She liked the wide staircase with its elegant curved balustrade, the long windows and the high moulded ceilings. The place had a romantic air of faded grandeur that appealed to her imagination.

There were six bedrooms, most of them now shrouded in dust sheets. Downstairs, on either side of the spacious hallway, there were a dining room and an enormous drawing room that ran the whole length of the house, with a large window at each end and a massive marble fireplace.

'We used to have parties in here,' Celia told her. 'At weekends. While the war was on Mum used to have a lot of American friends. It was good fun. But when Dad came home all that changed. He doesn't like parties much and I think he was a bit jealous. Once he accused Mum of – you know – *carrying on*.'

'And – did she?' Amy asked.

Celia looked thoughtful. 'I don't think so. I never saw anything. Mind you, one of them used to bring her an awful lot of presents, and when men give women presents it usually only means one thing.'

'What's that?' Amy asked.

Celia gave her a pitying look. 'Oh, *be* your age, Amy. *Services rendered* and all that. Like old baldy Reg. Anyway, Mum used to say how was she to know that Dad hadn't been carrying on while he was away?'

She led the way back out into the hall and closed the door. 'It looks as though Dad only uses the kitchen now he's on his own. I don't blame him. It's the warmest place in the house. It's hard to keep a place this size warm in the winter. I expect you've noticed. He'll probably sell up when the divorce comes through. That's what Mum says anyway. Then perhaps we'll have some money again.'

Later Celia's father came home again, bringing with him his new girlfriend, Candice, who, it turned out, was the new wardrobe mistress at the theatre. She was a little mouse of a woman with blonde hair and pinched features. Her nose was pink as though she suffered from a permanent cold. She wore a mouse-coloured fur coat and a chiffon scarf over her hair. And she carried a bulging shopping bag, which she began to unpack onto the kitchen table.

Celia nudged Amy. 'She looks like Mrs Tiggywinkle,' she whispered.

Celia's father, less harassed now that the matinee was over, turned out to be quite jovial, and Amy noticed for the first time that he spoke with a slight Scottish accent. He insisted that she must call him Jock, which she found acutely embarrassing until later, when she discovered that theatre people hardly ever used surnames at all.

Candice took off her coat to reveal an unfashionable mustard-coloured wool dress. The scarf had flattened the limp blonde hair so that it clung to her head like damp cotton wool. From the shopping bag she unpacked the ingredients for a surprisingly good meal, which she cooked and served to the four of them in the barn-like kitchen where a huge black range threw out a welcome heat. Jock Frazer kept up a flow of cheerful chatter all through the meal, questioning Celia about her new school and commenting on how much she'd grown, trying unsuccessfully to drag the obviously shy Candice into the conversation. As soon as the meal was over he and Candice left for the theatre once again, leaving the girls to clear away.

Celia looked ruefully at Amy as they shared the washing-up. 'A good thing you came with me,' she said. 'Wouldn't have been a barrel of fun on my own by the looks of it.'

That night, enjoying the novelty of sharing a room, the girls lay talking long after the light was out.

'Have you got a boyfriend?' Celia asked.

'No. Well, not unless you count Mike,' Amy said.

196

'Mike? Who's he? You've never mentioned him before,' Celia said eagerly.

'Michael Taylor. He's seventeen and he's going to college in the new year. He wants to be a journalist like his father. He's the son of the lady I was evacuated with in Suffolk.'

'Wow, *seventeen*,' Celia said, impressed. 'Is he handsome? Has he kissed you?'

'I suppose he is *quite* handsome,' Amy said thoughtfully. 'No, he's never kissed me. I've known him since I was seven. He's more like a brother than a boyfriend.'

'Got any photos?

'Yes, I've got some snaps at home.'

'You *must* show me when we go back. There used to be a boy here that I liked,' Celia said wistfuly. 'I thought I might see him this Christmas. He's probably found someone else by now, though.' She raised herself to lean on one elbow, peering at Amy through the darkness. 'What did you think of Candice Tiggywinkle then?'

'She's all right. She's a good cook.'

'Well, she must have *something*, I suppose,' Celia said scathingly. 'Dad seems besotted. Did you notice, his eyes went all gooey when he looked at her. God knows why. I think she's really wet. Can't see what he sees in her. Mum is much prettier – *and* smarter. That awful dress. I wonder if they'll really get married,' she mused. 'Hey – Amy, I've just had a gruesome thought – do you think she and Dad are too old to have more babies?' But Amy wasn't thinking at all. She'd fallen asleep.

What had started out as a slight disappointment for Amy turned into a week of sheer delight. The Christmas show at the Theatre Royal was to open on Boxing Day and Jock took both girls along to the dress rehearsal on the afternoon of Christmas Eve. Going in through the stage door, Amy found herself in a strange new world. Above her head, surrounded by a wooden gallery, was the scenic studio, from which the smell of varnish, paint and size floated down. Down a flight of stairs she found herself in a corridor with numbered doors – dressing rooms, she was told. The corridor gave onto the huge, cluttered prop room, which was like an Aladdin's cave, containing everything you could possibly imagine from table lamps to fire irons. In one corner she saw a rocking horse and an elephant's foot umbrella holder. In another hung a human skeleton, draped in an old net curtain. This was Jock Frazer's domain. He introduced Amy to his band of stage hands; a cheerful group of men in shirtsleeves

197

who showed Amy their own designated corner with a card table and gas ring where they brewed up tea and played cards between acts.

From the prop room they stepped out into the area that was the stage. Amy looked up to a forest of ropes and pulleys and batons of different coloured lights.

'Those are the flies,' Jock told her. 'All the drops – curtains and backcloths – are worked from there. And that . . .' He pointed to an opening high up. 'That is called the perch. It's where the lighting technician sits. From up there he can turn day into night and sunlight into storm clouds, all with his magic switchboard. He works most of the special effects from there too.'

Taking Amy by the hand, Jock led her through the wings and out onto the centre of the stage itself. The fire curtain was raised and she found herself looking out onto the orchestra pit and, beyond it, row upon row of empty red plush seats.

'Why does the stage slope?' she asked him, looking down at her feet.

'It's called the rake,' Jock explained. 'It was designed so that the audience could see the performers better, but you only find it in old theatres. Newer ones have better seating arrangements so it isn't necessary. And those are the footlights.' He pointed to the row of lights at the edge of the stage. 'If those were lit you wouldn't be able to see anything beyond them at all.'

'It's lovely,' Amy breathed.

Jock looked down at her. 'Ever been on a stage before?'

'I was in a play when I was at my old school,' she told him. '*Twelfth Night*. I played Viola.'

Jock looked impressed. 'Quite a part for someone as young as you. Did you enjoy it?'

'Oh, yes. But I'd like to be in a play in a real theatre like this,' she told him.

She was enthralled by everything she saw and when she and Celia took their places in the front row of the stalls to watch the dress rehearsal she completely lost herself in the sheer delight of it all. It was so much better than just seeing the finished show. The ordinary looking people she had seen arriving by the stage door, wrapped against the cold in scarves and mackintoshes, were transformed into ethereal fairy-tale characters in glittering costumes and fantastic make-up.

Watching as the rehearsal progressed she was fascinated to see how all the imperfections were ironed out and put right by the director. She was so impressed by the professionalism of real live

198

actors. The technical side of it absorbed her too; the lighting effects that could turn dull sacking into cloth of gold and a curtain of coarse grubby gauze into a mystical starlit mist. Then there was the music; the songs, worked at painstakingly over and over again, until the musical director was satisfied that they were as good as he and the actors could make them.

And the treat did not end with the end of the rehearsal. When the final scene was finished the girls went backstage again to have tea with the cast, some of them still in their costumes and make-up. Amy thought it was the most exciting day of her entire life. And if she had ever felt any doubt about what the future held for her it was completely erased during that magical afternoon.

'I'm going to be an actress when I leave school,' she whispered to Celia that night when they were in bed.

Celia laughed. 'You must be joking,' she said. 'There isn't any money in it. Ask any of them. If you ask them they all say they don't know why they do it.'

Amy said nothing. She knew why they did it. Because there was nothing else on earth that was so exciting and glamorous; because no one in their right mind could possibly want to do anything else, that was why. As she fell asleep she suddenly realised that she had completely forgotten that it was Christmas tomorrow. Nothing could possibly compare to the excitement of today. Surely when you were an actress every day must feel like Christmas. And she couldn't *wait* to leave school and begin.

Vincent ran down the basement stairs to where Roisan was making coffee in the kitchen.

'Don't bother with coffee for us. I've just rung for a taxi. I'm taking Maryan home. Oh, and don't wait up. I might be late.'

'All right Vinnie,' she said quietly. 'I suppose what you're really saying is that you might not come home at all.'

He stopped in his tracks and turned to face her. 'Don't look like that, Roisan. Surely you can see how I feel about Maryan. You like her too, don't you?'

She looked at him. 'Yes I do. I like her very much. But you're not being fair to her, Vinnie.'

'She knows the situation. We're neither of us children, Roisan. You surely don't grudge me a little happiness, do you?'

'I don't grudge either of you anything. I just think you're running your head – *and* hers – into disaster. If you thought as much of her as you say you do, you wouldn't be letting it go on. Do you want to see her hurt?' She stood facing him, her blue eyes looking into his in that disconcerting way she had. 'And what about that child of hers? Have you stopped to consider her at all?'

He sighed. 'She's away with her friend. You know that. You surely don't think either Maryan or I would risk her knowing . . .'

'*Knowing* – knowing what? That you're sleeping with her mother? You – a married man?'

He winced. 'You have a positive genius for making things seem sordid.'

'So what else would you call it?'

He sank wearily onto a chair at the kitchen table. 'Don't spoil it, Roisan. Maryan has made such a difference to me. She's given me back my life. It's been a hell of a long time since I've felt this happy. Is that such a crime?'

Relenting, she sat down opposite him and reached out to touch his hand. 'Ah, Vinnie – I know how unhappy you've been in the past, but you've got such a gem in Maryan. She's taken to the business like a duck to water. You don't want to ruin everything and lose her, just when the interior decorating side of the business is taking off so well and you need her at the shop, do you?'

'I shan't lose her. I'll make sure I don't. She's more to me than just an employee, Roisan. Don't you understand, I love her – really love her.'

'Well, if you really feel that serious, and if she feels the same, maybe you should get in touch with Fay and ask her for a divorce.'

He looked up at her with startled eyes. 'I never thought I'd hear you say a thing like that.'

She lifted her shoulders. 'We live in a changing world, Vinnie. The war has broken so many marriages. Maybe it's time for a change. Fay left you. It was she who did wrong and not you. It isn't fair that you should be forced to sin when you could marry the woman you love.'

'*Sin?*' he got to his feet. 'I don't see loving Maryan as a sin.'

'You know as well as I do that it is – while you're still married to Fay. There's no getting away from it.' She looked at him. 'Do you still go to confession? Have you talked to a priest about how you feel and what you're doing?' When he avoided her eyes she rose and went back to the Aga. Taking the percolater off the hotplate she said: 'It seems to me that you've given up your faith anyway, so why cling to the old rules? Ah well, I've said what I think, and probably too much at that. Now it's up to you. I think I can hear your taxi outside. You'd better go.'

He stood where he was, reluctant to leave in disagreement. 'Come up and say goodnight to us properly, Roisan. Maryan wants to thank you for the lovely Christmas you've given us. She'll think it odd if you don't come.'

Roisan turned to look at him and saw the silent plea in his eyes. It said: *Please don't send me away like this.* Ever since he was a small boy she could never resist that look. She sighed. 'Of course I'll come and say goodnight,' she said. 'But I'll not change my opinion, Vinnie, so don't you be thinking I will.'

Upstairs in the hall Maryan was buttoning her coat. She held out her arms to Roisan. 'Thank you for such a wonderful day,' she said. 'Dinner was delicious. I'm sure I won't be able to eat another thing till New Year.' The two women hugged each other warmly and Roisan stood on tiptoe to kiss her brother's cheek. As she patted his arm she whispered: 'Remember what I said.'

She stood at the front door and waved to them as they got into the taxi and drove away, her heart full of doubt and foreboding. In her experience, taking what you wanted when you had no right to it only led to one thing. You usually found yourself paying a far higher price than you could afford. But she'd had her say. There was nothing more she could do.

At Simons Mews Vincent paid the driver and went inside with Maryan. Upstairs, the flat was cold after being empty all day, but Maryan switched on the electric fire and drew the curtains.

'I'll make some coffee,' she said. 'Or would you prefer tea?'

Vincent came to her and slipped his arms around her waist. 'Neither,' he whispered huskily against her neck. 'All I want is you. His kiss betrayed the hunger he felt for her and she put her arms around him, grateful for his warm masculine strength – for his love and his wanting her.

'Oh, darling, it seems so long,' he said, his lips against her throat. 'I want you – need you so much. I wish we could be together always.'

In the bedroom they undressed silently and climbed into bed, shivering a little under the cool touch of one another's hands. Holding him close, Maryan felt a pang of guilt at being glad they had the flat to themselves. She had longed so much to have Amy back with her, but she was finding it hard going, re-establishing her role as Amy's mother. That and the strain of hiding her deepening relationship with Vinnie was beginning to take its toll of her nerves.

Tonight the world was theirs, though. In their first eager need of each other the act of love was swift and quickly over. But as they lay in each other's arms, growing warm and relaxed under the covers, kissing and caressing in the luxury of solitude, they soon became aroused again. And this time their lovemaking was unhurried and wonderful. It seemed to Maryan that each time they made love it was even more perfect than the last. She had known only two men in her life: Marcus, with whom love had been consummated only once and so briefly that she had scarcely had time to realise what was happening, and Tom. Poor, dear Tom, to whom she had never truly given herself. In Vinnie she could lose herself completely. With him she could let the heartache of the past go. He made her feel alive and free in a way she had never known before.

After the launch of the Marcus Leigh Collection every newspaper she picked up had been full of his name. There were countless stories of Marcus's tragic marriage and his bravery – his wife's untimely death and later, his own. Vincent had taken the sting out of it all for her, made her forget with his patient, loving tenderness until the hurt lessened and the gaping wounds healed over. She had been grateful to him for that alone, but soon her gratitude had blossomed into love. The sweetest, most fulfilling love she had ever known.

What had been leisurely lovemaking developed into a hungry passion as it approached climax. Maryan felt the familiar pulsating surge of sensation and arched upwards towards him, wanting to give all of herself, offering him her heart and soul as well as her body. Together they reached a stunning crescendo that left them both gasping and clinging to each other, and Maryan felt tears of joy well up inside her.

'Oh, Vinnie, Vinnie, I love you,' she said softly, her lips against his cheek.

He raised his head to look down at her. 'You've never said it before,' he said. 'If you only knew how much I've wished you would. I love you too, my darling. But I'm sure you know that by now.'

For a long time they lay quietly together, languorous with assuaged love, weightless with relaxation. Then with a resigned sigh Vincent roused himself and began to get up.

'I suppose I'd better go.'

Maryan reached out to pull him down again. 'Oh, please, not yet. Stay a little longer. There's nothing to prevent you staying till morning – is there?'

He lay back against the pillows with a sigh. 'Roisan knows about us. Oh, I didn't say a word. She guessed – in the way that sisters have of guessing what their younger brothers are getting up to.'

'She disapproves?' He nodded and Maryan looked up at him. 'Of me?'

'No, not of you.' He smiled, stroking her hair back from her face. 'Don't look like that my love. It isn't you she's angry with. It's me.'

'Because of . . .?'

'Yes. She actually suggested tonight that I should get a divorce. I never thought I'd hear her say a thing like that.'

Maryan held her breath. 'And – what did you say?'

He sighed. 'In divorcing Fay I'd automatically renounce my faith.'

'How can anyone *automatically* renounce their faith?' she asked. 'Surely whatever you do it can make no difference to the way you feel – what you believe in.'

He shook his head. 'I'm afraid the church doesn't see it quite that simply. And in spite of what Roisan thinks, it does still matter to me. But if Fay were to admit misconduct and desertion . . .'

There was a pause before Maryan said tentatively: 'Do you think she would?'

He shrugged. 'Who knows?'

She paused, searching his face with her eyes. 'But – maybe that isn't what you want, Vinnie.'

He reached out to pull her almost fiercely into his arms. 'Anything that would mean you and I could be married; could be together properly for always, is what I want. Surely you know that.'

'So – what happens next? Will you ask her?'

The question hung in the air between them. Vincent said: 'I could try. Knowing Fay, though, she'll probably refuse, especially if she gets an inkling of what it means to me. I refused to give her a divorce when she left, you see. On religious grounds, of course. She'll certainly throw that in my face.'

'Oh, Vinnie, what are we going to do?' Maryan felt a sudden despair. Why were there always such insurmountable barriers to happiness for her? Why did she always fall in love with men she couldn't have? Must she always have to steal love shamefully and secretly, like a thief? She had more than just herself to consider too. There was Amy.

'Why is life so difficult?' she asked him. 'I have to think of Amy. How will she react to it all? Since we've been together again she's been so difficult. It's been five months now and I seem to be getting nowhere with her. I never expected it to be easy, but I've tried so hard, Vinnie. Sometimes I think she hates me.'

He pulled her close. 'Don't be silly. Why should she hate you?'

'I don't know. I think she feels I've let her down in some way. Maybe I should have found a way for us to be together during the war. I did try once, but she didn't want to leave the Taylors.'

'Maybe you've been too soft with her, Maryan. I'll admit that there've been times when I've had to bite my tongue not to say something to her. The way she speaks to you sometimes makes me see red.'

Maryan shook her head. 'I try to make allowances. I'm afraid she isn't happy. But why? I'm her mother. I should be able to make her happy, shouldn't I?'

'She doesn't seem to feel any obligation to try to please you,' he said. 'It seems to me that all the trying is on your side. Maybe if you started thinking of yourself more . . .'

She shook her head. 'Perhaps you're right. I don't know.'

'Roisan is afraid I'll hurt you,' he said softly. 'I don't want to make any more problems for you, Maryan. Maybe she's right. Maybe I'm not being fair to you.'

'Shhh.' She put her fingers over his lips, then replaced them with her lips. 'At the moment you are the only brightness in my life,' she told him, her mouth moving against his. 'You've given me so much; a home, a wonderfully interesting job. And best of all, your trust and your love. Let's not think too much about the future. Let's just be grateful for what we have.'

They lay for a while at peace in each other's arms, then Vincent said: 'Talking of work, I've got something for you to do the day after tomorrow.'

'You have? What is it?'

'There's a big country house sale down in Sussex. From what I've seen of the catalogue there are some nice pieces to be had. The preview is in the morning, auction in the afternoon. I thought we'd go. Take a packed lunch perhaps. No one will expect the shop to open till Friday anyway.'

'That sounds like fun.'

'Yes, but this time there's going to be a difference.'

She raised herself on one elbow to look at him. 'What kind of difference?'

'This time it's going to be all up to you. You choose the pieces we go for, and you do the bidding.'

She stared at him, wide-eyed with apprehension. 'Oh, Vinnie, I *daren't*. I'm not ready.'

'Yes you are. You've been to plenty of sales with me. You know how it works and I believe you've learned enough about the business now to know what to look for.' She looked doubtful and he added: 'You have to take the plunge sometime, my love. Especially as I'm planning to put you in charge of buying eventually.'

'But – suppose I make a mistake – an expensive one?'

He laughed. 'Easy, I'll fire you.'

'Then I'd better look out, hadn't I?'

He reached out to squeeze her hand reassuringly. 'We'll go through the list of requirements for the jobs on hand tomorrow, so that you can see what we're looking for. Any *mistakes* as you call them can always go into the shop.' He reached across to kiss her. 'But you won't make any mistakes. I'm sure of that. I've got faith in you.' He reached out his hand to switch off the bedside light. 'And now, in case you don't know it, it's two a.m. We'd better get some sleep. Goodnight, my love.'

With a happy sigh, Maryan snuggled close to him in the warm darkness and closed her eyes. 'Goodnight, darling.'

Sam was happy. Mainly because Rachel was happy. He hadn't seen her looking so well or so radiantly fulfilled since before the war. The Marcus Leigh Collection had exceeded even her hopes for it.

The launch last September had been an enormous success. The press had been especially generous to them, taken as much with the story behind the collection as with the designs themselves. The romance of Marcus's wartime heroism, and the designs, created in secret for the beautiful young wife he had lost so tragically in childbirth, had made a wonderful story. Sometimes Sam worried a little that they might be exploiting their tragic loss, but Rachel clearly didn't see it that way.

The whole venture had been her salvation, and for that reason alone Sam was deeply grateful. He reasoned that Marcus would have wished for this outcome. He would surely have been pleased to see his designs becoming so successful. And he would certainly have chosen this way in which to be remembered.

Sam often thought about Maryan and Amy. He would have liked to see them both, but he curbed the desire. If Rachel found out she would be upset. He had paid Amy's new term's fees in advance and in return had received a letter from Maryan, thanking him and saying that Amy liked her new school and was doing well. Perhaps some day he would find the opportunity to see his granddaughter. But not if it meant disturbing Rachel. She had made it clear that she would never believe that the child had been fathered by Marcus and he knew that nothing he could say would ever persuade her otherwise. Best to let sleeping dogs lie.

Their son's prolonged absence during the war and, later, his terrible death had almost destroyed them both, but Rachel had suffered most; her grief aggravated by Maryan's revelation. There had been a time when Sam had feared for her sanity. It was nothing short of a miracle, the way she had discovered the designs and decided to promote and follow them through. It was almost as though some divine hand had been at work, giving Rachel help and strength at the very time when she needed it so desperately.

After the launch, most of the original designs had been ordered by exclusive little boutiques in and around London, but some of the large West End stores had bought a selection too. Now Gina Stern was working hard on a new summer collection, to be shown in early spring. Next year people would be thinking of holidays again. Summer outfits would need to be frivolous and gay, frothy and carefree. And the drawings Gina was creating were certainly all of those things. She had chosen light, colourful fabrics, designed romantic swirling skirts and flattering feminine tops with pretty sleeves. Rachel was delighted with the young designer's work. And it gave Sam a secret glow of pride that at last the garments that were receiving such acclaim bore the name of Leigh instead of Feldman.

After V-J Day Sam had suggested that they might move back to Hackney. He had re-established the Feldman Fashions' factory as soon as the bombing ceased so that he could re-employ some of his old workers who had remained in London and been thrown out of work by the bombing. But Rachel seemed reluctant to go back. He understood that the house held many sad memories for her. It was the same for him of course. But it had been the first home of their own they had shared. He had bought it for Rachel when, together, they had made Feldman's successful. And she had put so much of herself into making it theirs. It seemed so sad to let it go. On the other hand, there was a good train service from Hazelfield. It was pleasant in the country and they had both become accustomed to the peace and fresh air. If it made Rachel happy to stay there, then so be it.

On one of his thrice weekly visits to London he decided to do something positive about the neglected house and he went along to an agent and put 124 Hackney Road on the market. He also arranged for a firm of house clearers to empty it. When they moved to Hazelfield at the beginning of the war they had taken everything they valued with them. And Sam knew that Marcus's belongings had been cleared by Rachel herself. The rest could go. Let the past be buried, he told himself. So many people had suffered loss through the war. At least he and Rachel still had each other. And if she could make a new start, then he would too.

It was on the train journey home that Amy made a startling discovery. As the train chugged through the frosty countryside Celia happened to mention that her grandmother was contributing towards her school fees. Amy looked surprised.

'I passed my scholarship exam,' she said proudly.

'So did I,' Celia retorted. 'But St Hil's is a private school. Mum didn't like any of the London schools I could have transferred to, so Gran said she'd help her pay for me to go to St Hil's.'

Amy was silent. So Mum had lied to her about that too. Someone must be paying her fees and if not Mum, then who? And why was Mum keeping it from her?

'Didn't you know it was private?' Celia asked.

Amy shook her shoulders. ''Course I did. I just forgot,' she said dismissively.

As it was Saturday afternoon and as Maryan was working, Anne Frazer had offered to meet both girls off the train. The taxi dropped Amy off at the end of Simons Mews and she waved goodbye to her friend, then made her way gloomily towards the shop. Maryan had already closed for the night and the place was in darkness except for the one streetlamp near the side entrance. Finding the door on the latch, Amy made her way up the stairs. She felt dreary and flat. Her brief, thrilling sojourn in the world of the theatre was over and so, almost, were the Christmas holidays. School started again in a few days' time. Although she quite liked school the thought of the new term made her heart sink. It was all so dull and routine.

At the top of the stairs she paused in the narrow hallway. She could hear voices, her mother's and Vincent's. In contrast to her own mood they sounded in high spirits.

'I'm so proud of you,' Vincent said. 'You did wonderfully well. Getting that Regency table for the price you did was a real coup. I can soon fix that little bit of damage. I think we'll have to arrange some driving lessons for you next. Then you can take the van along to sales and save us the delivery costs. I'll have to make arrangements at the bank too, so that you can sign cheques.'

Amy had been about to step into the room, but something made her stop. There was an abrupt silence and even out in the hall she could feel the highly charged atmosphere. Instinctively she knew that they were embracing. Shrinking back, she stood for a moment in the shadows. After a moment she heard Maryan say breathlessly: 'Oh, Vinnie, you're so good to me.'

'*I* am. What about you?' came the reply, so soft that Amy barely heard it. 'I can't tell you how wonderful these last few nights alone together have been. It's going to be torture, having to leave you and go home to a lonely bed tonight.'

Amy slipped back down the stairs, her heart beating dully and a huge lump in her throat. So that was it. It must be Vincent who was paying her school fees. Paying them in return for – what was the phrase Celia had used? *For services rendered.* She shuddered. At the bottom of the stairs she opened the street door again and banged it hard. Then she began to ascend the stairs again, making as much noise as she could.

Maryan appeared at the stairhead, her face flushed and her eyes unusually bright. 'Amy. You're home then? Did you have a lovely time?'

Amy nodded, pushing past her mother unsmilingly. 'Smashing, thanks. Did you?'

Amy lay awake for a long time that night, thinking over her latest discoveries and wondering what to do. Once again there were two alternatives. She could demand to be told the truth about her school fees and make a fuss about her mother's relationship with Vincent, or she could keep quiet. If she made a fuss it might mean that Mum would be forced to give up her job. And that would mean the flat too. They would lose their pleasant, comfortable home. Amy thought of the horrid little house in Crimea Terrace and shuddered at the thought of returning to somewhere like that. Then again, if she made a stand about Vincent paying the school fees she might have to leave St Hildred's; change schools and go to one of the ones Celia had told her about; a school where there might be no drama or music lessons – and certainly no Celia. It would probably even be full of Lily Smiths. Was it worth it? No, she told herself decisively. She had to think of herself from now on. Herself, and her plan for the future.

She rolled restlessly onto her other side and listened to the wind as it rattled the window and tossed the dry leaves about in the mews outside. For a moment she felt like those little heaps of dry, used-up leaves. Useless and forgotten, unwanted, just cluttering the place up. She chewed a corner of the pillowcase thoughtfully. For the moment she had little choice other than to go along with her mother's bewildering behaviour – fall in with the promiscuity, lies and deceit if she wanted the best from life. But one day, she promised herself; one day she *would* have a choice. One day she would be someone special instead of just a child who was in the way. When she was a famous actress people would admire and look up to her. They'd be standing in a line to know her then. It wasn't just a dream either. She would *make* it happen – somehow.

Chapter Twelve

Mike's letter came a week before St Hildred's broke up for the summer holidays. Amy hadn't had a letter from him for some time and as soon as she recognised the distinctive chunky handwriting she tore it open eagerly. His news was mainly about his first year of college, which he seemed to be enjoying, but he went on to say that his mother was giving him a party for his eighteenth birthday on 4 August. He hoped that Amy would be able to come, and perhaps stay on with them for a few days.

Excited at the prospect of a visit to Rhensham, Amy passed the letter to her mother at once, watching her face anxiously for the necessary permission. Maryan read it through to the end and then looked up.

'I don't need to ask you if you want to go, do I?' she said with a rueful smile.

'Oh, *can* I? It'd be lovely to see Mike and Auntie Marjorie again,' Amy said. 'I've been wondering what on earth I was going to do once school broke up.'

Actually the invitation was a blessing as far as Maryan was concerned. She'd been telling herself that she really should try to take Amy away for a holiday of some kind, but she hadn't an idea how to fit it in. Vincent would gladly give her the time off, she knew that, but doing so would be bound to make things difficult for him. Besides, there was so much she wanted to do. Ever since spring she'd been taking driving lessons and she was due to take her test in August. After that she'd be able drive herself to and from sales independently in the van Vincent had bought for the business.

Then there was the shop, now fully stocked and doing a steady trade. Once the antique-loving public had rediscovered Vincente's they had had a flow of regular customers and Maryan was kept busy cataloguing and pricing the stock and keeping the books straight, as

209

well as attending to customers and dealers.

Last spring Vincent and Roisan had divided the business into two separate parts. Vincente Antiques still operated from Simons Mews and was run by Maryan, helped by Paul, the personable young apprentice Vincent had recently engaged, who looked after the shop when Maryan was occupied elsewhere. Decor Vincente was run from Roisan's home, where a secretary had been employed to deal with bookings and enquiries. Roisan had converted one of her ground-floor rooms into an office which the middle-aged, austere Miss Stokes, late of the NAAFI, ran like a well-oiled machine, leaving Roisan free to work away upstairs on her soft-furnishing and colour-scheme planning.

The interior restoration business had gone from strength to strength since that first refurbishment of the Grahams' house. They had a wide circle of friends who, having seen the transformation wrought by Decor Vincente, had positively clamoured to have their own war-tattered homes professionally made over. Vincent was busy from early morning till well into the evening, liaising with clients and supervising his team of painters and decorators. Some weeks Maryan hardly saw him at all, and he had very little time nowadays to spend down in his workshop on the antique restoration work he loved. She didn't even know whether he had managed to get in touch with Fay, regarding their divorce. He hadn't brought the subject up again since Christmas. And Maryan had not liked to broach it herself. She felt that the little time they managed to snatch together was too precious to spend discussing anything so delicate and tenuous.

She began to clear the breakfast table, and for once Amy helped, carrying her own plate, cup and saucer into the kitchen.

'I wonder if they'll think I've grown up at all,' she said, glancing at herself sideways in the mirror as she passed.

'Oh, they're sure to,' Maryan said with a smile. Even living with Amy, seeing her every day, Maryan could see that her daughter had developed dramatically over the past six months. She'd grown so tall, taller now than Maryan herself. And she'd grown her dark hair longer. She wore it curling softly on her shoulders or tied up in a bouncing pony tail. Luckily for Amy, she suffered from none of the usual adolescent problems. Her sapphire-blue eyes and her complexion glowed with health and she had a poise and grace that made her appear older than her fifteen years.

Maryan was very proud of her pretty daughter but she held back from telling her so. There was still a barrier between them that, try as she would, she could not break through. Occasionally they would find something to laugh at together, or a strong view that they

210

shared. There would be moments when they were almost close, when Maryan would feel she had almost beaten down the inexplicable reserve that held them apart. There would be a moment of heartening warmth between them, then Amy's eyes would cloud over and the shutters would go up again. At least this morning she had been able to please Amy; do something to make her smile. If only it could have been she who had been the cause of her happiness and not the Taylors.

At school that morning Amy showed Mike's letter to Celia. 'I'll have a week to get ready and then I'll be going,' she said, her eyes dancing with excitement. 'I can't wait to see them all again.'

'What do you mean, see them *all*?' Celia said, rolling her eyes. 'It's *him* you really want to see, isn't it – Mike? And I can't say I blame you from the look of those snaps you showed me. He's a smasher.'

'Mmm, I wonder if he's changed?' Amy said, looking thoughtfully into the cloakroom mirror and twisting a curl of dark hair round her fingers. 'Mum says I have. What about my hair? Do you think I should have it done in that new bubble cut?'

Celia had had her waist-length plaits shorn earlier that year. It had been her mother's idea, but when she had gone to visit her father at half term and he'd first set eyes on the jaw-length bob his daughter sported he'd been really angry.

'Men seem to like long hair,' Celia said. 'Remember the fuss Dad made when I had mine cut? No, keep it long. It's so pretty. Not poker-straight like mine.' She grinned. 'Mum says she'll treat me to a perm in the hols. It's a sort of consolation prize, because we can't afford to go on holiday.'

Amy looked at her friend wistfully. 'I wish I could take you along to Rhensham, Cee,' she said. 'Like you took me to your dad's last Christmas. I would if it were up to me, but I'm not related to the Taylors so I can't very well.'

'Course you can't. I know that. Don't be silly.' Celia slipped her arm good-naturedly through Amy's. 'I had hoped to go to Dad's when the theatre closes for a week in August, but he and Candice are off for a holiday in France, rotten pigs.'

'Maybe Reg will take you both somewhere,' Amy suggested.

Celia pulled a face. 'Reg hasn't been round for a couple of weeks. Mum says it's over. I miss the chocolate bickies, but I can't say I miss him.' She giggled. 'Never mind, when you get back we'll think of all sorts of mischief to get up to. We'll have to make the best of it. It'll be heads down and full steam ahead for School Cert. in the autumn, so we'd better have a smashing time while we've got the chance.' She grinned. 'If you and this Mike of yours haven't eloped to Gretna Green, that is.'

Amy coloured. 'Oh, *Cee* – how many times do I have to tell you? Mike and I aren't a bit like that. He's just like a brother.'

Celia winked and nudged her in the ribs. 'Go on, pull the other one. You can't fool me.'

Maryan went with Amy to Liverpool Street and saw her onto the train. All the way to Rhensham she sat looking out of the window in a state of high excitement. This felt more like going home than coming back to London had last year. As they crossed the boundary into Suffolk she watched the familiar landmarks slip past. It seemed to take an eternity. But at last here they were, sliding into Rhensham Station. And there was Mike standing on the platform, scanning the carriage windows as they passed him.

Amy could hardly believe how tall he'd grown, or how handsome he looked in his dark grey flannels and tweed jacket. As she stepped down from the train and saw him take the first hesitant step towards her she felt suddenly shy and tongue-tied. By the slightly puzzled expression on his face, he was having some difficulty recognising her. They met and looked at each other. Amy saw with surprise the pale beginnings of a moustache on his upper lip. He wasn't a boy any longer. He was a young man. Then Mike grinned and to her relief she saw that inside it all he was the same old Mike she had always known after all.

'Hello, Amy.'

'Hello, Mike.'

'It's good to see you.' He held out his hand, 'Here, better give me your case. Come on. The car's in the station yard.'

'Oh. Is Auntie Marjorie with you then?'

He smiled condescendingly. 'Heavens, no. I drove here myself. Passed my test in the spring.'

Captain Taylor's 1938 Hillman Minx had been laid up all through the war, but when he came home for good he'd had it overhauled and resprayed. It stood in the station yard looking like new, its dark blue paintwork gleaming in the sunlight. Mike proudly opened the front passenger door for Amy.

'Hop in. I'll just put your case in the boot.'

It felt so strange, being driven to Mitcham Lodge by Mike in the smart blue car. He drove carefully, keeping his eyes on the road all the time and sitting up very straight. Amy could tell he was trying to impress her, showing off a little in the way he always had. She smiled to herself. Nothing much had changed really after all.

At Mitcham Lodge Marjorie came out on the steps to meet them. She hugged Amy warmly, exclaiming at how much she'd grown.

'You're quite the young lady,' she said. 'And so smart in your London clothes. We can't buy anything as fashionable out here in darkest Suffolk and the coupons are always such a problem. We keep waiting for rationing to end but no sign of it yet.' She drew Amy inside the house. 'Now – I'm dying to hear all your news. I've put you in your old room so you're sure to feel at home. Tea's all ready. I can't wait to hear all about your new school and this exciting job of your mother's, so don't be too long, will you?'

Mike carried her case up the stairs and Amy followed him happily. It was almost as though she'd never gone away.

She unpacked her case and carefully hung up the summer dresses she'd brought. At the bottom of the case lay the new party dress. Maryan had insisted on going with her to Regent Street to Dickens and Jones to buy Michael a birthday present. Amy had chosen a smart pen and pencil set and a card to go with it. Afterwards her mother had steered her towards the 'Junior Miss' department, announcing that they must choose something special for her to wear for the party.

Amy took it out of the tissue paper it was packed in and put it on a hanger, shaking out the folds in the long skirt. Then she hung it on the wardrobe door and stood looking at it critically. It was a proper evening dress, the first she'd ever had. Made of crisp white watered silk, it had a heart-shaped neckline, puffed sleeves and a wide sash that tied in a big bow at the back. To go with it Maryan had bought her a pair of silver sandals and a silver ribbon hairband.

Amy stepped back and stared at the dress. She had mixed feelings about it. To begin with, she hadn't wanted her mother to spend so much on her and she knew that Maryan had been saving her clothing coupons for a smart new autumn suit she had her eye on. Deep down, she suspected that Maryan was trying to get round her and she hated the feeling of being indebted to her. To make matters worse, the dress was Maryan's choice too, and secretly Amy thought it was a bit childish. She would have preferred a slinky black velvet number she'd seen in the adult department. She'd even persuaded her mother to let her try it on and been cross and humiliated when Maryan had laughed and announced that it made her look like a little girl dressed up in her granny's cast-offs. She felt quite sure that none of the other girls Mike had invited to the party would be wearing anything as babyish as this. She was going to look like the fairy off the Christmas tree.

Jumping up from the bed suddenly, she pushed the white moire

213

evening frock into the wardrobe and shut the door on it. She wasn't going to let anything spoil her stay at Mitcham Lodge. She'd worry about the dress when the time came.

Downstairs, Marjorie had tea ready with all Amy's favourites. She wanted to know about the new school and Amy assured her that she liked it as much as her old school in Ipswich.

'I believe it's a convent,' Marjorie said.

'How does it feel, having nuns as teachers?' Mike asked, looking slightly superior.

'It felt strange at first,' Amy told him. 'I thought they'd be long-faced and serious all the time, but they're not at all. Some of them are really funny and make us laugh. They do all the things other teachers do too. When Sister Sebastian, the sports mistress, tucks up her habit and plays hockey or tennis she can outrun the best of us. And our dancing mistress, Sister Veronica, can dance like Ginger Rogers.'

Mike and Marjorie laughed at the images created by Amy's descriptions, then Marjorie said: 'I've been reading a lot about this new designer, Marcus Leigh, in the fashion magazines and papers. Are those the same Leighs your mother used to work for?'

Amy felt herself blushing. 'Yes. Mr Marcus was their son. He was killed in the war.'

'I know. I read all about him, poor young man. Such a sad, romantic story,' Marjorie said. 'But the designs he left behind seem to be making a terrific impact on the fashion world. So stunningly smart, and delightfully different from what we've been used to.'

'Yes.' Amy hid her face in her cup.

Over dinner Amy was a little shy with Philip Taylor. He was almost a stranger to her and he looked so completely different in his civilian clothes. But he did his best to be friendly and welcoming. When the meal was over Mike invited her upstairs to what had been the old playroom.

'Mum's turned it into a study for me now,' he told her. 'And I've got a portable radio. Radio Luxembourg is on in the evenings. They play all the latest hits.'

Amy was impressed by the room. The old toys were gone and the bookshelves were full of grown-up books instead of the familiar children's favourites. A carpet had replaced the old linoleum and rugs, there was a new desk over by the window and two armchairs drawn up on either side of the fireplace. Mike looked at her enquiringly.

'Like it?'

'Yes. It's smashing. I miss the old table where we used to paint and do our homework, though.' She walked round the room, touching the new books on the shelves. 'And I miss the old teddies and the rocking horse – and your Meccano set.' She grinned at him. 'Not that you ever let me play with it.'

'They haven't gone,' Mike told her. 'They're all up in the attic. Mum says she's saving them for when I have kids of my own.'

Amy sat down in one of the armchairs. 'Do you like being at college in Ipswich – coming home each evening, or would you rather have gone right away?'

He shrugged. 'I don't mind really.' To Amy's amazement he opened the desk drawer and took out a briar pipe, which he began to fill with tobacco. He cocked a nonchalant eyebrow at her. 'Do you mind if I smoke?'

'Er – no,' she said. 'Does Auntie Marjorie mind?'

He coloured. 'This is my room. I do as I like in here.'

'Oh, I see. Sorry.' She watched, fascinated, as he lit a match and held it to the bowl, puffing furiously, his cheeks growing pink when it became obvious that he was having trouble getting it to light. And when he put it aside and said gruffly, 'Think I'll leave it for now. You probably wouldn't have liked the smell anyway,' she had to bite her lip hard to keep from laughing. Mike sat in the other armchair, one leg draped over the arm.

'So – you've settled down in London after all?'

She shrugged. 'Yes. It's not so bad, I suppose.'

'School Cert. soon, isn't it?'

She pulled a face. 'Next spring. Waste of time really. I've already decided what I'm going to do.'

'What's that?'

'I'm going to be an actress.'

He showed no surprise. 'Well, everyone said you were good as Viola. Matter of fact I've got a job lined up myself.'

'You have?' Amy leaned forward with interest.

'Yes. When I've done my National Service I'm going to the local rag as a trainee reporter.'

'Mike, that's smashing. So you'll still be able to live at home then?'

'Mmmm . . .' He stroked his chin. 'I daresay I'll have to find some digs in Ipswich, I'll have to be on the spot when I'm working. Reporters work all hours, you know. Have to be ready to cover a story at the drop of a hat.'

'Gosh. It sounds exciting.'

He grinned sheepishly. 'Not really. Dad says I'll probably be a dogsbody-cum-tea-boy to begin with – covering the hatch, match and dispatch.'

She frowned. 'The what?'

'Births, marriages and deaths to you.'

She laughed. 'Oh, Mike, it *is* good to be back,' she said. He grinned the old grin.

'Good to have you back.' He looked at her thoughtfully. 'Amy – did you ever get that business sorted out? You know, about this Leigh fellow being your father?'

Amy blushed. 'No. Look, Mike, I've never told anyone but you about that – except Grandma, of course, and you can't count her. I've never mentioned it to Mum and I don't see how I ever can now. You haven't told anyone, have you?'

He shook his head, frowning a little. 'Crumbs no, of course I haven't. I did give you my word, didn't I?'

'I know. Thanks. I just thought . . .'

'His name seems quite big in the fashion world from what I can make out,' Mike went on. 'It seems funny, doesn't it, a chap becoming famous after he dies.'

'Not really,' Amy said. 'A lot of artists and composers get famous long after they're dead, don't they?'

'Doesn't it make you feel odd, though – knowing he was your father, I mean?'

'I haven't thought about it much,' she said. 'There's no point, as no one is ever going to know I'm his daughter. I suppose the best thing I can do is forget all about it, like Grandma said.'

'Yes, but *can* you? I mean, if his name is always going to be cropping up in the papers and so on it won't be easy. And you'll always know, inside yourself, won't you?'

'Yes. I'll always know – inside.' She lowered her eyes for a moment and when she raised them again she was smiling. 'Have you still got the horses, Mike? Can I help you muck out in the morning?'

'*Can* you? We've been saving it up for you. Haven't mucked out for a week specially.'

It was wonderful to be teased again. Her heart full of joy, she threw her cushion at him and he laughed, catching it and throwing it back. 'Hey, we're missing Luxembourg.' He got up and switched on the radio and was rewarded by the strains of 'A Gal in Calico'. He began to snap his fingers in time to the music. 'I like this one. Do you know the words?'

They were still singing along to the record when Marjorie tapped on the door and came in with two steaming cups of cocoa and a plate of biscuits on a tray.

216

She smiled indulgently. 'Come on, you two. Party tomorrow and a late night. Better not stay up too long.'

Amy sipped the hot, sweet brew contentedly. It was wonderful to be home.

Maryan opened her eyes. It was just getting light, but already the sounds of traffic on the King's Road reached her ears through the open window. She turned her head to look at the alarm clock. Five o'clock. Ages before it would be time to get up.

She turned her head to look at Vincent, still soundly sleeping beside her. Last night she had prepared a special dinner for the two of them, by way of a celebration. They hadn't had a chance to be together, undisturbed in the flat since last Christmas. She smiled, remembering how much Vinnie had enjoyed his meal. She hadn't seen him so relaxed for weeks. He really was working much too hard. But, as he told her, there was nothing else for it if they wanted eventually to expand the business. When they could take on more staff, things would get easier.

It had been a warm night and they had sat at the open window, finishing the last of the wine he had brought with him, then they had come to bed. Their lovemaking had been leisurely and ecstatic. It had been almost 3 a.m. when they fell asleep at last. Now Maryan lay relaxed and warm beside him, looking forward to the weekend they would spend together; a weekend Vincent had promised her, free from work or talk of work. A special time just for them.

He stirred a little and she thought he was about to wake, but he settled back into sleep again. She watched his face. He looked younger in repose, his face smoother and less craggy. Although the dark hair had streaks of grey, it was still thick and wavy. But his eyes were his best feature, dark as treacle; brown and melting. When they looked at her in the special way he had, her knees turned to jelly and she could have died for him. She was so lucky. Since Marcus she had been convinced that she would never love another man. Not that this was the carefree love she would have liked it to be. At the back of her mind the worry that never quite left her began to niggle afresh. Had he contacted Fay? Had he actually done anything about a divorce? Would they ever be in a position to marry?

While she was still looking at him, Vincent sighed and suddenly opened his eyes, looking at her for a second uncomprehendingly. Then he reached out and pulled her close.

'Maryan,' he said sleepily. 'I thought I was still dreaming for a

217

moment.' He sighed contentedly. 'So – what are we going to do today?'

'I don't mind – don't care, just as long as we can be together.'

'In that case, let's just stay right here in bed.' He laughed. 'I can see that I'm shocking you. No, I'm only teasing – I think.' He laughed light-heartedly. 'It looks like a grand morning. We could do anything you like.' He sat up and stretched luxuriously. 'I know. Why don't we take the van and have a run down to the coast – Southend?'

Maryan's heart gave a jerk. She hadn't been to Southend since before the war, not since that memorable Bank Holiday with Marcus. '*No*,' she said sharply. 'I mean – I don't fancy the seaside. It'll be so terribly crowded at this time of year. Let's go somewhere quieter.'

'Ever been to Hampton Court?' he asked. She shook her head. 'Right, then that's where we'll go. Get dressed in your Sunday best and we'll be away.'

'I'll pack some sandwiches.'

'You will not. We'll find a quiet little hotel and have lunch. This is our special day, remember?' He bent to kiss her. 'I love you, Maryan.'

'I love you too,' she whispered.

Hampton Court was a revelation to Maryan as they wandered hand in hand through the magnificent state rooms. She gazed in awe at the brocade hangings, the pictures and tapestries, the beautiful, centuries-old furniture. Just fancy a man giving a palace like this to the woman he loved. Not that any of his loves lasted long. Poor Henry. From what Maryan could make out, Henry VIII had the worst kind of luck, always falling in love with the wrong woman. Vincent laughed when she said so.

'He just wanted an heir to the throne,' he said. 'It wasn't anything to do with love.'

'But surely he must have loved some of them?' Maryan argued. 'Anne Boleyn and Catherine Howard, for instance. I read about them in one of the books you lent me.'

'Books – even history books – don't always reflect real life,' Vincent said. 'If he really loved them how could he bear to order their execution, whatever they'd done? Personally I've always thought Henry a manipulative, self-indulgent lout; bringing people's lives and everything they'd lived for crashing down, simply for his own ends. Think of the good people he murdered merely for their beliefs; the monasteries he overthrew.'

'I suppose so.' Maryan shuddered. 'I'm glad I didn't live then.'

She was reminded suddenly that Vinnie was a Catholic. Little wonder he felt no great sympathy for Henry VIII.

Having explored the palace, they came out into the sunlight and went into the maze, losing themselves and laughing helplessly as they tried this way and that. They wandered round the grounds for a while, appreciating their much cherished leisure and each other's company. But by the time they got back into the van for the drive home Maryan could contain her curiosity no longer. All the talk of divorce and the Catholic church had brought the subject that was never out of her mind to the surface. Knowing that she had to know, one way or the other, she turned to him.

'Vinnie, I've been meaning to ask you. Did you ever manage to get in touch with your wife – with Fay?'

He had already started the engine, but now he switched it off again and turned to look at her. 'I've been wondering when you'd ask.' He reached out a hand to cradle her cheek. 'You're patience itself, my Maryan. I should have kept you in the picture more. You deserve better than me, God knows you do.'

'Does – does that mean that you have?'

He sighed. 'Well, I wrote to her. I told her I thought it time we made the break final. It's been so long now. I think we could get an annulment quite easily if she was willing.'

'Yes . . .' She looked into his eyes, trying to read what she saw there. 'Vinnie, don't keep me in suspense. What did she say?'

'Nothing. She hasn't replied. I've written to her three times now. I wondered if she might have moved, or be out of the country or something, so I finally telephoned. His name – her lover's – is still in the book at the same address. I tried several times, but there was no reply.' He shook his head. 'Anyway, talking to her on the phone isn't likely to get me anywhere. She could always deny anything she'd said later, and, knowing her, she would. I need to get something in writing from her.'

'What will you ask her to do?'

'To divorce me on grounds of desertion.'

She frowned. 'But *she* deserted *you*.'

'I know, but it can be made to work both ways.' He looked away. 'She'll be required to say that I made life intolerable for her.'

She stared at him in horror. 'But that's so unfair, Vinnie.'

'Nevertheless, it's the only way I can get my freedom.' He sighed. 'If I knew she was still there I could go and see her, I suppose,' he said slowly. 'Or I could get a solicitor to write, telling her that I plan to apply for an annulment and need her cooperation. First I need to know for sure where she is.'

219

'What will you do next?'

He squeezed her hand. 'I still haven't decided. To tell the truth I've been putting it off. I've been too busy to think it out properly lately. It needs careful planning. It's not the kind of thing to rush into.'

'Vinnie . . .' She looked at him hesitantly. 'I've been wondering. If your church doesn't recognise your divorce will you really be free to marry again?'

He took both her hands in his. 'Not in the church, my love.'

'And – would you be happy with any other kind of ceremony?'

'I just want us to be together.' He squeezed her hands. 'And for your sake, I want it to be legally binding. Please, Maryan, let's not spoil the day talking about all the difficulties now.' He leaned forward and kissed her firmly. 'Now – shall we go back to the flat or will you let me take you out to dinner somewhere?'

Amy spent Saturday afternoon helping Marjorie with the party food. It was nice, being together companionably in the kitchen and catching up on all the village news. Marjorie told her that the Smith family had definitely made their presence felt. Apparently hardly a week went by that one of them wasn't the subject of local gossip for some misdemeanour or other. Lily's older brother, Norman, had been caught stealing bicycles and had been sent to Borstal for a year. Mrs Smith herself had made front-page news in the local paper, which reported a spectacular brawl she'd had with a neighbour. And Maisie, one of Lily's older sisters, had given birth to a baby boy, fathered, it was rumoured, by an American soldier.

'I miss living here,' Amy said wistfully. 'In London people don't seem to care about each other so much.'

Marjorie laughed. 'They mind their own business, you mean? But you and your mother have settled down together, I hope?'

Amy shrugged. 'Mum's always too busy to chat like we're doing now. I suppose we both are.'

For a minute Marjorie was silent, then she said: 'When Mike goes away to do his National Service I shall miss him terribly. I wouldn't tell him so, of course, because I want him to look forward to his first venture into the adult world and not feel bad about leaving home. And I've been so much luckier than so many other mothers, having him with me all through the war, and even after he went to college. You and your mother have a lot of time to make up. Make the most of it, Amy. All too soon you'll be gone and she'll be alone again. Whatever you might think, she does need you.'

Amy didn't agree. Maryan was clearly too wrapped up in her job

220

and in Vincent to care about her much. But she remained silent on the subject. The Jessops and the Taylors were totally different kinds of people, with two entirely different situations. It wasn't possible to compare them; never had been and never would.

The party was to take place in the large sun-lounge at the back of the house. The parquet floor had been cleared and chalked for dancing and the doors were open onto the garden, which Philip and Mike had decorated with coloured lights. As the day was hot and sunny they expected to be able to overflow onto the lawn until late into the evening. Amy thought the whole affair very sophisticated. She looked forward to the evening with a mixture of excitement and apprehension. Mike had obviously been to a good many such affairs, but it was her very first grown-up party and as the time drew near she was aware of a tingling sensation in the pit of her stomach.

When the time came for them all to get ready she closed her bedroom door and took out The Dress. Hanging it on the wardrobe door again she sat on the bed to stare at it in near panic. There were *so* many things wrong with it. Maybe she should have gone for a short dress. Suppose no one else wore long? She'd feel such a fool she'd just want to *die*. Then there was the neckline. If only it were lower and showed more of her chest. Not that she had all that much chest to show off. She briefly toyed with the idea of padding her bra with cotton wool. No, best not, she decided. If the padding fell out when she was dancing she'd die of shame. She took off the cotton skirt and blouse she had worn all day and went off to have her bath. Back in the bedroom she brushed her hair and secured the silver hairband in place, then she put on a little of the pink lipstick Maryan had allowed her to buy and dusted her nose with powder to take off the shine. Finally it was time to slip into the dress. She managed to do up the zip, but couldn't tie the sash to her satisfaction. Slipping out of her room she tiptoed along the landing and tapped on Marjorie's door.

'Auntie Marjorie, I wonder if you could tie my sash . . .' She stopped. Marjorie was staring at her. 'Oh – is something wrong?'

'Wrong? Good heavens, child, no. You look so lovely. Quite charming.' Marjorie drew her into the room and closed the door. 'I can hardly believe this is the little girl who came to me as an evacuee.' Philip came out of the dressing room fastening his cufflinks and she said: 'Look at Amy, Philip. Isn't she beautiful? I can't wait for Mike to see her. Here, let me tie that sash for you, then we'll make a grand entrance.'

Much to Amy's embarrassment, Philip insisted on taking her downstairs on his arm. The other guests were arriving and she was relieved to see that most of the other girls wore long dresses too. In the sun-lounge Mike stood talking to an older man who turned out to be one of his tutors. Feeling a little shy, Amy stood back, thinking how handsome he looked in his immaculate evening dress suit. He turned and saw her and his mouth dropped open in amazement.

His father laughed. 'All right, you can close your mouth now, Michael. May I introduce your guest of honour, Miss Amy Jessop.' He bowed low and handed Amy's hand to Mike. 'I suggest that you lead her into the dancing. I'll put on a record.'

The evening passed like a dream to Amy. She couldn't remember ever enjoying herself so much. She was glad that her school taught modern ballroom dancing as she was in great demand. Mike's friends were almost queuing up to dance with her. It felt so strange, dancing with boys. So far her only dancing partner had been Celia. It wasn't until after supper that Mike himself managed another dance with her.

'You've made a hit,' he told her. 'Everyone keeps asking me who you are. It's like Cinderella all over again.'

She looked up at him. 'Are you saying that I usually look ragged and dirty?'

'Well, you don't exactly dress like this to muck out the horses, do you?' He laughed and tightened his hold on her waist as he felt her trying to free one hand. 'Behave yourself. You can't thump me dressed up like that. It wouldn't look right.' He grinned down at her. 'You know, it's a relief to know you're still the tough little Amy I know. Seeing you tonight, I was beginning to wonder if you'd turned into someone quite different. I'm not sure I'd like that.' He slipped a finger inside his collar. 'It's getting so hot in here. Shall we go into the garden?'

They walked across the lawn to the little seat by the lily pond that was screened by a willow tree. Mike took out his handkerchief and dusted it carefully for her.

'Can't have that wonderful dress messed up, can we?'

'I wish you'd stop teasing me about it,' she said, sitting down. 'I know I look like a dog's dinner, but Mum would insist on buying it.'

'The last thing you look like is a dog's dinner,' he told her. 'I'm sure you know that you look absolutely marvellous.' He waved a hand towards the house. 'Ask anyone in there if you don't believe me.'

They sat for a moment in silence, then Amy said: 'Thanks for inviting me to your party, Mike. I've had a smashing time.'

'And thank you for my present. It'll come in really useful.' He laughed. 'Do you remember the birthday parties we used to have when you lived here? Jelly and blancmange and trifle, and cakes with candles for us to blow out? I didn't realise it then, but Mum used to stand in endless queues and hoard all her rations up for months to be able to do it.'

'I know.' Amy sighed wistfully. 'Auntie Marjorie did all the things for me that my own mum never did.'

'Only because she was here and your mother wasn't,' Mike said fairly.

'I still miss you all, Mike.' Amy turned huge blue eyes towards him. The coloured lights reflected in the water made them look luminous and Mike felt the breath catch sharply in his throat.

'We miss you too, Amy. And I'll tell you something else – I'm going to miss you even more when you go back this time.' He bent towards her and brushed his lips across hers. It was like the touch of a butterfly's wing, yet it made them both shiver. Amy lifted her arms and let them rest on his shoulders and he kissed her again, his lips firmer and more confident this time, his arms sliding round her waist to draw her closer.

'I thought you were still a kid last night,' he said when they drew apart. 'You looked grown up at the station, but then later you were the same Amy as always. Tonight though – tonight . . . Oh, Amy, I can't make up my mind which one I want you to be.' He kissed her again until they were both breathless and trembling. The moment hung suspended; bright and shining and magical as the coloured lights in the trees, then suddenly they were aware of voices calling from the house.

'I think they're looking for you,' Amy whispered. 'I expect people are leaving and want to say goodnight.' She stood up and held out her hand. 'Come on, we'd better go in.'

'Amy – wait. Look – when you go back. Will you go out with anyone else?'

She laughed. 'I shouldn't think so with School Cert. coming up. Why?'

'Because . . .' He stood up, laughing. 'Oh, I don't know. Because if you do I'll come up to London and punch his head. That's why.'

She laughed delightedly, catching at his hand. 'Oh, Mike, you are silly. Come on, we'd better go before they come looking for us.'

'Just a minute,' he pulled her down on the seat beside him again. 'Look, when I go into the Army, will you write to me as – you know, my girl?'

Happiness welled up inside her like a bubble. 'Oh, Mike, of course I will.'

Together, hand in hand, they ran through the trees and across the lawn. Two young people with childhood behind them. At that moment each of them felt the future beckoning, just waiting to be plucked like a ripe golden fruit from the tree of life; theirs for the taking.

Maryan was just closing the shop. It was only a quarter past five but business had been slack that afternoon. She'd let Paul, her young assistant, go home early and when no more customers had appeared by a quarter past she decided to call it a day. She was to take her driving test the following morning and she intended to have an early night so as to be fresh and alert.

She was just turning the sign on the door to 'closed' when a woman appeared in the mews outside. Maryan watched as she peered hesitantly through the shop window as though looking for something. It was so typical. No customers all afternoon, yet the minute she decided to close, they seemed to pop up from the cracks in the pavement. With a sigh, Maryan turned the door sign over again and went back to her desk at the back of the shop. Customers didn't like to be pounced on the moment they entered the shop. They liked to browse. She hoped this one wouldn't browse for too long, only to waste her time and walk out again empty-handed.

Her head down, Maryan heard the doorbell tinkle as the woman came in. She glanced up. The customer looked about forty, perhaps a little older. Her clothes were obviously expensive and yet she looked oddly ill at ease in them. She was a little overweight, her thickened waistline straining the buttons of the pink linen suit she wore. And her bleached hair was noticeably dark at the roots as though it was some time since it had seen a hairdresser. Even from the back of the shop Maryan could see that the too bright lipstick that clashed with the suit was badly applied as though she'd put it on in a hurry.

She made no attempt to browse, but hovered just inside the doorway, looking expectantly towards Maryan. Clearly she was looking for something very specific. Maryan rose and went towards her with a smile.

'Can I help you? Were you looking for something special?'

'Not some*thing* – some*one*.' The woman cleared her throat. 'Does Mr Donlan live here? Mr Vincent Donlan?'

'No. I'm sorry, he doesn't. He lives in Notting Hill with his sister. I can give you the address if you like.'

Maryan turned back towards the desk, reaching for a pencil and slip of paper, but the woman said hurriedly: 'Oh, no. It doesn't really matter. It's just that I was passing and I thought . . .'

'He's out of town today,' Maryan said, writing down Roisan's address, 'or I could have called him for you. This is where he lives. If I see him first can I give him a message?'

The woman glanced at the slip of paper Maryan handed her, then slipped it into her handbag. 'Thank you.' She looked up enquiringly. 'Er – you would be . . . ?'

'Me? Oh, I just manage the shop,' Maryan told her. 'And I live upstairs in the flat.'

'I see.'

Suddenly Maryan began to feel uneasy. Who *was* this woman? And what did she want with Vincent?

'Who shall I say called? Are you an old friend of Mr Donlan's?' she asked.

The woman nodded. 'The name's Briggs – Mrs Briggs. Well, I suppose I'd better go, Miss – er . . .'

'Jessop. *Mrs* Jessop,' Maryan supplied.

'Mrs Jessop. I'll call back sometime.' She hesitated, half turning. 'On the other hand – maybe you could . . . Oh dear.' The woman closed her eyes and swayed precariously, clutching at the back of a Victorian spoon-back chair. Alarmed, Maryan stepped towards her and put out a helping hand.

'Are you all right?'

'I – yes. I think so. I just feel a little dizzy, that's all. I'd better go. I've got quite a long journey home to face and the trains will be busy.'

'I don't think you should go anywhere at the moment. Not if you're feeling ill,' Maryan said. 'If you like you can come upstairs and sit down for a little while – wait till the rush hour is over. I was just going to close the shop anyway. I could make you a cup of tea.'

The woman smiled and looked relieved. 'Oh that *would* be kind. I'm diabetic, you see, and I have to be careful. I haven't eaten much today. I expect that's the trouble. Silly of me really.'

Upstairs in the flat Maryan opened the windows to let in some air. The afternoon had been hot and the living room was stuffy. She invited the woman to sit in an armchair near the window and went to the kitchen to put the kettle on.

The tea seemed to revive Mrs Briggs, who in spite of her indisposition seemed remarkably interested in her surroundings. Maryan noticed that while she talked her small pale eyes darted everywhere, taking in every detail of the room.

'So you live here, dear. Nice place, isn't it? Go with the job, does it?' Maryan nodded and the woman looked around her appreciatively. 'This your furniture?'

'No. It's Mr Donlan's.'

'I see. Quite fell on your feet here, dear, didn't you? I expect it's a well-paid job. I've seen the adverts in the magazines for Decor Vincente. Sounds very posh. And there's always been a lot of profit in . . .'

Prickling with resentment, Maryan said quickly: 'It's such a pity that Mr Donlan wasn't here. Shall I tell him you'll call again, or can I give him a number where he can telephone you?'

'No. I need to see him, dear – talk to him face to face, so to speak . . . It's really *very* important. I – oh dear, I'm so s-sorry.' She began to sniff and her eyes brimmed with tears. She fumbled in her handbag for a handkerchief and Maryan refilled her cup, watching anxiously as the woman struggled to compose herself.

'Look, is there anything I can do? Shall I ring his sister for you?'

'No. It's him I have to see. No one else will do.' She paused. 'I wonder. You look so kind and you've been so nice to me.' The woman gulped hard and lifted her teacup, peering at Maryan over the rim. 'I suppose it's all right to tell you as you're obviously a trusted employee. You'll have to know eventually anyway.'

'Know? Know what?'

The woman smiled coyly. 'I'm Vinnie's wife, dear. I'm not really Mrs Briggs. That's just what I call myself.' The pale eyes were sad and watery under puffy eyelids. 'Vinnie and I were married soon after the war broke out, in the spring of 1940. I let him down, I'm afraid. I met someone else while he was in the army. Eddie Briggs – that's where the name comes from. He was a businessman; clever, good-looking and well off – had this lovely house down in Virginia Water. Central heating and all mod cons. Quite swept me off my feet, he did. I'd never known such luxury. But it was a terrible mistake. Oh, Vinnie knew at the time. Refused point-blank to divorce me, he did. Said I'd find out and be sorry.' She smiled. 'He said I'd come back some day with my tail between my legs. Of course I thought he was just being spiteful at the time. Such a vulgar expression, I always think, don't you? But many's the time I've remembered his words and wished I hadn't been so hasty. Still, all's well that ends well, as they say. Just as well we never got divorced, eh?'

'How do you mean, just as well?' Maryan asked, her heart growing ice-cold with dread.

'Well, because I've come to tell him he was right.' Fay dabbed at her cheeks with the damp handkerchief. 'To throw myself on his mercy as it were and – and to ask him – oh, *ever* so humbly, to take me back.' She smiled. Watching Maryan with a sly shrewdness from under the puffy eyelids, she took in the sudden pallor and the clouded eyes. 'And I know he won't turn me away, bless him,' she went on. 'A good Catholic, my Vinnie is. Believes in the sanctity of marriage and all that.'

Amy travelled home in a state of euphoria. Her week with the Taylors had been the happiest she'd spent for ages. Mike had seen her off on the train and promised faithfully to write every week from now on. Amy had invited him to come and stay for a few days before the start of the new term. Sitting in her corner seat she planned happily how they would spend the days. They'd go to the theatre and the cinema. She'd be able to show him the London she knew; the parts she'd come to know since she'd been back. Kew Gardens and the Zoo. The West End shops.

Amy was certain in her heart of hearts that she loved Mike. Perhaps she'd always known it. It seemed so obvious and natural now, since the night of the party when he'd kissed her. Being in love was the most marvellous feeling she had ever experienced. She felt as though she could fly – as though she walked without her feet touching the ground, light as air. Everything she looked at seemed beautiful, the greyest skies brilliant, the dullest landscape inspiring. Even the rain was like silver spangles falling from heaven. Sitting in the train and thinking of Mike she thought she could understand her mother a little more. Was this how she had felt about Marcus? Her face suddenly grave, she imagined how she must have felt when he married someone else. And when he was killed – how it must have hurt. She resolved to be nicer, and less selfish when she got home. She would try harder to be what a daughter should be, close and companionable – the way she was with Auntie Marjorie. As the train drew into Liverpool Street Station and she stood up to reach down her case from the rack, she found that she quite looked forward to it.

Maryan was waiting to meet the train. Amy spotted her as she walked down the platform. She handed in her ticket and turned to her mother with a smile.

'Hello, Mum.'

'Hello, love. Have a good time?'

'Oh *yes*. It was wonderful. Mike's party was terrific and everyone said how nice the dress was.'

'I told you,' Maryan said abstractedly. 'A good thing you didn't have that awful black thing.'

'Mum, I've asked Mike up for a few days. Is that all right?'

Maryan was busy heading for the Underground and seemed not to have heard. Amy repeated her question.

227

'Mum – can Mike come and stay with us for a few days?'

'Oh, Amy, I'm not sure I want visitors at the moment. We'll have to wait and see. Things have been happening . . .'

'But *Mum* – he'll be going into the Army soon and I've already asked him.' Amy looked at her mother in horror. It would be too humiliating, not to say disappointing, to have to write and tell Mike he couldn't come after all.

'Well, you shouldn't have asked him till you'd checked with me,' Maryan snapped. 'I run a business as well as a home, you know.' They went down to the platform and waited in silence. A train drew in and the doors opened. Maryan took Amy's arm. 'Come on, Amy, don't sulk. And don't hang about. I can't leave Paul in the shop alone all afternoon.'

'Oh, the shop. It's always the *shop*,' Amy burst out. 'Why does it always have to come first? Why can't you ever think of *me* for a change?'

The train was crowded and they had to stand. Oblivious of the other passengers jostling and swaying against them in the packed aisle, Amy said, 'All through the war it was the Leighs. Now it's the shop and Vinnie, your – your *fancy man*. Everyone else in the *world* is more important to you than I am.'

Maryan rounded on her. 'Stop that at once,' she hissed. 'I won't have you speaking to me like that. We'll talk about this when we get home, young lady.'

Amy stood hanging onto the strap, her cheeks pink and her face sullen as she tried not to notice the amused glances of the other passengers. She hated them all. And she hated her mother more than all of them put together. Her week's holiday – the loveliest week she'd ever spent in her entire life – was utterly ruined. And it was all her mother's fault. She'd never, *ever* forgive her.

Maryan turned away from her daughter's dark expression. Amy's selfishness was the least of her worries. She detached herself from her surroundings as the train continued on its way, automatically counting the stations off one by one as they stopped, wanting nothing more than to be home again.

The past few days had been a nightmare. After Fay's visit she had waited with mounting tension to hear from Vincent. When two days had passed and he still hadn't come to the flat or telephoned, she rang Roisan and left a message that she needed to see him urgently. Roisan sounded strained and awkward on the telephone; something which Maryan viewed with foreboding.

He came that evening. Using his own key he let himself into the

228

flat, arriving as she was cooking herself a meal. The moment she saw his face she knew that he'd already seen Fay.

'You've seen her then – your wife?'

He sat down on one of the kitchen chairs and passed his hand over his brow. 'Yes. I've seen her.'

'She came here first.'

'I know. She told me.'

Maryan turned off the gas under the saucepan she was stirring and turned to him. 'She told me who she was. And that she wanted you to take her back.'

He sighed. 'She never got the letters I wrote her. She hasn't been living at that address for some time. It seems that the man she's been living with, Briggs, has found himself another woman – a younger one.' He lifted his shoulders. 'Some chorus girl or other. He threw Fay out so that he could bring this woman to the house. She's been living in some scruffy little bedsitting room for the past three months.' He looked up at Maryan. 'She hasn't said it in so many words, but she obviously blames me. She seems to think that if she'd been free to marry him four years ago it would never have happened.'

'She told me it was just as well that you'd refused her a divorce,' Maryan said. 'So – what did you say?'

He paused, shaking his head. 'He treated her appallingly, Maryan. Even knocked her about. Life hasn't been easy for her. She's certainly learned her lesson.'

She looked at him. 'The thing is, Vinnie – have you learned yours?'

He slumped on his chair, elbows on knees and head in his hands as he avoided her eyes. At that moment he looked ten years older and when he looked up at her she saw that he had already given in to Fay's demands. It was all over between them.

'You're taking her back,' she said quietly.

'Maryan, when she left, she was pregnant with my child. She didn't find out till later.'

Her heart froze. '*Vinnie*, that's the oldest trick in the book. How can you believe her? How can she possibly prove it was yours?'

'Because he – this Briggs – wasn't able to father a child. He was sterile and he already knew it. His wife had left him for that very reason. When she told him she was expecting a baby he knew it had to be mine and he gave her an ultimatum: get rid of it or leave. She had no option, Maryan. She had nowhere to go. She was ill and afraid. So she did it. She killed our child – *my* child, Maryan. Can you imagine how that makes me feel? The only child I'll ever have and it died – thrown away like a piece of rubbish.' He shook his head. 'Apparently she nearly died after the abortion. When she's been through so much, how can I turn my back on her?'

'She deceived you before, Vinnie. How do you know this isn't just a pack of lies to get you back?'

He shook his head. 'She was never that good at lying. If you'd seen her face, Maryan, heard her heartbroken sobbing. No, it's true. She's – she's still my wife when all's said and done.'

Her heart as heavy as a stone, Maryan straightened her back and faced him. 'I see. So when would you like me to leave, Vinnie?'

He looked up at her in alarm. 'I don't want you to *leave*, Maryan. You've become a tower of strength to Roisan and me. We couldn't manage without you.'

'But – the flat. You'll want to live here – with Fay.'

'No, we can stay with Roisan for the time being, just till I find somewhere else.' He stood up and came towards her, his hands outstretched and his eyes filled with pain. 'Maryan – I can't tell you what this is doing to me. It's tearing me in two. It's not what I want. You must know that.'

She turned away from him, her eyes stinging with tears. 'Then why do you have to do it?'

'I told you – because whatever's happened, she's still my wife.'

'She said you'd do what she wanted,' Maryan said bitterly. 'She said you were a great believer in the sanctity of marriage. It seems she was right.'

He took her shoulders and turned her to face him. 'Listen, Maryan. *I love you*. This makes no difference to the way I feel. It never will. But I made vows all those years ago – sacred vows, before a priest.'

'She made vows too.' She looked at him, the tears slipping down her cheeks. 'She broke them. Not you. You made a promise to *me*, Vinnie. Doesn't that count for anything?'

He dropped his hands to his sides, his shoulders slumping helplessly. 'I'll never make you understand, will I?'

'Does it matter whether I understand or not? I'm just an employee, after all.'

The bitter irony of her words went over his head and he looked at her eagerly. 'Does that mean that you'll stay on? Live here at the flat and keep working for me?'

The look of gratitude in his eyes pierced her heart like an arrow and she tried unsuccessfully to swallow the lump in her throat. Her pride wanted to refuse – to pack and leave that very evening and never see him again. But she had more than just herself to think of. There was Amy. This was her home. She'd already had problems settling down after the wartime parting they'd endured. Lately their relationship had seemed to be improving. Reluctantly she looked up at him and nodded. 'Yes, all right. I'll stay. But it isn't going to be easy.'

'Believe me, Maryan, it isn't going to be easy for me either. I love you. I'll always love you. He reached out to take her in his arms but she stepped back, holding him off.

'I don't want you to think because I've agreed to stay that I'm going to be here for you whenever you want me, Vinnie,' she told him. 'If you take Fay back then it's over between us. Over for ever.'

He swallowed hard. 'Of course – if you say so.'

'I do. I've never in my life meant anything more.'

When he'd gone she stood in the empty flat staring out of the window, her heart too heavy with misery to cry any more tears. She stood watching from the window as he came out of the side door and walked to the end of the mews. Before he turned into the street he turned back to look up at the window, but she drew back so that he wouldn't see her standing there. Why was it that happiness always eluded her? Why were the people she loved always beyond her reach? What terrible sin had she committed that fate should punish her so cruelly?

The train rattled to a halt at Holborn Station and Amy nudged her mother in the ribs. 'Well – are we getting off here then?' she demanded rudely. 'Or do you want to go on to Ealing?'

They changed platforms and this time when the train arrived there were seats, two separate ones, one at either end of the carriage. Maryan was relieved to be apart from her angry daughter for a while. She closed her eyes, swaying in her seat with the motion of the train, thinking of yesterday when Roisan had called to see her. Vincent's sister's placid face had been pink with rage, her mouth folded into an angry button when she arrived at Simons Mews. Maryan took one look at her expression and invited her into the office at the back of the shop.

'I had to come and see you, Maryan. I want you to know that I think he's taken leave of his senses,' she said the moment the door between them and the shop was closed. 'The woman's a devious bitch and always has been. I warned Vincent about her before they married. I always knew she'd let him down. And I knew she'd be back as soon as she thought there was any money to be had. She's seen the advertisements we placed in magazines and decided there were pickings to be had. That's why she's here. I don't for one moment believe that she never received Vinnie's letters asking for a divorce. And as for the story about the child . . .' She threw up her hands. 'Blatant, outrageous lies, all of it.'

231

Maryan sighed wearily. 'He's taken her back, Roisan. She's his wife and he has every right to do as he wants. There's nothing either of us can do about it. We don't have the right to interfere.'

Roisan sat down heavily. 'Let's face it, Maryan. I know what you and Vinnie feel about each other. This is no time for pretence. How can you just accept it? Fight for him, girl. You don't for a moment believe he really *wants* her back, do you? I know I don't. She's got him over a barrel. She knows he's a soft touch. We've got to stop her somehow.'

'We can't, Roisan. It wouldn't be right to try and come between them,' Maryan said. 'Vinnie's not soft. He has strong principles. He needs to do what he feels is right. He couldn't find happiness any other way. If I tried to push him into sending her away he'd resent me later.'

'Well, one thing's for certain. He won't find happiness with her,' Roisan said. 'She'll make his life a living hell if I know anything about her. She's already started nagging him to find a flat. That's an expense he can't afford at the moment. We need every penny to invest in the business as you know. And she won't be satisfied with anything but the best either. Mark my words, Maryan, he's heading for disaster. She'll ruin us all before she's done. And just when we were all getting along so well.' She looked at Maryan's determined expression and gave an explosive sigh. 'Oh well, if you won't, you won't. At least you're still working for us. That's something, I suppose.'

Maryan walked with her through the shop and saw her out, trying to reassure her that everything would work out for the best; a reassurance she didn't for one moment believe in. And as she closed the door behind her she was overwhelmed by the feeling that nothing could ever be the same again. The excitement of helping Vincent and Roisan to build their business; the way she had believed her luck was changing; her beautiful golden dream of a future with Vincent, all lay in ruins at her feet.

Someone was tugging impatiently at her arm and she opened her eyes with a start. She must have nodded off for a moment. Amy was standing over her, her face pink with irritation.

'Mum, come *on*, wake up. This is our station.'

Getting to her feet, Maryan followed her daughter out onto the platform, wondering how she would explain to her what had happened during her absence; asking herself how she would heal this new rift that had come between them, wishing there were someone she could turn to for comfort. As she came out of the Underground station into the afternoon sunlight and headed for Simons Mews she had never felt more alone in her life.

Part Three

Chapter Thirteen

'Now, put out all the candles with one blow and you'll be sure to get your wish.'

Roisan put the birthday cake with its lighted candles down on the table in front of Amy and stood back. 'Well, what are you waiting for?' She peered, frowning, at the cake. 'I did put on the right number, didn't I? I'm sure I counted out seventeen.'

Amy laughed, her eyes bright. 'Yes, they're all there. It's just that I wasn't expecting a cake too. Oh, Roisan, you are kind.' She jumped up and hugged Roisan till, laughing and misty-eyed, she extricated herself and put the cake knife into Amy's hand.

'Go on with you. It's nothing. Just a morsel of sponge cake and a bit of icing sugar. Can't let your seventeenth birthday pass without a cake, now can we? And your mother so busy. Come on now – blow, wish and then cut before we all die of starvation.'

Amy filled her lungs, then, watched by Roisan and Celia, she closed her eyes and blew hard. When all the candles went out Roisan and Celia clapped.

'Well done,' Celia said. 'You'll get your wish for sure now. And we've no need to ask what it was, have we?'

Amy cut the first slice and Roisan passed the plates round the table.

'Come on now. Tuck in. I don't want any leftovers.'

As Amy ate her cake she thought of all the other birthdays she'd had. Before the war it had been Grandma and Tom who had made them special. At Mitcham Lodge Auntie Marjorie had always given her a party with all her schoolfriends. This was the fourth birthday she'd had since she had been back in London. On the first two Mum had taken her to the pictures and out for tea afterwards. Last year she'd been too busy even to do that. And when Roisan had invited her round to tea for this one she'd shaken her head, telling her that

233

she was really too old for birthday tea parties now.

Roisan had thrown up her hands in horror. 'Sure you're *never* too old for a little treat on your birthday,' she said. 'And aren't you the only person I've got left to spoil? Now that my Colin has left home for good and Vinnie's gone too I've no one to make a fuss of.'

Roisan's son Colin had got married just over a year ago to a girl he'd met at college and they had set up home in Manchester, where Colin worked as a lecturer at the technical college and his wife taught at a primary school. Since Vincent's wife Fay had returned and they'd moved to a flat of their own, Roisan had been living alone in the little house in Notting Hill. When Amy's birthday loomed she had been only too glad of the excuse to spend some time in the kitchen, making all the things she never bothered with for herself. She'd telephoned Amy the week before.

'A little bird reminded me that a certain young lady has a birthday next week,' she said. 'Now – your mother tells me she has a sale to go to and she's likely to be gone all day, so as it's half term why don't you come and spend the day with me? You can help me in the workroom if you like – or give Miss Stokes a hand.' She laughed. 'If she doesn't scare the pants off you, that is. I know she does me.'

Amy was delighted. 'Oh, Roisan, that would be lovely. Thank you.' She loved Roisan's house with its homely, untidy rooms spilling over with interesting things. 'Can I ask Celia to come to tea as well?' she asked. Celia had taken shorthand and typing in her last year and had left school the previous July. She now worked as an office junior for the same magazine company as her mother in Southampton Street.

'Of *course* you can. Ask whoever you like,' Roisan said generously.

So here they were, sitting round the big table in Roisan's kitchen, stuffing themselves with all the good things that Roisan had made, ending with the sumptuous illuminated birthday cake.

The girls smiled at each other across the table. Apart from growing taller, Amy hadn't changed much in the past two years. Now in her final year at St Hildred's, she was restless. She had longed to leave last year with Celia but Maryan was adamant. As long as her daughter had the chance of a proper education she was going to have it. She'd passed her School Certificate with Matriculation and Maryan had been assured by her teachers that there was every chance the girl would get a good Higher Certificate too.

Celia on the other hand had changed out of all recognition. Gone were the long fair bob and chubby freckled face. Now her hair was cut and permed in the short, fashionable 'bubble cut' and her puppy

234

fat had been whittled away by the diet her mother had put her on. Her newly revealed facial bones gave her a attractive gamin look. She wore make-up every day now, foundation, powder and lipstick; she even got away with a little mascara to darken her pale lashes. Amy on the other hand was only allowed a dash of lipstick at weekends. Celia had smart fashionable clothes too, nylons and high-heeled shoes, which she bought with the money she earned. Amy envied her friend all this sophistication, though she'd never have let her see it. Celia was still her best friend and she never flaunted her new adult status or made Amy feel childish.

Later, as they were travelling back to Simons Mews together, Celia enquired whether Amy had heard from Mike.

'Not since he finished his National Service. He's really busy with his job now,' Amy told her. 'Journalists work long hours, and Mike is hoping to be offered the job of junior reporter on the *Clarion* soon.'

Celia looked suitably impressed. 'He must be coming up for twenty-one,' she said. 'I expect you'll get an invite to his party.'

Amy shrugged. 'Maybe – if he has one. Anyway, it's not for ages yet. Anything could have happened by then.'

Celia looked at her with interest. 'Oh? Like what?'

Amy shrugged. 'I don't know – anything.'

The 'anything' she referred to was her own gloomy theory that the way things were going it looked as if Mike might well be getting engaged on his birthday. His last three letters had been full of a girl he had met. She worked as a secretary on the *Clarion* and her name was Julia Honeywell and she was the same age as him. Deeply wounded by the news, Amy hadn't mentioned her to anyone, not even Celia. The thought of Mike falling in love with someone else hurt too much. At night she lay in bed thinking of Mike's eighteenth birthday party; the night when they had sat by the pond together and he had kissed her. Doris Day had recorded a song last year. It was called 'It's Magic' and the words described exactly how she felt. She'd bought the record and played it over and over when she was alone. Now she tortured herself imagining what this Julia Honeywell would be like. Mike had described her as a redhead. She'd be glamorous, of course. A bit like Rita Hayworth; a great cloud of wavy hair, endless, shapely legs and pouting red lips. And of course she'd wear fabulous, sexy clothes. Amy felt her angry teenage frustration burning her up. It was as if she was a woman trapped eternally in childhood. It wasn't *fair*. Other girls of her age were out earning their own living; allowed to look and behave like adults, whilst she still had to sit in a classroom all day, listening to the nuns droning on and on. She hated the school uniform she was still obliged to wear; the sensible shoes and thick stockings and the dreaded hat. She was quite tall now, almost five foot seven, and she felt ridiculous in her pleated skirt, blazer and Breton hat with its school badge. On the Underground each morning she was sure that people were staring at her – laughing behind their hands at this great tall girl dressed up like a *kid*.

Of course it was all her mother's fault. Amy was convinced that Maryan was determined to keep her dependent on her for as long as possible – just to humiliate her, or perhaps it was just to make herself appear younger. It certainly wasn't because she enjoyed having her around. Most of the time Maryan was preoccupied with her work. She lived and breathed it, having less time for Amy or any kind of home life than ever before. Then there was this mysterious business about Vincent's wife coming back. Instead of leaving when it happened, as Amy thought she would have done, Mum had been throwing herself into her job harder than ever, working long hours and sometimes weekends too. And of course Vincent never came round to see them any more except to talk business. Their love affair, if that was what it was, was definitely finished, and yet the school fees obviously still got paid. Maybe *that* was why Mum had stayed on. In which case Amy fervently wished she hadn't. Still, there was one consolation: at least she wouldn't be getting *Uncle Vinnie* as a step-father.

'Tell me what I've just said?' Celia had stepped in front of her and was staring challengingly into her face. Amy stopped walking and blinked guiltily at her friend.

'I – er . . . Oh, I'm sorry, Cee. What did you say?'

'I *said* I'd read in the paper that clothes are coming off coupons soon. Isn't that terrific?'

'Yes. Sorry. I was miles away.'

Celia gave an explosive snort. 'Huh! You don't have to *tell* me. You're only on this *planet* about half the time lately. What's up, Amy – something on your mind?'

Amy shook her head impatiently. 'It's just that I'm so fed up with school,' she confessed. 'I mean, for instance, it won't make much difference to me, clothes coming off ration, will it? I've got no money to buy any. Anyway, all I ever wear is my rotten school uniform. I feel so – so left behind, Cee. It's so irritating, being made to stay on when I know that all I want is to be an actress. You don't need Highers for acting, do you?'

Celia pulled a face. 'Don't know really. I suppose it's bound to help whatever you do. Anyway, cheer up, droopy-drawers. It's not for much longer, is it? And you've still got your gorgeous Mike.'

But Amy knew she hadn't got Mike. Not any longer. At least, not in the way she would have liked. Although they'd exchanged letters after he began his National Service, they'd met only infrequently. At first Mike had been stationed up north. Later he'd moved down to a camp nearer to London and had come up two or three times to stay with relatives. They'd spent a couple of hours together, usually in the company of others. On the last occasion he'd written to ask if she'd like to see the new musical, *Oklahoma*, and Amy had looked forward to it eagerly for weeks. It made her feel so grown-up to be seen with a young man in uniform. But to her disappointment Mike had brought three other friends along with him and although they sat together in the theatre he hadn't even held her hand – not even during the singing of the romantic hit song, 'People Will Say We're in Love'. She'd hoped to recapture the magic of that summer night in the garden at Mitcham Lodge, but when Mike had dropped her off at Simons Mews after the show he had left her with the briefest of brotherly pecks, his friends looking on from the taxi. As she waved them off she reflected that sometimes it was almost as though she had dreamed it all.

The letters Mike had written since his demob were friendly and filled with news. The Army seemed to have matured him out of all recognition. Now he was eager and full of enthusiasm to get his career off to a good start like Celia and so many of her other contemporaries. They were all moving on while she was still marking time. How could she expect him to be interested in hearing about St Hildred's school concert, or a visit to the Science Museum? He'd probably even be ashamed to admit to his friends that he was writing to a girl who was still at school.

For this reason it had been she who'd let the intervals between letters grow longer. And now Mike had found this girl – this super, sophisticated Julia Honeywell. Her life was over before it had begun, she told herself despondently. Not that anyone cared. Least of all her mother.

'I don't think I can bear school for much longer,' she told Celia. 'It's making my life a misery.'

Celia squeezed her arm affectionately. 'Poor old sausage. You are down in the dumps, and on your birthday too. Come on, I'll treat you to the pictures. I've been dying to see Bob Hope in *Paleface*, haven't you? Everyone says it's an absolute scream, and they sing that song, 'Button and Bows'. I love that, don't you?' She quickened her pace, pulling Amy along behind her, humming a snatch of the

237

song. 'Come on, we'll just catch the last house if we hurry. It's just what you need to cheer you up.'

It was dark by the time Maryan drove the van into the mews. It had been a good sale and though she was tired she had the feeling of satisfaction that a successful sale always gave her. With the help of Geoff Masters, Vincente Antiques' newest employee, she had bought three good pieces that she felt sure were just what Vincent was looking for.

Geoff Masters had been working for Vincente Antiques for a year and a half now. Vincent had discovered him working as a porter for one of the auction rooms. Geoff had been disabled by a war wound and the heavy work was clearly causing him problems. Talking to him, Vincent had discovered that he was an expert restorer and had worked for a well-known cabinet maker before the war. He had offered him a job on the spot. Now Geoff worked in Vincent's workshop in the basement at Simons Mews, restoring damaged and neglected pieces of antique furniture to their former beauty with loving precision. He always accompanied Maryan to sales, examining pieces and assessing their potential. But it was Maryan who had become the expert bidder, often getting valuable pieces that appeared worthless for knock-down prices.

She put the van away in the garage and locked it securely. She had dropped Geoff off at his home in Fulham on the way home. They would unload their purchases in the morning. Fishing in her bag for her key under the streetlamp, she let herself in at the side door and went up to the flat. The place was in darkness, but on the kitchen table was a note from Amy.

Gone to the pictures with Celia. Back at ten-thirty – Amy.

Maryan took off her coat and filled the kettle. She was hungry. They hadn't eaten much all day. It would have been nice to have had the kind of daughter who would have had a meal waiting. Then she remembered that it was Amy's birthday and felt guilty. Of course she should go out and enjoy herself with her friend, she told herself. After all, I couldn't offer to take her. I'm just being selfish.

But as she set about cutting bread to make herself a sandwich she felt depressed about the relationship that she and Amy shared. Even if she had offered to take Amy somewhere on her birthday she wouldn't have wanted to go – not with her. They were like two ships that passed in the night; communicating mostly like this, by leaving notes for each other. As she prepared her solitary meal she wondered what would happen once Amy left school and began to earn her own living. She guessed that she would want her freedom and independence. The closeness she had looked forward to all through the long war years had never materialised.

She felt guilty in some ways, but in others she blamed the war. If only there had been more time for them to spend together – time to try to understand one another. There was always so much to do, but it was chiefly for Amy that she had built her new career. And she reasoned that if it hadn't been for the war she would never have had this chance to prove what she could do. Life was strangely perverse sometimes.

Then there was that business with the Taylor boy. Amy had seemed so keen on him, wanting him to come and stay. Maryan had seen all the signs and been afraid. It was herself and Marcus all over again. However friendly, the Taylors weren't their class and never would be. Amy would be hurt just as she had. Now she saw that by trying to nip Amy's teenage passion in the bud she had only strengthened it, and made an ogre of herself into the bargain. The girl never confided in her; never wanted to talk about her feelings or ask for advice. Maybe it was all her fault. Perhaps she had never been cut out for motherhood.

Looking back, she felt that she should have left when Vincent's wife came back and their affair came to an end. With hindsight she felt that Amy would not have cared, one way or the other. This flat had never been a real home to the girl anyway. And a clean break would certainly have been much less emotionally difficult.

But in spite of all that had happened Maryan still loved her job. Each day brought with it a fresh challenge. And with the knowledge of the antiques business and the management skills she had acquired, she knew that she had become a valuable asset to the firm. Now that Paul and Geoff had joined the staff at Simons Mews her working life was more organised.

Hoping to prove what he thought of her, Vincent had given her a substantial rise in salary recently. Along with the cheque there had been a short letter, saying that the rise was in appreciation of all her hard work. The note had wounded her to the heart for reasons she was reluctant to probe.

They saw very little of each other these days; communicating mainly on the telephone or through Roisan. She had stuck firmly to her decision to end their love affair when Fay had come back. Not that it had been easy, especially at the beginning. Seeing him; speaking to him on a purely business level; trying to pretend that they had never been more than employer and employee had been torture. She suspected it was for him too. And for that reason she was grateful that he kept his visits down to the minimum.

Fay, on the other hand, was a regular visitor. She arrived at the shop at least once a week, usually at the most inconvenient time. Obviously determined to flaunt her position as the boss's wife, she would wander round the shop pretending to knowledge she didn't possess about antiques, checking for dust and looking for something to criticise. Her interference upset and offended Paul, who loathed her, and Maryan usually took her into the office for coffee just to get her out of his way.

'I can't think why you keep that young man,' she'd said to Maryan the previous week. 'He's got a shifty look about him if you ask me. You want to watch he hasn't got his fingers in the till, especially with you being away from the place so much.'

'Paul is very loyal and he's a hard worker,' Maryan told her stiffly. 'I'd be lost without him. He's always glad to stay on after closing time or help me in any way he can.'

Fay sniffed, arranging the folds of her new fur coat. 'Mmm, I wonder why? In my experience nobody works for nothing. Like I said, you don't want to be too trusting, dear. You want to take my advice and watch him. After all, *you're* the one who'll carry the can back if anything goes wrong, aren't you? Vinnie puts a lot of trust in you, but as I always say, people are only human.'

Maryan boiled with resentment but she held her tongue. She suspected that Fay would do her best to make trouble for any of the staff she happened to take a dislike to – herself included.

Vincent and Fay had moved to a flat in Kensington soon after Fay's reappearance. Roisan worried about him constantly. In the early days she'd made frequent visits to the shop, telling Maryan that he wasn't happy – complaining that she had never known him so withdrawn and worried, until at last Maryan was forced to ask her to stop. As she explained to Roisan, there was nothing either of them could do about it. Whatever Fay was like, it had been Vincent's decision to take his wife back. They must let him live his life as he had chosen.

When the kettle boiled Maryan made the tea. Taking her tray into the living room she went to draw the curtains, but a movement in the mews below caught her eye. Someone was standing at the side door. She waited for a ring at the bell, but the next moment she heard the street door downstairs open and close. Her heart quickened. It was much too early for Amy and only one other person had a key. As she reached the top of the stairs Vincent was already halfway up. When he saw her he paused.

'Maryan. I'm sorry if I startled you.'

'I – wondered who it could be,' Maryan said breathlessly. 'There's nothing wrong, I hope?'

'No.' He followed her into the room. Catching sight of the tray he said: 'Oh, you were about to eat. I'm sorry.'

'It's all right. Perhaps you'd like some tea? It's freshly made.'

'No.' He waved his hand. 'Do have yours, though. I can say what I've come to say while you're eating.'

'The sale was good,' Maryan told him. 'Geoff and I haven't been back long. We did quite well – got a Regency drum table and a lovely Chinese lacquered cabinet. Both badly distressed, but Geoff seems confident that he can restore them. There's a little Jacobean court cupboard too. When I tell you what I got them for you'll . . .'

'Maryan. I've come to ask you something,' he interrupted. 'Roisan and I are going to register Vincente's and Decor as a company. She and I will be joint managing directors, of course, but we'd like you to be on the board of directors with us. What do you say?'

She stared at him, stunned. A director of a company – *her* – Maryan Jessop? The offer was so totally unexpected that she was temporarily speechless. 'I – I don't know what to say – except . . . I mean, don't directors . . . ? Wouldn't I be required to put some money in? I'm afraid I haven't got very much. I've got some savings put by, but not enough to . . .'

'No, *no*.' He was shaking his head. That's not why I'm asking you, Maryan. Your contribution will be the hard work you've put in and the skills you've learned. You've been with us from the beginning of our venture. Four years of studying and learning; working hard right from scratch. You are our most valued asset now. We simply couldn't have done it without you. So we'd like you to be a real part of the company now that we're becoming established.'

Maryan felt herself blushing. 'But – I'm just – just an ordinary person.'

He laughed. 'And what do you think I am?'

Confused, she shook her head. 'I'm afraid I don't know much about company practice. What would I have to do as a – a director?'

'What it means is that you'd have a say in any future plans we might make; to share your ideas with us as well as reaping whatever benefits there might be. And of course you'd have a vote on any major decisions we might think of making, including the hiring of new staff – dismissals too, of course.'

Maryan was momentarily speechless. It was so unexpected, and so flattering. 'I can't think why you should make me this offer,' she said firmly. 'I've no qualifications for it. I just do my job as best I can. I'm nothing special, just someone who needed a job when you needed someone.'

'Don't sell yourself short, Maryan,' he said. 'The work you've put

241

in these past four years is worth far more than I've ever paid you for. Well . . . ?' He looked at her expectantly. 'Will you accept?' He was leaning forward in his chair. 'Please say yes, Maryan. Roisan and I have talked this over and it's what we both want.'

'Well, I don't know.' She bit her lip uncertainly. 'What about your wife, Vinnie? What about Fay? I take it she'll be a director too?'

'No.' He frowned. 'Why do you ask? What has Fay to do with this?'

'It's obvious, isn't it? Won't she expect to share in any company her husband is forming?'

At the mention of Fay's name Vincent's eyes clouded as he leaned back in his chair. 'Fay hasn't the slightest interest in the firm. Except to spend the money it makes. She's made it clear that she thinks it all a crashing bore and you can rest assured that she wouldn't be interested in getting involved.'

Maryan was silent, remembering the way Fay behaved when she came to the shop. She certainly seemed to enjoy exploiting her position as Vincent's wife on those occasions. 'Well – as long as you're sure.'

'I am. I promise you. Both Roisan and I are firm on that.'

She smiled. 'Well then. Thank you. I'd be honoured to accept.'

'Marvellous.' He beamed delightedly. 'I'll put your name down on the list of directors. You're one of us now, Maryan.'

For a moment they sat looking at each other and suddenly the atmosphere became charged. Anxious to break the increasing tension that was building between them, Maryan stood up.

'Well – thank you for coming – for asking me.'

'Not at all. I'd better go – let you get on with your meal. Your tea will be cold.'

'That's all right. I'll see you out.' They reached the door at the same time and as their hands reached simultaneously for the door handle their fingers touched. Maryan snatched her hand back as though she'd received an electric shock and he turned to look into her eyes.

'It's wonderful to see you, Maryan,' he said quietly. 'To have the chance to talk like this. When you're on the board with us we'll have more chances to meet.'

'Yes – perhaps,' she said, her eyes downcast.

He touched her shoulder. 'Maryan – I can't tell you how glad I am that you stayed on after – what happened. Are – are you happy?'

Stung by the question she looked up at him. '*Are you?*' In his dark expressive eyes she saw her own pain reflected and the breath caught in her throat. 'You'd better go now, Vinnie,' she said. But he stood where he was, his hand on her shoulder, looking into her eyes.

'I wonder if you've been through the hell I've been through,' he said huskily. 'I know I hurt you, but believe me, Maryan, I hurt myself even more. It's only the business that makes life worth living most of the time. That and knowing that you're still here. Believe me, Maryan, I've had ample time to ask myself whether it was all worth it. Fay and I . . .'

'*Please*, Vinnie. I don't want to hear this. I can cope if I don't have to be close to you too often. If I . . .' She stopped speaking to look at him, her eyes wide as she asked: 'You haven't offered me this directorship because . . . ?'

'*No*. My dear girl, I don't want you to think that; not for one minute. Everything I said is true. Roisan and I have talked it over and we want you with us. It was purely a business offer, because we – we *both* value your dedication.' His fingers tightened on her shoulder. 'I'm sorry, my dear. It's just coming here tonight and finding you alone – seeing you like this. Remembering the times when we . . .'

'*Don't*.' She tried to twist out of his grasp but he caught her other shoulder and drew her to him.

'Perhaps I'm being selfish, but I want you to know that I still love you, Maryan,' he whispered, his voice muffled against her hair. 'I always will, no matter what. I can't help myself.' His lips found hers and for a moment she remained stiff in his arms, then, unable to resist the passionate insistence of his kiss, she melted against him, responding with all the pent-up longing she had denied for so long, her knees weak and her heart pounding. When they drew apart he looked down at her, his eyes full of regret. 'It won't go away, will it, Maryan? It's as agonising for you as it is for me.' She nodded wordlessly and he went on with a sigh: 'But it's something I'm afraid we're both going to have to live with.'

Stung to anger, she pushed him away. 'Not *me*, Vinnie,' she said, almost choking with bitterness. '*I* don't have to live with it. I'm doing my best to forget what happened between us, and I'll succeed if only you'll let me. I'm trying to pick up the pieces and make a life for myself and Amy. I'm going to have to ask you not to come here again, like this – alone. If you can't guarantee that our future association will be on a strictly business footing, I'll have to reconsider the offer you've just made me. I'll have to leave.'

He dropped his hands to his sides and nodded, smiling ruefully. 'I deserved that. Of course I understand. What I've just said and done was very wrong. But please don't leave, Maryan. Without you . . .'

'*Goodnight*, Vinnie.'

He took one last look at her pale face, then turned and walked down the stairs, letting himself out without looking back. Maryan watched, holding her breath until the street door had closed behind him and the sound of his footsteps grew fainter. Then she gave a long, shuddering sigh and sank down onto the top step, one hand over her mouth, unleashing the torrent of harsh, choking sobs that threatened to tear her heart to pieces.

It was two weeks later that Sam arrived at Simons Mews. Over the past four years he had visited Maryan several times. Whenever he had occasion to come up to the West End on business he would look in on her to satisfy himself that she was still all right and that she and Amy had everything they needed. He always came when he knew that Amy would be at school, though. The thought of seeing the girl he could not acknowledge as his granddaughter was too much for him to contemplate.

Paul came into the office halfway through the morning to tell Maryan that Mr Leigh was waiting to see her. Smiling in anticipation, she came out immediately and saw him standing in the middle of the shop; a stocky, dark-coated figure, his black homburg hat in his hand. For the first time she noticed with a twinge of nostalgia that he was growing old. His hair was greyer and thinner than it had been, and he seemed to have shrunk since she last saw him. She felt a surge of affection towards the man who had been like a father to her for so many years. In spite of his unswerving loyalty to his wife, Sam had never let her down. She went to greet him, her hands outstretched.

'Mr Sam. How nice to see you. Come up to the flat and I'll make you some coffee.'

When they were seated in the living room she asked him how he was.

'Fine, my dear,' he nodded. 'Fine, thank you.'

'Business going well?' Again he nodded. 'And Mrs Leigh?'

'Aaah.' Sam sighed and spread his hands expressively. 'My Rachel works too hard. She worries me. But what does she care for my opinion?'

Maryan nodded. 'I knew there was something worrying you. Do you want to tell me about it?'

'It's the new line.'

Maryan smiled to herself. She could imagine how irritated Rachel must be when Sam insisted on referring to the Marcus Leigh Collection as, 'The New Line' – as though it consisted of mass-produced floral print dresses for sale on the street markets.

244

'Marcus's couture designs, you mean?' she asked.

He nodded. 'She works all hours. Up till the small hours of the morning – making contacts abroad, arranging shows, planning publicity. She won't rest until his name is a household word throughout the world. She's *killing* herself, Maryan.' He shook his head. 'I've told her – Marcus wouldn't have wanted her to ruin her health for him. He never wanted fame and riches. His life was spent in helping people.'

'I know,' Maryan said quietly.

'The thing is . . .' Sam crumbled the biscuit on his plate. 'The thing is that the designs we're selling now aren't Marcus's any more. They're the work of Gina Stern. She's talented, young and ambitious. I feel it's only a matter of time before she'll want to spread her own wings. What will Rachel do then?'

'Maybe by then Marcus's name will have achieved the fame she wants,' Maryan suggested.

Sam sighed. 'I can't see that ever happening. Rachel drives herself relentlessly. She is never satisfied. I don't think she ever will be. Gina has already suggested leaving once. Seems she had an offer from a rival firm. Rachel was devastated – didn't sleep for nights on end. She almost made herself sick with worry. In the end she offered the girl an enormous salary increase. I tell you, I was shocked. It was out of all proportion – just to keep her designing under the name of Marcus Leigh.' He shook his head. 'Well, then I knew for sure. My Rachel has always been such a sound businesswoman. This thing had stopped being an ambition and become an obsession with her.' He looked up at Maryan, his brown eyes sad and anxious. 'But will she listen to me?' He shook his head sadly. 'There's the money too.'

Maryan shook her head. 'The money?'

'The designs have made a fortune, both here and on the Continent. Now the Marcus Leigh look is sweeping America. But Rachel won't touch the money. She insists that all the running costs are met out of Feldman Fashions. She says she's putting it all in a high-interest, long-term investment.' He lifted his shoulders. 'But what *for*? I've asked her again and again, but she just shakes her head and says it's what *he* would have wanted. I don't know what to do about it, Maryan. It's almost as though she's still expecting him to come back. Sometimes I fear for her sanity.'

Maryan reached out and touched his hand. 'Try not to worry. I'm sure her own good sense will come to her rescue before long. Perhaps you could persuade her to go for a nice long holiday somewhere abroad where she could relax.'

'Maybe. I'll try. I hope you're right, my dear. I do hope you're

right.' He drained his cup and passed it to Maryan to refill. 'But –
tell me about yourself. And Amy. How is Amy doing?'

'Oh, we're both well,' Maryan passed him his cup. 'Something
quite exciting has happened for me. This firm – Vincente's – has
been registered as a company. And I've been offered a
directorship.'

Sam's sad eyes brightened with delight. 'But that's wonderful.
Congratulations. I'm sure you deserve it. You've worked so hard.'
He reached out to pat her hand. 'Sometimes, my dear, I believe that
leaving us was the best thing you could have done. You were always
wasted in domestic work.' When Maryan failed to agree he asked:
'And little Amy? Still enjoying the school?'

'She got her Matriculation as you know,' Maryan told him. 'Later
this year she takes her Higher Certificate. The Mother Superior tells
me she has every chance of doing well.'

Sam nodded with satisfaction. 'Wonderful, wonderful. I'm proud
of you both.'

'She couldn't have done it without your help,' Maryan said. 'She
doesn't know you pay her fees, of course. But one day I'll tell her
how much you've helped her – helped us both.'

He shook his head. 'No, no. It's enough for me to know she's
taken care of and getting the education that Marcus's daughter
deserves.'

'I wish you and she could get to know one another better,'
Maryan said wistfully.

'So do I, believe me, my dear. But it's better this way.' Sam got to
his feet and began to button his coat. 'I wish so much that Rachel
could have accepted things as they are. I'd rather she had put her
energy and love into the child than into this – this treadmill to
madness she's obsessed herself with.'

Maryan walked with him to the end of the mews and saw him into
a taxi. As she stood on the kerb, waving to him, a feeling of
depression engulfed her. If only her mother could have talked to
Rachel Leigh she might have made her see sense as she always had
in days gone by. For all the differences in religion, race and class,
Sarah and her beloved 'Miss Rachel' had shared the common ground
of motherhood and loss that makes all women equal. Theirs had
been a very special relationship. If only Sarah could have lived a
little longer, things might have been so very different for them all.
Maryan turned and walked slowly back to the shop with a heavy
heart.

Amy was bored. The Easter holidays stretched ahead and with Celia

246

working there was absolutely nothing for her to do. Maryan suggested that she might like to help in the office or the shop, but she wasn't really interested in antiques and just felt in the way there. She made herself useful around the flat and amused herself trying her hand at cookery, but before long the outdoors beckoned. With spring in the air she longed for Rhensham but had to make do with London streets instead, where the dusty sparrows twittered and quarrelled over discarded crusts under the stunted trees trying to burst into leaf at the pavement's edge. She spent a lot of time looking around the shops, gazing longingly at the colourful new spring clothes that now could be bought without clothing coupons, and wishing she could afford to buy herself something new that was her choice and not her mother's.

It was on the Wednesday of the second week when Celia rang. Amy was alone in the flat and answered the telephone herself.

'Hello, Amy, it's me. How about going out for the day?'

'Aren't you at work?'

'No. I had a bit of a tummy upset last night and Mum thought I'd better have the day off,' Celia explained. 'But I feel fine again now.' Seems a pity to waste a day off, so I thought if you felt like it . . .'

'But – suppose someone sees you?'

'Hard cheese. I'll say I was on my way to the doctor's.'

Amy giggled. 'Well, if you like. Did you have anything in mind?'

'Not really. We could have a look round the shops, then a snack and go to the pictures – or even a theatre. In the gods, of course. We'd get a front seat if we started queuing early.'

'Well, all right.'

'Meet me at Alaniano's in half an hour. We can have a coffee first.' Celia dropped the receiver quickly before her friend could change her mind.

Alaniano's was a milk bar the girls often frequented in the King's Road. It had a bar with high stools, freshly made doughnuts and a coffee machine that hissed and spluttered. It also had a coin-operated jukebox which attracted all the local teenagers. The owner's name was Alan Springer, but with his dark, swarthy looks he passed for Italian, in spite of his strong cockney accent, hence the name, *Alaniano's* emblazoned above the bar itself and inside, scrawled artistically across the mirror behind the counter in red and blue paint.

When Amy arrived Celia was already there, dressed to kill in her latest full-skirted dress in a brightly coloured plaid taffeta and a cut away jacket of black wool. She was flirting with Alan as he made up sandwiches behind the bar, and she'd already made her choice of record. Perched on her stool at the counter, she shook her shoulders provocatively, singing along to the record.

'All I need is loving you and music, music, music.' She caught sight of Amy and waved. 'Hi. Come on in. I've already got you a coffee.'

Amy was acutely aware of how dowdy she looked in comparison to her friend. She was wearing her 'best' dress, a button-through design in red wool jersey. She'd had it for over a year and in spite of the fact that she'd changed the buttons and stitched on a new white collar it still looked hopelessly unfashionable to her. She slid onto the stool next to Celia and caught sight of her friend eyeing the dress.

'Okay – go on, say it,' she said, blushing with discomfort.

'Say what?' Celia passed her the sugar in its giant shaker.

'My dress. It's awful, isn't it? You always make me feel like a real frump with your fashionable clothes.'

Celia put down her cup and leaned towards Amy. 'Listen, stupid. You haven't the slightest idea of how attractive you are, have you? You don't even *know* that whatever you wear the boys all stare at you. You're too busy feeling sorry for yourself.'

Blushing, Amy hid her face in her cup. 'It's not true. You know it isn't. I can't flirt like you do.'

Celia sighed with exaggerated patience. 'Of course you can't. And that's *exactly* what fascinates them,' she said. 'You're – oh, I don't know – all coolness and mystery and what-d'you-call-it, *enigma* – like Ingrid Bergman.'

Pleased, Amy laughed and gave her friend a push. 'Oh go on. You're full of rubbish this morning. Drink up your coffee and let's go.'

The girls caught the bus up to Oxford Circus and gazed at the shop windows. They were full of Dior's New Look: long, swirling skirts and figure-hugging jackets a bit like the one that Celia was wearing. But the Marcus Leigh look still seemed to be popular. It had changed subtly since the first designs had been launched, with the introduction of floating panels and looser, more flowing lines, reminiscent of the twenties. Recently Marcus Leigh hats and shoes had been launched too, to complete the Leigh ensemble. Celia stopped as they walked down Argyle Street, riveted by a particularly striking Leigh outfit in the window of an exclusive boutique. Its citrus yellow and gold made a splash of colour in the centre of the small window.

'Now *that* would suit you,' she said, her head on one side. 'It's so fresh and spring-like and the contrasting colours are like sunshine and shadow.'

'It's all right, I suppose,' Amy said, hurrying on. If only she could tell Celia that the famous Marcus Leigh was her father. But she had no right. She had no right to claim anything, it seemed. She was nobody – daughter of no one. Depression descended on her again. She grabbed Celia's arm. 'Come on. Let's get a bus and go down to Leicester Square. We can get something to eat at Lyons Corner House.'

After beans on toast and an ice-cream apiece Amy and Celia made their way to Shaftesbury Avenue to look at the theatres.

'There's *The Lady's Not For Burning* at The Globe or *The Little Hut* at The Lyric,' Celia said, looking up at the rival theatres. 'Which one do you fancy?'

'Don't know that I'm in the mood for either,' Amy said. 'It seems a shame to go inside when the sun's shining.' In actual fact she didn't think she could face seeing people doing the one thing she herself wanted so badly to do. Sometimes it seemed that she would never realise her ambition; never really amount to anything. Celia shrugged good-naturedly.

'P'raps you're right. Maybe a walk and then a news theatre later on. We can drool over the latest film of Princess Elizabeth's baby and have a good laugh at some cartoons, eh?'

They wandered until they lost themselves among the maze of back streets behind Shaftesbury Avenue and were just about to turn back when they noticed a queue of people standing outside what looked like a disused cinema. With her usual open curiosity Celia went up to the last person in the queue and asked what they were waiting for.

'They're auditioning at three,' the girl said.

'Who's "they"?' Celia asked. 'And what are they auditioning for?'

'It's Alex Keynan, the director. He's forming a new repertory company – to tour up north.'

'I see.' The girls walked slowly on in silence, each of them busy with her own thoughts, then Celia turned to Amy. 'Go on, I dare you,' she said.

Amy stared at her. 'Dare me to what?'

'You know damn well. Get in the queue. Audition for a job. You know you want to.'

Amy's cheeks burned crimson. It was as though Celia had read her thoughts. 'I couldn't,' she said. 'What – what about school and – and Mum?'

'Time to worry about that if they offer you a job,' Celia said. 'It'd be a lark just to have a go, wouldn't it? Good experience for you too.' She glanced scathingly at the queue. 'Anyway, I bet you can do as well as that lot. They look like a bunch of drips to me.'

'But they'll all have prepared something,' Amy argued, terrified and excited all at the same time. 'They'll have rehearsed and everything. I haven't got anything ready.'

'Oh, rubbish. What about all that poetry we did at school? And that Shakespeare play you were in – *Twelfth Night*? I bet you can remember some of that.'

In her mind Amy was already going over Viola's lines. *Make me a willow cabin at your gate*, her inner voice recited. She did remember it. *Could* she really do it? Dare she?

There was a sudden buzz of interest as the doors up ahead opened and the line of people began to move forward. Celia elbowed Amy into the queue and began to propel her forward towards the open door.

'Go on, kid,' she hissed in her ear. 'You're as good as them, I bet. *Better*. Tell you what, half a crown says you can do it.'

'All right. You're on.'

As they reached the door a young man with a clipboard took their names and gave each of them a slip of paper with a number on it, then they were ushered through into the empty auditorium which had been stripped of everything except a few rows of chairs in front of a hastily improvised platform. In the centre of the front row sat three people: a man with grey hair and a beard, a woman with glasses, and another man who stood up when they were all assembled, introducing himself as Alex Keynan.

Sitting in the back row, Celia nudged Amy. 'Ever heard of him?'

Amy shook her head. 'Don't think so.'

'Quite good-looking, isn't he?' Celia remarked. 'For his age, I mean. Thirty-five if he's a day.'

Amy looked at the slip of paper in her hand. 'Look, I'm number twenty-four. We'll be here for hours. Are you sure you want to stay?'

Celia grabbed her wrist and held her tightly. 'You just stay where you are, my child,' she instructed. 'I grew up in this game, remember. It won't take nearly as long as you think.'

Celia was right. The first few candidates were stopped midway through their audition piece and told to give their addresses to the man on the door. 'Thank you. We'll be in touch in due course,' Alex Keynan told them.

Celia pulled a face. '*Don't call us, we'll call you*,' she muttered under her breath. 'That's the kiss of death. Told you they were a bunch of deadbeats. You'll knock spots off 'em, kid.'

Amy's turn came round sooner than she'd thought. There had been several young actors and actresses who sounded really good to her. They'd been allowed to finish their pieces and, in addition, some had been asked to read from a script the assistant producer handed them. Now it was her turn and she seriously doubted whether her wobbling knees would carry her as far as the platform. To her surprise they did. For a moment she stood there, deeply conscious of the three pairs of expectant eyes that were concentrated on her.

'Right, begin whenever you're ready,' Alex Keynan prompted, looking up at her over the frames of his horn-rimmed reading glasses.

Amy took a deep breath to calm her hammering heartbeat, then began, playing both parts in her favourite scene between Olivia and Viola from *Twelfth Night*. As soon as the first lines had squeezed past her constricted throat she relaxed and forgot where she was. Her nerves calmed as she sank herself into the characters, speaking the lines of both with conviction. At last she came to the end of the scene with Viola's exit line: *Farewell, fair cruelty*. There was a short silence as she came down to earth again. She looked out at the three people lined up before her. Then Alex Keynan looked up, cleared his throat and said:

'Thank you, Miss – er . . .' He peered at the clipboard on his lap. 'Miss Jessop. If you'd like to leave your address with Peter over there we'll be in touch.'

Amy's cheeks were pink with embarrassment as she rejoined Celia at the back of the hall. 'I told you,' she whispered. 'I feel a fool now. Let's go.' But Celia shook her head. 'Don't be daft. You did all right. They let you finish, didn't they? Let's stay and hear the last few. We might as well.' As Amy sat down reluctantly beside her she squeezed her hand and whispered: 'You were better than any of them – honest.'

'No I *wasn't*,' Amy hissed back. 'I got the *don't call us* treatment. You said it was the kiss of death.'

They sat on, Amy with undisguised impatience and Celia placidly enjoying the entertainment. At last everyone had been seen and Alex rose to his feet and thanked them all for coming. They were filing out when the young man who had checked them in came up and touched Amy's arm.

'Miss Jessop. Mr Keynan would like to speak to you. Will you come this way please?'

Amy stared at him, and then at Celia who nudged her.

'Go on then. I'll wait,' she said.

Amy followed the young man back into the hall to where Alex Keynan was standing with his two colleagues, apparently absorbed in earnest discussion. She stood hesitantly on the fringe of the group until the young man touched Alex on the shoulder and drew his attention to her.

'Ah – Miss Jessop.' He turned away from the others to regard her, his arms folded. He was a tall man in his late thirties with thick dark hair brushed back from his forehead and worn fairly long. He had a typical actor's face: long, mobile mouth and strong nose, high cheekbones and bright, sharp eyes that seemed to Amy to look right through her. Then he smiled and his expression changed instantly, exuding a charm that quite took her breath away.

'I wanted a word with you before you left. Are you a drama student?'

'No.'

'How old are you?'

'Eighteen,' she lied. 'Well – almost.'

'And you want to make the theatre your career, I suppose?'

'Oh, yes. It's all I've *ever* wanted.'

He lifted one eyebrow with a hint of cynicism. 'Such enthusiasm. What it is to be young. Well, I should say right away that I've got all the actors I need for the present, but I was quite impressed by your audition. I do still have a vacancy for a student ASM.' Seeing her mystified expression he explained: 'Student-cum-assistant stage manager. What it boils down to is that you'd lend a hand wherever it's needed backstage: running errands, making coffee, sitting in the prompt corner with the script, that kind of thing, in return for learning the craft of acting. There would be the occasional walk-on part to help you get some experience and you might sometimes be required to understudy too.' Seeing excitement beginning to dance in Amy's eyes he added quickly, 'I warn you, we'd work your backside off and the money's abysmal. Just about enough to pay your digs, if you're lucky.' He peered at her quizzically. 'Well, I'm prepared to take a chance if you are. Do you want to go home and talk to your mother and father about it?'

Amy drew a deep breath. 'I haven't got a father and my mother lets me make my own decisions,' she said. 'I'd like to accept your offer, Mr Keynan.'

'Right.' He was already turning away. 'Just give your particulars to Peter over there and he'll give you all the details. The tour begins a month from Monday, but we'll be travelling up to Lancashire to begin rehearsals on Sunday. Peter will let you know the travelling arrangements.'

'Yes, I see. Thank you, Mr Keynan.'

*

'So – what do you think your mum will say?' Celia asked as they sat over frothy coffee in a nearby café. She was looking at Amy with open admiration, awed by the magnitude of the decision she'd just made. When she'd dared her to audition she hadn't dreamed that she'd actually be offered a job – still less that she'd have the nerve to take it.

'I doubt if she'll be interested,' Amy said, displaying a bravado she didn't feel. Only now was it beginning to sink in. The euphoria of getting her first job in the theatre was rapidly becoming overshadowed by the prospect of the reception her news would receive – both at home and at school. 'Ever since Vincent made her a director Mum's had even less time for me,' she added with a shrug. 'I should think she'll probably be glad to get rid of me.'

Celia pulled down the corners of her mouth. 'Well – I wouldn't bet on it. You do realise that she can stop you, don't you? You're still under age.'

Amy tossed her head. 'She'd better not try.' But as the girls made their way down to Piccadilly to the Underground Amy's stomach was quaking. She wanted to go to Lancashire with Alex Keynan's theatre company more than anything in the world. But she was already wishing with all her heart that the next few hours were behind her.

Maryan had been glad when Amy announced that she was going out for the day with Celia. She'd been mooning around the place, bored and taciturn, ever since St Hildred's had broken up for the Easter holidays. Sometimes Maryan despaired of the relationship between them ever improving. She'd tried to interest her in the shop and its contents, even given her some filing to do in the office and encouraged her to serve in the shop when Paul was at lunch. But the girl had shown no enthusiasm for any of it. She didn't even seem interested in doing the necessary revision for her coming exams. Getting her out of the flat for the day was frankly a relief and Maryan was glad to be able to apply herself more fully to her work.

She was deep in her monthly book-keeping when Paul tapped on the office door and announced that Mrs Donlan was here and would like to see her.

'I did tell her you were busy,' he added in a whisper.

Maryan laid down her pen with a sigh. Just when she had promised herself an uninterrupted afternoon on the books. But before she had time to speak, Fay, resplendent in fur coat and matching hat, pushed rudely past Paul and into the office.

253

'I think you and I have got to have a little talk, Mrs Jessop,' she said stridently, her eyes flashing.

A feeling of apprehension stirred uneasily in Maryan's breast. It was clear from the expression on Fay's face that the 'little talk' was going to be anything but pleasant. She had a fair idea of what it was about, too. Rising from the desk she nodded to Paul who was still hovering uncertainly in the doorway. 'Thank you, Paul.' To Fay she said: 'Perhaps you'd like to come upstairs to the flat?'

Fay followed her upstairs in bristling silence. When they reached the living room and Maryan asked if she could take her coat, Fay declined, pulling it round her protectively.

'No thank you. It isn't very warm in here. What I have to say won't take long anyway.'

'Well, have a chair at least,' Maryan said. 'Perhaps you'd like a cup of tea?'

'This isn't a social call,' Fay said with a sniff. 'And you might as well know that I don't take kindly to being told by that – that *upstart* downstairs that one of my husband's *employees* is too busy to see me.'

'That was my fault, not Paul's,' Maryan said calmly. 'I told him I wasn't to be disturbed as I was having an afternoon on the books. Now, is there something I can do for you, Mrs Donlan?'

'Yes, there certainly is.' Fay fixed her with an icy look. 'And I might as well come straight to the point. I want to know what the relationship is between you and my husband?'

Maryan felt as though all the blood in her veins had turned to ice. 'I – don't understand,' she said. 'I work for him. I run the shop and do some of the buying.'

'I know all *that*,' Fay snapped. 'It's what you've been getting up to out of business hours that concerns me.'

'There is nothing between Vincent and me,' Maryan said quietly. 'Ever since you came back to him . . .'

'Ah – so I *was* right then.' Fay was on her feet, her eyes glittering. 'There is something. I knew there had to be a reason for him making you a director.'

'Mrs Donlan, please. Making me a director in the firm was purely a business gesture. I was about to say that since you came back Vincent and I have hardly met at all. Most of our communication is done by telephone.'

'Huh. You expect me to believe that? Why did he give you a seat on the board then, while I – his own wife – am left out of it? I'm completely left in the dark about how the business is doing. All I hear are constant complaints about the money *I* spend.' She paused

254

briefly for breath, looking round her. 'And another thing, this flat; if he's so anxious to save money why should you live here, rent-free in comfort in *our* flat, while Vinnie and I have to pay rent for another place?' She drew herself up to her full height. 'I've decided to give you a month's notice, Mrs Jessop. Now that you're going up in the world I'm sure you'll want to buy a place of your own.' Her eyes glinted triumphantly. 'You'll kindly be out of this flat – shall we say by the first of May? That be convenient to you, will it?'

'I'll take notice from my employer and no one else,' Maryan said, her heart pounding. 'I don't think you really have the right to evict me.'

Fay fumed, her face turning bright scarlet. 'No *right*? Well, we'll see about that. If I say you're to get out, then out you go – understand? I'm still not convinced that you and Vinnie aren't carrying on behind my back. Why would he pick up an uneducated, penniless *nobody* like you, send you off on God knows how many courses and then make you a director? It stands to reason there's something fishy going on. I'm not stupid, you know. I'll prove to him that I can be careful with his money. I'll save him the rent on our flat for a start. We can move in here.'

It was during this tirade Maryan heard footsteps on the stairs and realised with dismay that Amy had come home and was on her way up. She mustn't hear this woman's wild accusations, whatever happened. She held up her hand. 'Please – you'll have to excuse me. My daughter is home and . . .' She edged towards the door and Fay gave a triumphant little laugh.

'Oh, *no*, you wouldn't want her to know what a devious mother she's got, would you?' To Maryan's horror she sat down on the settee. 'I'll wait,' she announced stubbornly. 'There are one or two more things I'd like to say to you while I'm here.'

Maryan came out onto the landing and closed the living room door just as Amy reached the top of the stairs. 'I've got a visitor,' she said quietly. 'Will you . . .'

But before she got any further Amy burst out: 'Mum – I've got a job. I'm leaving school.'

Maryan stared at her daughter. 'You've *what*?'

'A job – in the theatre – a touring company. Student ASM, it's called. I went for this audition. I didn't mean to but it was on when we were passing and Celia dared me. It was just for fun really but then they offered me a job and – and I said yes.'

Maryan frowned. 'That was a very irresponsible thing to do, Amy. You're still at school. You know you can't take it.'

Amy's mouth set into the stubborn line that Maryan knew all too

255

well. 'I'm going to take it, Mum. There's nothing you can do to stop me.'

'Oh yes there is. You're under age. I do still have some say in what you do.'

'I don't care what you say, I'm going. I'll only run away if you try and stop me.'

'Don't be so silly, Amy.' Maryan stepped across the landing and opened the bedroom door. 'Just wait in your room for a few minutes. We'll talk about this after . . .'

'*No*. I won't be sent to my room like a naughty child.' Amy stamped her foot. 'This is the chance of a lifetime and you're not going to stop me. You've done enough already to ruin my life.'

'Do as you're told at once,' Maryan hissed, desperate to bring the altercation to a halt. 'I've told you, I've got a visitor.'

'It's always someone else who gets priority with you, isn't it?' Amy snapped. 'I almost have to make an *appointment* to speak to you. Well, it isn't going to make any difference. I'm taking this job no matter what you do.'

Maryan felt her nerves stretched almost beyond endurance. She was dangerously close to losing her temper when she reached out and made a grab at Amy's shoulder. 'For heaven's sake be *quiet*,' she hissed. 'I've told you, I can't talk now.'

Her eyes full of angry tears, Amy shook off her mother's hand. 'Why pretend? You'll be glad you're getting rid of me,' she shouted. 'You left poor Grandma on her own just so that you could come here. Left her in that awful bombed-out house in Hackney to die of the damp and cold.'

Maryan gasped. 'Amy. That's not true. It was for you. I took this job and the flat for *you*.'

'Don't tell *lies*, Mum,' Amy lashed out. 'Nothing has ever been for me. I was a mistake right from the first, wasn't I? Nothing but a great big *mistake*. Why did you never tell me who my real father was? Why did you let me go on all those years, believing I was a Jessop when I was another man's child? Oh yes, I know all about it. I've known for ages. Well, now I'm going for good so you won't have to hush me up any more. And you can tell your boyfriend – *Uncle Vinnie* – that he needn't pay my school fees any more either. So you see, I'm doing everyone a favour, aren't I?'

Maryan winced as the door slammed in her face. She felt stunned. Amy *knew* about Marcus. But how? Who could have told her? Apart from the Leighs, only two people knew – Vinnie and her mother, and neither of them would have . . . And the remark about *Vincent* paying the school fees. Where on earth had she got that idea? She was still trying to make sense of it all when a voice behind her startled her.

'Well, *well*. Quite a revealing little outburst, wasn't it?' Fay stood in the living-room doorway, a smile of spiteful triumph on her face. 'Now I'm really glad I stayed.' She stepped up to Maryan, so close that her over-applied perfume was almost suffocating. 'You and he have known each other longer than you let on, haven't you? *A lot longer*. You and your spoilt, nasty-tempered brat are just a couple of little skeletons, rattling away here in your rent-free cupboard. And to think he accused *me* of promiscuity. When I think of the way I've had to grovel and ask his forgiveness when all the time . . .' She poked Maryan in the chest with a sharp forefinger. 'Tell me – did you *blackmail* him into giving you this job and flat? Is that the price poor Vinnie had to pay you to keep your mouth shut about his bastard?'

Maryan's heart throbbed in her throat and her mouth was dry, but she kept her head. 'You're jumping to all the wrong conclusions, just as Amy did,' she said, outwardly cool. 'Blackmail is a very serious accusation. I think you should be careful.'

There was a momentary flicker of doubt in Fay's eyes. 'Never mind,' she said. 'Now that I know what a hypocrite my dear husband is I'll make sure he pays. By the time I'm done with the pair of you you'll wish you'd never set eyes on each other.'

Chapter Fourteen

As the train rattled through the unfamiliar landscape Amy sat quietly in her corner looking out. It was like nothing she had ever seen before. She had always equated the countryside with leafy rural Suffolk. This raw, wild moorland scenery clothed in granite and olive green seemed bleak and unfriendly; almost awe-inspiring by comparison. Staring out at the massive craggy sweep of it she relived the two traumatic days prior to her leaving Simons Mews.

She had burned her boats; she knew it now. And although she recognised that taking this job was the most adventurous thing she had ever done there were still twinges of doubt and guilt about the way she and her mother had parted. She knew that she had behaved deplorably, making things difficult for her mother by blurting out suspicions that later turned out to be partly untrue. But instead of displaying the anger Amy had expected, Maryan had been strangely silent. Her silence unnerved Amy. It was almost as though her mother had finally given up on her. She had won her fight for independence. But it was a hollow victory.

When she had slammed the door in her mother's face on the afternoon of the audition she had thrown herself onto the bed in a torrent of emotional tears. But once the tears were shed she felt relief that at last the secret between them was out in the open. Maybe she should have told her mother long ago that she had overheard her confession to the Leighs all those years ago. She decided to apologise; to make it up with Maryan. Maybe she would even give up the job if her mother seriously wanted her to.

But when she went downstairs to the office she found Maryan white-faced and ominously silent.

'Mum – I'm sorry . . .' She began.

Maryan laid down her pen and met her daughter's eyes levelly. 'I hope you realise just how much damage you did this afternoon,

258

Amy,' she said. 'It was Mrs Donlan who was waiting in the living room. She heard your disgraceful outburst and she's gone away with all the wrong ideas.'

'Oh.' Amy bit her lip. 'What wrong ideas?'

'If you can remember what you said, you can use your own imagination. You've put me in an impossible position.' She looked up at her daughter. 'And, for your information, Amy, Vincent does *not* pay your school fees.'

Amy gasped. 'I'm sorry. I didn't know. Mum – do you think – could we talk about my real father some time?'

'I don't think there's anything to be gained by that. I don't think there would be much point. But I would like to know who told you.'

'You did. I mean – I heard you telling Mr and Mrs Leigh that night at Whitegates – just after Mr Marcus – my father, was killed.'

'Oh. I see.' Maryan sighed, relieved that at least no third person was guilty of betraying her secret.

Amy stood biting her lip, bewildered at her mother's lack of response. She had said she was sorry, but it seemed that Mum was determined to make her grovel. 'Look – if you like I'll go and ring Mrs Donlan,' she offered. 'I'll tell her it isn't how she thinks. I'll even turn the job down – if you want me to.'

'The damage is done now.' With a resigned sigh Maryan picked up her pen again. 'Talking to Mrs Donlan will only make things worse. And you might as well take the job if it really means so much to you,' she added wearily. 'I've been given notice to leave the flat. From the first of May we won't have anywhere to live.'

Amy's heart sank. Could her outburst really have caused such disaster? 'Is – is that my fault too?' she asked.

Maryan shook her head. 'No, not entirely. What you said didn't help, though. I'm afraid neither of us is popular here any more. Perhaps it's time I looked for another job and you and I went our own ways. Perhaps I've looked on you as a child for too long. You're a woman now, after all.'

Since that afternoon Maryan had been unnaturally quiet. Amy had hardly seen her except at mealtimes, and even then they exchanged scarcely a word. The one thing Maryan had insisted on was that Amy herself went along to St Hildred's to tell the Mother Superior that she was leaving. This she had done yesterday morning and she still cringed inwardly when she remembered the witheringly stern looks and words she had received.

'You are throwing away a golden future, Amethyst.' (The nuns always used the girls' proper names.) 'The sisters have worked hard with you because they felt that you were a highly promising pupil

259

and worthy of all their skills and expertise. Now, on the kind of reckless whim I would have expected of some ignorant guttersnipe, you are tossing all that dedication back in their faces.' She leaned forward, the palms of her hands on the desk and her spectacles glinting ominously. 'You are jeopardising your whole future life, child. You will bitterly regret this decision. And the tragic part is that when you do it will be too late.'

Unable to think of a suitable reply, Amy had sat mesmerised by the formidable dark-veiled figure on the other side of the massive mahogany desk. For one electrified moment their eyes had locked in a wordless, uncompromising duel. Mother Superior was first to avert her gaze. She waved a dismissive hand. 'Very well, that is all, child. If your mind is made up you had better go.'

The train for Lancashire was due to leave Euston at seven forty-five on Sunday morning. Amy had set her alarm clock for six o'clock, risen quietly and made herself a hurried breakfast. Nothing had been said the night before. There had been no last-minute reprieve, no forgiveness or loving reconciliation. It seemed that Maryan had meant it when she said it was time for them to go their own ways.

Amy was careful not to wake her mother. She fought shy of the parting. It would be awkward. She wouldn't know what to say. Instead she scribbled a note and left it on the kitchen table along with her key to the flat, then she picked up her suitcase, crept quietly down the stairs and let herself out into the mews. Closing the street door behind her she suddenly felt very small and alone. Recognising that she was taking her first independent step into the adult world, she shivered a little, half excited, half afraid. If only she could have taken it with everyone's blessing. But she was learning fast that being a rebel didn't come cheaply.

As she came out of the Undergound at Euston Station the first person she saw was Celia. Her eyes lit up in surprise.

'Cee – what are you doing here?'

'What do you think, dope? I've come to see you off.' Celia hugged her hard. 'I hope you appreciate the fact that I've sacrificed my Sunday morning lie-in for you.'

They looked at each other, both girls' eyes bright. 'You *do* want to go, don't you?' Celia asked anxiously. 'I mean – don't feel you have to see it through just for the sake of pride. No one's going to think any the less . . .'

'I *do* want to go. Honestly.' Amy hugged her friend. 'But I do appreciate you coming to see me off.' She picked up her case and together they walked to the barrier.

'Was it awful?' Celia asked. 'Your mum and everything?'

'Pretty awful. But she accepted it in the end. Mother Superior was something else though.'

'Oh, hell, poor you. I can imagine.' Celia pulled a face. 'Hey, that looks like your lot over there. There's that Peter whatshisname running around like a headless chicken trying to organise everyone.' She hugged Amy so hard that all the breath was knocked out of her. 'Look, goodbye, kid. I'm off now. I hate standing waving at the back end of a train. Anyway, I might make a fool of myself and blub. You will write and tell all, won't you?'

''Course – you bet. Cee . . .'

'What?'

'I'm going to miss you.'

'Me too. Bye then – have a good time. Make it to Hollywood, or break a leg, or whatever it is they say.' Then, with a final wave, she was gone, to be quickly swallowed up in the mass of people congregating on the platform. And Amy was really alone, facing the future and the results – whatever they might be – of her first major decision. And feeling very far from confident.

Vincent arrived soon after ten, while Maryan was still eating her breakfast. He let himself in and walked up the stairs, pausing to tap on the kitchen door before entering. Maryan knew who it was the moment she heard the street door opening. No one else had a key except Amy, and she had left hers on the table, along with the note she had written. At his knock she called out to him to come in.

He stood in the doorway, taking in her pale face, devoid of make-up. There were traces of tears still on her eyelashes.

'Maryan,' he said quietly. 'My dear, I had to come.'

'Does Fay know you're here?' She got up and turned to the sink to refill the kettle. 'I'll make some fresh tea.'

He sat down at the table. 'I've just come from Mass. And I did tell Fay that I intended to look in on you.'

'Did you manage to calm her?'

He lifted his shoulders expressively. 'Not really.'

'I'm sorry about Amy's outburst. I've no idea what gave her the notion you were paying for her education. It gave entirely the wrong impression. If it caused you any embarrassment . . .'

'Embarrassment's hardly the word for it, but believe me, Maryan, it couldn't have made things any worse than they were already. Every day there's some new outrageous complaint or accusation. I'm getting used to it. I'm just sorry that she came here, interrogating and upsetting you.'

261

Maryan sighed. 'I should have been straight with Amy as soon as she was old enough to understand. You always said I should, didn't you?' She looked at him. 'I've lost her, you know – Amy. She's gone, taken this theatrical job. She left early this morning.' She pulled Amy's crumpled letter out of her pocket. 'She left this. It's all I have to prove that I once had a daughter.'

Vincent took the note and read.

Dear Mum,

I'm really sorry for any trouble I've caused. I didn't mean to. I didn't wake you because I hate goodbyes and I think we've said all there is to say. You were right when you said it was time we went our own separate ways. Maybe this way I can find out what kind of person I really am. I hope you find somewhere nice to live soon and another job.

Good luck, Amy.

He looked up at Maryan in alarm. 'What does she mean about another place to live – and another job?'

'I thought you knew. Fay gave me notice – of the flat, that is. It's my decision to give you my resignation.'

He stared at her, appalled. '*No*, Maryan. I refuse to accept it. And Fay had no right . . .'

'I think she did,' she interrupted. 'She wants to make this flat your home. She expected to have a directorship in Vincente's. She resented you offering me one. And perhaps she's right, Vinnie. She is your wife, after all.' She glanced up at him. 'And we can't deny that her suspicions about us were partly justified, can we? It's better that I leave – make a complete break. Perhaps it will make things easier for you too.'

He got up from the table and began to walk up and down. 'I won't accept this, Maryan. You are part of this firm. An important part. I can't – I *won't* let you go.'

'But you have to. There's no choice, for either of us.' She reached out to catch at his wrist as he passed. 'If you care anything for me at all, Vinnie, you'll accept my resignation and let me go. There's no future for me – for us. And staying on here isn't going to make things easier.' She looked up at him pleadingly. 'Please – I mean it.'

His face stricken, he pulled out a chair and sat facing her, grasping both her hands. 'But where will you go? How will I know you're all right?'

'I'll be fine. You don't have to worry.' She gave him a wry smile. 'I could always go back and work in the market again if the worst comes to the worst. Summer's on its way and it isn't so bad when the weather's fine.'

'Please – don't joke.'

'I'll keep in touch with Roisan.'

'Will you? Promise me you'll do that?' he asked earnestly. 'I know she'll want you to.'

'All right. I promise. I'll go and see her soon; let her know what I've decided.'

He stood up, drawing her to her feet. Searching her eyes he said: 'Oh, Maryan, what have I done to you, my love? I feel like a man being torn in half.' He looked at her. 'Fay thinks Amy is mine, you know – that we were having an affair long before she left me. Nothing will convince her it isn't true. She's even managed to persuade herself that she knew it was going on at the time and that was her reason for leaving me.'

'I'm sorry. That makes it all the more necessary for me to leave.'

'Sometimes I feel I should have listened to Roisan when she urged me to get a divorce,' he said vehemently. 'Fay is so neurotic – either over-excited or deeply depressed. Perhaps it's something to do with her diabetes.' His eyes clouded. 'I believe that losing the child must have affected her deeply. God, Maryan, what a mess I've made of everything.' He drew her close and held her for a long moment, till she gently pushed him away.

'Go now, Vinnie,' she said. 'I'll leave at the end of the month. If you want me to help choose someone else to run the shop, I will, but I think Paul is quite capable of managing now. And Geoff could easily take over the buying. Perhaps you could manage with someone to come in and do the book-keeping.'

'Just you look after yourself,' he said. 'You'll get the best reference I can write. The rest is my problem.' He tilted her chin with one finger to look deeply into her eyes and his voice was husky as he said: 'I'll always – *always* love you, Maryan.'

She smiled gently. 'Life will be easier without me, though. Admit it.'

'It will be bleaker, I know that,' he said with a shake of his head. 'You brought the sun back into my life again. Without you . . .' He lifted his shoulders. 'God only knows.'

The three-week rehearsal period was a revelation to Amy. A revelation and, if she were truthful, a slight disillusionment too. Alex Keynan had warned her that the life of a student ASM was hard work, but it sometimes seemed to her that the job was nothing more than that of an errand girl. At the beck and call of every member of

263

the company, she was run off her feet all day long. It sometimes seemed that the principal actors regarded her as some kind of personal maid, and as well as slipping out to buy cigarettes, newspapers and aspirins from the local shops, she was expected to climb ladders and hold tools for the carpenter and electrician, help paint scenery and go round the local shops begging various articles and items of furniture for props on the promise of a free advertisement in the programme. If she'd expected to be able to learn anything about acting she was to be disappointed in those early weeks. She wrote to her mother to let her know that she was safe and well and to send a temporary address, but Maryan did not reply. It looked as though the break between them was permanent, and gradually, as the days passed, she hardened her heart, telling herself she'd been right all along. Maryan had never really wanted her. It would be best if they didn't communicate at all.

The company was to tour several northern towns with a repertoire of plays, working for three weeks in each venue. The plays were varied: Coward's *Tonight at Eight-Thirty*; Shaw's *Pygmalion* and Emily Brontë's *Wuthering Heights*. Once the first three weeks of hectic, intensive rehearsal was over and they had settled into a routine of nightly performances and the occasional morning runthrough, things became quieter and Amy was at last able to find more time to observe and glean what she could from Alex Keynan's direction and the professionalism of the cast. The first thing she learned was that it was all very different from school plays.

To begin with she had been quite shocked by Alex's method of direction. It seemed to her that he was rude and insulting to his actors. He frequently shouted and swore at them and often made them go over a scene again and again. She had seen the leading actress in tears more than once. But when she asked Peter King, the stage manager, why they never threw down their scripts and walked out, or swore back at him, he just smiled and said: 'They know he's a good director, the best, and that they're damned lucky to be working with him. They've got the sense to know that he can really bring out the best in them and that doing as he says will further their career. He's tipped for the top, you know.'

'If he's that good why is he taking out a small-town tour like this?'

Peter looked at her in surprise. 'Didn't you realise that this is an Arts Council sponsored tour? The other two bods at the auditions were from there. Alex was just beginning to make a name for himself before the war. He was one of the youngest directors Stratford had ever had, and he was directing in the West End when he was still only twenty-five. He hasn't done much since he came out of the RAF. I think this tour is his way of getting his hand in again.'

Amy was impressed. 'The RAF? Why wasn't he with ENSA?'

'Seems he wanted to have a bash at the Luftwaffe. He was a pilot. He flew Mosquitos. They were death-traps, you know. Not much of a chance of getting out if you were hit. He volunteered for them when his wife was killed in an air raid in '41. They'd only been married a couple of weeks.'

'Oh, I see. How awful.'

After that Amy looked on Alex Keynan with a slightly different attitude. She watched him working whenever she could and soon she began to see that Peter had been right. Alex knew how to coax and cajole as well as bully the very best out of his actors. It all depended on who he was handling as well as the role they were playing. And he certainly got results. They played to packed houses and the local press was generous in praise of the company.

As the weeks went by and Amy performed her endless thankless tasks, running errands, making coffee, fetching and carrying, she longed for a chance to experience for herself the direction of the Keynan Players' brilliant, charismatic director. She already knew most of the lines of each of the leading female roles. She fantasised about one of the leading actresses being stricken by some virus or knocked down – very gently, of course – by a bus, so that she could step into the vacant role just once and prove her worth. But, much to her disappointment, all the members of the cast, both male and female, seemed to have cast-iron constitutions and never succumbed to as much as a headache

Their first date was in Minsdale, a small market town on the Lancashire-Cumbrian border. It was early summer now and on the first Sunday Peter took her walking up onto the fells on the outskirts of the town. The air was sparklingly fresh and larks sang high above the hills, joyful specks hovering in a clear blue sky. A gentle breeze stirred the grass and wild flowers sprang from cracks in the rocky outcrops that scattered the climb to the ridge of the fell. They'd taken a packed lunch and at midday they sat down among the wiry grass to eat. Amy shaded her eyes and pointed to where a sheet of water gleamed in the distance like beaten silver.

'What's that water?'

'Lake Windermere. It's very beautiful – popular too. It'll be getting full of summer visitors soon. We're playing there later in the season. I'm afraid that might mean the digs'll be expensive.'

Amy sighed. 'That's all I need. I hardly have anything left over at the end of the week as it is.'

'I know. The pay is a bit stingy, isn't it?' He took the sandwich she handed him. 'Thanks. Apart from the money, how are you liking it, Amy – now that we're really into the tour, I mean?'

'It's okay.' Amy munched her sandwich thoughtfully. 'I'd like it better if I got a chance to act, though. Alex said there might be the odd walk-on part, but all the parts are taken so I can't see how I'm to get a look-in at all.'

'I expect what he meant was when someone dropped out or wanted time off,' Peter said. He glanced at her thoughtfully out of the corner of his eye. 'Look, if I tell you something will you promise to keep it to yourself?'

Catching the scent of conspiracy she turned to him, her eyes beginning to shine. 'Of course, anything you say. What is it?'

'Well, one of the girls is going to give in her notice shortly. She's had the offer of a part in a film. Only a tiny part, but it's a start and . . .'

'Yes, yes – *who*?' Amy knew that if it was one of the leading actresses someone else would have to be engaged. If it was someone who played smaller parts she might just be in with a chance. 'Come on – who is it, Peter?'

He chewed his lip before replying. 'You do promise not to let it out, don't you? She only told me because I was there when she got the telegram.' At her emphatic nod he said, 'Okay. It's Natalie Bentham.'

Amy's heart sank. She was an established actress; a woman in her early thirties. She played the leading parts in two of the plays and substantial roles in the others. There was no chance that Alex would risk a raw beginner in parts like that.

But the following day Alex asked her to stay on after the morning run-through. She found him in his cubbyhole of an office, close to the side of the stage in the small theatre they were playing. She tapped nervously on the half-open door and he called out to her to come in.

'Ah, there you are, Amy. You may have heard that we are to lose a member of our company.' Amy shrugged noncommittally and he went on: 'Natalie is leaving us and Rosalind Decker will be taking over her parts. It's going to mean some shuffling around; and it's going to leave some of the minor parts vacant. I intend to start rehearsing again tomorrow with everyone in their new parts.' He took a sheaf of scripts from the table in front of him and handed them to her. 'Perhaps you'd like to begin studying the parts I've marked. There are two: the maid in *Pygmalion* and the little kitchen skivvy in *Wuthering Heights*. I think you'll find the costumes will fit you.'

266

Amy took the scripts, her heart thudding with excitement. 'Thank you, Alex. I promise you *faithfully* I'll do my very best.'

He raised an eyebrow at her. 'I don't need your undying gratitude, darling. Just say the lines and try not to bump into the scenery, that's all I ask. After all, that's what you're here for – to fill in where necessary. If you turn out to be a bloody disaster I'll have to send for someone else, but we'll see.' He grinned at her. 'Don't look so crestfallen. I said I'd give you a try-out and this is it.'

Slightly deflated, she retreated, clutching her scripts, to spend all afternoon in her tiny bedsitter, learning the lines. By the time rehearsal was called at ten next morning she knew her few lines and moves perfectly. Nevertheless her stomach churned with apprehension as she stood in the wings waiting for her cue. Alex's casual words about sending for someone else if she proved 'a bloody disaster' had made her determined to prove beyond a doubt that she was a born actress.

Halfway through rehearsing the first act of *Wuthering Heights* Alex called out for them to stop.

'*Amy* – what the hell do you think you're doing?' he thundered from his seat in the front stalls.

She looked up, broom in hand, her face pink as all eyes were turned on her. 'Me? Er – sweeping.'

'Ever heard of the expression *upstaging*?' he demanded.

Amy looked nonplussed as a muted titter went round the other members of the cast. 'Yes. But I . . .'

Alex gave an exaggerated sigh and raked a hand through his hair. 'I know you're supposed to be a kitchen maid and realism is very commendable, but you don't *sweep* when the other characters are speaking their lines – *right*?'

Amy blushed crimson. 'Oh, no. I mean, yes. Sorry.'

When the rehearsal was over Peter found her in a corner of the prop room, frantically tidying the shelves, her face flushed.

'Oh, there you are. I've been looking all over for you. We're going to the pub for a sandwich and a beer. Are you coming?'

She shook her head without turning round. 'No. You go. I'm not hungry.'

He paused, then came over to her. 'Amy. You're not upset, are you? I've just heard Alex saying how good you were. How clearly you spoke the lines.'

She turned to look at him. 'You're just saying that. I was awful. Anyway. I've only got three lines *to* speak.'

'Yes, but you got the accent right – spot on.'

267

'I just copied my landlady. It's supposed to be Yorkshire, but suppose it's Lancashire really.'

He slipped an arm around her shoulders. 'Never mind, Alex thought it was okay anyway.'

She brightened. 'So you don't think he'll send for another actress then?'

He laughed. 'When he can get you to do it for next to nothing? You must be joking.'

It was a backhanded compliment, but it was all Amy needed to cheer her up.

Later that evening Alex came to find her and obliquely confirmed that she was to keep the part.

'Amy, I'm getting next week's programme roughed out for the printer. Do you want your own name on the cast list?'

Her heart gave a little leap. Seeing her name on the programme as a member of the cast for the first time would be quite a thrill. 'Oh – yes please.' At his slightly doubtful expression she asked: 'Why? Is something wrong?'

'No – but . . .' He stroked his chin. 'Amy Jessop's a bit on the mundane side, isn't it? I wondered if you'd thought about adopting a stage name.'

A *stage* name. The idea stirred her imagination; it would be a bit like casting a skin – taking on a new identity. 'My first name is really Amethyst,' she told him. Then she had a sudden flash of inspiration. 'I think I'd like to be called Amethyst Leigh,' she said.

Alex smiled. 'Oh, *very* exotic. It has a gypsyish ring to it. I like it. Amethyst Leigh it shall be. And we'll keep you in as Amy Jessop, Assistant Stage Manager.'

And the fact that when the programmes were printed it came out as Amethyst *Lee* made no difference to Amy. She had a whole new persona. She was Amethyst Lee, the actress. A real person in her own right at last.

By the time Amy had been gone a week Maryan was already packed and ready to leave the flat in Simons Mews. On the Saturday morning after Amy's departure she had left the shop in Paul's capable hands and gone to visit Roisan. The older woman greeted her warmly.

'Come in, my dear. Vinnie said you'd be coming to see me. I can't tell you how upset I was to hear what had happened.' She took Maryan downstairs to the kitchen where she was busy cooking lunch. 'You will stay and eat with me, won't you?' she asked.

'There's plenty for two and it's always more enjoyable than eating alone.'

Maryan sat down at the table. 'I came to tell you what happened,' she said. 'But I don't know where to start.'

Roisan tested the potatoes bubbling away on top of the Aga, then replaced the lid. 'You don't have to. Vinnie has already told me everything; the whole unfortunate business. He's devastated at the thought of losing you.' She joined Maryan at the table. 'In more ways than one, as I'm sure I don't need to tell you.'

'I can't bear the thought of Fay thinking Vinnie is Amy's father,' Maryan said. 'I feel so responsible and I keep thinking that there must be something I can do to put it right.'

Roisan shook her head. 'Take my advice and don't even try. Fay will believe what she wants to believe and if you thwart her she's likely to make matters worse. Taking that woman back was the worst day's work Vinnie ever did. I'm sorry to say it, and God knows I've been a devout Catholic all my life, but if ever there was a good case for changing the divorce rule, Fay is it. I sometimes wonder if she's actually sane.'

'I'm packed and ready to leave the flat,' Maryan said. 'I just want it all to be over now.'

'Have you found another job?' Roisan asked. 'And somewhere to live?'

Maryan lifted her shoulders. 'Not yet. Flats are hard to find in London, as you know. And the rents are so expensive when you do find one. I've been thinking of moving out of town altogether.'

'Well, you're more than welcome to stay here till you get sorted,' Roisan said. 'I've plenty of room and I'd enjoy your company.' She rose to dish up the meal, but as she brought the plates to the table her face was thoughtful. 'I've just had a thought,' she said. 'A young woman I know is about to set up in business on her own and she's needing a secretary – no, a bit more than that; someone to organise things for her. It might be just your kind of thing.'

Maryan looked up. 'What line is she in, antiques?'

'No, fashion. I met her doing the decor for a show and I've run into her a few times since when I've been buying fabrics. You've worked in the rag trade too, haven't you? Would you like me to put in a word for you?'

'Well, yes. Yes please, Roisan.'

'Better than that, I'll ring her and then you can get in touch yourself. I've got a card somewhere. I'll find it for you before you leave.'

Maryan felt better for Roisan's good beef casserole and apple

269

sponge pudding. Alone in the flat since Amy's departure, she'd hardly eaten at all. Now, with the offer of temporary accommodation and the prospect of a job in view she felt much more optimistic.

'Have you heard from Amy?' Roisan asked as they ate.

Maryan shook her head. 'Not so far. I wonder if I shall.'

'Oh, surely she'll write and let you know she's safe and well,' Roisan said. 'I've always found her a considerate girl.'

'Maybe she has been – with you,' Maryan said. 'The truth is, she and I have never really got on. She was closer to my mother than to me, but I think she still looks on Marjorie Taylor, the woman she lived with all through the war, as more of a mother than me.'

'That can't be true,' Roisan said. 'Blood is thicker than water after all. And you've done your best for her. It must have taken a big slice of your salary to send her to St Hildred's.'

Maryan was thoughtful. Amy knew it had not been she who paid the school fees. How she knew that was still a mystery. She'd been tempted to tell her that Sam Leigh had paid for her education, but she had held back in deference to Sam's wishes. There was always the possibility that Amy might try to get in touch with him and cause trouble between him and Rachel. 'I didn't pay,' she said in answer to Roisan' s question. 'Amy's grandfather did. But he wanted it kept secret. Believe me, Roisan, I've always tried to do what was best, but somehow everything I touch seems to go wrong. I daresay I'm to blame. But it's too late now to ask where I went wrong.'

'You mustn't be so hard on yourself,' Roisan said. 'Circumstances have been against you. You've had bad luck.'

'I wish now that I'd tried harder to put things right between us.' Maryan sighed. 'But maybe it's better this way. After all, Amy's a young woman now. Time for her to find her own place in the world.'

'And what about you?' Roisan asked quietly. 'Where do you go from here, Maryan? You deserve a decent life too. I know this is a dreadful setback for you after all the hard work you've put in, but don't give up. Go out and get the best for yourself. You deserve it. And I'll be here to help in any way I can.'

'Thank you, Roisan.' Maryan's eyes filled with tears. She wished she didn't have so many secrets. If only she could lay her head on Roisan's shoulder and tell her everything. It would have been such a relief.

'Don't thank me, girl. I only wish there was more I could do.' Roisan got up to make coffee. Her back to Maryan she said: 'For a short while you made Vinnie happier than I've ever seen him. It was you who helped him get this business on its feet. It's us should be thanking you. It's a crying shame we have to lose you.'

It wasn't until Maryan was leaving later that afternoon that Roisan remembered something. She rushed off to find her large, battered handbag and rummaged in its capacious interior. 'I know I put it in here somewhere,' she muttered as she heaped the bag's miscellaneous contents onto the table.

'Don't worry about it,' Maryan said pulling on her gloves. 'Any time will do.'

'No, it won't. You want to apply for the job as soon as you can. I don't want her to go and get . . . *Ah*, here it is,' she said, triumphantly holding up the small rectangle of cardboard. 'Now, I'll telephone her myself tonight and when you have a minute why not ring her yourself? She's a charming person. I'm sure the two of you will get along like a house on fire.'

Maryan tucked the card into her bag, hugged Roisan and made her way to the bus stop. It wasn't until she opened her bag to pay her bus fare that she took out the card and looked at it properly. When she did her heart missed a beat. Inscribed on it in clear black letters was a name she had heard before: Gina Stern. Haute Couture Designer.

When Fay had received no reply to her ring at the bell, she let herself in through the side door at Simons Mews with the key she'd recently had cut from Vincent's. She needed to measure for new carpets and curtains. There was no way she was going to put up with things that woman had half worn out. As she pushed the door open it caught against a bundle of mail, delivered after Maryan had left. Fay picked up the handful of letters and was about to put them to one side when her eye was caught by the rounded, childish writing on the top one. She turned the envelope over. On the back was a name and address: *Miss A. Jessop. Theatre Royal, Minsdale, Lancashire*. It was from the girl.

For a moment Fay stood tapping the letter thoughtfully with her fingers. There might be more information in this letter – things she'd find useful. The girl might make some further reference to the row she and her mother had had. She might even mention her father by name. Proof positive that Vincent was lying. Without further hesitation she slid a finger under the flap of the envelope. Inside was a single sheet of paper which she scanned eagerly. To her frustration it contained nothing of importance. It was just a brief note to say she was all right and enjoying her new job. *Damn*. Fay crumpled the letter angrily and thrust it into her pocket. The stupid girl needn't have wasted her time writing such trivia. And the Jessop woman certainly wouldn't be missing anything by not receiving it.

*

Amy's first week as an actress was one she would always remember. Getting dressed in the costume; waiting in the wings to go on; speaking her few lines and then, at the final curtain, taking her place in the line-up with the rest of the cast and listening to the applause – it was a heady experience and all she'd ever dreamed of. She loved every minute. And when a member of the cast fell victim to a migraine the following week and a chance came for her to play a bigger part in one of the Coward one-act plays she was delighted. The play was *Fumed Oak*, which told the story of a henpecked husband who kicked over the traces. Amy played the whining schoolgirl daughter and enjoyed it very much. She could identify and sympathise with the male character who, having been undervalued and misunderstood by the other members of his family, finally walked out. She'd done the right thing in leaving home, she told herself. Maryan had cheated her of a proper family life. She'd lied to her from childhood and never put her first as a mother should.

On the Saturday night after the performance she stayed on at the theatre. She'd been sharing a dressing room with two other members of the company and her digs were noisy too. She wanted an hour to herself to study the part of Cathy in *Wuthering Heights*. It was the part she coveted most of all and she was sure that one day she'd get the chance to play it. When that opportunity came she would be sure of the lines and ready to step into the role confidently. The theatre was quiet and after a while she made her way up onto the stage where she began to act out one of Cathy's scenes. The fire curtain was raised and the stage was lit only by the small pilot light in the prompt corner. Imagining the rows of seats in the empty auditorium filled with people, she completely lost herself in the part. She spoke her own lines out loud and Heathcliff's under her breath. So she was startled when a deep male voice began to speak them for her. She froze, recalling the tales of a theatre ghost, told by the elderly stage-doorkeeper. Then to her shocked surprise she saw a shadowy figure making its way towards her across the darkened stage.

'Cathy – Cathy, my love, my life.' The voice was heavy with emotion and the figure held out its arms as it advanced towards her. Amy's heart almost stopped in terror, then the figure stepped into the thin beam of light and she saw his face.

'*Alex*! You frightened the life out of me.'

He laughed. 'I'm sorry. I couldn't resist it. Besides, you gave me a bit of a start too. I thought I was alone and when I heard someone ranting away on stage I wondered what the hell was going on. Why aren't you at home in bed? Don't you know it's after midnight?'

272

'I didn't know you were still here,' she said, acutely embarrassed at being caught out.

'It's a dammed good job I was. Think yourself lucky you didn't get locked in for the night.'

'Sorry. I never thought.'

He chuckled. 'Don't be sorry. I'm quite impressed. Tell me – do you know *all* the lines?' He was looking at her with an expression of amused tolerance.

'Yes. Look, I'll be going now.'

'Hang on. Wait a minute.' He caught her arm as she passed him. 'You're really keen, aren't you, Amy? That's good, of course. But you haven't really got a clue when it comes to a character like Catherine Earnshaw.'

She felt her face stiffen. 'I'm awful, you mean?'

'No. I wouldn't say you were awful. You put up quite a presentable little try just now. But to play a part like that you need to be able to feel as deeply as the character feels. Do you have any idea how Cathy feels when she says those things to Heathcliff? Do you know what it is to be – not just in love, but *obsessed* by a man – even *po*ssessed?' He took her by the shoulders and looked down at her. In the dim light she could see the gleam of his eyes. 'No, of course you don't. You're much too young. And until you know, Amy, my sweet, you're never going to be able to get under Cathy's skin.'

'But – but it's *acting*, isn't it?' she said breathlessly. 'It's imagining. A good actress should be able to imagine how she felt.'

'You think that's possible?'

'Yes, why not?'

'Have you read *Wuthering Heights* – the book, I mean?'

'Yes. At school.'

'What school?'

'St Hildred's. It's a convent.'

He gave a brief bark of laughter. '*Nuns*? That explains a lot.' For a long moment he stood there, looking down at her, then he took her hand and began to stride off the stage. 'Come with me. It's late, I know, but I'm going to give you an acting lesson.'

He closed the door. The tiny office was lit by a single light from the Anglepoise lamp on the desk. Also on it was an open bottle of Scotch and a glass. He indicated a chair and took another glass from a drawer.

'Drink?' He picked up the bottle and looked at her enquiringly. She'd never tasted whisky before but she nodded.

'Oh, yes please,' she said casually, trying to sound as though she drank it every day.

He poured her a generous measure and sat down in the chair opposite. Taking a deep draught from his own glass he said: 'Catherine Earnshaw was the only daughter of a widowed Yorkshire farmer who had high hopes of marrying her into the local gentry. He wanted his daughter to become a lady, and Cathy quite liked the idea too – some of the time. But Cathy was basically a child of nature. She loved the moors. They'd been a part of her ever since she could remember. She was as much a moorland creature as the animals that lived there, as untamed and untamable as the wind and the storm clouds. Heathcliff with his mysterious background and passionate, unpredictable nature was her soulmate. He understood her as no one else ever could. He was all she had ever wanted. Her alter ego. She couldn't live without him. But she couldn't live *with* him either. She both loved and hated him. She resented him for the mirror image of herself that he held up to her and for the irresistible hold he had on her. She tried to be rid of him by marrying another man, but she couldn't.' He leaned across the desk to look into her eyes. 'Can you imagine the intensity of a relationship like that, Amy – *can you?*'

She lifted her glass and took a drink of the whisky. The bitter, fiery liquid almost stopped her breath and it was all she could do not to gasp. 'I suppose not, but I – I could try,' she said, her cheeks pink.

'You could try, could you?' He laughed. 'Have you ever been in love, Amy?'

She took another sip and managed this time to swallow it without wincing. 'Yes,' she said boldly. 'Yes, of course I have.'

He refilled his glass and leaned back in his chair, putting both feet on the desk in front of him. 'Okay – tell me about it.'

'Well – his name was – *is* Mike. We grew up together and I always looked on him as a brother. Then I went to his eighteenth birthday party and I knew – knew that I – I loved him.'

'So he's the same age as you?'

'Oh no. That was ages ago. He's done his National Service since then. He's a journalist now.'

'I see. And did you go to bed with him?'

She blushed crimson. '*No*. Of course not.'

'No?' He looked at her thoughtfully over the rim of his glass. 'No, you'd be pretty young at the time. Have you ever made love with a man, Amy?'

She got to her feet, her heart beating fast. 'I – I think I'll go home now.'

He was on his feet instantly. Coming round the desk he stood

274

between her and the door. Reaching out, he took her hands. 'Amy, I'm sorry. I've shocked you. I've had too much of that damned stuff.' He indicated the whisky bottle. 'I didn't mean to pry into your personal life. I just wanted to assess you as a person – an actress; to find out what you might be capable of, because you do show promise, you know.' He held her hands warmly in his and smiled gently at her as he went on: 'Do you know that when George Bernard Shaw first wrote *St Joan* and a certain celebrated actress asked him to let her play the part, he told her to go away and have a child first? He meant that she should experience emotion at its very deepest before attempting anything as intense. Do you begin to see what I'm trying to tell you?'

She nodded, though she didn't really know what he was getting at at all. She was feeling slightly dizzy and she couldn't decide whether it was because of the whisky or the compelling eyes that held hers so hypnotically. All she was really aware of was that she wanted him to kiss her. It was giving her the most peculiar sensation in the pit of her stomach. 'I – I think so,' she whispered.

'So you see, my sweet little Amy, I hardly think that a few chaste kisses with your childhood sweetheart behind the bike sheds qualifies you to play a part like passionate, tortured Cathy.' For a long moment he looked down at her. He found the upturned face with those huge, appealing eyes and the soft, slightly parted lips sorely tempting. Didn't the girl know what power she wielded? Was it possible she could really be this naive, or was the wide-eyed innocence merely an act? The next moment she gave him the tacit answer to his unasked question by reaching up and slipping her arms boldly around his neck.

He did what any man would have done. He kissed her; experimentally at first, then, finding her lips warm and yielding, he kissed her again, drawing her close so that her supple body was moulded against his.

Amy was shaken. Never in her wildest dreams had she imagined that a kiss could be like this. When Alex kissed her for the second time he took her completely by surprise. As he pulled her close she was aware of the uncompromising hardness of his body, of his lips moving sensuously on hers. When his tongue parted her lips to explore her mouth she held back for a moment, unsure. She and Celia had talked about this kind of kiss, both of them vowing that they would never allow it; denouncing it in their girlish way as 'disgusting and horrid'. But now that it was actually happening to her she found that it stirred and excited her in a way she could never have imagined possible. She let her lips part, and found that

275

surrendering to this demanding assault on her mouth was deeply erotic. It quickened her heartbeat and sent the blood roaring dizzyingly through her veins. It aroused all kinds of feelings she had never experienced before. She closed her eyes, wanting it to go on for ever. When he released her she felt almost too weak to stand and clung to him for support. He looked down at her, his eyes dancing with a mixture of amusement and surprise.

'Well, *well*. For one so innocent you're a passionate little thing, aren't you?'

She looked up at him. 'Am I?'

'Are you telling me that you've never kissed anyone like that before?' He took her arms from around his neck and held them against his chest. 'I confess you have me puzzled, Amy. You look like a little angel, yet I have the feeling there's a firebrand in there, just waiting for someone to light the touch-paper.' He chuckled softly. 'Come on. It's late. I'll take you home.'

As they walked the deserted streets together Amy had a feeling of anti-climax. She wasn't quite sure what she had expected – or wanted – to happen, but Alex's abrupt decision to take her home was a distinct let-down. The summer night seemed to her to be made for falling in love. It was warm and mellow and although it was still barely two o'clock the sky was already luminous with the promise of dawn. In the shadows near the doorway of her digs she turned to him.

'Thank you – for the acting lesson.'

He laughed softly. 'Don't mention it.' He reached out and pulled her to him. Pinioned to the wall, she could feel his body pressed hard against hers from shoulder to thigh. She caught her breath as, slipping his hand inside her coat, he cupped one breast and stroked it firmly. 'There are lots of things you're going to have to learn, my sweet,' he whispered against her ear. 'And not all of them have to do with acting.' Then his mouth found hers again and this time it opened for him eagerly and without hesitation. At last he stood back, away from her, his arms dropping to his sides. 'I think you'd better go inside now,' he said with a sigh. 'One thing I'm sure I don't really have to tell you is that there's only so much a man can take . . .' He leaned forward to kiss the tip of her nose. 'Without making a beast of himself, that is.'

Amy looked up at him, her eyes tantalising. 'How do you know that's not what I want?' she said daringly.

His eyes opened wide, feigning shock. 'It's a good job it's me you're talking to,' he said sternly. 'And not some unscrupulous cad.' He laughed. 'Go in, girl, before I forget myself and ravish you right here on the pavement.'

276

On that light-hearted note they parted and Alex went on his way, lightened and cheered by the little encounter. When he'd decided after the show to stay on at the theatre it had been out of a feeling of bleak depression. He'd opened the bottle of Scotch, intending to drink himself into a stupor out of sight of everyone. It was a remedy he resorted to when the memories became nightmares and the heart-wrenching longing grew to unbearable proportions. Amy had unwittingly rescued him from that. He found that innocent eagerness of hers, that adolescent trembling on the brink of sensuous womanhood, quite irresistible. She was like summer morning, warm and untouched, just waiting to be enjoyed. She made him feel young again, as though the war with all its sorrows, its waste and destruction had never been. And he went on his way with a lighter step; refreshed.

But for Amy it was more than a few carefree kisses. She climbed the stairs with stars in her eyes. Alex Keynan had noticed her – not only as an actress but as a person – no, better still, a *woman*. Now anything could happen. Lying in her narrow bed she realised that a metamorphosis had taken place in her tonight. She was suddenly acutely aware of herself; her body and its sexuality – her unexplored potential. Was this what Alex had meant by experiencing deep emotion? Was she falling in love – *really* in love? And if she was, would it make a real actress of her? It was all so exciting – like opening a magic box full of wonderful gifts of which she had so far only unwrapped the first. What other delights lay inside, just waiting for her to explore and experience? She tingled with anticipation. Alex had unlocked the box for her and given her the key. Now she could open it again whenever she wished. And she would. Oh yes – she would.

She fell asleep as dawn was breaking, his name on her lips.

The house was in Gower Street. Maryan found it easily and mounted the steps to ring the bell by the newly painted front door. It was opened by Gina Stern herself. She was a small woman with large, expressive brown eyes and glossy dark hair, cut in a short, fashionable style. She was wearing – surprisingly – a pair of decorator's overalls at least two sizes too large for her, but she smiled unselfconsciously as she invited Maryan in.

'I hope you'll excuse me for a moment while I change into something more suitable,' she said, unbuttoning the overalls as she spoke. 'I couldn't wait any longer for a decorator. They take an age to come these days. I decided I might as well have a go at it myself.'

She led Maryan through a hall shrouded in dust sheets and into a small room at the back of the house, inviting her to make herself at home while she waited.

'Just give me a moment,' she said on her way out. 'I'll be with you in a jiffy.'

The room was furnished as an office and Maryan looked around her with interest. As well as the desk there were two comfortable chairs and a table heaped with fashion magazines. On the other side of the room, close to the window, which looked out onto a small walled garden, a drawing board was set up. On it lay a sketch of a winter suit with a stylish half-cape. It was coloured in crimson and black. She was still looking at it when Gina returned, wearing grey trousers and a crisp white blouse.

'I'm sorry to have kept you, Mrs Jessop. Until I get the place shipshape I'm having to use this room as a combined office and studio. Now . . .' She took a seat behind the desk and looked at Maryan's application which lay on the desk. 'I see that you began your working life as a machinist, went into domestic service and then later worked at Vincente's for the Donlans.' She looked up with a smile. 'You've had a very varied career.'

'Yes. Mainly because of the war,' Maryan said. 'I've been running the shop at Simons Mews since the end of the war, when I came back to London. I've learned a lot about organisation there. I took a business course when I began; shorthand and typing, book-keeping – that sort of thing. I learned the antique trade as I went along, studying from books and going to sales with Mr Donlan – working in the shop.' She opened her bag and took out Vincent's reference, handing it across the desk to Gina, who read it carefully. Coming to the end, she looked up.

'Well, Mr Donlan obviously thinks a great deal of your ability and efficiency, and I'm sure you know that Roisan has given you a glowing report too. But may I ask why you decided to leave? Weren't you happy there?'

Maryan drew a deep breath. This was the tricky question; the one she'd been expecting and dreading. She wasn't quite sure how much Roisan might have told Gina. 'I loved my job,' she said slowly. 'And I got along very well with Mr Donlan and Roisan. It was for purely personal reasons that I decided to make the break.' She looked at Gina, who appeared to be waiting for more. Looking down at her hands, she went on: 'It was Mrs Donlan who . . . I believe she felt the need to make – certain changes.'

Gina held up her hand. 'No need to go on. I think I get the general idea. Sometimes personalities clash, don't they? For no special reason. Call it chemistry. It wouldn't do for us all to be the

278

same. But I feel it's essential to like the people I work closely with. I would never engage someone I didn't feel I could look upon as a friend as well as an employee. I daresay you feel the same.' She smiled. 'I'm pretty sure from what I've seen and heard that you and I would work well together. What do you say we give it a month's trial – on both sides, of course?'

Maryan had warmed to the young woman facing her across the desk. There was nothing she would have liked more than to agree. But first there was another hurdle to get over.

'I'd like that very much, Miss Stern – but there is something I feel you should know before we go any further.'

Gina, who had half risen from the desk, sat down again. 'Oh dear, that sounds ominous. Please tell me.'

'I know that you used to work as a designer for the Leighs of Feldman Fashions. I worked for them too. From leaving school till the end of the war.' She opened her bag and took out the reference that Sam had written for her.

Gina looked slightly puzzled. 'Well, that's a coincidence, of course, but they obviously valued you, so I don't see why it should be a problem.'

Maryan bit her lip. 'I've kept in touch with Mr Sam Leigh, and because of that I know the circumstances of your employment with them. I realise that Mrs Leigh won't be altogether happy about your leaving and setting up on your own.'

Gina shrugged. 'That's true. But why should any of that affect your coming to work with me?'

Maryan shook her head, at a loss to put into words what she feared. 'I just wanted you to – to be aware of the connection between us,' she said. 'I didn't want you to find out later and think I was spying for them.'

Gina laughed. 'Thank you for being so honest with me, but I'm sure you'd never do anything so underhand. If it doesn't worry you it certainly won't worry me. Now – shall I try and tell you a little of what I have in mind?'

Gina was easy to talk to, and so enthusiastic that it was impossible not to catch some of her bubbling enthusiasm and be carried along by it. She told Maryan that she had been saving hard towards starting her own business whilst working for the Leighs and then she'd had a windfall in the shape of a sizable legacy from her grandmother, including the house in Gower Street.

'The house hadn't been lived in for a number of years,' she said. 'Nanna spent the war years in Devonshire. There was some slight bomb damage and it was terribly neglected, of course. But I'm

279

getting it all into shape gradually. I intend to live and work here.'
She looked at Maryan. 'By the way, I see that your present address
is Simons Mews.'

'Yes. I live in the flat above the shop.'

'Obviously you'll have to move out. Have you found somewhere
else to live?'

'I'm living at Roisan Freer's at the moment,' Maryan told her.
'But it's only temporary. I've tried to find a flat, but they're so few
and far between – and so expensive too.'

Gina nodded. 'I know. That's why I decided to live here. I hope
you find something soon.'

She went on to explain her plan to Maryan. She'd been working
on some designs for the middle-of-the-range market, for chain and
department stores; a line which she hoped would keep her going
until she was ready to launch her innovative top-of-the-range collection, possibly early the following year.

'So you see it's essential for me to find someone I can trust to deal
with selling and organisation – oversee the production too,' she said
earnestly. 'Take all those things off my shoulders while I get on with
my designing. If I'm to have my designer collection ready for next
spring I need all the time and space I can get.'

'Are you engaging your own workers?' Maryan asked. Gina shook
her head.

'I hope to later, of course, but for now I'm leasing the work out to
a really good firm in Islington. I've already negotiated terms with
them. It's not ideal, of course, but I know the firm well and I'm sure
I can trust them to turn out the standard of work I require.' She
leaned back in her chair and looked at Maryan enquiringly. 'Well,
Maryan – I hope I can call you that. I think I know all I need to
know about you. Do you have any questions you'd like to ask me?'

Maryan shook her head. 'No. It sounds very interesting.'

'I do have one or two others to interview,' Gina said. 'But I can
tell you here and now that I believe you would be perfect for the job
– if you want it. I'll telephone you at Roisan's, shall I? Shall we say
the day after tomorrow?'

Maryan was glad of the small respite. There was something else she
had to do before deciding finally. Instead of going straight back to
Notting Hill that afternoon she took the Underground out to Hackney and paid a visit to Feldman Fashions. She was in luck. It was
one of Sam's working days and he was in his office. His face lit up
with pleasure when he saw who his visitor was.

'Maryan. How nice to see you. What brings you all the way out

280

here?' He stood up and pulled out a chair for her. 'Would you like some tea? I can get you some . . .'

Maryan shook her head. 'It's business really. I'm leaving my present job. There are personal reasons – a disagreement that can't be resolved. I've applied for another job. It would suit me very well and I'd like to take it.' She glanced at him apprehensively. 'But I wanted to talk to you about it first.'

Sam gave her a puzzled smile. 'Well, I'm flattered you should ask my advice, my dear, but it's your life and I'm sure you know best . . .'

'The job is with Gina Stern, you see.'

The smile left Sam's face and he sighed heavily. 'Ah – Gina.' For a moment he was silent, then he looked up at Maryan again. 'Gina is a brilliantly talented designer and a very nice young woman. She deserves to get on. It's high time she spread her wings and I wish her nothing but good luck. As for you working for her, why should I mind? You're free to work for whoever you wish.'

'Thank you, Mr Sam. I just didn't want you to think I was being disloyal to you.'

He smiled gently. 'I hardly feel you owe us any loyalty, my dear. Not after what happened. But I appreciate your candour. Take the job by all means – with my good wishes.'

'Thank you.' She looked at his face. It seemed to her that he looked a little older every time she saw him. 'Are you well – both of you?'

'Well? I'm fine, but Rachel . . .' He spread his hands expressively. 'Ever since Gina left she has been in a state of emotional turmoil. I tell her it is high time she retired. If she would only agree I would retire too. We could go for a long holiday, a world cruise maybe. We both deserve some time together, to relax and enjoy life again. We could even go and live abroad. Somewhere in the sunshine. But Rachel . . .' He sighed and lifted his shoulders. 'She cannot forget this obsession of hers; cannot let Marcus rest in peace. It's ruining her life. And mine too.'

'I'm so sorry. Have you asked her to see a doctor?'

'I have tried everything. I am so afraid she will make herself really ill.' With an effort he shook off his worried expression to smile at Maryan. 'But why should any of this worry you? Go and work with Gina, my dear. Go with my blessing. It is for people like Gina to carry the flame now. I tell Rachel this. Soon we will have completed the first half of this century. So much anguish and suffering we have seen these past fifty years. Surely now the world has learned its lesson and things will improve.' He smiled. 'It is up to the young to build a better world for the next generation. There is so much work to be done to put the world to rights, but Rachel and I are too old to take any part in that. I tell my Rachel that the world belongs to the young – to the *living*. There are so many others who have lost loved ones. We must let go as they have done.'

'Thank you,' Maryan said. 'I couldn't have accepted the job happily without telling you first.'

As she made to get up Sam said, 'Maryan, I've been meaning to get in touch with you. I was surprised to have my cheque returned from St Hildred's the other day. There was a letter with it to say that Amy was no longer a pupil at the school. Is that right?'

With a sigh, Maryan sat down again. 'I'm sorry. I should have let you know. Amy has left home. She got herself a job with a theatre company in Lancashire. There was nothing I could do to stop her.'

Sam looked concerned. 'Oh, my dear. Is she all right? Have you heard from her?'

Maryan shook her head, her throat tightening. 'No. I'm afraid I've lost her. Since the war we just don't seem to have settled down together. I blame myself. I feel I must have failed her.' She looked at his drawn face. 'I won't worry you with the details. She's grown up now. She wants to go her own way and there's nothing I can do about it.'

Sam touched her hand. 'I'm so sorry. I'm sure she'll come back when she needs you. Children always need their mothers.'

'I'd like to think so,' she said, without conviction.

Maryan made her way back to Notting Hill that afternoon with a heavy heart. If Rachel Leigh had only accepted Amy as Marcus's child so much suffering would have been avoided: for Rachel and Sam; for herself and Amy. If it hadn't been for Rachel's abhorrence she and Vinnie would never have met, loved and parted again. That in itself would have saved so much heartache. Sometimes, fate had a strange way of working.

Chapter Fifteen

To Amy's disappointment Alex ignored her when they met at rehearsal on the Monday following that Saturday evening. Days
passed, and then weeks, during which Alex continued to treat her as
a very junior member of his company and nothing more. It was as
though the encounter between them that night in the empty theatre
had been a dream. Amy tried hard to forget, but Alex's arbitrary
treatment and the lack of opportunity to play more important roles
gradually turned her disappointment into discontent. One morning
as she and Peter prepared the stage set for the evening performance
he remarked on it.

'Anything wrong, Amy? You haven't seemed yourself lately.'

She shrugged the enquiry off. 'It's nothing. I haven't been sleeping
very well lately.'

'I see.' He gave her a curious look. 'Any particular reason?'

'No,' she said. 'Except . . .'

'Yes? Except what?'

'It's just that I'd like a chance to show what I can do. A real part,
I mean, instead of all these walk-ons.'

He chuckled. 'You have to learn to walk before you can run.
Anyway, why not concentrate on stage management? You could do
a lot worse. There are always good openings for stage managers, you
know. I've got my eye on working for television. It's the coming
thing. More and more people are getting sets. They're saying it'll
soon put the theatre out of business.'

'God forbid.' She turned away to put the kettle on for coffee.
Peter went on talking about television but his remarks went over her
head as she remembered Alex's remarks that Saturday evening, all of
which were indelibly printed on her memory. Her lips still tingled
every time she remembered his fiery, exciting kisses. He had seemed
so sincere. It had all seemed so real to her, yet he behaved as though

he'd forgotten the episode. Some days he looked at her as though he could hardly remember who she was.

When Peter left for lunch, Amy stayed on, finding some small jobs with which to keep herself occupied. She liked working alone in the theatre. It was quiet – a friendly silence that gave her space in which to think. She felt as though she had come to a watershed. Maybe she should give up all thoughts of being an actress and go back to London – try for something else. Recently she'd had a letter from Celia. Her mother had remarried and moved out to Richmond. Celia herself had moved to a job as junior secretary for a firm of family solicitors in York. She seemed really happy; earning a good salary and enjoying an independent life in the bachelor-girl flatlet she could now afford. She had even started going out with the boss's son, newly out of uniform after National Service and studying law at university. Celia wrote enthusiastically about their relationship and of how Brian was working hard towards becoming a partner when his father retired. Amy envied her as she sat reading the letter. Celia, always the scatty one, seemed to have her life under control and her future all sewn up, while she still floundered between an insecure past and an unsure future, the one as ephemeral and unsatisfactory as the other.

The lack of a reply to her letter home seemed to confirm that Maryan meant to be done with that part of her life once and for all. There was nothing for it but for Amy to go along with the decision and do the same.

'Good God, you scared the daylights out of me. I didn't know there was anyone here.'

Startled, Amy looked up from the prop bench to see Alex standing in the doorway. Her heart jumped painfully. He wore black corduroy trousers and an open-necked shirt and she noticed that he didn't appear to have shaved this morning. Turning away so that he wouldn't see her blush, she said, 'I thought I'd stay on and finish laying out the props bench ready for this evening.'

'Ah – that's what I like to see,' he said. 'Very commendable.'

He was laughing at her and she felt an impotent fury rising in her breast. 'Time I was going,' she muttered. 'I've got some shopping to do.' But as she made to pass him he stood in her way, his face serious.

'What's wrong, Amy?'

'Nothing. Nothing at all. May I pass, please?'

'You may when you've told me why you're so angry.'

'I'm not angry.'

'You're lying.' Seeing the hot blush that coloured her cheeks he

284

reached out to rest his hands lightly on her shoulders. 'Amy. I think you and I should have a talk. Shall we find a quiet place to have lunch?'

'There's no need – really.'

Disregarding her protest, he rubbed a hand along his jaw. 'When I've been back to my place and shaved, that is.' He grinned at her. 'I overslept this morning. Can't take a nicely brought up young lady out to lunch looking like this, can I?'

'I told you. There's . . .' He took her arm and steered her firmly towards the stage door.

'You can come back to the digs and wait for me. It won't take long.'

He was staying at the Olive Tree, one of the town's best pubs. His room was at the front, overlooking the busy market place. Amy sat in the room's one armchair while Alex took his things into the bathroom and shaved. He reappeared looking clean and spruce in a fresh shirt. Reaching out, he drew her to her feet.

'Now – are you going to tell me why you've been going round for the past few weeks with a face like thunder?'

'I didn't know I had.'

'Oh, I think you did.' He bent to look into her eyes. 'Is it something I did – said?'

Acutely embarrassed, she shook her head, but he persisted.

'You're unhappy about something. Tell me.'

'No. There's nothing. I wish you wouldn't . . .' Her voice trembled perilously and she tried to pull away.

He sighed. 'Oh dear. It's worse than I thought.' He drew her towards the bed and made her sit down beside him. 'Amy – come and sit down. Tell me about yourself.'

'There isn't much to tell,' she said awkwardly. 'I was born in the East End of London, but I was evacuated to Suffolk when the war started. I lived with a family called Taylor.'

He nodded. 'Ah yes, I remember. The famous Mike.'

'Then, when it was over I went back to London and lived with my mother in a flat over the antique shop she runs.'

'And that's all? No dramas, no joy, no pain?'

'Well, my grandmother died, then there was school . . .'

'And – your father?'

She looked at him sharply. 'He – died in the war. My real father, that is. Tom Jessop – the man my mother married – died when I was little.'

He nodded slowly. 'I see. So you never knew him – your real father?'

'I *knew* him. But not that he was my father. I only found that out by accident.' She looked away. 'It was a shock. He was dead by then, you see. It was too late – too late to . . .'

'Get to know him – as a father?'

She nodded. 'There's so much I'd like to know about him. I don't even know if he knew I was his.'

'Have you talked to your mother about it?'

'No.' She shook her head vehemently. 'She let me down; cheated and lied to me all those years. She and I don't talk. I don't suppose she ever wanted me really. She's never really understood me and I certainly don't understand her.'

'What don't you understand?'

'She puts her work before everything.'

He smiled wryly. 'From what you tell me she's probably had to.' He laughed gently. 'You're thinking, what the hell does *he* know about it?' he said, slipping an arm around her shoulders. 'But life is never one-sided, Amy. Maybe if you just let her tell you her side . . .'

'If she'd wanted me to know, why didn't she tell me before? Anyway, she needn't bother because I'm not interested any more,' she said abruptly. 'I'm thinking of *my* work now. And I'm not going home again until I've made a success of it. Probably not even then.'

'Oh dear.' He rolled his eyes ceilingwards. 'Heaven preserve me from avenging angels.'

She sprang to her feet, blushing hotly. 'If you're just going to sit there and make fun of me – treat me like a child . . .'

'I'm not. I'm sorry, Amy.' He caught at her hand. 'It's just that you're so earnest that I can't resist teasing you a little. I do want to understand, believe me.' He looked into her eyes. 'But we still haven't got down to the reason you're so quiet and preoccupied, have we?'

'Do we have to? I mean, why should you be interested – in me?'

He drew back his head and looked at her thoughtfully. 'Ah – so *that's* it. It was our little encounter the other Saturday night?'

She coloured. '*No*. Not really.'

'It was. I can tell.' He gave her shoulders a squeeze. 'You must learn not to take things so seriously, Amy.'

'I don't – *didn't*. If – if you want to know, I'm fed up because I never get the chance to play a real part,' she told him in a rush. 'You promised me when you gave me the job that I'd get the chance. But I – haven't.'

'Oh, but I think you have,' he corrected.

'Bit parts. Walk-ons. I want to do something *real* – something that counts.'

'Like Cathy?' His eyes twinkled.

She bit her lip hard. 'All right, *yes*. Like Cathy.' She looked up at his slightly amused, quizzical expression and something seemed to erupt inside her. 'Oh, it's all very well, you telling me not to take things seriously,' she told him stridently. 'But how am I to get that emotional experience you speak of if I'm not supposed to *feel* anything?' To her horror tears filled her eyes. She blinked them back, swallowing hard, but it was no use. They brimmed over to slip down her cheeks. She got up, making for the door in a panic. But he was there before her, barring the way.

'Amy. Please don't be upset. I didn't mean to hurt your feelings. I thought it was a very pleasant little interlude. I thought you did too. I don't see why you're so upset.'

'I don't go about kissing people I don't care about,' she said angrily. 'When it – happened – I thought it was because – because you – you liked me. And then afterwards when – when you ignored me . . .'

'I'm sure I never ignored you,' he broke in.

'You *did*. You hardly knew I was there. It's *you* who can't feel things. You're the one who's emotionally immature.' She knew she was being silly and childish. To her own dismay she heard the break in her voice, its tearful shrillness. With one determined effort she tried to push him out of the way before he could witness her complete humiliation, but he grasped her arms and held her fast.

'*Amy*. Amy, listen. If you knew the truth about me you wouldn't say a thing like that. We all have to protect ourselves. We all start off soft and vulnerable, but we get hurt so we build a protective shell around ourselves. You'll have to learn to do the same, otherwise life will batter you to death.'

She stared at the floor. 'I know. I'm – sorry.'

'Poor baby. You're very young, aren't you?' He drew her close and kissed her very gently. At once all the passionate feeling she held for him flared up and she clung to him helplessly, her heart beating fast against her ribs. 'If I hurt you I'm sorry, darling,' he said. 'Come and sit down. I want to tell you something.'

Once again they sat together on the edge of the bed. Her hands firmly held in his, he looked into her eyes. 'I was married once,' he said. 'Just once in my life, very briefly I knew what it was to be blissfully happy. Chloe and I met, fell in love and married all within a few weeks in the summer of 1941. I was in the RAF, she was a WAAF working at the War Office. I came home on leave. My first since the wedding. We'd looked forward to it so much. Her parents lived in a village in Essex, but they had a tiny flat in Earls Court that they used when they came up to Town for shopping or the theatre. We'd planned to spend my leave there. Chloe met me at the station that afternoon. We were going out to dinner to celebrate. I left her at the flat, changing, while I went down the road to buy cigarettes. I was gone just a few minutes, but when I came back there was nothing left. The street had received a direct hit. At three o'clock that afternoon my life came to a halt. I was reduced to a kind of mindless machine, going through the motions of life.' He paused and Amy squeezed his hands.

'She was – killed?'

He nodded. 'The emergency services were there. They tried to make me go away but I wouldn't. I helped them dig – tearing at the rubble with my bare hands – hoping against hope. Everyone had miraculous stories of people buried in the rubble who were found alive. But when we found her . . .'

He broke off with a shudder and she saw suddenly that he was no longer with her. He was reliving that part of his past that haunted the darkest recesses of his mind. His eyes were bleak and filled with such raw, naked pain that she couldn't bear to look at him. After a moment he went on: 'We should have gone together, Amy. I'll always be convinced of that. Being left alone like that seemed to me the most cruel thing imaginable. I volunteered for the most dangerous job I could think of, all the time hoping that the danger would take the pain away – even that I'd be killed. But I wasn't. I came through the whole bloody nightmare without so much as a scratch, while friends – good men with wives and families and everything to live for – died. That was my worst punishment. I felt as though God was mocking me. Playing cat and mouse. Can you believe that?'

Amy couldn't answer him, her throat was too tight for words. Instead she put her arms around him and drew his head down to hers, pressing her lips against the corner of his mouth. To think she had accused him of being emotionally immature. She felt ashamed – longed to take his pain away, to be someone special who could make him forget. He sighed and squeezed her shoulders.

'You should thank God you were still a child. Sorry to put you through all that, Amy.'

She shook her head. 'I'm glad you felt you could,' she said. 'I'm flattered that you can trust me enough to confide in me.'

'I just wanted you to understand. You see sometimes, when the memories are too much, I drink. Not because I enjoy it, but to blunt the pain. When I've had too much, I'm not a very nice person. I do things I shouldn't.'

'Are you trying to tell me you were drunk that Saturday?'

288

He smiled wryly. 'No. That would be rather insulting, wouldn't it? I'd had too much, but I knew what I was doing and saying. I admit that I enjoyed it too. But whisky releases all the inhibitions, makes one forget one's responsibilities. I suppose I was a little ashamed afterwards because I knew I'd no business to let it happen.' He looked into her eyes. 'And you've confirmed that for me, haven't you?'

'Because I behaved like a silly schoolgirl and took it all too seriously? I won't do that again.' Without waiting for his reply she went on: 'Alex – you can't go on for ever living with only memories. She'd want you to be happy again, wouldn't she – Chloe?'

'Not at someone else's expense.'

'But why should it be that?'

'Because I don't – I couldn't . . .' He shook his head. 'We're getting much too serious again. Come on, let's go and have that lunch.'

She laid her hand on his arm. 'Alex. Now that you've told me; now that I know, I won't mind if you can't feel as I do. I just want . . .' He stopped her with a finger across her lips.

'Shhh. Don't, Amy. I know what you *think* you want, but you don't. Not really. You're young and sweet. You deserve a nice young man who'll appreciate you. I'd only make you miserable, you know. Write to that nice Mike of yours. Get him to come and see you play Cathy. I guarantee that if he isn't already in love with you he'll fall on the spot.'

She stared at him. 'Play Cathy?'

'Yes.' He held both her hands tightly in his. 'Look, I wasn't going to tell you this and you must promise to keep it to yourself for the moment, but I think you need some good news right now. Remember Minsdale?' She nodded. 'Well, the group of businessmen who own the Theatre Royal have written to ask me to form a resident repertory company there. I've accepted the offer, but as a good many of the present company have commitments to follow this tour, I'll be looking for some replacements. There's a vacancy for a juvenile lead.' He smiled into her eyes. 'So, I'm offering it to you, Amethyst Lee. If you want it, that is.'

When Maryan was officially offered the job with Gina Stern she was delighted and relieved. She had already been staying at Roisan's for six weeks and she felt she couldn't impose on her hospitality much longer. The moment she had read the letter she telephoned Gina.

'I can start next week if you want me,' she said. 'I just have to find somewhere to live that isn't too far from Gower Street.'

'Fine . . .' Gina hesitated. 'As a matter of fact I've got two rooms to let at the top of the house,' she said. 'I've been thinking of converting them into a flat. I think I might be able to get a government grant for that. I would have offered you accommodation before, but I thought you might be put off by the thought of living in.'

Maryan laughed, delightedly. 'You needn't have worried about that, the room will be a godsend.'

'Right, as long as you know you'll be free to move out any time you find somewhere better, that's settled then. Move your things in whenever you like.'

Roisan gave a little supper party for Maryan on her last night. She invited Paul and Geoff. Together the three of them had clubbed together to buy her a parting gift. It was something from the shop that she'd admired for a long time: an exquisite Baccarat glass paperweight. When she unwrapped it her eyes filled with tears.

'Oh, how lovely. Thank you. I'll always treasure this,' she said. 'I've loved working with you all and I'm going to miss you so much. I hope we won't lose touch.'

Paul grinned sheepishly and Geoff cleared his throat. ''Course we won't,' he said gruffly. 'Don't think you can get rid of us that easily.'

Roisan was downstairs making coffee when Vincent walked in. His arrival brought an air of tension down on the little gathering. Paul and Geoff didn't know the true reason for Maryan's leaving and they still blamed Vincent for it. After an awkward half hour when no one quite knew what to say, Paul looked at his watch and got to his feet.

'Time I went,' he said. 'Don't want to miss my bus.'

Geoff seized the opportunity to join him. 'Me too,' he said. 'The missis'll think I've run off and left her if I don't put in an appearance soon.'

When they had gone Maryan and Vincent looked at each other. 'They're smashing chaps, both of them,' Maryan said. 'You were lucky to find them.'

'They think I've sacked you, don't they? They hate my guts at the moment. It sticks out a mile.'

'They know I'm leaving from choice,' she told him. 'I told them I'd found a better job.'

He looked at her. 'And have you?'

'I've found a job, it's true. It's a good one and I'm lucky to get it.'

'They're lucky to get you.' He raised an eyebrow at her. 'Do I know them? Is it one of my rivals?'

Clearly Roisan hadn't told him about Gina. She was grateful to her for that. 'No,' she said. 'It's going to be a case of starting from scratch again – learning a new business – well, not quite new. I've worked in the rag trade before. I'll be glad to keep busy, what with – with one thing and another.'

'Have you heard from Amy?'

She shook her head. 'She hasn't written. I tried to get in touch with her friend, Celia Frazer, but she and her mother seem to have moved. I rang Marjorie Taylor in the end.' She looked up at him with a sigh. 'That took some doing, I can tell you; having to admit that I didn't know where my own daughter was. And when I heard that she'd written to Marjorie it hurt.'

'It must have. Did she give you Amy's address?'

'All she had was the address on Amy's letter. They're on tour, you see; moving around. But she said Amy sounded well and happy. That's all I really wanted to know. Maybe one of these days she'll contact me again.'

'There are ways of tracing people, if you're worried,' he said, his face concerned. 'I hear that the Salvation Army . . .'

'No.' She shook her head. 'As long as I know she's all right. She knows that if she needs me she has only to contact Roisan.'

'I suppose so.' He reached out to touch her hand. 'Maryan, I . . .' but at that moment Roisan pushed the door open and came in with the tray of coffee.

'Pity the fellers had to go,' she said, looking pointedly at her brother. 'I was hoping they'd stay on and talk for a while. This is the last chance Maryan will have to be with them.'

'Maybe I shouldn't have come,' Vincent said, quick to pick up her annoyance.

'Maybe you shouldn't,' Roisan said bluntly. 'I'd have thought you'd have more . . .'

'How is Fay?' Maryan broke in. 'I daresay you must be looking forward to moving into the flat. It'll be so much more convenient for you.'

Vincent avoided his sister's accusing eyes as he said, 'Fay's fine – as long as she keeps taking the insulin injections.'

'That's good.' Maryan got to her feet. 'Well – I think I'd better go to bed now. I've got an early start in the morning.'

Vincent stood up. 'Please don't go – not yet. I want . . .' He shot his sister a pleading look. 'Roisan . . . ?'

Reluctantly she got up and moved towards the door. 'I seem to have forgotten the biscuits.' At the door she paused and looked at Vincent. 'I'll only be a few minutes, so you'd better say whatever it is you have to say briefly and be done with it.'

When she'd gone, leaving the air heavy with her disapproval, Vincent looked at Maryan. 'There's no need to look so apprehensive. I just wanted to wish you well.'

'There's no need.' He looked so drawn and unhappy and she longed to be able to help him. 'It's going to be interesting and exciting, joining a brand-new venture,' she said brightly. 'And in the fashion business too. Back where I started, you could say.'

'Maryan – can I see you sometimes?' His hand covered hers and her eyes came up to meet his.

'I – don't think that would be a very good idea,' she said shakily.

'And *I* don't think I can exist without the prospect of seeing you occasionally. I don't mean to make any demands on you.'

'Then don't.' Unable to bear the tension a moment longer, she got up and walked to the door. 'Tell Roisan I've gone up, will you? Goodnight, Vinnie.'

'Maryan – please . . .' He was on his feet, reaching out for her, but already she had the door open.

'Don't make it harder, Vinnie. It's over. It has to be. There's no other way. Please be kind and let me go.'

Sitting on the bed in her room she heard Roisan's angry recriminations as she admonished her brother downstairs. A little later she heard the front door slam and after a moment Roisan tapped gently on her door.

'Maryan, love. Are you all right?'

'I'm fine, thank you, Roisan. Just fine.'

'Can I get you anything?'

'No. No, thank you.'

She heard Roisan's footsteps going back down the stairs as she sat there on the edge of the bed, her eyes dry and her heart cold and spent. Then, every muscle in her body aching with tension, she got up and began, very slowly, to get ready for bed.

The Keynan Players moved to Minsdale to take up residence at the Theatre Royal at the end of October. Alex immediately put them into rehearsal. Three members of the company had been replaced. Amy had taken the juvenile lead and another student ASM had been engaged; this time a young man called David Handley. The playbills and programmes had already been printed and they were to open 'by popular demand' with *Wuthering Heights*; Amethyst Lee playing the leading role.

In rehearsal Alex was tireless and demanding. At times Amy wondered if she would ever be good enough for him. He bullied and coaxed her by turn, often driving her to distraction as they repeated

292

scenes over and over. But in a strange way his relentlessness exhilarated her. Although she alternated between tears and fury, she knew inside herself that the roughness of his language and his harsh criticism were drawing out the best in her; stirring her emotions and igniting a deep-seated passion within her of which she had so far only touched the edge.

On the opening night she felt as though she would die of nerves. Her stomach churned and her heart pounded every time she thought of stepping onto the stage. Twice she was physically sick, throwing up wretchedly in the backstage lavatory. An hour before curtain-up, convinced that she was too ill to appear, she went in search of Alex to tell him. To her surprise he wasn't angry. He behaved almost as though he'd been expecting it. Taking her hands he drew her calmly into the office and made her sit down.

'Now listen to me. You are Amethyst Lee, the star of this show. You are about to give a stunning performance. I'm your director and I know what I'm talking about. You know your lines. You love the part. You *are* Cathy. Understand?'

'Y-yes, Alex.'

'Right.' Dragging her abruptly to her feet, he pushed her towards the door. 'So go and get your bloody make-up on and try and behave like a pro instead of an hysterical fifth former.' At the door he cupped her chin with one hand and kissed her hard. 'That's for luck. You won't let me down, Amy. I know you won't.'

She didn't. By the time the curtain came down on the last act she was physically exhausted, but her spirits were soaring higher than the moon. It had gone perfectly. The audience had been with her all the way and so had the other members of the cast. Terrence Troy, the actor who had played Heathcliff, led her forward as the cast took their final call and the audience roared and clapped their approval. For Amy, it was a moment to cherish, a dream come true.

Later, as she was taking off her make-up, Alex came to her dressing room. 'What did I tell you?' he said with a smile. 'You were terrific, just as I knew you'd be.'

She jumped to her feet to throw her arms around his neck. 'Oh, Alex, wasn't it *wonderful*? I enjoyed it so much once I'd made my first entrance. I can't *wait* for tomorrow night.'

'Good.' He laughed. 'But you'd better get your beauty sleep first. You look completely frazzled.'

'Oh, Alex, I can't,' she said. 'I can't just go tamely back to the digs and go to bed. Not after tonight. This has been the most exciting night of my entire life.'

He sighed. 'Oh God, Amy, you make me feel so old. I wish I

could get that excited about something again.' He took her face between his hands. 'Make the most of it, darling. Enjoy it while you can. It doesn't last very long.'

The smile faded from her face. 'Alex, don't. I hate it when you say things like that. I want you to be happy too. I want you to share it with me.'

He kissed her briefly. 'Come on, I suppose you do need to wind down a little. I'll take you out for a drink, to celebrate.'

'Can I come home with you afterwards?' she asked, her eyes large and pleading. 'Just for a little while – please?'

For a moment he looked into the blue eyes wistfully. 'If I didn't know how innocent you are, Amethyst Lee, I'd suspect you of trying to seduce me.'

Several other members of the cast were in the Swan, the pub opposite the stage door. Everyone was in high spirits. The Keynan Players' first night in their new resident venue had been an outstanding success and Amy was the toast of the evening. She felt intoxicated by the sheer headiness of it; it was a feeling no mere alcohol could produce, as she told Alex on the way home. He had taken a flat; the ground floor of a Victorian house in a quiet tree-lined street on the town's outskirts. As they walked among the fallen leaves Alex remarked that winter would soon be on them.

'I expect it's colder here than in London,' he said. 'But young blood like yours doesn't feel the cold like my old bones, I daresay.'

'Why do you always make yourself sound so old?' she asked as he unlocked the door. 'You can't be more than – what, thirty-four?'

He grinned at her. 'Don't fish. I'm far too old for you, Miss Lee.'

'Who says so?' She reached up and pulled his head down to hers. He resisted her for a moment, then drew her into his arms and kissed her soundly. 'I'm very nearly old enough to be your father,' he whispered as they drew apart.

'I don't care.' She pressed close to him. 'What does it matter? What does *anything* matter tonight?'

'Mmm. I'll make you a coffee and then I think I'd better take you home,' he said.

'No, Alex. You're not going to get rid of me as easily as that,' she told him.

'Why – what did you have in mind?'

'I'm going to stay here with you. I want to spend the night with you.'

'Oh, no . . .' He removed her arms from around his neck.

'Alex, I'm serious. I don't want to be a virgin any more. I want to be an experienced, mature woman. And I want you to be my first

294

lover.' Her eyes twinkled up at him. 'Just think how good it will be for my art. It's your duty really when you think about it, isn't it?'

He laughed. 'You wouldn't be using me for research purposes by any chance, would you?'

She looked up at him, her eyes clear and candid. 'No, Alex. I promise you it's not that.'

The laughter left his eyes. 'Amy, listen. Don't throw yourself away. I'm no good for you – for anybody, for that matter. You're on a high tonight and you don't know what you're saying. I don't want you to do something you'll regret.'

'You don't get it, do you? I love you, Alex. I *want* you. It's all very simple.' Her arms snaked seductively around his neck again.

'I don't believe I'm letting you do this,' he groaned. 'You're going to hate yourself – *and* me, in the morning.'

'I'll never hate you.' She nuzzled her face into his neck. 'The morning's a thousand light years away,' she whispered. 'Tonight is now, and it's magic. It belongs to us.'

It was just getting light when she woke, but in spite of her unfamiliar surroundings she knew at once where she was. Her whole body still tingled from Alex's lovemaking. She would never have believed anything could be so wonderful. Now she knew beyond the slightest doubt that she loved him. He'd made love to her so passionately that she couldn't believe that he didn't love her in return. He was just being cautious when he said he wasn't good for her. Surely he must know that they were made for each other. And as for the age difference, it was trivial – a mere detail, an accident of birth. She trailed a finger down his cheek and he wakened instantly, looking up at her with eyes slightly unfocused. Then, seeing her face above him – remembering, he groaned.

'Oh, Amy, what the hell have we done?'

She laughed. 'Don't you remember? Would you like me to remind you?' Under the covers she began to caress him. 'We've got hours before we need get up. Plenty of time to . . .' His lips were on hers and he had rolled over onto her so swiftly that it took her breath away.

'You goddamned little temptress, you're enough to drive a man mad. You deserve a damned good hiding, do you know that?' His body was heavy and she could feel his arousal throbbing against her thigh as he lay on top of her. His face was raw with desire as he looked down at her. 'What the hell are we letting ourselves in for, Amy? It's madness and you bloody well know it – don't you?'

She reached up and pulled him down to her. 'Just love me,' she whispered as she arched her body invitingly towards him. 'Just love me and leave the worrying to me.'

The first weeks at Gower Street were hectic. There was so much to do – not only arranging Gina's busy work schedule, but helping her to finish decorating the house and, in particular, Maryan's own flat, so that she had somewhere to lay her head. Gina had promised to have a small bathroom and kitchen installed as soon as she could find a willing plumber who wasn't inundated with work. She had lent Maryan a few essential pieces of furniture until she could buy some of her own and Roisan had offered to make curtains.

Gina worked late into each evening on the designs for her collection, but during the day Maryan and she worked together, making business calls and organising a working plan in the office in the mornings. In the afternoons they worked on the house, donning overalls and turning their hands to whatever was necessary, from scrubbing and cleaning to painting and distempering.

During this time, working side by side, they grew to know one another well. Gina learned of Maryan's family problems and her estrangement with Amy, while in her turn Maryan learned that not all of the funds to set up the business came from Gina's grandmother. The house had been hers and there had been a small legacy to go with it, but Gina confessed that she'd obtained a sizable loan from a businessman friend too.

'Was that wise?' Maryan asked. 'I mean – did you have a legal agreement drawn up so that he can't demand his money back if the whim takes him?' Seeing Gina's expression she blushed. 'Oh – I'm sorry. It's really none of my business, is it?'

Gina smiled. 'I understand what you're saying, but it's really more of a friendly agreement.' She hesitated. 'I might as well tell you. You'll be seeing him around quite often anyway. Robert is a boyfriend.'

'Oh, I see. That's all right then. Are you – I mean will you be getting married?'

Gina shook her head. 'That's the snag. He's already married to someone else.'

'Oh, *no*.' Maryan's face dropped in dismay and at once she bit her lip. 'Forgive me, Gina. I've no business to make remarks. It's just that I've suffered from the same situation myself. I wouldn't like you to be hurt as I've been.'

'I won't.' Gina laid down her paintbrush and sat on the stairs. 'Robert hasn't been happy for years,' she said. 'I didn't break up his marriage. He has two sons and he's waiting till they've finished their education. Then he'll ask his wife for a divorce.'

'I see.' Maryan hoped it was as Gina said and that this Robert, whoever he was, wasn't just playing her along. But she kept silent. She was desperately trying to think of a new subject when Gina did it for her.

'Maryan. I think we know each other well enough now for me to say this to you. You have a nice figure and you're really a very attractive woman.'

'Oh.' Maryan blushed. 'Thank you.'

'But – if you don't mind me saying so, you don't really make the best of yourself,' Gina went on. 'Would you be offended if I gave you some advice about clothes?'

'No, of course not. You're the expert.'

'Then there's your hair and make-up.' Gina smiled apologetically. 'Oh dear, I'm making you sound like a complete frump and you're not. It's just that I know that with a little help you could be quite stunning.' She smiled. 'When we've got some time at the weekend, shall we do a little make-over?'

'That might be fun.' Maryan looked at her enquiringly. 'But what about your friend – Robert?'

Gina sighed. 'That's one of the disadvantages of being the mistress of a married man. He always spends the weekends with his family.'

On Saturday they went shopping. Bearing in mind what Maryan had to spend, Gina picked out the nucleus of a wardrobe for her: a classic suit and blouse, a plain black dress that could be dressed up or down, a smart winter coat and a couple of hats. Then they went on to Gina's favourite beauty parlour for a complete make-up, hair restyling and manicure. Gina insisted that it was to be at her expense; a special thank you to Maryan for helping with the decorating.

When the expert staff at Maxine's had finished with her Maryan stared disbelievingly at herself in the mirror. She hadn't changed her hairstyle since the war ended and now, with the shoulder-length tresses cut into a fashionable short bob with a little half fringe, and the new make-up with its soft colouring and subtle eye-shadow – something Maryan had never worn before – she looked quite a different person. She realised for the first time how dowdy she had grown. Throwing all her concentration into Vincente's, she had quite forgotten to attend to her own appearance. Now she saw that if she was to spend part of her time representing a fashion designer she must be suitably groomed for the job and this was Gina's subtle way of telling her so. Outside in the street she couldn't resist stealing glances at herself in the shop windows they passed. Gina caught her doing it and laughed.

'You should have done this long ago, Maryan,' she said. 'That hairstyle does wonders for you.'

Briefly and wistfully, Maryan wished that Vinnie could see her, then she pulled herself up sharply. This was a new beginning. However much she might regret it, Vinnie was part of the past. She owed it to herself to make a new life. From now on she must look forward and not back.

In the weeks that followed the two women visited the buyers of dress shops and department stores together, showing Gina's portfolio of off-the-peg designs and taking along samples to show the workmanship. Her innovative flair was well known to many of the buyers who remembered her as the designer responsible for the Marcus Leigh label, and most were delighted that she had branched out on her own. Her up-to-the-minute styles interested them and so did her competitive prices. The order book rapidly filled up and after a while Gina was able to leave the selling trips to Maryan, remaining in her studio to work hard on the new season's designs.

One day each week Maryan visited the clothing factory at Islington to supervise the making up of garments. Ken James, the manager, and his head cutter, Ethel, were pleasant and obliging. It was a small, friendly factory and the sound of whirring machines and female voices uplifted in song as they joined in with 'Music While You Work' on the radio brought back memories to Maryan. Those far-off days before the war, when she'd worked at Feldman's, seemed like another world to her now. Watching the girls bent over their work, she was reminded poignantly of the day when Marcus first joined his father's firm and she had shown him how to thread a machine. Poor Marcus. She had loved him right from that very first day: so handsome and gifted with his dark, laughing eyes and curly hair. He had so much charm and talent. He should have had a golden future; a life filled with love and success. Yet the whole of his brief life had been dogged by tragedy and sadness. At times like this she could understand Rachel's endless grieving and Sam's despair.

A date had been set for Gina's show. It was to be at the end of January. Her haute couture collection was of spring and summer clothes to celebrate 1950. The venue was to be the ballroom of a Mayfair hotel, hired at what seemed to Maryan enormous expense. She guessed – correctly – that Robert Kemp was paying for it. Gina had already made out a guest list and given Maryan the task of sending out the invitations. As she worked through it, addressing envelopes, she was a little surprised to see that Sam and Rachel

298

Leigh were included. As she sealed their envelope she wondered if they would accept.

Gina worked through most of Christmas, hunched over her drawing board and breaking only to share the meal that Maryan cooked for them both. Maryan spent most of the holiday decorating her own flat and trying not to think about Amy. There had been no word, not even a Christmas card. Things could have been so very different between them. She was sure that Amy would have got along well with Gina and enjoyed living here. She hoped that, wherever she was, she was happy. She found her thoughts drifting wistfully towards Vincent too. She pictured him with Fay in the flat at Simons Mews and wondered what kind of Christmas they were sharing.

She now had her own bathroom and a tiny kitchen, hastily installed by a plumber whose services had been arranged for Gina by Robert Kemp. Robert seemed to be the kind of man who could pull strings and make things happen. Gina had only to say that she was having difficulty in obtaining something or getting some job done, for it to be attended to next day. Maryan had met him a few times, passing him on his way in or out. He was a tall, well-built man of about forty-five, handsome in an almost saturnine way with his deep-set grey eyes and lantern jaw. She sometimes wondered what vivacious Gina could see in him, but if her employer seemed happy with the far from ideal situation who was she to question it? And she could not deny that he was a great help in getting things done.

As the weeks rushed busily by and the day of the show drew closer, life grew hectic. There was no time to brood over the past or to speculate about the future and Maryan was glad of it. She was busy and fulfilled. She enjoyed her work and at the end of the day she was too tired to think very much. It was enough.

At Minsdale Christmas and New Year were busy and exciting. The Keynan Players put on a production of *Cinderella*; performed more as a musical play than the traditional pantomime, with a male actor in the role of Prince Charming. Amy played Cinderella and had her first experience of playing a musical role. Alex had persuaded a choreographer he knew to come up to Lancashire and teach the dance steps while Harry Palmer, the theatre's musical director, coached them in the singing. It worked well and Amy loved it. She thought about the first time she had stood on a stage, at Northmere Rep with Celia's father. This was her dream come true. Life was good. She had achieved her ambition to be an actress and found the only man she would ever love. She was so lucky. The only problem was that for the moment Alex didn't see things in quite the same way. She was confident that she could make him change his mind, but when she had begged him to let her move into his flat he had been adamant.

'I don't want the other members of the cast to get the wrong idea,' he told her.

She laughed. 'What wrong idea?'

'The moment we let ourselves be seen as a couple they'll start getting suspicious. They'll see every part you get as preferential treatment. Let's just leave things as they are, Amy. Being together at the weekends will give us something to look forward to, eh?'

She said nothing, biding her time and waiting for the right moment, when she would prove to him just how committed she was. She was confident that he would come round to her way of thinking then. And she couldn't help but agree about the other members of the company. Her relationship with Alex had caused a few pointed remarks, especially when she was cast in a coveted leading part. Alex insisted that she was only cast in roles that suited her, and she was sure this was true. He wasn't the type to jeopardise his productions just to please her. But some of the older women in the company would have questioned this. Catty remarks were made and Alex had to be scrupulously fair in order to retain his credibility. He warned Amy not to flaunt their relationship too openly.

'That kind of thing can break a company up,' he told her. 'I've seen it happen. And we've got a very nice rep here. I know you won't want to spoil it, especially when so many provincial theatres are closing down.'

It was true. Peter's prediction about the popularity of television was clearly being fulfilled. As more families bought sets and stayed at home to watch them, one theatre after another closed through lack of business. Experienced actors were thrown out of work and valuable training ground was lost to newcomers. The profession was in the doldrums.

They played *Cinderella* for two weeks instead of the usual one, and on the last night Alex gave them a party. The stage was cleared and everyone invited friends. They ate, drank and danced until the small hours of the morning. After the party Amy walked happily home with Alex, light-hearted and high on wine and success and looking forward to the ecstatic weekend they were about to share.

The night was cold and frosty and the sky was bright with a full moon and stars. She hugged his arm and looked up at him. 'Are you happy, Alex?'

He laughed. 'What kind of damn-fool question is that?'

'A simple one,' she said, slightly put out. '*I'm* happier than I've ever been in my life. Are you?'

He looked down at her. 'It's a long time since I asked myself whether I was happy or not. I've got out of the habit.'

'Couldn't you try and get back into it?' she asked. 'Go on – ask yourself now. Just try.'

He stopped to take out his key, disengaging his arm from hers. 'Isn't it enough for you that you're happy?'

As they stepped into the dark hallway she reached up to wind her arms around his neck. 'No. I want you to be happy too. I want you to be happier than you've ever been before – just as I am. When you love someone it isn't enough to be happy on your own.'

He sighed. 'Let's go to bed. I'm tired.'

She laughed softly. 'What kind of reason is that?'

'It's a bloody good one when you get to my age,' he told her. 'You'll find out.'

'I don't believe you.' She pulled him towards her and began to undo the buttons of his shirt. 'Now, let's see just how tired you are.' Confident that her hands on his bare flesh would make him forget his tiredness, she continued to unfasten his shirt, then slipped her hands inside to caress him. For a moment he stood passively and let her, then, with a roar of angry submission, he swept her up in his arms and carried her to the bedroom.

Their lovemaking was as passionate as ever. Over the months Amy had learned the things that pleased him. She knew how to touch him in ways he found irresistible; how to kiss and caress; when to urge him on, and when to hold back. For her, loving Alex had become almost as much of an art as her acting. When at last they were both spent she lay drowsily in his arms thinking about the request she had wanted to make for some time.

'Alex . . .' She twisted her head to look up at him as she lay with her head on his chest. His eyes were closed and he looked perfectly relaxed. This seemed to her like the perfect moment. 'Alex – will you marry me?'

His eyes flew open. '*What* did you say?'

She laughed. 'I asked you to marry me. Well, if I wait for you to ask *me* we could both be old and grey.' She sat up and looked down at him. 'Well – will you?'

He sat up abruptly, swinging his legs over the side of the bed and reaching for his cigarettes and lighter. She watched as he lit one, inhaled deeply and blew out a cloud of smoke.

'Alex – please say something,' she said quietly.

301

He drew hard on the cigarette again. 'You're a child, Amy. I've told you so many times before. I'm all wrong for you.'

'You're not. I . . .'

He turned and silenced her with a look. 'I *am*. I'm too old and too – I don't know – world-weary – call it what you like. I don't want to get married. Not now. Not ever.'

Swallowing her disappointment, she reached out to touch him. Angry tears and recriminations would do nothing to help her cause. She knew him well enough to realise that. 'Alex. I'm not a child. You know that. You need someone. You need me. You've been alone too long. I love you. Please don't close your mind to the idea of us being together.'

'We are together. It's enough for me the way we are. Why can't it be enough for you?'

Her hand tightened on his shoulder and she pulled him towards her but he shook her off angrily and stood up, pulling on his dressing gown. 'You don't know what you're saying, Amy – don't know what you're asking. I believe losing your father has a lot to do with this. I think you see me as some kind of father figure.'

She laughed aloud. 'Oh, what *rubbish*. Can you really say that I've treated you like a father?'

He shrugged impatiently. 'It's just a theory, but whatever the reason, I mean it, Amy. Marriage is out.'

She looked at him. He did mean it, she could see that by the determined set of his mouth. The time had come to play her trump card. She had kept it as a kind of treat; the icing on the cake. But now suddenly she saw that it was nothing of the kind. A chill went through her and the thought of what she was about to reveal filled her with dread. Nevertheless, she had to say it. She took a deep breath.

'I'm pregnant, Alex. I'm going to have our child.'

He closed his eyes, rocking back on his heels for a moment. When he opened them again she shrank from the look in them. Glaring furiously down at her he thundered: 'What the *hell* do you think you're playing at, Amy? You said you were taking care of that.'

'No.' She shook her head bemusedly. 'No, I didn't.'

'*Leave the worrying to me*, you said. I thought . . .' He broke off. Stubbing out his cigarette savagely he turned his back to her. 'Christ, what a bloody mess.' He paced the room for a moment then turned to face her. 'Look, there are doctors in London who can fix it. I know where I can get the name of one. A good one. You'll be safe. I'll give you the money and you can . . .'

'*No*. I won't do that.'

He rounded on her. 'You'll do as I bloody well say.'

'No, I *won't*. Not that. You can't make me.'

He raked his fingers through his hair. 'You'll *have* to, Amy. Can't you see? It's not my fault if you've been stupid enough to get yourself into this. Don't you care anything for your career? Or mine? How do you think this is going to look to the rest of the company?'

She was crying now, tears slipping unchecked down her cheeks as she looked up at him. She'd thought she knew him – she'd been so sure that he loved her. 'I don't care about the rest of the company,' she said in a choked voice. 'I only care about you – and me and – and our baby. No one will think anything about it if we get married. Why should they?'

With a despairing sigh he sat down and drew her into his arms. 'Amy – *Amy*. A baby will wreck your career as an actress and I'd make you miserable. Within a year we'd be at each other's throats. You'd wish you'd never met me.'

'I won't. I *won't*. Please, Alex – *please*.'

He grasped her by the shoulders, holding her away from him, his eyes burning into hers. 'Amy, listen to me. I'm trying hard not to be unkind, but you're forcing me. The simple fact is, *I don't love you*. I don't love you and I never will. I can't love anyone – ever. And I can't marry anyone either, because I'll only ever have one wife – Chloe. And I'll never be able to stop loving her.'

She began to sob like a child. 'I don't believe you. It isn't true. You can't love a dead person. You *do* love me. I'll prove it to you, Alex. I'll make you. I'll *make* you.'

With a sigh he held her in his arms and let her cry. It was his fault. He should have seen from the beginning how immature she was. For all her passion and her beautiful woman's body, she was still a child – vulnerable and trusting and naive. He should never have let the relationship develop. God only knew there were plenty of women willing for a quick fling with no strings attached, so why had he chosen Amy? He knew the reasons why. He'd been touched by her innocence; flattered by her admiration; and all his predatory instincts had been aroused by her vulnerability. Christ, how arrogant he'd been. Deep inside he'd known it was folly, seen all the danger signals, so why had he ignored them? Now it was too late. His heart sank despairingly. What in God's name was he to do?

They were married three weeks later, two days after Amy's eighteenth birthday, at the register office in Minsdale. One or two members of the company were present at the ceremony and they all went for lunch at the Swan afterwards. Feeling she wanted someone of her own there, Amy had written to Celia, and to her great delight, she came over from York for the day. After the ceremony they found a few moments to be alone together in the cloakroom at the Swan. Celia hugged her friend warmly.

'Well, you made it before me in the end,' she said. 'Are you happy, kid?'

Amy nodded. 'Do you like him, Cee?'

Celia hesitated just a fraction of a second too long. 'Of course. He's terribly handsome and romantic-looking. But . . .'

'Go on, but what?'

'He's quite a bit older than you, isn't he?'

'Not all that much. He's thirty-six.'

'That's twice your age.'

'What does it matter anyway when we love each other?' Amy said, instantly defensive.

'Nothing. Of course it doesn't matter. Where will you live?' Celia asked. 'Have you got lots of exciting plans about working together? I expect you're planning a great theatrical partnership like Kay Hammond and John Clements.'

Amy looked down at the shiny new gold band on her finger. 'I'm going to have a baby, Cee. So my career plans will have to be shelved – for a while at least.'

Celia looked into her friend's face and her heart sank. In the blue eyes she thought she could already see the seeds of unhappiness. Swallowing her dismay, she hugged Amy hard.

'Hey, that's terrific. Congratulations. Promise you'll let me know when it's born, won't you? Maybe I could be a Godmother.'

'Alex has a house in Mill Hill,' Amy went on. 'It belonged to his parents and they left it to him. I'm going to live there when I have to give up my job with the company here.'

'I see. And what about Alex?'

'He's going to try for some film or television work in London when his contract is finished here. But in the meantime he'll travel down to Mill Hill to be with me at weekends.'

Celia was silent. She hoped Amy wasn't about to be dumped and forgotten, like some unwanted animal. She didn't quite know why she should feel this. After all, she had only just met Alex Keynan. It was just an uncomfortable feeling she had. Forcing herself to smile, she said: 'Sounds exciting.' She hesitated, then asked, 'Amy – does your mum know – about you getting married, I mean, and – the baby?'

Amy shook her head. 'I did write when I first came up here but she never answered. I doubt whether she'd be interested.'

304

'Oh. Well, maybe you're right.' Privately Celia wished that she didn't live so far away. She wished Amy hadn't fallen out with her mother too. She had a horrible feeling that she was going to need someone close to her before too long.

Chapter Sixteen

Gina's first collection was a bigger success than she had dared to hope. The venue she had chosen for the show was a wise choice. Almost everyone who had received an invitation turned up on the day of the show, including – much to Maryan's surprise – the Leighs.

She caught sight of them when she was ushering people to their seats just before the start of the show. For a moment she stood where she was, on the far side of the room, watching as they settled into their seats. They both looked so old and tired that she felt a stab of pity and regret as she watched Sam attentively making sure that his wife was comfortable. Should she go across to them? She stood hesitating. Rachel might be upset – might snub her. Did she even know that she was working for her ex-designer? But at that moment Sam caught sight of her and his face broke into a smile. He waved, beckoning her over. Taking a deep breath, she walked across.

'Hello. How nice to see you both.'

Sam took her hand warmly in both of his. 'Maryan, my dear. Rachel and I were so pleased to be invited. This is a very special day for Gina. We're proud of her, aren't we, Rachel? And we feel so honoured to be asked to share this day with her. I know she must be busy, but if you see her before the show begins, wish her the best of luck from us, will you?'

'Of course I will.' Maryan glanced at Rachel. 'And how are you, Mrs Leigh?'

Rachel turned to give her a brief nod. 'I am very well, thank you.' It was clearly an effort for her. Maryan saw her throat constrict as she swallowed. 'It's – been a long time, Maryan. It – it's good to see you again.'

Maryan reached across Sam to take Rachel's hand. 'It's good to see you, too – very good.' She looked up as the small orchestra they had hired began to play. 'It looks as though we're about to start, so I'm afraid I'll have to go now. But I'll come and see you again in the interval.'

Behind the scenes all was chaos as the models prepared for their appearance. Hairdressers were busy combing and pinning, while the make-up girls worked briskly with their brushes and pots of colour. Gina herself seemed to be everywhere at once, checking hemlines, pinning a seam here and tweaking a sleeve there. As she passed her Maryan managed to say: 'Gina – the Leighs are here. Both of them. They asked me to say good luck.'

Gina looked up with a smile. 'Oh, that's wonderful. Thanks, Maryan.'

In the interval Maryan made a point of joining Sam and Rachel, taking them a tray of tea and picking out a plate of the choicest cakes for them. She found them looking more relaxed, though Rachel seemed a little flushed.

'How are you enjoying it so far?' she ventured.

Sam nodded eagerly. 'Gina has done wonders. Her designs are delightful. We both think so, don't we, Rachel?'

Rachel looked up. 'They are certainly different.' She smiled diffidently. 'I mean that in a complimentary way. I'm so relieved, you see. I dreaded that they might be too like – too close to . . .'

'Too close to Marcus's styles,' Sam said in a hushed whisper. He turned to his wife. 'But I told you, darling. Those styles are out of fashion now anyway. Gina has such flair. She is a trend *setter*, not a follower.' He leaned across to Maryan with a conspiratorial smile. 'Rachel and I are going on holiday next month. I've persuaded her at last. We're going on a cruise to the Greek islands.'

'Oh, how lovely. You'll enjoy it so much.'

Rachel nodded. 'I can't remember when we last had a proper holiday. There was the war and everything.' She smiled reminiscently. 'Though I always felt that working to promote Marcus's name was a holiday for me. I loved it all so much.'

'But it will be so nice to be together,' Maryan said. 'To have no one else to think of but each other.'

Sam smiled and squeezed his wife's hand. 'A second honeymoon, I tell her.' He chuckled. 'Though she tells me not to be a sentimental old fool.' He looked at Maryan. 'We are thinking of winding up Feldman's – maybe even selling up,' he said quietly.

Maryan glanced at Rachel, wondering how she felt about this. The firm had been started by her father and left to her. It had always been meant as a family business, to be handed on. But now there was no one to hand it to. She must feel that. 'I see,' she said. 'Well, whatever you decide, I'm sure it will be the right decision.'

Gina joined them and Maryan left her to speak to the Leighs alone. She felt happy to have seen them and spoken to Rachel. Although no one had mentioned Amy or the circumstances in which they had parted, she felt instinctively that she had been forgiven. And she was glad that they bore Gina no ill will.

The fashion magazines and trade papers were full of praise for Gina Stern's spring and summer collection and she was soon receiving invitations to exhibit her work at larger shows both in England and on the Continent. By summer she was inundated with orders, both for her range of off-the-peg fashions and for her more exclusive designs, so much so that the factory in Islington could no longer cope with her orders as well as their other commitments. After a meeting with her bank manager to find out just how much she could afford to spend, Gina decided that there was nothing for it but to hire a whole factory instead of just a few machines. She discussed it with Maryan over supper one evening.

'It's going to be so expensive,' she complained. 'And where will I find a place like that anyway? In the end the only answer is to buy, and that would mean taking on a big mortgage. I'd rather wait till I'm more established before taking a step like that.'

'Would Mr Kemp – Robert help you?' Maryan ventured.

Gina stirred her coffee pensively. 'I'd rather not ask,' she said. 'I want to stand on my own feet. I already owe him a lot. Too much, in fact.'

Maryan was surprised at Gina's tone. 'I'm sure, from what you tell me, that he doesn't look on it like that.'

Gina looked up at her. 'You might have noticed that Robert hasn't been around much lately,' she said. 'I'm afraid it's on the cards that our relationship is coming to an end.'

'I see. His wife . . . ?'

Gina shook her head. 'No. That I could come to terms with. Robert is going in for politics. He's standing for Parliament in next year's General Election. He's been selected for a constituency in Essex. It's something he's always wanted, so I'm sure I don't have to tell you that he won't allow a scandal to ruin his chances.'

'I see.' Maryan looked thoughtful. 'It's bound to be expensive, organising an election campaign. Is he asking for his money back?'

'No. But he's going to get it,' Gina said determinedly. 'Every last penny, which is why buying a factory could be something of a problem just now.'

'Yes, of course.' A gloomy silence descended between them. Then Maryan had an idea. 'Why not ask Sam Leigh if you can rent Feldman's premises? He's talking of winding the business up – even selling it off. He might be willing to let you rent the workshop for a while with the option to buy later, when you're ready.'

Gina stared at her. 'My God, Maryan, that's brilliant. Do you really think he would? It seems an awful cheek to ask after I left them.'

'They don't hold that against you,' Maryan said. 'Anyway, there's only one way to find out. Ask him.'

Gina's eyes lit up with excitement. 'I will. I'll ring him tomorrow. No – better than that, I'll go and see him.'

Number twenty-two Willow Drive hadn't been lived in since 1947, when Alex's widowed father had died. One of a row of neat semi-detached residences built between the wars, it had once been the ideal suburban home. Now it was sadly neglected and run down. The garden was a wilderness of weeds and long wiry grass and the house itself, closed up for the past three years, smelt musty with damp and was badly in need of decoration.

When Amy saw the place for the first time she was deeply disappointed, and the thought of living there alone depressed her beyond measure. The removal of dust sheets revealed ugly, old-fashioned furniture; dark in colour and heavy in design. The curtains were dusty and in need of washing, the carpets were worn almost threadbare and cobwebs festooned every corner.

'I think Dad became a bit of a recluse after Mother died,' Alex told her. 'He wouldn't have a cleaning woman in or help of any kind.'

'I can see that,' Amy said dryly. She had wandered into the kitchen, where the first thing to catch her eye was an ancient black gas cooker which squatted in one corner on four bandy legs. It was encrusted with grease, welded in position by layers of dust. Its rusting plate rack held two cracked dinner plates and a filthy tea towel. The half-tiled walls, once white, wore a film of grime and the linoleum on the floor was cracked and torn, showing the floorboards in places.

Seeing her look of dismay, Alex said cheerfully, 'It just needs a bit of a clean. You'll soon get the place shipshape. It'll be something to occupy the time, won't it?'

Despair gripping her chest like an iron band, she wrapped her arms around his waist and laid her head on his chest. 'Oh, Alex, do I really have to stay here on my own? Why can't we be together? I know I can't act at the moment, but I wouldn't be a nuisance. I'd help backstage if you like. Anything so's we could be together.'

He put her from him impatiently. 'Amy, look, we talked all this through and we decided. It's better for you to be here in a stable home, at least until after the baby's born. Later – well, we'll see.'

'But we could make a stable home in Minsdale. I don't know anyone here.'

'You'll soon make friends. I daresay you'll be going to some sort of clinic where there'll be other young mothers-to-be. You'll be fine.' He kissed her. 'Look, I know this place looks pretty awful now, but at least it's ours and it's paid for. When my contract runs out at Minsdale I'll be getting work in London. This will make a good central base for me.'

'But it's so – so shabby and creepy,' Amy said, looking round at the dark green paintwork and peeling ceilings. 'Couldn't we sell it and find something nicer?'

'That's easier said than done,' Alex told her. 'Houses like this are at a premium. You have to go through heaven knows how much red tape, not to mention building permits, to build a new place and even then it wouldn't be as sound as this.' He ruffled her hair. 'Cheer up. You won't know the place once we get a bit of paint slapped on and some new furniture.'

'I don't really know how to paint. You will help me, won't you?'

'Of course.'

'When, Alex?' she asked him eagerly. But he shook his head.

'Might have to wait a bit,' he hedged. 'I'm tied up in Minsdale for the next twelve months. After that – well, we'll just have to wait and see.'

In the early weeks she occupied herself by cleaning the house. At first she found that she couldn't even light the boiler for hot water. Whenever she tried clouds of smoke filled the kitchen, almost choking her, until she realised what the trouble was. Once she had found a local sweep and had all the chimneys swept it was easier. Then, armed with buckets of hot water, soap and soda, she scrubbed the house from top to bottom until her hands were red and raw. She washed the curtains, hanging them out to dry in the spring breezes. She'd already discovered that the beds were not too bad. The double one in the front bedroom had an interior spring mattress, and after a good airing it was warm and comfortable. The airing cupboard was full of good quality linen, too, yellow with age and disuse, but whole and some of it exquisitely embroidered; a relic of better days when Alex's mother was alive, she guessed. To add to this there was good cutlery and china in the sideboard downstairs. It seemed that Alex's father had put it all away, using only the two cracked plates in the kitchen and a pathetic chipped cup with a saucer that didn't match.

All through the hard-working weekdays Amy looked forward to the weekends when Alex would come. But to her disappointment he didn't always get away. She knew of course that it was difficult for him, making the long drive down from Minsdale after two shows on Saturdays, then driving back on Monday to arrive in time for the evening performance. Because they had no telephone she often waited in vain, sitting up until the small hours of Sunday morning, hoping against hope that he would come. The usual reason he gave for not coming was that the second-hand car he had bought soon after they married had let him down.

She wrote long letters to Celia, making her marriage and pregnancy and settling into the house sound like an exciting adventure. Celia wrote back with news of her busy and interesting life. She was training to be a legal executive, now; studying in her spare time. She invited Amy to go up to York and stay with her at the flat for a weekend. Amy declined, saying that Alex always drove down to spend the weekends with her. Of course this wasn't strictly true and she suspected that he would be only too happy for her to have an alternative to occupy her weekend. The real reason was that she was short of money. Alex's weekly cheque often failed to arrive and she had to eke out the previous week's money as best she could. Dearly as she would have loved to see her friend, the train fare to York would have been beyond her means. She often toyed with the idea of writing to her mother. She had sent her a note, telling her that she was to be married, addressing it to Simons Mews, confident that one of the Donlans would forward it to wherever Maryan had gone. But, as before, she had received no reply.

She did write to Marjorie Taylor, however. As with Celia's letters, she made everything sound much happier and grander than it really was. As well as passing the time, writing letters boosted her confidence and made her feel that things were going to be all right. Marjorie replied, telling her that Mike was working for the BBC and hoping eventually to become a foreign correspondent. She promised to pass on Amy's good wishes.

Month by month the baby grew inside her. She was remarkably well. She had registered with a local doctor and had her monthly checks without fail. She had been booked in at a local hospital for the birth and everything seemed to be going according to plan. As Alex had predicted, she did meet other young mothers-to-be, but no one with whom she felt she had anything in common. When she told them she was an actress they looked at her with open suspicion and

311

disbelief, preferring to talk amongst themselves about babies and shopping and what they were going to give their husbands for tea.

Alex declared that pregnancy suited her. In the early days when he came home he loved to lie in bed and watch her undress. Seeing the nymph-like figure growing increasingly ripe and voluptuous excited him. It was like making love to someone new. He was delighted too at the way pregnancy seemed to increase Amy's appetite for love. But as the months passed and the pleasantly rounded figure grew larger, his interest waned. Privately he thought she looked bloated and grotesque. Making love to her became little more than a duty. The list of stock excuses for staying away lengthened and the weekend visits grew even more infrequent.

His obvious lack of interest was a cause of anxiety and distress to Amy. She lay awake at night, worrying about it. He had made no attempt to hide the fact that he no longer found her desirable and it hurt unbearably. Surely once the baby was born and she regained her figure he would find her attractive again? In the meantime she was lonely, lonelier than she could ever have imagined. She often thought nostalgically about the happy times at Rhensham, and of the Taylors; of her schooldays and Celia. And she thought of her mother too. It would have been nice to have had a proper mother at this time in her life – someone she could talk to about the pregnancy, sharing her fears and apprehension about the coming birth with someone close who loved her. Her feelings towards Maryan swung between anger and wistfulness, resentment and regret. But however much she might want it, her pride would not allow her to beg for her mother's attention. Maryan had always been too busy for her in the past. Clearly nothing had altered.

As spring evolved gently into summer her thoughts turned to the garden. Looking out of the windows at the tangle, she realised that something would have to be done with it. With the warmth and the gentle spring rain the weeds and grass were shooting up. Day by day it grew increasingly out of control. She was struggling to cut the front lawn one afternoon in late May when she made her first friend.

'You'll never make no headway like that, missie.'

The voice made her look up. A little man with a brown face and bright blue eyes stood looking over the front gate. She straightened her back and he noticed for the first time that she was pregnant.

'Oh,' he said, taking off his cap and scratching his head. 'Sorry, I didn't notice you was a missis. Like me to give you a hand with that, would you?'

Amy smiled and wiped the sweat from her forehead with the back of her hand. 'I'm afraid I couldn't afford to pay you, but if you could just show me how to get it started . . . I don't know anything about gardening, you see.'

'I can see that all right.' A smile lit up the blue eyes as he eagerly opened the gate and came in. 'Bless your heart, I don't want no paying. Glad of something to do. Since my retirement I've been getting under my missis's feet something chronic.' He held out his hand. 'Jack Shaw from number twenty-nine.'

Amy smiled and shook the large knobbly hand. 'How do you do, Mr Shaw. I'm Amy Keynan.'

Jack slapped his cap back onto his head and looked pointedly at her thickened waistline. 'Apart from anything else, m'dear, you got no business doing heavy work like this in your condition, if you don't mind me saying so. Hubby work away, does he?'

'Yes.'

'Right. Better let me get on with it for you then, eh?'

Amy handed over the mower gratefully. 'Well, if you're sure. I'll make a cup of tea. I expect you'd like one.'

'Well now. That'd be very nice.'

Jack did wonders with the garden. Having convinced him that the exercise was good for her, Amy helped, and once they had cleared the tangle of weeds they found a pleasant lay-out underneath, with borders and a shrubbery. Jack brought bedding plants from his own greenhouse to plant in them. It wasn't long before he brought his wife across to view his handiwork and to meet Amy.

Addie Shaw was plump and motherly with tightly permed hair. The sharp blue eyes that twinkled behind her spectacles missed nothing that went on in Willow Drive. Right from the first she showed a friendly curiosity towards her new young neighbour. She admired the work that Amy had put in on the house and then, as they sat down to a cup of tea together, showed a lively interest in her private life.

'Hubby work away from home then, does he, luvvie?' she observed, her little finger crooked as she drank tea from one of Alex's mother's bone china cups that Amy had brought out of retirement.

Amy explained that the house had belonged to Alex's parents and that he was up north for the time being.

'He's running a repertory theatre in Lancashire at the moment, but when his contract is up he'll be looking for film work,' she said. Addie was impressed.

'There now. Just fancy. A film producer. We never saw much of old Mr Keynan, of course. Kept himself very much *to* himself, if you know what I mean. There's plenty would have been willing to help him after his poor wife passed on, but he wouldn't have it. Oh no,

313

very independent.' She looked up over the rim of her cup. 'Tell you the truth, dear, we never even knew he had a son. Your hubby didn't visit much – hardly ever that I can remember.' She looked around her. 'Always wondered what sort of a state this place was in. A man on his own usually lets a house go to pot, don't he? But it's all good stuff, you can see that. And you've made it quite nice, dear – considering.' She nodded in the direction of Amy's stomach. 'When's baby due then?'

'The end of August.'

'Oh. Not long to wait now then, eh? Exciting, isn't it – the first baby.'

But in spite of the improvement to the house and garden, Alex bristled with annoyance when he knew that the Shaws were partly responsible.

'Interfering old fools. Who asked them to poke their noses in? I hope you haven't been telling them too much. People like that have nothing better to do but ferret out other people's business and gossip about it all over the neighbourhood.'

'That's a horrible thing to say,' Amy retorted. 'They've been so kind. I don't know what I'd have done without them. It hasn't been easy, getting this place shipshape as you call it. I haven't noticed you doing much – when you ever bother to turn up, that is. It seems you never came to see your parents, though, so it's nothing unusual, I suppose.'

'There, you see? They've already started making trouble.' He rounded on her angrily. 'Thanks a *lot*, Amy. That's what I call *real* gratitude. I work bloody hard all week, then wear myself out, driving all the way down here as often as I can, to make sure you're all right. And you reproach me because I don't spend all day Sunday digging the damned garden or sloshing a paintbrush about.'

'You hardly ever come any more,' Amy said reproachfully. 'I don't think you really give a tuppenny damn whether I'm all right or not.'

'Oh. I see.' His face darkened. 'Well, if that's what you think I might as well go now. There are plenty of other things I could be doing that are a bloody sight more rewarding than this.' He strode into the hall and began to put on his coat. 'Maybe it'd be better if I didn't bother coming home any more,' he said, shrugging his arms into the sleeves. 'Maybe you prefer the Shaws' company to mine.'

Heaving herself out of her chair, she hurried after him. 'Oh, Alex, don't. You know I didn't mean it. I get so lonely, that's all. I miss you. And I can't do everything on my own, specially now.' She put

314

her arms around his neck, attempting to pull off his coat as she did so. 'Don't go, darling. Come up to bed.'

'It's the middle of the afternoon.'

She smiled up at him. 'So – when did that ever bother you?'

He frowned, pushing her away. 'No, Amy. I can't. It isn't – isn't good for you.'

She let her arms fall to her sides and stood looking at him. 'You could give me a cuddle,' she said, her lip trembling. 'You never cuddle me any more.'

He turned away, his expression a mixture of guilt and distaste. 'Oh, Amy – don't be so childish.'

She managed to persuade him to stay, but for the rest of the day he was morose and silent. In bed, when she reached for him he kissed her briefly and turned his back. Long after his breathing had deepened she was still awake, staring at the ceiling, the tears drying on her face. Perhaps she should have done as he wanted in the first place and gone to London for an abortion, she thought despairingly. As though responding to the thought, the child inside her stirred and she clasped her stomach with protective hands.

'I didn't mean it,' she whispered. 'I didn't really mean it, baby. I'll never let anyone hurt you.' She promised herself that whatever happened, whatever came out of this, she would have her baby to love; someone who truly belonged to her. And she vowed that she would always be honest and truthful with her son or daughter. There would be no secrets between them. No shocking surprises. No lies or deception. Never.

Alone in the house she often thought about the couple who had lived there before her; Alex's parents. She was always coming across things – little things, clues to the life they had led here, which she gradually fitted together like the pieces of a puzzle. A photograph album she found at the bottom of a drawer held all the Keynan family memories. A wedding photograph bearing the inscription, *Henry and Florence July 9th 1910*, showed Alex's parents as a young couple on the day they'd wed: a shy young man with a waxed moustache, wearing a high, stiff collar and Windsor knotted tie; and his bride, her face almost hidden under the enormous cartwheel hat loaded with flowers. Further on there were pictures of Henry as a young soldier in the Great War and Alex as a chubby infant on his mother's knee. He was their only child. They must have been so proud of him. She often wondered why he had neglected them and tried to imagine their puzzled sadness and, later, the loneliness of poor widowed Henry, left in this house with his memories and his solitary grief. Sometimes in the night when she couldn't sleep she held imaginary conversations with them in her head, and wondered if she was about to be abandoned too in this house of disillusionment and loneliness.

It was six weeks before Alex came again, arriving unannounced one Friday evening. The baby's birth was less than a month away now and Amy, lonely and tired of the endless waiting, forgot all her fears in her delight at seeing him. Everything was ready now. She had made most of the baby's clothes herself, finding Alex's mother's old sewing machine carefully put away in the boxroom. The needle-work lessons she had complained of so bitterly at St Hildred's had finally come into their own. She proudly showed Alex the little flannel nightgowns and the vests and jackets she had knitted. Addie Shaw had found her a second-hand pram in good condition. She'd made some baby clothes for her too, but Amy kept those at the back of the drawer, in case Alex might be annoyed again.

But he showed scant interest in the baby clothes. He'd driven down earlier that afternoon to attend an interview for a job he'd applied for with Gainsborough Films, but by the end of the afternoon he knew that the job he wanted so badly had gone to someone else. He had repaired to the nearest pub in an attempt to dull the pain of disappointment. But drinking only made him feel worse, and by the time he arrived at Willow Drive the mixture of alcohol and disillusion-ment had plunged him into the blackest of moods.

'What's the matter?' Amy asked. 'Aren't you interested?'

He waved a hand at her impatiently. 'I've got more on my mind at the moment than bloody knitting and baby clothes.'

Stung, she rounded on him angrily. 'Well, isn't that nice for you? I wish *I* had other things on my mind. All I've got to look forward to is the baby, Alex. You might try to take an interest in it, if only for my sake.'

'If it's all you've got, then you've only yourself to blame,' he said, erupting hotly into anger. 'Do I have to remind you that you forced me into this marriage? That it was *you* who threw yourself at me and *you* who was careless enough to get yourself pregnant? Well, now you've got it all your own way and I'm stuck with a wife and child I don't want. So if I were you I'd just keep my mouth shut.'

She turned away, tears springing to her eyes. 'If you're trying to punish me, Alex, you're succeeding. I wonder if you know how cruel you are.'

He got up and flung out of the room. She followed him. 'You're bored with me, aren't you? God knows you've made that clear enough these past months. Do you want a divorce? Is that it?' she

316

demanded. 'If it is, just say so. You obviously don't love me any more.'

He spun round, his face a mask of fury. 'I've *never* loved you, Amy. I thought I'd made that clear to you right at the beginning. What we had was meant to be just a fling – a bit of fun. I thought you knew that. I thought you were keen on a career and that you'd take proper care.'

'So – it's over then?' She stood staring at him, her eyes wide and her lip trembling.

'*Over?* How can it be over now that you've landed us with *that?*' He threw a look of disgust at her swollen belly. 'We're trapped, Amy. You and I are well and truly up the creek in the same bloody boat, and I just hope you like it.'

Her hand to her mouth, she went into the kitchen and shut the door. How could she have come to this? she asked herself. She wasn't even twenty yet and her life was over. She'd had such plans. She'd been so determined to make a success of her life. And she *would* have, too. She was a good actress, everyone said she had promise. Everything had been going so well. And in spite of that she hadn't been unhappy when she found out about the baby because she loved Alex. But if he resented her so much; and meant to go on blaming her, then there could be no future for them.

She felt bleak and alone. Standing at the kitchen window, she gripped the edge of the sink and tried hard not to cry. Tears cured nothing. She'd already proved that. She must let Alex go. Somehow or other she must manage on her own. How could she stay with a man who clearly despised her? She couldn't take it any more.

When the first pain gripped her it came as a shock. She'd always thought labour began slowly and gently, besides there were still three weeks to go yet. It caught her low down in her back and abdomen, like a giant hand gripping and squeezing her. The intensity of it took her breath away and left her gasping. She gave an involuntary cry and bent almost double, clutching at the kitchen table for support. Slowly the contraction relaxed its iron grip and she was able to breathe again. She was crossing the kitchen when another pain seized her, sharper and even more intense this time. Her scream brought Alex, running down the stairs and bursting into the kitchen.

'What's the matter? Have you hurt yourself?'

'I think – think it's the baby,' she said between clenched teeth. 'I've got to go – to the hospital.'

'I'll take you.' His face was white with shock. 'I'll get the car started.'

317

Minutes later they were on their way. Amy sat hunched in the passenger seat, her teeth clamped over her lower lip to stop her from crying out. There was scarcely a break now between the pains. They were fierce and relentless. It was as though something else, some demon, had taken her body over. She was no longer in control, however hard she fought. With every contraction she wondered just how much longer she would be able to bear it. Already her breath was coming in hiccuping gasps. Would they get there before the baby thrust its way into the world?

When they reached the hospital the staff took over. She was lifted onto a trolley and whisked away, leaving Alex to wait in the corridor.

Amy's son was born less than an hour after her arrival at the hospital. Although he was three weeks premature he weighed almost eight pounds and cried lustily at birth.

'Here he is. Little master impatience.' The nurse smiled as she put the baby into Amy's arms. 'He had no intention of waiting around for anyone, did he? A real go-getter he's going to be.'

Amy looked down in wonder at the enormous blue eyes that stared up at her. His dark lair lay against his little round head in flat, damp curls. She adored him instantly, and from that very first moment she knew exactly what his name was going to be.

'Mark. I want to call him Mark, after my father,' she told Alex when at last he was allowed in to see her.

He looked down at his son. 'Yes. It suits him.' He bent over Amy. 'Darling, I'm sorry – about earlier. I didn't mean what I said. It's all the rushing up and down from Minsdale and the partings. We haven't had a chance to settle down to marriage really, have we?'

She smiled, pushing aside the memory that living apart had been his idea. The baby's birth seemed to have made everything else insignificant somehow. 'Never mind. Everything will be all right now, won't it?'

'Of course it will.' He took her hand. 'Poor love. I felt so useless out there, waiting.' He lifted the hand he held and kissed the fingers one by one. 'Was it ghastly?'

'It was, a bit.' She smiled sleepily. 'But at least it was quick.'

'I didn't tell you. I had an interview this afternoon for a job with Gainsborough. I didn't get it. It hit me hard. That's why I was so bloody to you.'

Her eyes clouded as she looked up at him. 'Why didn't you tell me, Alex? We should share the disappointments as well as the happiness. I'm your wife.' She held his hand against her cheek and closed her eyes. Suddenly she was terribly tired. She wanted to talk to him. There was so much she wanted to tell him, so many promises and plans for their future, theirs and Mark's. But her eyelids felt as though they were weighted with lead and try as she would she could not make them stay open.

Alex stood looking down at them both. His wife and child, both sleeping peacefully. It was hard to take in. Through all the past months, haunted by doubt, he'd kept telling himself that once it happened – once the child was born – he would be able to come to terms with the fact that he was a married man again. But as he looked down at the girl sleeping so serenely in the bed the image of Chloe's face seemed to superimpose itself on Amy's. Not Chloe's face as he wanted to remember her, but the image that haunted his worst dreams of that horrific day when he had helped to dig her out from under the debris of the bombed building.

He closed his eyes in an attempt to shut out the dreaded pictures but it was no use. Even behind his closed eyelids he could still see the fair hair caked with dirt and the lovely face bruised and blackened, streaked with blood. The grotesquely twisted limbs. His stomach heaved and bile rose in his mouth. It was a sight he would never get out of his mind if he lived to be a hundred. One regret would torture him for ever. He should not have left her that afternoon. They should have gone together.

Fighting his nausea and blinded by tears, he stumbled out of the room and along the corridor. The birth of his son should have marked a new beginning; this should be the day when the past could finally be laid to rest and he could start again. But even today the past would not free him from its grip. Maybe it never would.

Sam Leigh agreed happily to let Gina rent the old Feldman premises. Refreshed after his holiday, he was feeling buoyant and optimistic. She was to have first refusal to buy whenever she felt ready.

'You gave up so much for us, my dear,' he said. 'You gave us the benefit of your talent for far longer than we deserved. The least we can do is to help you get established in your own career.'

He and Rachel were to live in peaceful retirement at Hazelfield, he told her. But by letting Gina rent the factory they would be able to remain in touch with the trade and take an interest in the progress of her career. It seemed that Rachel had at last given up trying to keep Marcus alive. She was content now to live with her memories and let him rest.

But in spite of having the problem of factory premises solved, Gina still seemed restless and uneasy. When Maryan asked her why,

319

she admitted that she was still going to be short of money once she had repaid her debt.

'I'll have machinists to engage, twelve at least; a good cutter and someone to supervise.'

'Do you really have to pay back the money you owe Robert right away?' Maryan asked. 'I'm sure he wouldn't mind waiting a little longer.' But Gina's mouth set in a firm line.

'*He* wouldn't, but I would. I want it over and done with,' she said. 'While he still has a financial interest in the business I'll have to go on seeing him from time to time. I want to make the break complete.'

Maryan looked at her employer. The end of the affair had obviously hit her hard and she wanted no loose ends to prolong the agony. She understood that well enough. But tying them up could prove costly. 'I suppose there's nothing you could sell, is there?' she suggested.

Gina shrugged. 'All I have is the business and the house – apart from a few old sticks of Nanna's furniture down in the cellar.'

Maryan's heart jumped. 'What kind of furniture?' she asked. 'Can I have a look?'

'If you like, but there isn't much. She took anything of value down to Devonshire with her when the war started. Other things she gave away to friends and relatives. The house was virtually empty when I inherited it. There are just a few items of furniture that have always been down in the cellar as long as I can remember.'

'Never mind. They might be worth a look,' Maryan said. 'Shall we go down?'

At first glance it seemed that Gina had been right. The few effects that Gina's grandmother had left behind were stacked at one end of the cellar and covered in dust sheets. On removal, Maryan saw that there was a hide-covered Victorian chaise longue; some balloon-back chairs and an enormous and quite hideous Edwardian sideboard. Gina stood back and folded her arms.

'You see, I told you.'

'Mmm, none of it is really old enough to be called antique.' Maryan opened one of the sideboard cupboards. 'Did you know it was full of china?' Taking out a plate she turned it over. 'Limoges. An early design. I wonder how much of it there is? If it's a complete set it might be worth quite a bit.'

Excited, Gina bent to help Maryan take out the pieces, counting them one by one as they stacked them carefully on the floor. 'I remember this dinner service,' she said as she brought out an ornate tureen. 'Nanna always used it when the family came for Christmas

320

when I was little. There should be two dozen of everything if I remember rightly. Four kinds of plates, soup cups, four tureens, two sauce boats, four meat plates . . .' She was kneeling now, surrounded by the dinner service, and she looked up at Maryan with shining eyes. 'I do believe it's all here. It's a miracle. What do you think it'll fetch?'

Maryan shook her head. 'I can't say offhand, but you should get a good price at auction.' She looked at Gina, whose smile faded.

'But not enough to repay my loan, eh?'

'Well – not really, I suppose. Is there anything else?'

'There's a picture over there against the wall, but I don't think it can be worth anything,' Gina said doubtfully. 'Nanna surely wouldn't have let it moulder away down here if it'd been anything valuable.'

'You can never tell. Often it's just a matter of taste,' Maryan said. 'Let's see.'

The picture was covered and leant against the wall. She pulled off the sacking that covered it. It was a mediocre still life, Victorian and probably a copy. Gina was looking at her hopefully.

'Any good?'

'Sorry, I'm afraid not. And this is all?'

Gina was pulling out the sideboard drawers. 'I think so, except – there's a box in here.' She drew it out and took off the lid. 'Oh, look, aren't they pretty?'

Inside was a collection of miniatures. It was a subject that Maryan had found fascinating when she was studying the books Vincent had lent her, and as she looked at the tiny, detailed portraits she felt excitement stirring inside her. There were eight in all, exquisitely painted and carefully wrapped in tissue paper and laid on a bed of cotton wool in the box. The fact that every one of them was gold mounted and painted on ivory told her that they were important, but when she peered closely and saw that some of them were signed too her heart began to drum with excitement.

'Are they any good?' Gina asked.

Maryan looked up. 'I think we've got a real find here,' she said. 'I don't want to get your hopes up too high in case I'm wrong, but I believe that at least two of these are by Fragonard and this one . . .' – she held up a miniature portrait of an eighteenth century-beauty – '. . . is by Richard Cosway. See – it's signed.'

'Oh. Does that make them valuable?' Gina asked, holding her breath.

'It certainly does. And if we could find out who the sitters are as well it would make them worth even more.' Maryan sat back on her heels, wishing she had Vinnie's book with her. 'You really should get an expert opinion,' she said. 'Perhaps you could get someone from Sotherby's to look at them.'

'I'll get onto it at once,' Gina promised. 'Thanks, Maryan. I'd never have thought of looking down here for the answer to my problems.'

It was later the following day that Gina told Maryan what she'd arranged. 'Last night I rang Roisan,' she said. 'I can't think why we didn't think of it before. She's promised to get her brother, Vincent, to come and look at the miniatures.'

Maryan's heart lurched and she felt the colour drain from her face. 'Oh,' she said faintly. 'Well, he'll certainly be able to help value them.'

She looked forward to Vinnie's visit to Gower Street with a mixture of excitement and dread. Working hard over the past months, she had been able to put aside her own heartache. But the thought of seeing him again, of being close to him, filled her with apprehension. Determined to be strong, she steeled herself as the day drew nearer. She would not let him see that she had suffered. She'd hold up her head and greet him as a colleague and friend.

Gina had arranged for him to call at about eight-thirty, when the day's work would be over and they would have plenty of time to examine and discuss the miniatures. After she had eaten, Maryan waited in her flat for Gina to call her. As the time drew near she found her nervousness increasing and when at last she heard the doorbell ring downstairs and Gina's voice calling up the stairwell to summon her, the breath caught in her throat. Admonishing herself for being a fool, she took a deep breath and went downstairs to meet them.

He looked tired and drawn, but when he saw Maryan his eyes lit up and he held out both hands.

'Maryan. How nice to see you. It's been so long.'

She put her hands into his and smiled, wishing that her heartbeat would steady. Surely by now she should be able to greet him calmly? It was ridiculous.

'It's nice to see you too, Vinnie,' she said. 'Are you well – and Fay – how is she?'

He smiled and nodded. 'We're both well, thank you.'

'I can't wait for you to see what we've found,' she went on. 'There is definitely a Cosway and I think there are two Fragonards. I hope I'm right about them.'

Gina had the box of miniatures all ready and she took off the lid with a flourish, holding her breath with suspense as Vincent took out the loupe he always carried in his pocket and examined them minutely one by one. He took a lot of time over his examination, putting four of the eight miniatures on one side. When he had finished he looked at Maryan.

'You were right about the Cosway and these two are certainly Fragonards,' he said. 'I think I know who the sitters are, too, but it shouldn't be difficult to verify. The Cosway is of Mrs Fitzherbert.' He picked up the fourth one. 'This is by John Smart; late eighteenth century.'

'And the other four?' Maryan asked him.

'Military souvenirs. A lot were done of young soldiers at the time of the Napoleonic Wars. They're all good, but they need a little more research.' He looked at Gina. 'Would you mind if I came back again and made a closer study? I'll do some more research in the meantime. I believe you have a very important find there. I'd insure them well if I were you. I'll let you have a firm valuation figure when I've done some more research.'

'They're for sale,' Gina told him.

He stared at her for a moment. 'Are you serious?'

She sighed. 'I know they're beautiful and I'd love to keep them, but I need the money. They could save my business. At the moment that is the most important thing in my life.'

He nodded. 'I understand. Well, if you're quite sure that's what you want, I can arrange it for you so that you get the best deal. I'll look into it and tell you what reserve to put on them. I'd advise auctioning them and I think they should be sold individually and not as a collection. I believe you'd do better that way.'

Gina looked mystified. 'Reserve? I don't understand.'

Vincent smiled and looked at Maryan. 'Maryan will explain it all to you. In the meantime put them away somewhere safe.'

Gina's face was flushed with excitement as she stowed the miniatures carefully back in their box.

Vincent smiled. 'Well, it's nice to be the bearer of good news for once. Now I'd better be on my way.'

Gina looked up. 'Oh, how rude of me. Can I get you a drink, or a coffee or something?'

He shook his head. 'No thank you. I'll be on my way. I'll be in touch in a day or two if that's all right.'

Seeing that Gina was engrossed in the task of putting away her treasures, Maryan went with him to the door. In the hall he looked at her.

'You look wonderful, Maryan,' he said softly. 'You've done something different with your hair. It really suits you.'

'Thank you.'

'It's obvious that you're happy in your job with Miss Stern. I'm glad.'

'Yes. It's very interesting.'

'We still miss you at Vincente's.'

'I'm sure that can't be true.'

'It is. If you only knew . . .' He broke off to sigh. 'Paul has left us, you know.'

'No, I didn't. I haven't seen Roisan for some time.'

'Fay and he never got along. And with her working in the shop . . .' He lifted his shoulders. 'But I don't need to burden you with my troubles. Roisan was saying the other day that it would be nice to see you.'

'I know. I feel bad about it, but we've been so busy, what with Gina's show and everything. Tell her I'll come round to see her soon, will you?'

'I will.' They stood by the front door now. Maryan made to reach for the handle but he stood in her way. 'Will you be here when I come again, Maryan? It's so good to see you.'

'I might be,' she said brightly. 'It all depends.'

'On what?'

She shrugged. 'All sorts of things – what time of day it is. How busy I am . . .'

'Of course.' His eyes sought hers. 'If I come in the evening – at the same time as this? Please be here, Maryan.'

'I – I'll try.'

'There can be no harm in our seeing each other now, can there? Not after all this time.'

'No, I suppose not.'

He moved aside to allow her to open the door. 'I'll be in touch again soon,' he said as she let him out. 'Goodnight.'

'Goodnight.' She closed the door firmly behind him and leant against it, her heart hammering. Why had she said she would be here when he came again? Why had she meekly agreed to subject herself to all that agony again? She would not let it happen. When he came again she would be out. She had all but convinced herself that she was over him; that seeing him this evening wouldn't affect her at all, and it *mustn't*. But when she closed her eyes she could still see the sadness in his dark eyes and the fine network of lines that unhappiness had etched on his face.

Inwardly she screamed in protest. 'No. *No*. I won't give in. He made his decision. He made it impossible for us to be together and now he must live with it.'

324

'Maryan – *why didn't you tell me?*'

Startled at the voice interrupting her inner struggle, Maryan opened her eyes to see Gina looking at her. 'Tell you – what?'

'That you and he were – that close. It's why you left, isn't it? Because he's married.'

'Is it that obvious?'

'Only to someone who's been through the same mill. I saw it the moment you looked at each other. If you'd told me I would have asked someone else to value the miniatures.' She took Maryan's arm. 'Come and sit down. Tell me about it – if it would help.'

The first days of looking after little Mark and settling down to motherhood were serene and happy ones for Amy. It was as though his birth had put all her worries and fears to rest. While she was still in the hospital a trolley came round with things to buy. There were little cards announcing the baby's birth. On impulse Amy bought one and sent it to her mother. On the front was a picture of a stork carrying a baby suspended from a blue ribbon. Inside she wrote, *Announcing the arrival of Mark Alexander Keynan – July 24th 1950. Seven pounds fifteen ounces.* But the weeks went by and, as before, there was no response, and Amy's time was too consumed with the baby to brood over the reason why. Mark thrived and grew bonnier every week and for a little while life was better, and when Alex got a job with the Rank Organisation it looked as though their luck was changing.

He was making travel documentaries and was away from home even more than before, but the money was good and they began to improve the house a little. Alex had a telephone installed, as he said it was essential now that he needed to be available.

Mark's first Christmas came and went. His first tooth appeared and, a week before his first birthday, he took his first steps. Amy was so proud of him. He was a happy baby, placid and contented. Jack and Addie Shaw adored him and sometimes came across to spend the evening at number twenty-two, while Amy went to the first house of the local cinema for a treat.

Now that Mark was no longer a baby, Amy itched to get back to the stage. She reminded Alex that they'd said they'd think about her resuming her career when Mark was old enough. But Alex, fiercely protective of his son, was adamant.

'It's out of the question, Amy. How can you be a mother and have a stage career?' he said. 'No child of mine is going to be brought up by strangers.'

And with that Amy had to be satisfied. She loved little Mark and enjoyed being with him and watching him grow. But privately she promised herself that she would somehow find a way of returning to the stage before too much time had passed.

Alex's new job was taxing. When he was at home he was irritable and terse, snapping at Amy for the smallest thing. It became obvious that he was drinking too much. The smallest thing would trigger off a row and when he found out that she often left Mark in the Shaws' care while she went to the cinema he was furious.

'How could you?' he demanded. 'Suppose something went wrong? What use do you think they'd be if anything happened? Why can't you grow up and think of the child for a change, Amy?'

His harsh criticism stung her. 'That's not fair,' she shouted. 'I hardly ever get out. A couple of times a month – if that. I have to have *some* time to myself. And you're wrong about Jack and Addie. They love Mark. They'd never let anything happen to him.'

'You're right. They won't, because he won't be left with them again, do you hear? You wanted a baby, but now it seems it's too much trouble to stay at home and look after him.'

Amy turned away, swallowing the defensive retort that she longed to make. The more she tried to defend herself, the guiltier she sounded. And she wasn't guilty. Alex was never at home. He had no idea how demanding a small child could be, or how boring and repetitive her days were. His criticism hurt her deeply and he knew it. It seemed to her that all he wanted was to sting her into retaliation and start a row so that he could say the things he knew would hurt her.

In September, just a month after Mark's first birthday, Alex was assigned to a film that was to be made on location in the north of Scotland. It meant several months away from home. And for the first time Amy felt nothing but relief at the prospect of parting.

Chapter Seventeen

Autumn came to Hazelfield early that year. By the beginning of September the nights were too cold for Sam and Rachel to spend idyllic evenings sitting on the terrace at Whitegates. Log fires were lit in the pleasant drawing room and they resigned themselves to the end of summer.

The news of the King's illness and operation in September had shocked everyone. Having a lung removed seemed so frighteningly serious. And when Rachel caught a bad cold which went to her chest she dwelt on the subject more and more.

Sam grew increasingly worried about her. Her cold refused to clear up and her persistent cough became troublesome and exhausting, robbing her of sleep and making her look haggard and drawn. To Sam's concern she seemed to lose interest in her appearance and grew more and more depressed. She began once again to dwell on the past and fret for Marcus. Sam begged her to see a doctor, but every time he suggested it she became so upset and agitated that he was obliged to let the subject drop.

One night he woke to find her standing at the bedroom window in her nightgown, her feet bare. Shocked, he got up at once and went to her.

'Rachel, my love, what are you thinking of? You'll catch your death.' He picked up her dressing gown and wrapped it around her shoulders, feeling the chill on her skin as he did so. 'What is it, darling?' he asked, peering anxiously at her. 'Why won't you talk to me? Are you ill?'

She leant wearily against him. 'Oh, Sam, I think I am – very ill indeed. I – I'm afraid I haven't much longer to live.'

Sam was shocked, but he tried not to show his fear. Putting his arms around her he said: 'Rachel! You mustn't say such things. Whether you want me to or not, I'm sending for the doctor

327

tomorrow. You're feeling low after your cold. You should have had treatment for it long ago. He'll give you something for the cough and a tonic too. Then we'll take a nice long holiday in the sun.' Very gently he led her back to bed and tucked her in. 'I'm going downstairs to make you a hot drink. I won't be long.'

'But she grasped his wrist, refusing to let go. 'Sam, no. Stay here with me. There's something I want to tell you.'

He sat down on the edge of the bed, glad that at last she was ready to talk. 'Well – as long as you don't tire yourself. What is it?'

'I have a confession to make. It's been preying on my mind for so long. I have to tell you now, while I have the courage. While there is still time.'

He pressed her hand. 'Surely it can't be anything so terrible.'

She looked up at him, her brow furrowed with anxiety. 'Oh, but it *is*, Sam. You don't know how terrible. I've deceived you and it was wrong of me.'

He shook his head, clicking his tongue at her. 'Now, now, you really mustn't get things so out of proportion, Rachel. You're depressed.'

'No, Sam, hear me out. When I've told you you'll probably be angry with me but I can't help it. It couldn't be any worse than carrying this burden of guilt around. I can't bear it any longer.' The rush of words made her cough a little and Sam poured her a glass of water frown the carafe beside the bed. When she had finished drinking she lay back against the pillows and looked at him.

'You remember the time I went to Hackney Road at the end of the war and brought back Marcus's things?'

'Of course. The day you found his designs. It was the turning point. It seemed to cheer you – give you a new reason for living.'

'Yes. But later, going through his papers, I found a letter he had left for us – in case he was killed.'

His eyes clouded. 'A letter? And you didn't tell me? Never showed it to me?'

'I didn't show it to you because I couldn't.' She pressed his hand even more tightly. 'You see, in the letter he explained about Maryan's daughter. About Amy. He *was* her father, Sam.'

He sighed deeply. 'Oh, Rachel.'

'You always believed her, didn't you?'

'Of course. I know she would never have lied about a thing like that. I think you knew it too, but you wouldn't let yourself believe it.'

She nodded. 'Are you very angry with me, Sam?'

'I can't be angry with you. You know that. I do think it's a pity that we have missed so much, though. Amy was such a lovely child. She would have given us so much pleasure and comfort. We could have done so much for her – Maryan too. She was good to us, Rachel. She didn't deserve what we did to her.'

'I know. I *know*. And I haven't told you everything.' Rachel moistened her dry lips before going on: 'There were two other letters. One to the bank and one to Maryan. I – still have them. I never passed them on.' She looked up at Sam anxiously. 'But I did carry out Marcus's wishes.'

'His wishes?'

'About the money. I didn't go to the bank, as he asked, to have all the money from his estate invested for Amy. But I did put aside all the proceeds from its fashion collections. Apart from the charity donations, I invested it all. It's still there, untouched. And it's for Amy. That's why I had to tell you before anything happened to me. You must see that she gets it. If I died without making sure she got it I'd have betrayed Marcus.'

She burst into tears and, deeply moved, Sam gathered her into his arms and held her. So much was clear to him now. This was the reason that she wouldn't touch any of the money – why she had insisted so adamantly that all expenses must come out of Feldman's. 'Please, my love, don't cry. Everything will be all right, you'll see. Tomorrow we'll get the doctor to take a good look at you. I'm sure he will soon have you fit and well. Then after that we'll go and see Maryan. Or ask her to come here. We'll tell her everything you've just told me.'

Rachel shook her head. 'How will she ever forgive me, Sam – for keeping Marcus's letter from her all this time?'

He smiled. 'She will. I know she will.' He wiped the tears gently from her cheeks. 'And I'll tell you why. I've got a confession to make to you too. Although I knew nothing of all this I kept in touch with Maryan. I paid for Amy's education. Not because I wanted to go against your wishes, but because I wanted what was best for the child I truly believed was our granddaughter.' He looked into her eyes. 'So – do you forgive *me*, my Rachel?'

For the first time she smiled. 'Forgive you? Oh, Sam, you're such a good man. I don't deserve such a husband.'

Next day Sam summoned the doctor, who diagnosed acute bronchitis and prescribed complete bed rest and one of the new antibiotic drugs. Tired and run down, Rachel was content to stay in bed and allow Sam to spoil her, but she responded to the treatment very quickly. Sam secretly felt that unburdening herself of the secret she

329

had kept from him all these years was better medicine for her than anything the doctor could have prescribed.

As soon as he felt Rachel was well enough to receive visitors he telephoned Maryan and invited her over to Hazelfield for the day the following Sunday. She sounded slightly apprehensive, but he was able to reassure her that Rachel was anxious to see her and that they had something of importance to impart.

It was with mixed feelings that Maryan returned to Whitegates. The last time she had seen the place had been on the day she had left after Rachel's hostile reaction to her disclosure and she wondered what her ex-employers could possibly have to say to her. When she got down from the bus by the church gate the village looked much as she remembered it. Leaves were falling from the tall elms in the churchyard. They swirled around her feet as she walked, dry and rustling in the wind. The sky was dark and heavy with threatening storm clouds. Somehow the weather seemed to reflect her mood. Whatever the Leighs had to tell her now, it was too late to heal the breach she had created when she had confessed her secret to them.

Sam opened the door to her himself. He looked pleased with himself. Inviting her in, he took her coat. 'Rachel has been ill,' he said. 'A bad bout of bronchitis. But she's better now, and she wants to see you – to tell you something. Do come into the drawing room, my dear. We'll have lunch in an hour, but first we'll talk.'

Rachel rose to greet her, but in her smiling eyes Maryan saw her own apprehension mirrored.

When Rachel explained the contents of Marcus's letter Maryan was stunned.

'But – I never told him about Amy,' she said. 'When he came back from France I'd married Tom Jessop. Then he met Jessica and everyone seemed so happy. If I'd told him about Amy it would have upset everything – caused so much trouble. I couldn't do it.'

Rachel smiled sadly. 'He must have guessed. Marcus was always a sensitive man. I suppose he must have felt as you did – that to bring it to light would upset too many people. And you never seemed unhappy with the man you had married.'

'No. Tom was a good man and a good father to Amy. That's why I never told her either.'

Rachel reached for the large envelope into which she had put the three letters. Drawing out the opened envelope, she passed it to Maryan. 'Here is the letter Marcus left for us, Maryan. Read it for yourself.' She passed a second, sealed envelope to her. 'And this is

330

the one he meant for you. I hope you can forgive me for keeping it from you all these years.'

Maryan felt her throat tighten as she read Marcus's words to his parents. To think that all the time he had guessed that Any was his child and never spoken of it to her. But he had tried to make it up to her – done his best to see that she was provided for. She tried to stifle the resentment she felt against Rachel for keeping his letter secret for so long, and for not passing on this other, personal letter intended for her. It seemed that even when Rachel knew the truth her bitterness would not let her accept it. When she came to the end of the letter she passed it back.

'Thank you for letting me see it,' she said. 'If you don't mind I'll keep my own letter for later. I'd like to be alone when I read it.'

Sam and Rachel both nodded their agreement. 'Marcus didn't have a lot to leave, as he says in the letter,' Rachel went on. 'But I invested all the money we made from the Marcus Leigh Collections for Amy. It's all in an account for her. I had to keep faith with his wishes.' She paused, then looked at Maryan. 'It's such a long time since we last saw Amy.' She smiled wistfully. 'I was always very fond of the child. Do you think she would come and see us if I wrote and asked her? I would like to tell her about her inheritance myself. Would you mind?'

Sam looked at his wife in dismay and Maryan said quickly, 'I'm afraid Amy left home two years ago. I haven't heard from her since. I'm sorry to say that I don't even know where she is.'

Rachel's face fell. 'Oh dear. Was there some kind of quarrel between you?'

Maryan cleared her throat, glancing at Sam before she said, 'It seems that on the night I told you about Marcus being Amy's father she overheard the conversation. She said nothing at the time and I never suspected until just before she left home. She was waiting for me to tell her and I let her down. I'm afraid it caused a rift between us. She hasn't forgiven me. She was very young at the time. What she heard must have made her feel rejected. I think she decided to show me she didn't need me; didn't need any of us.'

'And she never even wrote to you?' Rachel looked upset. 'Oh my dear. How hurt you must have been.'

Maryan sighed. 'Perhaps it was no more than I deserved. I should have been honest with her from the first. Now it's too late.'

Rachel was frowning. 'But we must find out where she is. I want to see her – to get to know her before it is too late. And above all, I want her to have the money that is rightly hers.'

Sam laid a hand on his wife's arm. 'The money will be there when she needs it,' he said calmly. 'I'm sure that Amy will come home to Maryan again one day soon. And if she doesn't, then we'll find her somehow. The main thing is that the three of us are reunited.' He reached for Maryan's hand, linking the three of them. 'I'm so happy that now at last I can say that.'

In the train on the way back to London, Maryan opened Marcus's letter. It felt so strange, drawing out the sheet of paper and knowing that the last eyes to look at it had been his. Tears blurred her vision as she read the words he had written.

My dear Maryan,

If you are reading this you will know already that we shall not meet again. I know that you will look after my parents and help to ease their grief. I know that they look upon you almost as the daughter they never had, and I thank you for all you have done for them in the past and no doubt will do in the years to come.

I want you to know, Maryan, that I guessed a long time ago that Amy was mine. She is a daughter to be proud of and I only wish that I could have acknowledged her openly before this. I needn't go into the reasons for not doing so. I think they were shared by us both. We were young and thoughtless, but that makes my omission none the less regrettable. I will never forget the young love we once shared, Maryan. I think of you often and I pray that you won't remember me as a coward who shirked his duty.

Because I want to do what is right I am leaving Amy all my money, such as it is. And – if you feel it is appropriate – I would like you to tell her that I was her father and perhaps speak of me sometimes.

Take care of yourself, Maryan. Take care of Amy too. I hope and trust that you will love her for both of us.

Goodbye, my dear. Ever yours, Marcus.

Blinking back the tears, Maryan slipped the letter back into her handbag. Perhaps one day she would get the chance to show it to Amy. She hoped so. If only Rachel had given it to her all those years ago, their lives might have turned out so very differently.

On fine days Amy always took Mark to the park. He loved to get out of his pushchair and play on the grass. They would take bread to feed the ducks on the pond and sometimes a ball to play with. He enjoyed it so much, and usually came home happily tired and ready for his tea. But when Amy had bathed him and put him to bed the evenings felt endless. When Mark was tiny she had sometimes put

332

him into his carry cot and taken him over to Jack and Addie's. Now he was too big for that and would only fall asleep in his own bed. They had been in the habit of coming across to sit with her some evenings, but they had recently bought themselves a television set and now spent their evenings in their darkened living room, their eyes glued to the small flickering screen, oblivious of everything else.

Alex's absences on location grew more frequent and she had almost come to welcome them. When he was at home he constantly picked quarrels with her, criticising her housekeeping and her cooking and, depending on his mood, accusing her alternatively of spoiling or neglecting Mark, in whom he now took an almost obsessive interest.

Sometimes, she asked herself how she could have fallen in love with him. When he had told her bluntly that he could never love her she should have realised that the marriage wouldn't work. But naively, she had imagined she could change him; that she could make him love her – that the baby would draw them together. How wrong she had been. His irritation and resentment of her were all too obvious. Sometimes, when he looked at her in that withering way of his, she was convinced that he hated her. She hadn't meant to trap him. She'd loved him so much when they'd married. But loneliness was preferable to putting up with his constant carping and the cruel criticism that wounded her so much. Now, as she sat alone night after night in the silent house, it was her turn to feel trapped. Trapped by a man who had neither love nor need for her, and by a child who had. She felt her youth and her talent slipping away like sand in an hour glass. Inside, a voice nagged her constantly to do something about it. But what could she do? She had a child dependent on her, no money and nowhere to go.

It was one wet Monday afternoon in early November when the front doorbell rang. Mark was playing happily in his playpen and she was ironing. Switching off the iron, she went to answer the door and gasped in shock. A man stood there, a smile of anticipation on his face. For a moment Amy stared at him, then her face almost split in half with delight.

'*Mike*. How lovely to see you. But what are you doing here?'

'I had to be in this area and I've got some time to spare, so I thought I'd look you up. Mum gave me your address.'

'Come in.' As she ushered him into the hall she took a quick look at herself in the hall mirror. She was wearing an apron and her hair was tousled and untidy. She'd been playing with Mark and he'd been pulling it. Quickly tucking a loose strand behind her ear she laughed. 'Heaven knows what I must look like. Come and meet my son.'

Mike was enchanted by the chubby toddler standing clutching a toy bear in the playpen. Suddenly shy at the sight of a stranger, he looked up at Mike with huge solemn blue eyes, then, after a moment, offered him his teddy.

Amy laughed. 'You're honoured. Teddy's his favourite.'

Mike accepted the toy graciously. 'Thanks, old chap.' He looked at Amy. 'What a terrific kid. He looks just like you. Same blue eyes and curly hair.'

She laughed. 'Thanks. Look, just let me put this lot away, then we'll have some tea and a good old natter. I want to hear all about this job of yours at the BBC.' She began to bundle the linen basket and iron into the hall cupboard.

'And I want to hear all about this producer bloke you've married,' Mike called to her. 'I hope he knows how lucky he is.'

As she filled the kettle at the sink she smiled wryly to herself. 'Far from it,' she said under her breath.

They talked over the tea. Mike told her all the news from Rhensham. His parents were well and Lily Smith had added twin boys to her family and now worked as a daily cleaning woman for the vicar.

'I think when Lily applied for the job he felt obliged to be charitable,' he said. 'Fallen women are a hobby-horse of his. Mum tells me that Lily's mother looks after the kids. I don't suppose she even notices another two among her own brood.'

Amy was silent, reflecting that even the feckless Lily had a mother who was willing to support her.

Mike told her about his work with the local rag and how he had come to get his present job with the BBC.

'I'm only very junior at the moment, of course,' he said modestly. 'But I'm in the news room and working my way up.'

'You'll get there,' Amy told him with shining eyes. 'I can just see you reading the news on TV in your dinner jacket. Very posh and suave.'

He laughed. 'So, what about you?' he asked. 'As I remember, you had ambitions too.'

She shrugged. 'They went by the board when Mark came along, I'm afraid. But I did do well, Mike. I joined the company as a student but I did get to play leading parts before Alex and I married.' She went on to tell him how she had played Cathy in *Wuthering Heights* and all the other things she'd done with the Keynan Players. When he had first arrived, Mike had been dismayed

334

at her appearance. She'd looked hollow-eyed and weary, but now, as she spoke about her brief career in the theatre, he saw a change in her. She became animated. Her eyes sparkled and the colour came back into her cheeks.

'You must miss it.'

'Oh yes. I do.'

'Obviously you'll be going back as soon as you can.'

The sparkle in her eyes snapped off. 'Not in the foreseeable future,' she said. 'Not now that I've got Mark.'

'Why not?' he asked. 'I mean, there are nannies and nurseries. He's getting older now and . . .'

'Alex doesn't believe in working mothers. In the theatre the hours are so erratic. Besides, people soon forget. If you stay out for more than six months your chances of getting back are poor – even if you've already made a name for yourself. Apart from all that, television is killing off all the provincial reps.'

Mark chose that moment to remind them that he was still with them and, looking at the clock, Amy saw that it was past his bedtime. When she scooped the little boy up in her arms Mike looked at his watch and got hastily to his feet.

'Heavens, I didn't realise it was getting so late. I'd better go and let you get this chap to bed.'

'Oh, don't go, Mike,' Amy begged. 'I mean, not unless you want to, of course. I get fed up spending every evening on my own. You can help me put Mark to bed if you like and then I'll make us a meal.'

He looked pleased. 'Well, if you're sure . . .'

'No, if *you* are. You've probably got some glamorous girl waiting for you somewhere?'

His eyes twinkled with mischief. 'Well, if I do, what the hell? It'll do her good to wait.' He laughed. 'No – there's no one – honest injun.' He gave her the Scout's salute and she laughed aloud. Suddenly she was back at Mitcham Lodge and they were children again.

Upstairs in the bathroom Mark was delighted to have two attentive people to play with him in the bath, and Mike volunteered to sing him to sleep while Amy went down to start the meal. Downstairs in the kitchen she could hear his pleasant baritone rendition of 'Baa Baa Black Sheep' and she reflected sadly that if only Alex was at home more they would be more like a real family. Nowadays he only seemed interested in talking to Mark. He didn't even talk to her about his work any more. She might never have been an actress at all.

335

She laid the table and made a quick meal of fried eggs and chips. Coming into the kitchen Mike sniffed appreciatively.

'You remembered,' he said. 'Egg and chips was always my favourite meal. Mum wouldn't let me have it when I lived at home – said too much fried food would give me spots. But now on the rare occasion when I get to Rhensham she spoils me rotten.' He sat down at the table. 'That's the best of leaving home, don't you find? It makes going back special.'

Her back towards him as she worked at the stove, Amy shrugged. 'I wouldn't know,' she said. 'I haven't been home for two and a half years. Not since I left to join the Keynan Players in fact.'

'Oh, why's that?'

She sighed. 'A lot of reasons. Mum and I never really hit it off, not since I found out about my real father. She never really seemed to have much time for me. And when I said I was taking the job with the Keynan Players – leaving school before taking my Highers – well, you can imagine.'

'But she knows you're married?'

Amy shrugged. 'I wrote when I first left, and again when I got married. Then I sent her a card when Mark was born. I don't know why I bothered. She never replied to any of them. I think I've got to accept the fact that she's written me off.'

Mike frowned. 'That doesn't sound like the Mrs Jessop I remember.'

'No – well, you never really got to know her, did you?' Amy ate in silence, her eyes downcast, and Mike watched her for a moment, his face concerned.

'So – you haven't been home – tried to see her?'

'I don't think there'd be much point. I haven't even been up to Town since I came to live here, even though it's only a short tube ride away.' She smiled wistfully. 'I must be the only person in England who hasn't seen this fantastic South Bank Exhibition. My neighbours went up when it first opened in the summer and they came back full of the Dome of Discovery and the Skylon and Battersea Park Funfair.'

'What a shame. Maybe you'll get up to see it before winter sets in.'

'Oh, I doubt it.'

He looked at her. It was plain that all was not as it should be. 'Tell me about your husband. He must be quite a bit older than you?'

'Yes. Nineteen years to be exact. He was beginning to make a name for himself before the war began. He was in the RAF. A

336

fighter pilot. He was married and his wife was killed in an air raid. After that he didn't care much about anything.' She looked down at her plate. 'Nothing's changed. He still doesn't.'

Her words were almost inaudible and there was a silence between them as Mike began to guess the reason for her obvious unhappiness. 'Does that mean what I think it means?' he asked.

She looked at him, her eyes dull with pain. 'I wanted him, Mike. I thought I could make everything all right for him again. Make up for what he'd lost. I wanted him so *much* and I thought he wanted me.' She looked down at her hands. 'I got wanting and loving all mixed up.'

'And – now?'

'Now it's neither. Sometimes I think we just torment each other. His work takes him away from home a lot, and frankly I think it's a relief for both of us.'

'Oh, Amy.'

She looked up at him quickly. 'It wasn't always like that. When Mark was on the way I used to long for the weekends. I looked forward to seeing him so much. I *did* love him, Mike. It was real. I know it was. But now it's just – gone – dead.'

'I'm so sorry, Amy.'

'It's my fault really. He warned me, you see. He kept saying he was too old for me. He told me quite openly that he'd never love me. He still loves her, you see – his first wife. He was completely frank with me. I should have listened.'

Mike tried to conceal his amazement that Amy had walked into a marriage so obviously doomed. 'What about the baby?' he asked. 'Has his arrival made no difference?'

'Oh, he loves Mark,' she said. 'He's fiercely protective of him. That's why he won't even think of letting me go back to work.'

'I'd no idea about all this, Amy. You sounded so happy in your letters to Mum.'

'Of course. I don't really want people to know. I'm slightly ashamed, I suppose. And I shouldn't really be telling you all this. It's just that there's no one else and sometimes I think . . .' She got up and took her plate to the sink. As she filled the kettle for coffee she said, 'Let's talk about something else. In a minute you'll be so depressed you'll wish you hadn't come.'

By the time coffee was made she had swallowed her depression and put on a show of light-heartedness. She amused Mike with stories about the struggle she'd had with the neglected house, turning her inept attempts at decorating and her worst domestic failures into amusing anecdotes. She left out the times she had sat in the middle

337

of the floor, surrounded by pots of paint and distemper, weeping helpless tears at her own inadequacy. Or the times she'd cried herself to sleep, sick with sheer loneliness and fears about the future.

She describe Jack and Addie Shaw, their well-meaning kindness and their preoccupation with their newly acquired 'telly'. And made him laugh with her description of the chimney sweep and her struggles with the overgrown garden. When Mike finally looked at his watch and announced that it was almost eleven o'clock they were both surprised.

Getting up to leave, he hugged her briefly and said, 'Thanks for a super evening, Amy. I can't tell you how wonderful it's been to see you again.'

'Thanks for coming. I don't get many visitors. Come again if you're at a loose end.'

At the front door he paused. 'Look, I've got two tickets for the new musical at Drury Lane, *South Pacific*. One of the perks of my job. Do you think you could come?'

Her eyes lit up. 'Oh, Mike. I'd *love* to. When are they for?'

'Next Monday. I'll be going straight from the office, but if you could come up on the train I could run you home afterwards.'

She bit her lip. 'Oh, it does sound tempting. I wonder if Addie would have Mark for me. I'll ask her. I'm sure she wouldn't mind, just this once.'

'Fine. Give me a ring if you can make it.' He found a scrap of paper and scribbled his number on it. 'You can get me there in the evenings. I share a little house in Chiswick with two other blokes. They're never off the phone, so if it's engaged do keep trying, won't you?'

'I will. Thanks, Mike.' Standing on tiptoe she kissed his cheek. 'It's lovely to see you again. Give my love to Auntie Marjorie when you see her – your father too, of course. Oh, and Mike . . .'

'Yes?'

'Forget all that gloomy nonsense I bored you with, won't you?'

Mike put his hands on her shoulders. 'Listen, silly. What you told me is strictly between ourselves. We never split on one another, do we?'

She stood on the step and waved as he drove away in his smart little Ford Prefect. It had been wonderful to see Mike and to have someone understanding to talk to; reminiscing over old times and hearing about what was happening out there in the world of work and entertainment. Would she ever be part of that world again, she wondered?

Closing the door and locking up for the night, she climbed the stairs. At least she had something to look forward to for once. She'd read about the exciting new American musical, *South Pacific*. And now – if she was lucky – she was actually going to *see* it. Maybe her luck was changing.

On 26 October Robert Kemp was elected Conservative Member of Parliament for Bradfield with a very healthy majority. By a narrow margin the Tories were in power again, with Winston Churchill once more at the helm. But it wasn't for political reasons that Gina received the news with relief.

'I think Robert's planning to move to his constituency,' she said. 'I've heard on the grapevine that his wife has been looking for a house in Bradfield for some time. All I have to do now is to pay off my debt to him, then I can start to get on with my own life again.'

The date for the antiques auction in which the miniatures were to be sold was set for Monday 10 November. Vincent had advised Gina to use an auctioneer he knew well and who could be trusted to make sure she had the best deal possible. Meanwhile the miniatures were in safe hands at the bank and now all they had to do was to wait.

Then, on 6 November Gina had a telephone call. Maryan put it through to her in the studio and five minutes later the office door flew open and a flushed Gina stood on the threshold, her eyes shining with excitement.

'I've been asked to fly to Paris on Monday,' she said breathlessly. 'To discuss plans for a fashion show being organised at the *Musée des Art Décoratifs* for next spring. Only top designers are being invited to exhibit. Oh, Maryan, imagine – *me*, Gina Stern – showing alongside people like Fath, Dior and Chanel. Thank God I've been working flat out on my new collection.'

'That's wonderful. Congratulations.' Maryan was looking at the calendar. 'When did you say it was?'

'Monday, the tenth.' Gina's face fell and her hand flew to her mouth. 'Oh, *no* – the sale.'

Maryan smiled encouragingly. 'Never mind. You must go to Paris. It isn't essential for you to go to the sale.'

'Oh, but I wanted to be there. Maryan, will you go? It won't matter if we close the office just this once. And you must take the car, of course. Oh dear, I'm so excited I can't think straight. What shall I take to wear? It's *so* important to create the right impression. There's that black suit I wore for the last show. It'll have to do. There isn't time to have anything new made up. You don't think I've put on weight, do you? Suppose I can't get into it? Oh – will you ring and book my flight? They want me there for three o'clock, so it'll have to be an early one. Oh – and a hotel too.'

She was like a whirlwind as she flew around the house, making one decision after another and changing her mind every five minutes. Maryan remained calm and smiling as she busied herself with the telephone, booking the flight and hotel and rearranging appointments that seemed to have gone right out of Gina's head.

Gina left Gower Street in a taxi at six o'clock on Monday morning. Maryan had made sure that she would have plenty of time to check in at her hotel and have lunch and a breathing space before the meeting. It was with some relief that she waved the taxi off. All weekend Gina had been in an agony of indecision. Would she make the right impression – say the right things? Was her schoolgirl French good enough or would she sound provincial and unsophisticated? And what about her portfolio? Would her spring collection be considered avant-garde enough to exhibit in a show of this calibre? She had promised to ring Maryan that evening, when they would exchange news about the day's events, though Maryan suspected that the importance of the sale had temporarily taken secondary importance in Gina's mind.

The sale was to take place in a country house in Surrey. Maryan drove down in Gina's car and arrived in plenty of time to look round before the start of the sale. Queensthorpe Hall was an imposing Georgian manor house standing in grounds which swept down to the river. It had clearly been very elegant indeed once, but during the war it had been requisitioned by the Army and after being abused and neglected for so long it had now acquired an air of crumbling grandeur. But in spite of its ill-kept appearance, it was the perfect venue for the sale with its spacious oak-panelled rooms and carved staircase.

When Maryan arrived there were already a good many people wandering round inspecting the numbered lots, ticking off items on their catalogues and making notes. She recognised one or two dealers from sales at which she had represented Vincent. The miniatures had pride of place, displayed in a room set aside for smaller articles, under glass in a locked cabinet to avoid excessive handling. They looked very special and she saw that they were described in the catalogue as being 'of outstanding quality – a rare find'. She felt a little frisson of excitement as she wondered what they would fetch and if it would be enough to relieve Gina of her debt. Their lot number was sixty-four, so she calculated that they would not come up until the afternoon. She would have a lengthy wait.

The auctioneer arrived, a small, dapper man in a grey pinstripe suit and bow tie. He had a pencil-thin moustache and quick, bright eyes, and the moment he arrived things began to happen. Two porters carried lot number one, an ornate Louis XVI console table, down to the front of the hall and the auctioneer's clerk tapped his gavel and asked everyone to take their seats as the sale was about to begin.

The bidding had been in progress for about half an hour when Maryan saw Vincent arrive. From her seat at the side of the hall she saw him slip quietly in and take a seat at the back. Her heart gave an involuntary lurch and she chided herself sharply. She was reacting like a schoolgirl. All that was over long ago. Surely she was too old for such nonsense? But when, a few minutes later, during a lull in the proceedings he slipped into the empty seat beside her and whispered a greeting, she could scarcely reply for the traitorous drumming in her chest.

'Maryan – hello. Isn't Miss Stern with you?'

'No.' She turned to look into the dark eyes, steeling herself to remain calm and unruffled. 'She was called away to Paris on business. I'm here to represent her.'

'I'm glad – that you're here, that is. I was wondering whether I'd see you today.' He bent towards her. 'Look – the lot I'm interested in won't come up until after lunch and neither will Miss Stern's miniatures. There's a very good pub in the village. Shall we slip out after this next lot for a bite of lunch?'

She intended to refuse – to tell him she'd brought sandwiches – anything. She actually opened her mouth to do so – and, to her astonishment, heard herself saying: 'Yes. I think that would be very nice.'

They left the sale just before twelve and under his direction Maryan drove the mile and a half to the Fox and Grapes in Gina's car.

'They always get really busy by one,' he told her as they parked. 'This is the best pub for miles. They do what they call a ploughman's lunch.'

Maryan laughed. 'What's a ploughman's lunch when it's at home?'

'Cheese, pickle and crusty bread with salad,' Vincent told her. 'Very satisfying.'

The pub was small and cosy with a welcoming fire crackling away in the huge open fireplace of the bar. There was an evocative scent of ale that reminded Maryan nostalgically of the old Prince of Wales in Crimea Terrace where she and Tom had celebrated their wedding twenty years ago. That pub was long since gone, bombed to the ground along with so much of the old East End she remembered. And here the smell of ale was mingled with the country scents of beeswax and burning apple logs. She settled happily in a corner by the fireplace to enjoy the atmosphere while Vincent went to the bar for drinks. When he rejoined her he was smiling.

'This is a real treat. I never thought when I left home this morning that I'd be sitting here having lunch with you.'

'You wouldn't if it hadn't been for Gina's business trip.' She took a sip from her glass of sherry. 'But it's good to see you too, Vinnie,' she added quietly. 'How are things with you? Is the business doing well?'

He sighed. 'Not as well as I'd like.'

'Oh – why is that?'

He looked as though he was about to say something, then changed his mind and shrugged. 'My fault, I daresay. I haven't the same enthusiasm I once had.'

'I'm sorry to hear that. You worked so hard to build the business. It always meant so much to you.'

'*We* built it, Maryan. Roisan and you worked hard too. And it meant everything once. But lately business has dwindled. God knows why. We give the same service we always have, Roisan works as hard as ever and so do I.' He held her eyes with his. 'The truth is that since you left nothing has been the same. Paul left as I told you. Fay does the job you did and runs the shop as well, but sometimes – sometimes I wonder . . .' He trailed off. Covering her hand with his, he said, 'All the zest has gone out of life. I'm sure I don't have to tell you why, do I?'

She tore her eyes away from his. 'But there's nothing to be done about it, is there?'

The landlord's wife brought their food and Maryan applied herself to it, but somehow her appetite had gone.

'Tell me about your work with Miss Stern,' Vincent said. 'You seem happy with her. It's good that you were able to have a flat in the house.'

She told him a little about Gina's work, trying hard to sound interesting and light-hearted, but all the time she was wishing she was anywhere but sitting here with Vinnie, skirting around the subject uppermost in both their minds.

They finished their meal and Vincent looked at his watch. 'Better be getting back,' he said. 'Don't want to miss seeing the miniatures come under the hammer, do you?'

As they threaded their way among the customers now crowding

the bar he remarked that he would have liked to buy the miniatures himself. 'They're not really my line though,' he explained. 'My customers like to choose their own pictures. I always think they're a very personal . . .' He broke off as the door opened and a familiar figure stood facing them on the threshold.

'*Ah. I thought I'd find you here.*' Fay's bleached hair looked unkempt but her eyes were bright with triumph as she confronted them.

Vincent looked shocked. '*Fay.* For heaven's sake. What are you doing here?'

'You might well ask. Thought you were safe out here, didn't you? Thought you could meet your *whore* in secret.'

Her voice was shrill and piercing and the other customers in the bar stopped talking to look curiously at the irate woman in the fur coat. Vincent took her by the arm and tried to guide her outside.

'Please, Fay. Don't make a scene in public.'

She shook his hand off and stared venomously at Maryan. 'I heard him talking to his sister on the telephone,' she hissed. 'He confides a lot in her, you know. They're both in this thing against me. Can't you see that they're just using you to get at me?' She shook her head. 'No. You're only too willing to fall in with their plans, aren't you, you devious *bitch*. Why can't you keep out of our lives? Why don't you leave us alone?'

Maryan stared from one to the other in horror. 'You've got it all wrong,' she said. 'It was sheer chance that we met here today. Gina Stern, my employer, should have been here, not me.'

'*Liar.*' Fay's lip curled into a sneer. 'If only you could see yourself. You're *pathetic* with your innocent blue eyes and your outraged expression. Butter wouldn't melt in your lying mouth, would it? But you don't take me in. Not for one moment. I know your sort.' She laughed, her eyes glittering with rage. 'You think I don't know that you've been meeting secretly for years? To talk about your bastard daughter, no doubt. But I could tell you things about *her* that you don't know yourself.'

The colour drained from Maryan's face and Vincent made another attempt to steer his wife away.

'Fay, for God's sake let's get away from here. You're making an exhibition of yourself.'

'What do I care?' she shouted. 'If they want to listen, let them. Let them all know what I've had to put up with all these years. A cheating husband who fathered another woman's child.'

'It's *not true.* Why won't you believe it?' Vincent made a move towards her but Maryan intervened.

343

'Wait. I want to hear what she has to say.' She looked at Fay. 'What do you know about my daughter that I don't know?'

Some of the triumph went out of Fay's eyes and they took on a wary look. In the heat of the moment she'd almost given away the fact that she'd opened and kept the letters that arrived at Simons Mews addressed to Maryan. But what did it matter? Who could prove anything? Serve the bitch right anyway.

'I can tell you she's *married* for a start.' Fay spat the word out triumphantly. 'Got herself into trouble, I shouldn't wonder. Like mother, like daughter. Bad blood will out, they always say, don't they?' She watched with satisfaction as Maryan's colour changed. 'Yes, she's got a child.' She looked at Vincent, a spiteful gleam in her eyes. 'She's a grandmother, your bit on the side. You didn't know that, did you?' She laughed bitterly. 'But then I suppose that makes you a grandfather too.'

White-faced, Maryan looked at Vincent. 'Did you know this? Did she write to Roisan?'

His face was as shocked as hers. 'If she did I knew nothing about it. It's probably all lies anyway.'

'It's not *me* who's the liar,' Fay screamed. 'It's *you* two.' She turned to Maryan. 'You'll find out. You'll suffer for what you've done. Even your own daughter walked out when she found out what kind of woman she had for a mother.'

Maryan turned and ran blindly for the car, Fay's hysterical voice following her as she got in and fumbled with the ignition key. Through the windscreen she could see Vincent struggling to calm her. She felt as though she was deserting him but she couldn't help it. She had to get away. She couldn't listen to any more of the woman's ravings. Was it true? Could Amy have married and become a mother without even trying to get in touch with her? Although no letter had come from her she had always believed, as Sam said, that Amy would come home to her eventually; that somehow or other they would be reconciled. Now she knew without a doubt that it would never happen. Now that Amy had her own life – her own family – she knew she had truly lost her, just as she had lost everyone she had ever cared for.

As Mike drove Amy home to Mill Hill she hummed the memorable tunes from the show she had just enjoyed. 'Some Enchanted Evening', It was such a beautiful, romantic song and it summed up what this evening had been for her – enchanted. It was so long since she'd been able to lose herself in an evening of pure pleasure. Mike's seats in the stalls had given them an excellent view of the stage. He'd taken her for dinner first and now she would have the memory to take out and enjoy whenever she felt low.

Mike glanced at her. 'It was a good show, wasn't it?'

She stopped humming to look at him. 'Oh, *yes*. Thank you so much for taking me, Mike. I haven't enjoyed myself so much for ages.'

'Mary Martin was terrific, wasn't she? That bit where she washed her hair.'

Amy laughed and sang a snatch of the song. 'I'm Gonna Wash That Man Right Outa My Hair.' She sighed. 'Oh, Mike, I *wish* I could get another acting job. I miss it so much.'

'I know you do.' For a while they drove in silence, then he said, 'Look, I've just had a thought. I hear they're planning a daily radio serial at the Beeb. The sort of thing the Americans call a "soap opera". They seem to think it could really take off. Why don't you audition for a part?'

Amy shook her head. 'How can I take anything on when I've got a child to look after?'

'It's only a fifteen-minute slot and as far as I can make out they record a number of programmes in one session,' he told her. 'It might mean you'd only need to come up about once a week. Couldn't you get someone to have Mark for you just for one day?'

A tiny twist of excitement made her heartbeat quicken. 'Well – I don't know. Maybe I could.' She turned to look at him. 'Oh, Mike. Do you think I'd stand a chance?'

He laughed. 'I haven't a clue, but I'll make some enquiries for you if you like. It's worth a try.'

'If I could get another job it would help in so many ways,' she said thoughtfully.

'With cash, you mean?'

'Not just that. You know, ever since I found out that Tom Jessop wasn't my father I've felt sort of lost.'

He glanced at her. 'In what way?'

'Oh, I don't know. So many ways. I keep looking for something in myself, yet I don't know what. I never knew my real father properly, so even if I was like him how would I know? I suppose I feel that I don't really know who I am – or what I might be.'

'*I* know who you are,' he said. 'You're Amy Jessop, the girl I grew up with. You'll never be anyone else as far as I'm concerned.'

'It's not as simple as that, though.' She sighed. 'When I was acting up in Minsdale I took the stage name of Amethyst Lee. I was happy with it. I really thought then that I'd found the real me. Now I'm not sure all over again. I'm Amy Keynan, and yet I'm not Alex's

345

wife. She was called Chloe and she died in the blitz ten years ago. But she's the only wife Alex will ever have. She's the real Mrs Keynan.'

'It's more than just a name though, isn't it? You're Mark's mother,' Mike said firmly. 'That's a *real* identity. Never forget that. And never let Mark forget it either.'

'Oh, I *won't*,' she said fervently. 'Whatever happens I'll always be there for him. I'll never lie to him or let him down.'

Mike dropped her off at the end of the road with a promise to ring and let her know about the audition. There was still a light burning at the Shaws' where Mark was staying for the night, so she decided to go across and make sure that he was all right.

Jack opened the door, but before she could speak he said, 'The little lad's gone. Right upset, Addie was. Just come across and insisted on taking him, he did. And the little'un fast asleep in bed too.'

Amy stared at him, her heart thudding with fear. '*Who*? Who took Mark?'

'Mr Keynan, of course. Come home unexpected. In a right temper he was. Said some real nasty things to Addie and me – uncalled for things. Insisted on taking the baby. Poor little mite cried something chronic, being woken up so sudden like.'

Amy apologised, thanked Jack and told him not to worry. Then, her heart in her mouth, she hurried across the road to let herself into number twenty-two.

Alex was in the dining room. He sat at the table, his collar and tie loosened and his hair awry. On the table beside him stood a glass and an almost empty whisky bottle. He looked up at her with bloodshot eyes, his voice slurred.

'Where' er bloody'ell've you been?'

'I've been to Drury Lane to see *South Pacific*,' she told him. 'Mike Taylor came to see me last week. He had two tickets and he asked me . . .'

'You – *what*?' He got to his feet to stand swaying in front of her. 'You left my son with those two old cretins while you went off gadding with one of your ex-lovers?' His face took on a dark red flush. 'I ought to give you a bloody good hiding for that.'

'Mike isn't an ex-lover,' she said. 'I never had a lover before you, Alex. You know that. You had no right to do what you did tonight.'

'No right? No bloody *right*?' The dark red flush turned to purple. 'You go off and leave my son and you say I've no right.' He made a lunge for her but she side-stepped his flailing arms and he staggered against the wall.

346

'I suppose you think you're the right person to look after a child,' she said contemptuously. 'Look at you. You can hardly stand up. He was fast asleep. You could have dropped him.'

He laughed dryly. 'And you're the devoted, caring mother, I suppose? You're the one who abandoned him.'

'I'm shut up in this house seven days a week, Alex. I never get a break. I hardly see anyone but tradesmen from one week's end to the next. I needed an evening out. I *deserved* it.'

Alex picked up the bottle and poured the last of it into his glass, regarding her with distaste as he did so. 'Fed up, are you? Well, what a *shame*. I might remind you, Amy, that it was you who wanted to be married.'

She swallowed hard at the lump in her throat. 'I wanted to marry *you*, Alex. There is a difference.'

'Oh yes. You wanted me. You even got yourself pregnant just to prove it. Well, now that you've got me the least you can do is take proper care of my child.' He swallowed the contents of the glass and slid it across the table. Steadying himself, he glared blearily at her, his eyes dark and hostile. From above came the sound of Mark's frightened crying, wakened by the commotion. But when Amy made a move towards the door Alex grabbed her by the shoulder and pinned her against the wall, leaning all his weight against her.

'*Leave him.* I'll see to him.' He pushed his face close to hers, breathing the sour odour of whisky into her face. 'You've got a choice, Amy,' he said. 'You can leave me any time you like. I don't give a damn what you do. But don't think you're taking that child with you. Don't you ever try to take my son away from me.' His fingers pressed into her throat until she could hardly breathe. 'If you decide to stay, you'll stay on my terms, understand? You'll behave as a mother should. And that means that you will not leave my son with strangers any more. Step out of line once more and out you go – got it? Out on your arse – and *on your own*. Got that, have you, Amy?'

Chapter Eighteen

Amy sat up, dozing fitfully in the armchair all night. After Alex had stumbled off to collapse on the bed upstairs she had remained where she was, numb; too stunned to think straight. An hour passed and she went upstairs to check Mark. He was sleeping peacefully, but when she went into the room she and Alex shared she found him sprawled across the bed, snoring loudly and still fully dressed. As she stood looking down at him he stirred and mumbled something. She couldn't make out what he was saying except for the name, *Chloe*. Going out quietly, she closed the door and went downstairs again, resigned to spending the rest of the night in the armchair.

Watching the hours pass she tried to make some kind of sense out of the tangle of thoughts milling around in her brain. Her marriage to Alex would never work. She had to face the fact. He had never got over losing Chloe and he never would. Now she recognised that his understanding of the character, Heathcliff, the interpretation that had impressed her so much, was based on his own experience. Alex himself was tortured in much the same way. He too knew the torment and slavery of obsession, and the crushing power of a lost love that refused to die. He was incapable of loving another woman. He'd warned her of that. But he adored Mark; adored him with a fierce, possessive love that frightened her in its intensity. Surely he must realise, though, that if she were to leave he couldn't possibly care for the child himself? It wasn't possible. She should call his bluff, take Mark and leave. But where could they go, and what would they live on?

It was getting light when she finally slept, only to be wakened an hour later by Mark's hungry cries from above. Rubbing her stiffened neck muscles, she went upstairs to wash and dress him. Her own bedroom door was still firmly shut. Alex was obviously still sleeping off the effects of the whisky.

But Alex wasn't asleep. Mark's cries had wakened him too. At first he couldn't make out where he was and why he was lying across the bed, fully dressed, then the events of the previous night slowly filtered up through the alcoholic fog inside his head. He heard Amy's footsteps as she came upstairs to attend to the child and her voice as she spoke softly to him.

He rolled onto his back and lay staring at the ceiling. The sick pounding in his head reminded him painfully of the previous night's excesses and he felt a stab of fear – a fear that was becoming frighteningly familiar. He knew his drinking was getting out of control but try as he would he didn't seem able to overcome it. It helped him forget; chased away the images that haunted him. He could no longer ignore that fact that his work was suffering. He'd already received a couple of warnings about being late on the set and, more recently, turning up too drunk to do his job. Not that he cared about that. Trivial little travel films were a waste of his talent anyway. He had a better job in the offing if only he could pull it off. If he did he'd stop drinking. He'd have the motivation then, something more interesting to absorb himself in.

The most worrying part was that lately he found he was unable to remember things he had done and said during one of his drinking sessions. All he really remembered about last night was his anger at finding Amy out when he had arrived home; his son farmed out like a dog with neighbours while she went to the theatre with another man. He hadn't been drunk when he arrived home. Last night's drinking bout had been down to her.

Had he been offensive to that old couple over the road? He hadn't meant to be. Well, he was damned if he was going over there to grovel and apologise. It wasn't his fault if he had an ineffectual wife. Let her go and apologise.

What had he said to Amy? Had he threatened – struck her even? He knew he'd been angry enough. He remembered the anger. Whisky always did that to him. Well, whatever he'd done and said it was no more than she deserved, going off like that.

He rolled onto his side, turning his back to the window and closing his eyes against a shaft of sunlight penetrating a chink in the curtains. It gouged through his eyes and into his brain like a red-hot gimlet.

Since Mark had been born he'd felt different. It was as though the boy was an extension of himself; a replacement, waiting in the wings, ready to step into his shoes. An understudy. If he died now he would have done at least one worthwhile thing. He had fathered a son. And Mark was no ordinary son. He was special. Born into a better world – destined for a better life than he had led. Watching the baby grow into a little boy he had seen himself mirrored in the child. And strangely, he could see a likeness to Chloe too. So much so that at times it was almost possible to imagine that Mark was Chloe's child and not Amy's; to persuade himself that through some mystic power beyond his comprehension Amy was the mere vessel for the child he and Chloe were destined to create.

'I'll take good care of him, my love,' he whispered drowsily into the pillow. 'I'll see that she does too. Some day we'll all be together. It might take time, but we will, never you fear.' And, as he drifted between sleeping and waking, he thought that he saw Chloe smile her lovely smile and nod her approval. He thought she looked happy again.

Mark had been fed and was playing happily in his playpen when Amy heard Alex stirring. Above her, there was the sound of doors opening and shutting – footsteps, the bath running. Her heart quickened. What mood would he be in this morning? Would he still be angry with her for going out? What right did he have to threaten her? She was his wife, a woman with rights of her own, not his prisoner. She stood at the sink, her hands trembling as she busied herself with the baby's washing. She dreaded Alex's appearance and wished that their confrontation could be over. Suddenly, to her horror and dismay, she realised for the first time that she was actually afraid of Alex – afraid of the unpredictable and increasingly violent behaviour that drink induced in him.

When at last he walked into the kitchen he looked grey and haggard. Amy glanced at him.

'Do you want breakfast?'

He groaned. 'God, no. I'd like some coffee though. Black. And a couple of aspirins if you've got any.'

She put the coffee on and fetched the aspirin bottle from the medicine cupboard. As she tipped two into his outstretched palm he looked up at her.

'Was I a bastard last night?'

The tightly wound spring of her emotions was suddenly released and she turned away as her throat constricted. 'You – were drunk,' she said. 'Mark was perfectly safe with the Shaws, you know. I hardly ever go out and leave him.' She spun round to face him. 'I don't care what you say to me – or what you *think* of me. I do the best I can, Alex, and I can't do more. But I won't have you upsetting the Shaws. They've been kindness itself to me. They've been there to help me when you haven't.'

350

He winced as he washed the bitter tablets down with the strong black brew she poured for him. 'Oh, Christ, don't start giving me a hard time, Amy,' he growled. 'I can't take it this morning. Look, to be honest I really don't remember much about last night. It's all a bit of a blur. I'd been out for a drink with some of the film crew. I've been shortlisted to direct a major film for Ealing. I made the journey all the way home specially to tell you about it. And then, when you weren't here . . .' He shrugged irritably. 'Oh, what the hell? Why am *I* apologising? It was you who let me down. Not the other way around.'

'You told me I could get out any time I liked,' she reminded him. 'But that I couldn't take Mark.'

He laughed uneasily. 'Oh, come *on*, surely not. You must have misunderstood.'

'I didn't misunderstand anything, specially when you started pushing me about,' she told him. 'You said I wasn't to go out again, and that if I did I'd be – I'd be out on my arse.' She was angry now. The previous night's hurt and bewilderment combined with lack of sleep brought her simmering anger to boiling point. '*Out on my arse,*' she repeated. 'That was the delightful phrase you used. I didn't misunderstand you, Alex. *On my own*, you said. Without Mark. Without my baby.'

He frowned. 'A man will say anything when he's had a few drinks, Amy. You should have known there was nothing in it. Just the whisky talking.'

'I don't know how much more of this I can stand, Alex,' she said, ignoring his alleged memory lapse. 'I should have listened when you told me you didn't want a wife. You certainly never wanted *me* – or Mark either – *before* he was born. Now you're using him as a kind of weapon to threaten me with.'

'That's not true, Amy, and you know it. I love the boy. I care more for him than anything else in the world. That's what this is all about.'

'You care for him, but not for *me*, Alex. That's what it's really all about. You live the life of a single man, use this house like a hotel and you treat me like dirt. I don't deserve that.'

'Oh, don't be so bloody melodramatic, Amy.' He got up and refilled his coffee cup from the percolator on the stove.

'If you really want me to go, I will. But let's get one thing clear. I won't leave my baby. You couldn't look after him yourself and you don't want strangers caring for him. If you don't want me any more you'll have to provide somewhere for Mark and me to live – and money for us to live on until he's old enough for me to get a job.'

Seeing the logic of her argument, he put down his cup and looked at her. 'Look, I'm sorry if I upset you last night, but it's nothing to get in such a state about. We're married and we've got Mark. Life might not be ideal for either of us at the moment but there's nothing else for it but to make the best of it.'

Amy bridled. Now that he'd sobered up he wanted to soft pedal the whole thing. Well, she wasn't going to be as easily talked down as that. 'And – if I say I'm sick of making the best of it? That I don't want this kind of life any longer?' she challenged. 'If what *I* want is a divorce?'

He took a deep draught of his coffee. Normally her truculence would have angered him, but all last night's fury had evaporated in the cloud of alcohol that filled his head. Instead a warning bell tinkled softly. Divorce meant she'd get custody of Mark. They'd live apart. He'd hardly see the boy. It was out of the question. He took a deep breath to control the pounding inside his head, and looked up at her.

'But you *don't*, do you? Not really.' He stood up and went to her, lifting her chin with one finger. 'Look, I'd had a few last night. I went over the top a bit. I'm sorry. If you want to go out occasionally, okay, I understand that. But pay someone to come and sit with Mark. The Shaws mean well, but they're past it. You must admit that they are.'

'And what am I supposed to pay a sitter with?' she asked him. 'You keep me so short of money we hardly have enough to eat.'

'Oh, that's a bit of an exaggeration, surely. Anyway, all that will change when I get a better job.' He pulled her to him and nuzzled her neck. 'Come on, love. Come down off that high horse of yours. I've said I'm sorry.' He blew gently into her ear. 'Hey, tell you what – I was a damned fool to get too pissed to make the most of being home last night. We didn't even get to sleep together – did we?'

'Don't you remember that either?'

For a second he looked unsure, then he laughed. 'You're teasing me. That's better. That's more like the Amy I know.' He caught sight of the kitchen clock and gave a gasp. 'Christ, is that really the time? I should have been away from here half an hour ago.'

'When will you be home again?' she called to him as he hurried into the hall and began to pull on his coat.

'God knows,' he called. 'We've got to go over to Ireland the day after tomorrow. Could be gone for anything up to a month, depending on the weather.'

She heard him go into the living room and pick Mark up. Heard the child's gleeful shriek and Alex's laugh as he tossed the child into the air and caught him. It was Mark's favourite game, and when Alex put him abruptly back into his playpen and hurried off the little boy let out a dismayed wail of disappointment. Amy sighed. She'd be half the morning pacifying him now. Alex didn't have a clue what it meant to be with a small child twenty-four hours a day.

Maryan was in the office at Gower Street on the morning after the sale when the door opened and a familiar face looked round it. She looked up from her typewriter in surprise.

'Roisan. How nice to see you.'

'Well, if Mohammed won't come to the mountain . . .' Roisan smiled. 'Actually I've come on a business errand, but I've been meaning to come and see you anyway.'

Maryan got up from the desk and fetched a chair. 'I was just going to make some coffee. Will you have some with me?'

'I certainly will.' After Maryan had plugged in her electric kettle Roisan opened her handbag and handed her an envelope. 'This is the cheque for the miniatures,' she said. 'Less the auctioneer's commission, of course. Vinnie asked me to bring it. He said to tell you they went well over the reserve price. Gina should be well pleased.'

'Thank you.' Maryan fingered the envelope, longing to look at the cheque – to know what the miniatures had fetched. But it was sealed and addressed to Gina. She must wait patiently till she came home to find out.

'I hope Vinnie has taken his commission too,' she said as she slipped the envelope into a drawer.

Roisan shook her head. 'Not a bit of it. He was only too happy to be of help.' She peered at Maryan, noticing her pale face and red-rimmed eyes. 'My dear, I heard what happened,' she said. 'Vinnie was so upset that you had to be humiliated like that.'

'I had no idea that Vinnie would be at the sale,' Maryan said. 'And certainly no notion that Fay might turn up. But she seemed to think we'd planned to meet.'

'I know. And once she gets an idea into her head . . . He would have come in person to apologise. But he thought you might not want to see him after yesterday. Anyway, he's leaving this afternoon for a sale in North Wales.'

'Fay is still convinced that he is Amy's father,' Maryan said. 'Nothing will persuade her otherwise. She made a terrible scene. I felt bad about leaving him with her like that, but my presence was making things worse.'

Roisan nodded understandingly. 'She's paranoid. I'm very worried

– for Vinnie's sake. Living with her is such a strain. And since she's been running the business side of things the orders have fallen off dreadfully. We're not getting half the contracts we were and business at the shop is almost at a standstill. Apparently, when she's in a bad mood she's appallingly rude to the customers. At the rate we're going Vincente's will be bankrupt before the end of next year, and Decor won't be long after it.'

Maryan was appalled, but not surprised. 'It's such a pity Paul left,' she said. 'He was so good with people. He knew the job too.'

'Never mind our business problems.' Roisan touched Maryan's arm. 'You were badly upset by the scene with Fay yesterday. I can see that. I wouldn't mind betting you didn't sleep last night.'

'I'm all right,' Maryan said. 'I just wish I hadn't gone to the sale. It was just that Gina had to go to Paris and I promised I'd be there.'

'And then you had to leave before the miniatures came up.' Roisan smiled. 'Still, I think Gina will be delighted with the price they fetched.' Her smile faded and she said quietly, 'You're still in love with Vinnie, aren't you? Oh my dear, I'm so sorry. I know it won't help when I tell you that he feels the same. If only he'd applied for an annulment as I wanted him to – before she came back.'

'It's just that I can't bear to see him so unhappy,' Maryan said. 'And the business he's worked so hard for – all going to waste. Isn't there *anything* you can do, Roisan?'

'I only wish to God there were.' Roisan was thoughtful for a while as she sipped her coffee. 'I've got all kinds of suspicions. I know I shouldn't say this, but I can't help thinking that the fall-off in business has something to do with her. I don't know what she's up to and even if I did I couldn't prove it, but if I could only . . .' She sighed. 'Ah, but that's only wishful thinking. She's convinced Vinnie that he owes her his loyalty and protection. God knows what lies she's told. Personally I wouldn't believe that woman if she had a halo and wings.' She looked at Maryan. 'Do you mind being here on your own? I could go and get my things and stay with you till Gina gets back.'

Maryan shook her head. 'No. It's good of you but I'm all right. There's plenty of work to do and Gina should be back in a couple of days' time.'

'Well, you know where I am if you need me.'

Roisan rose to leave but Maryan said quickly, 'Roisan – you haven't had a letter from Amy, have you?'

'No. You know I'd have let you know at once if I had.'

'Of course. It's just something Fay said yesterday. She said she knew things about Amy that I didn't know. She said she was married – that she had a child. I've been wondering if Amy did write to me after all. But surely Vinnie would have seen any letter that went to the flat?'

'Ten to one she made it all up to hurt you,' Roisan said. 'That woman is capable of saying anything that comes into her head. She's either as gloomy as doom or as high as a kite. Vinnie puts her changing moods down to her diabetes, but I'm not so sure. No other diabetic I've ever known has behaved as she does.'

Maryan sighed. 'I suppose you could be right. It's just that I've had this feeling.'

'What kind of feeling?'

'I don't know – a sort of intuitive feeling – that Amy isn't happy; that something is wrong. Oh, Roisan, I wish I hadn't let her go like that. She was so young. Anything could have happened. And if she did write letters . . .'

Roisan put her hand on Maryan's arm. 'You couldn't have stopped her, Maryan. She'd made up her mind. That job was what she'd always wanted. But leave it with me,' she said. 'I'll see what I can find out. If there were any letters I'll get to the bottom of it.'

'But – how?'

Roisan winked and tapped the side of her nose. 'I'll play it by ear as they say. Try not to worry. I'll be in touch.'

Amy was coming in from the garden, a basketful of washing, rescued from a sudden rain storm, on her hip. She heard the telephone ringing as she opened the back door and, dropping the basket on the kitchen floor, she hurried into the hall to lift the receiver.

'Hello,' she said breathlessly. 'Amy Keynan here.'

'Amy, it's me, Mike. Look, I've only got a minute, but I've got those audition details I promised you. I'll give you the address. You have to apply, giving your age, experience and so on. Then, if they think you might be what they're looking for, they'll send you a script and an audition date.'

'Will I stand a chance with the little training and experience I've had?' she asked doubtfully.

'Anyone's guess,' he said briefly. 'Just write in and take it from there. It's got to be worth a try.'

Amy took down the address as he gave it to her. 'When will I see you again, Mike?' she asked.

'Heaven only knows. They're sending me on an assignment to Derbyshire this afternoon. There's been a pit accident up there and

I'm to interview some of the victims. It's my first solo assignment, so it'll be quite a challenge.'

'Mike, that's marvellous. Congratulations.'

'Listen out for me on the nine o'clock news tonight,' he said. 'And don't forget, when you come up for the audition ask someone at the reception desk to ring me. We could have a drink – lunch even.'

'Right. I'll do that – if I get an audition. Thanks, Mike.' She hung up with excitement tingling in her veins. Mike's enthusiasm was infectious. Would they really allow someone as inexperienced as her to audition for a BBC serial? Well, as Mike said, it would do no harm to give it a try.

She wrote her application out carefully while Mark had his afternoon nap, signing it with her stage name, Amethyst Lee. Then, when Mark woke up, she walked down to the post box with him in the pushchair. As she dropped the envelope into the box she wondered what she had started. If she did get an audition, and if by some miracle she was actually offered a part, what would she do about Mark? And, even more to the point, what would Alex's reaction be?

She turned the pushchair and set out towards home. I'll meet that when I come to it, she told herself. Might as well worry what I'd do if the moon dropped out of the sky.

The room was small; much smaller than Amy had imagined it would be. The girl who had shown her up had taken her coat and pointed out the microphone.

'Someone will tell you what to do and when to begin,' she said as she left.

What she hadn't prepared her for was that the instructions would come via a loud speaker on the wall, and when the disembodied male voice addressed Amy for the first time she almost jumped out of her skin.

'Good morning, Miss Lee.'

'Oh – er – good morning.'

'I take it you have read the script we sent you.'

'Yes – thank you.'

'Good. I'd like you to read the piece of your own choice first. After that I'd like you to read the part of Estelle in our script. It begins on page three. Have you got that?'

With trembling fingers Amy turned the pages and found the place. 'Yes, I've got it.'

'Someone will read the other character for you. You may begin when you see the red light and there is no need to wait in between. Just carry straight on.'

'Right. Thank you.' She stood poised, staring at the bulb. Her heart was beating so loud that she was sure the microphone must pick up the sound, but she didn't dare move away in case they couldn't hear her. The light flashed on. She took a deep breath and began to read.

She had chosen a piece from *Wuthering Heights*. It was a longish speech, highly charged with emotion, and reading it reminded Amy of Minsdale and the Keynan Players. Life had been so full of hope then. Hope and love, so soon to be shattered.

When she had finished she paused, picked up the other script and began to read as instructed. The character of Estelle could not have been more different from that of Cathy. Having read the script she knew that Estelle was a teenage girl, the flighty daughter of an East End family. It gave her the chance to use the Cockney accent she had grown up with. As she relaxed she found herself slipping easily into the familiar accent; a language that brought its own memories – of her visits to the brewery mews and the big gentle horses; her early schooldays and playing the fairy in the pantomime; of Lily Smith's envious spite. Of the death of Tom Jessop, the man she'd mourned as her beloved 'Daddy'.

After she'd conquered her initial nerves, Amy thoroughly enjoyed the audition. It was wonderful to be doing the work she loved best, even if it was only for a short while. It was with regret that she laid down the script when it was over. She waited. When the voice addressed her again it was cool and impersonal.

'Thank you very much for letting us hear your work, Miss Lee. You may leave the script on the table. Someone will be in touch with you very shortly. Thank you for attending. Good morning.'

'Good morning.' Amy went down in the lift, wondering if the brief dismissal meant the same as 'Don't ring us, we'll ring you.' Thank goodness Mike would be waiting for her in the entrance hall. He was taking her out to lunch. Going straight home would have been such an anti-climax. She couldn't wait to tell him all about her audition.

Gina came home bubbling over with the visit to Paris and the sightseeing she had managed to squeeze into her brief visit to France's romantic capital. But she had serious news to impart. It was too important to blurt out, especially as it concerned Maryan herself. Realising that tact and diplomacy were needed, she invited Maryan to have dinner with her on the evening of her return, booking a table for two at her favourite restaurant.

When they were seated Maryan handed over the envelope

containing the cheque for the miniatures. So far Gina hadn't asked about them.

'I've been saving this. It's the money for the miniatures,' she said, waiting in anticipation as Gina tore open the envelope.

'My God, I'd completely forgotten.' When Gina saw the amount written on the cheque she gasped. 'I hadn't expected them to fetch quite this much.'

'It's enough to cover your debt then?'

'Yes. And plenty to spare.' Gina looked up, puzzled. 'But – you were there, weren't you?'

Maryan sighed. 'Well, I was – and I wasn't. I was forced to leave before the miniatures came up.' She went on to tell Gina about Fay's sudden appearance and the scene she had created. When she had finished her employer shook her head.

'She sounds impossible. How on earth does Roisan's brother stand her?'

'I think it's hard for him. But he's a Catholic. Divorce is out of the question.'

Gina looked thoughtful. 'If you and he still love each other . . .'

'There's no chance it can ever come to anything,' Maryan interrupted. 'It's better if we don't see each other under the circumstances.'

'That's what I thought,' Gina said. 'In which case the proposition I have to put to you might be just what you need.'

'Proposition?' Maryan looked up.

'Yes.' Gina took a sip of her wine. 'While I was over in Paris I had an offer. The real reason that I was invited was that my designs had impressed one of the big houses. Word had got out that I was responsible for the Marcus Leigh Collection. Well, to cut a long story short I've been offered a job – by Fath.'

Maryan looked puzzled. 'But – you're a designer in your own right. You're building your own house – your own name.'

'A very small house and a very small name. It'll take me years struggling alone.'

'But it's why you left the Leighs. I thought you'd always wanted to be on your own.'

'Of course. I still do.'

'Then – what about your new designs?'

'They're to be shown at the spring show. Fath will buy them. I'll be working for them by then – if I take up their offer.'

'But – I don't understand. Won't that put you back where you were before?'

'No. Not at all.' Gina leaned eagerly across the table. 'With a

358

name like Fath behind me I could come back after two or three years with a real head start. The Marcus Leigh label did well, but only as long as I was there. It was a flash in the pan. How could it be anything else when the original designer was dead? The public is fickle, Maryan. People want a face – a personality to put to a name. When they don't get it they soon forget.'

'Yes, I see.' Maryan felt her heart contract and Gina reached across to touch her hand.

'I'm sorry. Did that sound hard and insensitive?'

'No. I see what you mean. It's a wonderful opportunity for you. Will you take it?'

'Well, I'm seriously considering it,' Gina said. 'There's an awful lot to think about, of course. I'd keep the house on. I might let it on a short lease. I haven't started working it all out yet.'

'Then I'd better start looking round for another job and somewhere to live.'

'Oh *no*. That's what I was coming to. If I go I'd like you to come with me.'

'*Me*?' Maryan stared at her.

Gina laughed. 'Yes, *you*. I'll still need a secretary and the salary they're offering will certainly run to it. I'd have the rent from the house and what's left over from this too.' She waved the cheque. 'We could share a flat. Oh, just think, Maryan. It'd be such *fun*. I know you'd *love* Paris. And we'd both be getting away from the unhappy memories we'd rather forget.'

'I don't know.' Maryan shook her head. 'I've never thought of living anywhere but England.'

'You've nothing to keep you here, have you? Your daughter has her own life now, and you've said that there's no future for you and Vincent Donlan. Anyway, I wouldn't be going until early next spring. You'll have plenty of time to make up your mind.'

Maryan slept little that night. The thought of leaving England and spending two or three years in Paris had taken her completely off guard. It was something she had never even dreamed of. Yet suddenly it was a real possibility. And it was certainly tempting. As Gina had said, there was plenty of time to weigh up the pros and cons, but even so, Maryan had the feeling it wasn't going to be easy to decide. If only she didn't have this uneasy feeling about Amy. If only she knew where she was. And just how much truth there was in Fay's spiteful allegations.

The letter came with a batch of cards just a few days before Christmas. Amy opened the cards first, trying not to look at the other, smaller envelope lying face down on the mat. There weren't many. She'd lost touch with most of the people she used to know, and Alex seemed to have few friends. There was one from Celia, one from Mike and another from Marjorie and Philip Taylor. She bent and picked up the remaining letter. It had **BBC** printed in one corner, so she knew at once what it contained. She carried it through to the living room, put it on the table and sat down to stare at it. It would be brief and to the point, politely declining her services and thanking her for attending. Oh well, might as well get it over with.

She tore open the envelope and drew out the sheet of paper inside. She read the letter through once. Then, the words dancing before her eyes, she read it again, slowly and carefully, hardly able to believe what she read. *They were offering her a part.* Not the part she'd read for, but another, better part. If their offer was acceptable she was to go in and meet the producer and sign her contract on Friday, 21 December. It was a wonderful Christmas present, the best she'd ever had. She tried not to think about the new set of problems it brought with it. A reliable person would have to be found to take care of Mark while she was working. Preferably someone who didn't charge too much. And then, even more difficult, there was Alex. She must break the news to him. He had telephoned at the end of last week to tell her that he'd got the job he wanted. He was to direct a feature film for Ealing. The crew and cast, which included two big-name stars, would be leaving for location work in Greece right after Christmas. Should she tell him before he went, or wait and see how things worked out? She decided on the latter. If she got everything well organised and Mark wasn't suffering he would have nothing to argue about.

'It went really well, Mike. All the cast were there – and the producer. Even the writers, four of them. We talked about the main storyline and we each got a chance to say how we thought of the characters we will be playing.'

They faced each other over tea in the canteen. Amy's eyes were bright with excitement. She hadn't enjoyed herself so much since her days at Minsdale with the Keynan Players.

Catching some of her enthusiasm, Mike urged her to tell him more. 'Go on, what's the title? Have they got one yet?'

'Yes. It's to be called 'This Year, Next Year',' she told him. 'It's about two families. The middle-class Owens who own a printing business and a group of their workers, most of them from the same East End family.'

He grinned. 'Sounds good. So when do you start work?'

'Right after the Christmas holiday. We'll be working two days a week, one for rehearsal and one for recording a set of five fifteen-minute programmes.'

'Have you got a crèche or a sitter of some kind arranged for Mark?'

'Addie Shaw has put me onto this young mother who takes care of several children while their mothers are at work. She's a qualified children's nurse and very capable. I went to see her yesterday and took Mark. They seemed to take to each other on sight and she's actually got a vacancy coming up after Christmas, so everything looks like working out well.'

'That's good news.' He smiled at her. 'You know, you look like the old Amy today,' he told her. 'Your eyes are shining and you're full of excitement and enthusiasm. It's good to see you looking happy again.'

Suddenly embarrassed, she avoided his eyes. 'Thanks, Mike. If it hadn't been for you I'd never have had this opportunity.'

'Rubbish. I only told you about it. You got the job because you're talented.' He raised an enquiring eyebrow. 'Was Alex pleased for you?'

She sighed. 'I haven't told him yet. I wanted to have everything cut and dried first. Besides, he hasn't been home. I could hardly tell him over the phone, could I?'

'I suppose not. How will he take it?'

'He can hardly object to me earning extra money, especially when he can see that Mark is going to be well taken care of, can he?'

Her confident tone belied the uneasiness in her eyes and Mike smiled encouragingly. 'Of course not. What are you doing for Christmas by the way?'

'Alex will be home. He'll want to spend Christmas with Mark before he goes on location to Greece. He's likely to be away for at least six weeks.'

'Oh, that's all right then. I was going to invite you to Rhensham if you were going to be alone.'

'Oh, Mike. Were you really?' Amy sighed wistfully. 'It'd be lovely to spend another Christmas at Mitcham Lodge. I'd love Auntie Marjorie to see Mark. And to show him the village and the horses. Does she still help at the stables?'

He smiled. 'Yes. She's still got a couple at home too. Never mind. Some other time, eh?'

'That would be wonderful.'

'Amy . . .' He looked into her eyes. 'Look, Amy – you do know that if ever you need anything – if ever you need me, I'll be there.'

361

'I know, Mike. Thanks.' For a moment they looked at each other, then Amy noticed the time and jumped to her feet. 'Heavens, I must fly. Mark is with Addie this afternoon. I must go and collect him or she'll think I'm taking advantage.'

This year Mark was old enough to understand and catch the excitement of Christmas. He loved the coloured lights in the streets and the shop windows, and his own small Christmas tree, decorated with lights and tinsel and placed out of reach of his grasping little hands, was a source of sheer delight to him.

Alex arrived home on Christmas Eve. He'd had a drink, but to Amy's relief he wasn't drunk. He played with Mark until bedtime then he and Amy ate supper together before creeping upstairs to fill the stocking, hung up at one corner of Mark's cot. For once he was in a good mood and seemed to be looking forward to the challenge of the new job. He even discussed it with her, sounding more animated and enthusiastic than she'd known him for some time. Maybe it would make him less frustrated, she told herself hopefully. Perhaps it would bring about that change in their lives that he had promised.

All through the Christmas holiday she meant to tell him about the BBC job. Once or twice she even began, but each time something happened to stop her and when he left on the day after Boxing Day she still hadn't broken her news. As she stood on the doorstep with Mark in her arms, waving to him as he drove off, she regretted not getting over that one final, very important and difficult hurdle. But things had been so much better between the three of them. She couldn't bring herself to spoil it. It wasn't really that she was too cowardly, she told herself.

When Gina told Maryan that she had definitely decided to accept Fath's offer Maryan realised that the winding down process must be put into operation at once. One of her first tasks was to contact Sam and tell him that they would no longer need to rent the Hackney factory.

As soon as Christmas was over she telephoned, asking him to meet her for lunch. The purpose of her meeting with him was twofold. Besides asking him to release Gina from their arrangement, she was badly in need of advice and could think of no one better than Sam.

He agreed at once to meet her, suggesting lunch at a quiet restaurant in Soho. He was waiting when she arrived and had already ordered her a glass of wine. When they'd studied the menu and ordered their lunch he looked up at her with his kindly smile.

362

'You sounded a little anxious on the telephone, Maryan. You're looking peaky too. I hope everything is all right.'

'I'm fine. It's just that I've got some news.'

He looked up hopefully. 'About Amy?'

She shook her head. 'No. It's Gina. She was invited over to Paris last month with a view to taking part in a show next spring at the *Musée des Arts Décoratifs*.'

Sam looked impressed. 'That sounds wonderful. Marcus told us so much about the *Musée* when he went to Paris before the war. It's marvellous that it's up and running once again.'

'She took her portfolio with her new collection and had a terrific time. But while she was there she had an exciting offer – of a job with the house of Fath.'

Sam nodded. 'I see. She should take it, of course. I presume she accepted at once.'

'Not right away. She's been thinking it all out carefully. But now she has decided to take up the offer.'

'So she will wish to be released from our agreement about the Hackney premises.' Sam smiled. 'Tell her not to worry. It's not a problem. I can easily re-let the factory.'

'Thank you. I'm sure that will be a relief to her.' She hesitated and Sam peered at her, sensing that there was more on her mind.

'You didn't ask me to meet you just for that, did you, my dear? There's something else.'

'Well – yes. The fact is, she's asked me to go with her and I don't know what to do, Mr Sam.'

The old man reached across the table to squeeze her hand. 'Maryan, I think it's time you dropped the Mister, don't you? After all, we're almost related. So – you're finding it difficult to decide, and you want me to help you make up your mind. Is that it?'

She sighed. 'I can't go without knowing what's become of Amy,' she told him. 'I must find her before I can even begin to think of leaving the country. Do you understand?'

'My dear, of course. Rachel and I would like to know where she is too. Rachel in particular worries about her. She hasn't been well again. The doctor says her heart isn't strong. Worrying is so bad for her.'

'The problem isn't so much finding her,' Maryan said. 'That would be fairly easy, I imagine, if I put my mind to it. The question is, does Amy *want* me to find her?'

'Maybe to begin with we could make some discreet enquiries – just to be sure that she's all right,' Sam said. 'If you knew she was well and happy you could go to Paris with peace of mind, eh?'

363

She looked uncertain. 'It would help. But what I really want is . . .'

'A reconciliation?'

'To be forgiven, I suppose.' Maryan looked at her old employer. I wasn't a very good mother, Sam. Looking back now I can see where I went wrong. I should have made more effort to spend time with her – not kept secrets from her. Everyone deserves to know the basic truth about their parentage. I was so wrong not to tell her.'

'And Rachel and I made so many demands on you. Oh yes, we are to blame too.' He looked at her with his gentle brown eyes. 'Maryan, listen to me – do you really want to go to Paris?'

She sighed. 'I know I'm lucky. It's a wonderful opportunity. One I might never have again . . .'

He waved a hand at her. 'Putting all that aside – do you *want* to go?'

For a long moment she looked into the wise, candid eyes. 'No, Sam. No, I don't.' She sighed, suddenly filled with relief. 'This is the first time I've really admitted it. I feel I ought to want to go. But I don't, not really. I'm a Londoner, you see – born and bred. This is where I belong and I know I'd be homesick. I know now how Mum felt in the war when we tried to get her to stay with us at Hazelfield. If I went I'd feel I'd abandoned Amy. Even if she doesn't want to see me any more, I'd still feel that.'

'And all this has been keeping you awake at nights, eh?' He patted her hand. 'Making those blue eyes of yours so sad? I do know how you feel, my dear. Perhaps more than you can guess. So – what will you do when Gina goes?'

She shrugged. 'I haven't got as far as thinking about that yet.'

'How would you like to work for Feldman's again?'

She stared at him. 'But – there *is* no Feldman's. You retired.'

His smile was almost impish. 'I want to come out of retirement, Maryan – to start again. Maybe with your help I could do it. You see, I feel like you. Feldman's has been my life since boyhood. It *is* me. Without it I'm nothing. I've been thinking about it so much lately. Now that I have someone to leave the business to I can't let it die. I could do a lot of the work from Whitegates as I did before. I just need a good, reliable manager to run the factory for me – be on the spot. The job is yours if you want it, Maryan. I can think of no one better. It would be like having my own daughter run it for me.'

Maryan's heart lifted. She had started as an apprentice machinist at Feldman's when she left school at fourteen. Now she was going back as factory manager. Back to the East End where her roots were. What would her mother have said, she wondered? She could just imagine her shaking her head and saying that she should have the good sense to know her place. But life had changed since Sarah's day.

'You could have free rein,' Sam was saying. 'Use your own initiative and ideas with the workforce. After all, who better to understand their needs than you? And you're so much more up to date with the world of fashion than I am now. What do you say, my dear?'

She looked up with a smile. 'Oh, Sam – I'd *love* to come back to Feldman's.'

He squeezed her hand tightly. 'And maybe – just maybe we could look for Amy together?'

She smiled. 'Yes. Maybe we could.'

With the New Year came the usual crop of bills. At Decor business was at a virtual standstill and trade at Vincente's was no better. Things were even worse than Vincent had visualised. There seemed to be a slump in the antique and house refurbishment business in London and the Home Counties. If he wanted to continue he was obviously going to have to widen his sights and look further afield for work. He placed advertisements in the county 'glossies', offering to go as far as Scotland, and when he received a telephone call from a man in Caithness who had just bought a castle and wanted to refurbish it he was filled with new hope and excitement. He promised to travel up to Scotland to look at the property and give a brief assessment of its potential, and a date was made. But early on the morning of the day he was to drive north Roisan received an urgent telephone call.

'Roisan . . .' He sounded worried. 'I wondered if you could come over to Simons Mews today?'

'Of course, if you need me. Is something wrong?'

'I can't go into detail.' He lowered his voice so that she had to press the receiver close to her ear to hear what he was saying. 'I can't talk at all really. It's Fay. She isn't well, and there's no one to open the shop. I wouldn't ask you, but I might need to be away for at least three days.'

Roisan sighed and raised her eyes to the ceiling. Fay was up to her old tricks again. 'You must go, Vinnie,' she told him firmly. 'This could be the turning point for Decor. You mustn't let it slip through your fingers. I'll cope at this end. Is Fay in bed?'

'Yes. She couldn't sleep. She was up half the night, walking up and down, shivering – sweating. I tried to help but she didn't want me near her and she refused point-blank to let me send for the doctor. I dropped off myself in the end and when I woke, about four-thirty, she wasn't in the flat. God knows where she went. Maybe she thought some fresh air ... Anyway, she seemed a bit better when she came in.'

'Did she have some insulin?'

'Yes, when she came in. She's asleep now.'

'How long was she away?'

'I don't really know. About an hour – it could have been longer.'

Roisan clicked her tongue in exasperation. 'What was she thinking of, wandering about in the middle of the night? She might have caught pneumonia. All right, Vinnie, I'm on my way. Just you get off, and don't worry. I'll take care of everything.'

On the way over to Simons Mews Roisan worried about Vincent, driving all the way up to Scotland after so little sleep. It was typical of Fay to spoil his chances. Surely if she had felt ill she could have allowed him to help instead of worrying him by taking off into the night like that. It was so typical.

She had her own key to the flat and it was just before nine o'clock as she let herself in at the side door. At the top of the stairs, she paused to listen. There was no sound. She tiptoed into the bedroom. Fay was lying on her back, her mouth open and sleeping like a log. Roisan looked at her in disgust. If she hadn't known better she'd have thought Fay was drunk. She closed the door and went down to open the shop.

At lunchtime she put up the 'closed' sign and went upstairs to the flat to make herself a snack lunch. She put the kettle on, then put her head round the bedroom door. Fay would most likely be awake and hungry by now.

The moment she saw her she knew that something was wrong. She was a bad colour and her breathing was deep – much too deep. Maybe she wasn't asleep at all, but unconscious – in a diabetic coma. Roisan knew enough about the disease to know that if insulin wasn't administered the result was a coma. Yet Vinnie had said she'd had insulin in the small hours. Something wasn't right. In the living room she dialled for an ambulance. While she waited for it to arrive she collected up the syringes and ampoules from the bathroom cabinet. Then she remembered that diabetics carried a card. They would need to see that at the hospital. She went through Fay's handbag, but to no avail. There was nothing among the contents to certify a medical condition at all. It was as she heard the ambulance turn into the Mews that she found the slit in the lining. Slipping her hand inside she felt an envelope, but already the street doorbell was ringing downstairs. Cramming the envelope into her pocket, she went down to open the door.

The ambulance man agreed immediately that Fay was unconscious. When Roisan mentioned that she was diabetic he looked puzzled.

'This doesn't look like a hypo to me,' he said, bending over Fay's prone body and sniffing. 'But you'd better bring along her insulin and any other medication she's on.'

'It's all right, I've already done that.' Roisan held up the paper bag and saw that the ambulance man was examining the puncture marks on Fay's arm with a thoughtful expression. Straightening up, he looked at his assistant.

'Better get her to hospital right away.'

Fortunately, the journey to the hospital was short and as soon as they arrived in Casualty Fay was whisked away. It was while Roisan was waiting that she remembered the envelope in her pocket. They would need the card. She pulled it out and looked inside. There was no diabetic card, just two crumpled letters and a small card with a picture of a stork on it. She caught her breath. Amy's letters, and a card announcing the birth of a baby boy. So this was where Fay's information came from.

'Are you the lady who brought Mrs Fay Donlan in?'

Roisan looked up to see a tall man in a white coat looking down at her. She rose to her feet, thrusting the envelope back into her pocket. 'That's right. How is she?'

'Are you a relative?'

'I'm her sister-in-law.'

Looking around the crowded waiting area, the man said, 'I'd like a word in private. If you could just come with me.'

Mystified, Roisan followed him to a small office where he closed the door and indicated a chair. 'I am Doctor Leverton, the Casualty Officer,' he said. 'And you are?'

'Mrs Freer.'

The doctor nodded briefly, making a note on a pad. 'Now – the ambulance man who brought your sister-in-law in tells me that you told him she was diabetic.'

Roisan nodded. 'That's right. I brought her insulin and syringes with her, but I couldn't find a card.'

He looked at her thoughtfully. 'Does she live with you?'

'No. She lives with my brother – her husband.'

'Do you happen to know the name of her GP?'

'I'm sorry, no.'

'So you wouldn't know if she'd been ill lately?'

'Not that I know of. At least, not till this morning. My brother telephoned me earlier on and said she wasn't well. He had to go

367

away on urgent business and he asked me to go and stay with her.' Roisan frowned. 'Is she all right? What's happened?'

'How long had she been unconscious before you called the ambulance? Please think carefully, Mrs Freer. It's very important.'

'I don't know. Not long. I arrived at about half-past nine. She was sleeping then, quite peacefully, I thought. My brother has a shop, so I was busy till one. When I went up to the flat I found her collapsed. Apparently she'd injected some insulin early this morning . . .'

'Your sister-in-law is *not* diabetic,' the doctor said abruptly.

Roisan stared at him. 'She's not . . . ? Then what's wrong with her?'

'I have reason to believe that she has administered an overdose of a narcotic. The substance in the ampoules you brought with her is diamorphine, not insulin.'

Shocked, Roisan stared at him. 'But – I thought . . . Diamorphine, you said?'

He nodded gravely. 'Perhaps better known to you as heroin.'

Chapter Nineteen

It was much later that evening when the hospital telephoned to tell Roisan that Fay had regained consciousness and could be visited. She lay in bed in the small side-ward, her face grey against the white of the pillowcase. When Roisan closed the door and sat down by the bed she turned her face away.

'Why did you do it?' she muttered. 'Why did you have to bring me here?' She turned her accusing eyes on her sister-in-law. They burned like hot coals in her white face. 'You've always hated me, haven't you?'

'I thought you were in a diabetic coma. What was I supposed to think? You're addicted to that vile stuff, aren't you? How long has it been going on?'

'I told the doctor the drug was prescribed abroad when I broke my arm and afterwards I couldn't get off it.'

'And is that the truth?'

'What business is it of yours?' Fay glared malevolently at her sister-in-law. 'And what does it matter, as long as they swallowed it? You'd guessed anyway, hadn't you? This is just the chance you've been waiting for. It must have seemed like a godsend, finding me flaked out like that.'

'You're wrong,' Roisan said. 'I didn't guess, not about the drugs. It was a complete shock when the doctor told me. But if I had, Fay, and if you'd been anyone else but Vinnie's wife, I'd have blown the whistle on you right away. Make no mistake about that.' The two women looked at each other for a moment, then Roisan asked: 'So what happens next? Are they giving you any treatment?'

Fay grimaced. 'They've offered me a spell in some drying out place, to get off it. It sounds ghastly. I shan't go.'

'I would if I were you,' Roisan said dryly. 'As it happens I've had my eyes opened in more ways than one since this morning.'

369

'What do you mean?'

'I've spent the afternoon in the office – going through the books and checking bank statements.'

Fay raised herself on one elbow, her eyes staring. 'You've *what*? You have no right . . .'

'I have *every* right. It's my business you've been cheating too, remember? I've also been in touch with some of our previous clients. I know now why the business has been failing. You've been quoting exorbitant prices and creaming off the profits to supply your habit, haven't you?' When Fay turned her head away Roisan bent her head closer. '*Admit it*' she hissed. 'There's a name for what you've been doing, you know – one the police might well be interested in.'

'They can't charge me with cheating *myself*,' Fay said. 'Vinnie is my husband. Decor is my business as much as his.'

'The Inland Revenue might see things differently,' Roisan put in. 'You see, I found a bank book and statements too, Fay. The account is in the name of Kendal. Your maiden name, I think. The receipts tally with the extra cash you quoted clients. And the statements show some interestingly large cheques paid out regularly to the same person. It doesn't look good, does it?'

Fay swallowed hard. 'How dare you go through my personal papers – snooping and poking your nose into what doesn't concern you?'

'Doesn't concern me?' Roisan's face was flushed with anger. 'You've cheated, lied and stolen from Vinnie and me. Now you've been found out and you're going to pay for it.'

Fay turned her head on the pillow. 'Go away, or I'll ring for a nurse,' she murmured. 'I'm supposed to be resting.'

'I've no wish to spend a second more than I have to in your company, Fay, I promise you that. But I haven't finished with you yet. There are things I must say. You deserted Vinnie – went off with this man who you thought had more to offer. Then you came back and shattered Vinnie's life just when he was finding success and happiness again. Since then you've made his life a living hell. Well, now your little game is over – understand?'

'I'm still his wife,' Fay said with a maddening smile. 'You know Vinnie. As long as he feels he has a duty to me . . .'

'But he *hasn't*,' Roisan interrupted. 'There never was any pregnancy or abortion, was there? You made the whole thing up to use as emotional blackmail.'

'You can't prove that,' Fay snapped.

'I don't have to. I have enough proof of other things to put you behind bars if I choose to. You've almost wrecked the business

370

Vinnie, Maryan and I worked so hard to build. You're going to pay for that.'

'We'll see. When Vinnie gets here . . .'

'He isn't coming,' Roisan interrupted. 'I haven't told him about this little episode.

Fay's eyes blazed. 'I'll telephone him myself. I'll ask the doctor to.'

'I wouldn't if I were you.' Roisan took a small bundle of crumpled papers out of her handbag. 'While I was looking for your non-existent diabetic card I found these. You kept the letters that Maryan's daughter wrote to her. Vinnie might just be saintly enough to forgive you for stealing his money and wrecking his business. But this – never.'

'So – the girl *is* his child then?'

Roisan smiled wryly. 'You'll never know, will you, Fay? You'll never be able to prove it either way. On the other hand, all the cards are stacked against you.'

The defiant look faded from Fay's face and for the first time Roisan dared to feel confident that she was winning.

'It wasn't all for me – the money,' Fay said quietly. 'He – the man I was living with – has been blackmailing me. When he got tired of me and threw me out he promised to keep quiet about my habit and to keep supplying me with – what I need, if I made monthly payments.' She looked at Roisan. 'All right. What now?'

Roisan drew a deep breath, trying hard not to let it sound like a sigh of relief. 'I'm prepared to offer you a deal, and if you're wise you'll take it. Make yourself scarce. Get out of Vinnie's life and I won't go to the police. They tell me you'll be discharged from here tomorrow. I'll bring your clothes and the bank book. You can keep the money that's left in it. It'll be worth it to see the back of you. Later, you'll put divorce proceedings into action; set Vinnie free.'

'You don't want much, do you?'

'I want what's due to my brother,' Roisan said. 'He deserves it.'

'What's going to become of me?'

Roisan shrugged. 'That's up to you. You've been offered a cure. Why not take it?'

'And – if I refuse to co-operate?'

'Simple. I go to the police with the evidence I've got first – and tell Vinnie what I've done afterwards.' She raised an eyebrow. 'Well – what do you say?'

Fay made one last effort. 'I say you're bluffing.'

'*Try me*,' Roisan challenged, her mouth set in a determined line. 'The jail sentences for embezzlement are quite stiff, I believe. Illegal

371

possession of narcotics is probably even stiffer, I wouldn't know. And of course your friend and supplier would be involved too. He might not be too happy about that. Think about it, Fay. So far you've been lucky. Damned lucky.'

There was a long pause. Then the door opened and a nurse came in.

'I'm sorry, Mrs Freer. I'm afraid I'll have to ask you to leave now.'

Roisan got to her feet and walked to the door. She paused and looked back. 'Well?'

Fay nodded briefly, her face bleak with defeat. 'All right,' she said quietly. 'I'll do as you say.'

Roisan felt drained as she walked out of the hospital into the March evening. It was raining. Raincoated figures hurried past, the wind tugging at their umbrellas. The traffic swished by on the wet roads, throwing up a fine spray of oily water, and the pavements glistened underfoot. But as she joined the bus queue she saw that the woman in front of her carried a bunch of flowers, and as she breathed in their fragrance her heart suddenly lifted. The air seemed filled with the joyous promise of spring.

Since reopening Feldman's Sam had taken over the flat above the garage at Whitegates, using part of it as his office, as Rachel had done when she launched the Marcus Leigh Collection. He felt happier and fitter than he had for a long time. He was back in harness, running Feldman Fashions once again. And what was more, he had Maryan to help him. Every Friday he went up to Town to spend the day with her at the Hackney factory; going to the bank, paying the wages and helping out in any way he could. He loved to do the rounds, chatting to his workers, enquiring after their families and their health. He prided himself that he could remember all their names and personal details. He knew that it made them feel a valued part of the firm and encouraged them to take a special pride in their work. Maryan seemed happy too. She had found a flat nearby and settled into her job well. And she was certainly efficient. The factory had never run so smoothly or so profitably.

Rachel, on the other hand, was taking life quietly these days. The King's death in February had affected her deeply, but since the Princess Elizabeth had become Queen and the papers had been full of the new young royal family and the exciting arrangements for the coming coronation, she seemed to have cheered up. She had taken up an old hobby, embroidery, and was busy making a set of elaborate cushion covers to commemorate coronation year. While

372

Sam worked she seemed quite content to stitch away, listening contentedly to the wireless as her needle flew in and out.

It was as Sam was working one Wednesday morning that Rachel burst into the office. Her face was flushed with excitement and she was quite breathless from hurrying across the garden and climbing the stairs to the office. He looked up in surprise at her sudden entrance and admonished her sternly.

'Rachel, my love. How many times has the doctor told you you mustn't rush about like that? You know you . . .'

'Samuel – *listen* to me,' she interrupted impatiently. 'Something wonderful has happened.'

Frowning, he got up from his desk and took her arm. 'Sit down and catch your breath. Whatever it is, it can't be so wonderful you would kill yourself for it. Now – take your time.'

But Rachel flapped her hands at him frustratedly. 'Oh, do stop *fussing* and listen to me. I was listening to the wireless just now. A new programme was on. I was interested to hear it because they said it was all about an East End family who run a printing business – it sounded rather like us. Well, as I listened it struck me that one of the characters sounded just like . . .' She looked up at him. 'I know you're going to think I've taken leave of my senses, but she sounded just like – Sarah.'

Sam looked blank. 'Sarah?'

'*Our* Sarah – as she was when we first knew her. Sarah Brown.' She waved her hands again, anticipating his next remark. 'Yes, I *know* you're going to say that Sarah has been dead for years, but hear me out, Sam.'

Nonplussed, Sam sank back into his chair. 'All right – all right, I'm listening.'

'Well – when the programme came to an end I listened for the cast of actors. The name of the one who sounded like Sarah was . . .' She bit her lip with suppressed excitement. 'It was *Amethyst Leigh.*'

Sam shook his head. 'I'm sorry, but I don't . . .'

'Oh, *Sam*, how can you be so slow? It's Amy, don't you see? Amethyst is her full name, don't you remember? We know that she left home to be an actress. And obviously she has taken Leigh as a stage name.' She spread her hands. 'What other name would she choose but her true father's?'

Sam still looked doubtful. 'It's most likely all coincidence,' he said. 'I wish you wouldn't get yourself so worked up about it, my love. It isn't good for you.'

'Good for me? *You're* not good for me.' Rachel was on her feet. 'Can't you see how frustrated you're making me? At least we can find out, Sam. We can write to the BBC and ask for the address of this actress. Better yet, we could telephone them.' She clasped her hands together. 'Oh, Samuel, just think – our granddaughter might be no further away than the end of our telephone.'

'Now, Rachel, you must calm yourself,' Sam said firmly. 'All right. It may be as you say. But first we must go and see Maryan and tell her what you have heard. We can't do this without her permission.'

'Yes, yes – so when can we go?' Her eyes were bright with anticipation as they looked hopefully into his.

'You can come with me when I go up on Friday.'

'*Friday*?' She stared at him. 'How can you expect me to wait until Friday? Oh, Samuel, please – can't we go now – today?'

When she looked at him like that Sam had never been able to refuse his wife anything. He sighed resignedly. 'Oh, very well, if it will satisfy you – anything. But only if you promise me not to build up your hopes too high.'

By the beginning of March the first week of 'This Year, Next Year' had already been broadcast and the reaction had been marvellous, even better than the predictions. Letters flooded in from listeners to say how much they had enjoyed the heart-warming show with its memorable characters. The producer and cast settled down confidently to a long run.

Amy was radiant. Over the past two months she had learned so much about herself. Not only was she sure now that she could act – and act without Alex to guide her – but she could successfully combine her other roles of housewife and mother with her artistic career. It helped, of course, that she was working away from home on only two days of the week. There was plenty of time for her household jobs and for being with Mark. She usually studied her scripts in bed when the house was quiet. And of course there was the added advantage that radio work did not involve memorising lines.

Since Christmas she had seen a lot of Mike. On her two days in London they usually lunched together and he had been out to Mill Hill to spend the occasional Sunday with her and Mark, who was growing fond of him. Alex wrote from time to time and he had telephoned her twice. But he gave her little indication of how the film was progressing. Greece was fine, he told her. The weather was warm and sultry but they had been held up by a lack of sunshine. He had no idea when they would complete the location filming. On the two occasions he had telephoned he had made it unflatteringly clear that his chief reason for ringing was dire necessity. He needed her to

374

wire him some money. Boredom and inactivity were proving expensive, he said enigmatically. He rang off without saying once that he missed her. But then she didn't expect him to.

On the day that the first programme went out Mike suggested they celebrate. He rang to say he had booked a table at a restaurant by the riverside in Richmond and would pick her up at eight. Amy went across to ask Addie if she would have Mark for the evening. The older woman agreed at once, but Amy noticed that Jack looked less than pleased.

'Mr Keynan isn't likely to come back, is he?' he asked meaningfully.

'Oh no. He's in Greece, filming,' Amy reminded him. 'That other time was a misunderstanding, Jack. It won't happen again.'

Jack looked doubtful. 'Does he know about you and this Mr Taylor?' he asked.

'*Jack.*' Addie looked scandalised. 'Fancy saying a thing like that to Amy. It's none of our business.'

'It will be if he comes back and blames us for colluding,' Jack muttered ominously.

'Mike is a very old friend. We grew up together during the war. He's like a brother,' Amy told him.

'Yes, but he's *not* your brother, is he?'

Amy looked at Addie. 'Maybe I should ask someone else to sit for me,' she said. But Addie would have none of it.

'Take no notice of *him,*' she said, throwing her husband a reproachful look. '*I* know there's nothing going on that shouldn't be. That's good enough for me. You've worked hard and you deserve a little celebration. She smiled. 'Jack and I both listened to "This Year, Next Year" on the wireless and we thought you were ever so good in it.'

The restaurant was cosy and intimate. Checked tablecloths covered the small tables and on each was a small candle lamp. Lights along the river bank made the flowing river look like rippling black satin and Amy sipped her wine with a feeling of happy satisfaction. She smiled at Mike.

'Since I've been working again I feel like a real person,' she told him. 'A whole person. Acting is what I was meant to do. I'm sure of it. And everything seems to be working out really well. Mark is happy. He looks forward to going to Rosemary's two days a week and I'm sure I'm a better mother now that I feel more fulfilled.'

Mike took a thoughtful sip from his glass and looked up at her. 'And Alex?'

Her smile faded. 'Ah – yes, Alex.' She twisted the stem of her glass between her fingers. 'When I didn't manage to break it to him at Christmas I thought I'd write and tell him.' She looked up at him. 'But I couldn't put it in a letter. It wouldn't be right, would it?'

'I don't think you're being quite honest with yourself, Amy.' He looked at her. 'You're afraid he'll make you give it up, aren't you? That's your real reason for not telling him.'

She sighed. 'I suppose so. I couldn't bear it if I had to give the job up now, Mike.'

'Then don't. Telling him doesn't mean you have to give in. You have a right to your own life too. You've made it work, after all.'

'You don't know what he can be like.' She avoided his eyes.

'Amy . . .' He reached across the table, touching her hand – making her look at him. 'Are you afraid of him?'

'It's when he's been drinking. He's so unpredictable. I sometimes feel he isn't quite . . .'

'Isn't quite what?'

'In control of himself.'

'Then tell him when he's sober.'

'Yes. Yes, I will. When he comes back from Greece, I'll tell him. And I'll insist that I'm keeping the job. After all, I do have a contract to honour.'

'Leave him, Amy.'

Her eyes widened, startled by the sudden bold statement.

'I mean it,' he went on. 'You're terribly unhappy and you're afraid of what he might do to you. For God's sake, get out while you still can.'

Amy closed her eyes briefly and swallowed hard. 'Do you think I haven't thought of it?' she said almost inaudibly. 'But it was *my fault*, Mike. I forced him into marriage – into this situation. Anything that's happened to him is my fault. And there's Mark now. Alex loves him. I couldn't take his son away from him.'

'You're overrating your own part in this,' Mike said. 'And Alex could have access to his son. After all, how much time does he spend with him now?'

'But – where would I go?'

'You have a job now, Amy. You're independent.' He pressed her fingers lightly. 'And you could always come to me – if you wanted to. And bring Mark of course.'

She looked at him. 'You mean – to the house you share with . . .'

'I mean to a place of our own. Amy, I'm asking you to free yourself and marry me.' For a long moment they looked at each other, then Mike smiled wryly and said, 'Does that sound terrible? I suppose I'm what the Victorians would have called an "unprincipled cad".'

376

She smiled in spite of herself. 'It's not terrible at all, Mike. You're very sweet. I can never repay you for all you've done for me.'

He winced. 'Oh dear, that sounds ominously like the prelude to goodbye.'

'I didn't mean it to. It's just that I'd hate you to feel you have to be responsible for me.'

'But I want to be.' He looked into her eyes. 'I've always loved you, you know,' he said. 'I can hardly remember a time when I didn't. I think it might have started that day we went to London to see your grandmother, and got caught in the air raid.'

She smiled. 'I remember. Did Auntie Marjorie ever find out about that?'

He shook his head. 'She'd have had forty fits if she had. Do you remember the time you came to Rhensham for my eighteenth birthday party?'

'How could I forget?' she said, her eyes misty. 'It was my first grown-up party and I was so shy. You all seemed so sophisticated. Mum chose my dress and I thought it looked so babyish.'

'It was a beautiful dress. You looked like a princess in it.'

She looked up at him. 'You made the evening for me when you said you liked it. And you kissed me. It was my very first kiss – so romantic. I fell head over heels in love on the spot. But later when you were in the Army and came to London you seemed so loftily grown up. And then when you started your job as a journalist, I felt sure that you wouldn't want to be bothered with me any more. Especially when your letters were all full of that girl, Julia Honeywell.'

'Julia Honeywell?' He looked astonished. 'Oh, there was nothing going on there. I admit I had a brief crush on her, but we never really had anything in common. It fizzled out.' He laughed. 'So I was loftily grown up, was I?'

I felt you must be ashamed to be seen with a school kid.'

'What a pair of idiots.' He chuckled. 'That *terrible* convent school uniform.'

She winced. 'Please – don't remind me.'

'I suppose you don't want to be reminded of the time Lily Smith blacked your eye, either.'

She grinned wryly. 'It was after the play, remember? *Twelfth Night*. She thought I'd forgotten my origins and needed taking down a peg. Perhaps I did.'

Their mood lightened and they enjoyed their meal, but later, when they were alone together in the car, Mike turned to her.

'I meant what I said earlier. You still haven't answered.'

377

In the darkness she looked straight ahead, afraid to look into his eyes – afraid that she would see her own longing mirrored there. 'I know you meant it, Mike. And I love you for it.'

'Only for that? Only for meaning it?' He turned her face, making her eyes meet his. 'Just say what you have to say. Just tell me the truth, Amy. Don't worry if the answer is no. I won't get upset and I won't let it spoil our friendship, I promise. I have to know, though.'

With all the courage that was in her she tried to tell him that she didn't love him. But she couldn't. Tonight they had reached a watershed in their relationship. Nothing could ever be the same between them now. She couldn't tell him she would marry him. Yet losing him would be like losing a limb. Not just because he had become a vital lifeline, but because she now knew that the teenage love that had flowered on that lovely August evening had developed into something strong and sweet and infinitely enduring. She drew his face down to hers and kissed him gently.

'Of course it isn't just for that, Mike. I loved you when I was fifteen and I still do – for everything you are. For always. Whatever happens I want you to remember that.'

Flight 218 from Athens circled London airport. Passengers were requested to extinguish their cigarettes and fasten their safety belts in preparation for landing.

Alex swallowed the last of his whisky. He had been drinking ever since take-off. Ever since this morning if the truth were known – and before that. In fact he had hardly stopped for long enough to sober up since arriving in Greece with the cast and crew at the end of December.

Directing the film had not been the happy experience he had expected. Right from the start it had been one long series of catastrophes. To begin with he'd had a severe stomach upset – something to do with the food, or the water, he decided. After that the weather had been against them and there had been endless days of boring inactivity, waiting for the sun to shine. He'd started drinking seriously then – local wine, retsina, ouzo, anything he could get his hands on. There had been a brief and torrid affair with one of the starlets, until he had realised she was just using him to make her cameraman boyfriend jealous. That had led to a sordid brawl in which he had come off worst, collecting a bruised jaw and a warning cable from London. Apparently someone had had the bloody cheek to complain about his behaviour to central office. It was when he found out who that someone was that the real trouble came. After an evening's heavy drinking at the local taverna he'd gone out looking for the offending actor; finally hauling him out of a restaurant where he was dining with friends and challenging him to a fight. But his informant had omitted to point out that the actor in question was the nephew of a major shareholder.

His arbitrary dismissal came by cable. A few words, short and very much to the point. Two days later his replacement arrived and he was on his way home.

An hour after landing he was at the studios, clearing his desk. In the filing cabinet he found a whisky bottle still a quarter full. He took out the hip flask he carried and filled it, tipped the surplus into his mouth, and dropped the empty bottle into the wastepaper basket. His head was pounding with a fury fuelled by alcohol and a sense of injustice that tortured his guts even more painfully than the booze. 'They'll go a long way before they find another director as talented as me,' he muttered as he emptied the desk drawers into his briefcase. All his pre-war experience seemed to count for nothing. 'Inept, short-sighted bloody fools, the lot of them,' he growled. Just because some jumped up little ham took exception to his having a few drinks to break the monotony he was dismissed without warning, like some bloody shop assistant with his fingers in the till. If he'd had any say in the matter that cretinous little stuffed shirt wouldn't have got a job in a bloody sausage factory, never mind a part in a major film. Well, he wouldn't forget. Oh no. 'If ever I get the chance to get even with the little swine I'll do it,' he vowed as he stormed his way out of the building.

He collected his car from the parking lot behind the building and set out on the drive to Mill Hill. It was mid-afternoon and the roads were busy with heavy lorries. His tongue was like thick dry felt in his mouth and his head felt as though it was stuffed with cotton wool. He found it difficult to judge distances and twice other drivers hooted at him for almost hitting them. Finally he decided that what he needed was coffee, strong and black, and he pulled off onto the forecourt of a transport café.

The café was steamy and cheerful. Only a handful of customers sat at the plastic-topped tables. On the counter a radio played some nameless, mind-numbing music. He collected his coffee at the counter and carried it to a table near the window, but his hands were shaking so much that by the time he got there half of it was in the saucer. It was then that his fury suddenly drained away and the reality of his situation hit him. Christ, but he was in a mess. He had no job and no prospect of getting one – all through no fault of his own. He was a brilliant bloody director, damn it. He could knock spots off all the rest of them. Why could no one see it? Why were they all so petty and small-minded? To make matters worse, he had a wife and child at home, dependent on him.

Resting his elbows on the table he dropped his head into his hands. Why in God's name had he taken up with Amy in the first place? Young and naive, her gamin charm had flattered him. At first she had made him feel young and alive again. He'd enjoyed moulding her raw talent and seeing her blossom into a promising actress under his direction. Why on earth couldn't he have left it at that? How could he have been fool enough to fall for such an age-old trick – to let her trap him into a marriage he didn't want? She'd misled and used him all along, just like any little back-street tart on the make.

Mark was the only good thing to come out of it. And now he had let him down. Tears of maudlin self-pity coursed down his cheeks. 'I'm sorry, Chloe,' he muttered. 'I wanted to do well for our boy. And I will. I know you'll help me. Tell me what to do, darling. For Christ's sake, tell me what to do.'

Suddenly he was aware that the radio had stopped playing music and an announcer was introducing the next programme. One of the waitresses called out to another: 'Hey, Doris – it's that new serial. You gonna come and listen, or shall I turn it up?'

Alex looked up to see the two women lean their arms comfortably on the counter and prepare to listen as the introductory music faded and the episode began.

Radio drama. That was an idea. Maybe there might be an opening for him there. It was something he would have to look into. Who did he know at the BBC? Then, while he was still mulling the notion over, his attention was suddenly riveted by the sound of a familiar voice. Good God. He could have sworn ... The coffee machine hissed and spluttered, drowning the radio. When it stopped someone else was speaking.

He downed his half-cold coffee and went to the counter for a refill. As he did so the serial episode came to an end and the announcer began to read out the cast list. Alex found himself listening intently. One or two of the older actors' names were familiar to him. Then, to his astonishment, the announcer said: '*The part of Freda Owen was played by Amethyst Lee.*'

'That'll be fourpence, please sir.' The waitress held out her hand to the stunned-looking man on the other side of the counter. He stared at her.

'What?'

'Fourpence – for the coffee.'

Pushing his hand into his pocket he threw the coins onto the

380

counter and hurried out, his open mackintosh flapping behind him. The girl stared at his retreating back.

'Sir – don't you want your . . . ?' But he'd gone, leaving the door swinging open behind him. Through the window she saw him get into his car and the way he swung off the forecourt onto the road without even looking left or right made her gasp. It was nothing short of suicidal. She sighed and shook her head. *Honestly* – some people. You got all sorts in here.

'You mean you haven't heard it?'

'I'm sorry, no. I haven't.' Maryan had sent one of the girls to make tea for her unexpected visitors. Rachel was so flushed and animated that she felt slightly alarmed. Clearly Sam was concerned about her too.

'There's a radio in the factory,' she went on. 'The girls like to sing along to "Music While You Work". But I'm afraid I can't concentrate if I don't have quiet. I usually close the door while it's playing.'

'Of course you do,' Sam said. He turned to his wife. 'How do you think Maryan can listen to the wireless and do her work properly?' he admonished.

The girl came in with the tray of tea and Maryan poured Rachel a cup and passed it to her, hoping it would help to calm her down.

'It's a new daily serial, you say?' she said. 'And you think Amy is playing one of the parts in it?'

'I don't think, I know.' Rachel leaned forward. 'I ask you – how many people do you know with the name Amethyst?'

'Well, only the one, I admit.'

'And why would Amy take the name of Leigh?'

Sam broke in. 'I bought a copy of the *Radio Times* on the way here,' he said. 'It's spelt L double-e, not L e i g h.'

Rachel waved her hand at him dismissively. 'It could be a printing error. I just know deep inside that this is our Amy – your Amy, Maryan. Even if those silly people at the BBC wouldn't give us her address.'

Seeing Maryan looking puzzled, Sam explained, 'We asked them – on the telephone this morning. It isn't their policy to give addresses. Well, it's hardly surprising, is it? I told Rachel they'd say that but she wouldn't listen.'

'If you were to write a letter,' Rachel went on. 'Addressed to Amethyst Leigh, care of the BBC.'

Maryan hardly knew whether she was on her head or her heels. Just this morning she'd had a telephone call from Roisan – with news so stunning that Maryan had already had difficulty

381

concentrating on her work. Fay had gone. Gone for good, or so Roisan said. She sounded quite sure about it. Vincent was to get his divorce at last. She said mysteriously that she couldn't go into details over the phone but promised to come and visit as soon as she could, adding that she had other news too, and something to show her. Now here was Rachel, insisting that she had found Amy. It was almost too much for one day. Thank heaven for Sam's steadying influence.

Maryan took several deep breaths, trying hard to calm the churning excitement in her stomach. *Mustn't hope for too much*, she warned herself. And yet she couldn't help feeling that there was a distinct possibility that Rachel was right. Amy might well be the person in this radio serial. It was certainly worth investigating further.

'Look,' she said. 'Tomorrow morning I'll make a point of listening to this programme myself. And if I'm convinced that it is Amy, I'll do as you say and write.'

Recharged by several deep pulls from his hip flask, Alex drove like a maniac. Hardly able to focus on the road ahead, he pressed his foot down hard on the accelerator. He was dimly aware of going through two sets of red traffic lights – of angry motorists hooting at him – a lorry driver lowering his window to yell an obscenity. He ignored it all. All he could think of was that Amy had disobeyed – defied him. She was working again.

At the back of his mind and unacknowledged, he burned with the thought that Amy – an inexperienced girl of twenty on whom he had lavished the benefit of all his experience – could find work when he couldn't. It made her the breadwinner. The thought of living on his young wife's earnings was overwhelmingly humiliating. He wouldn't tolerate it.

He told himself that it meant she must be leaving Mark alone. His son – his son and Chloe's – was at the mercy of some stranger. He'd warned her what would happen if she did that again. Well, now he would teach her that he did not make empty threats. She wasn't up to caring for his son. Chloe would never have left their child alone. Amy must suffer the consequences of what she had done.

Net curtains twitched in Willow Drive as the car drew up with a screech of tyres outside number twenty-two and Alex leapt out of the car. The house looked deserted as he let himself in with his key. He sensed that the house was empty as he stood in the hall, but still he ran upstairs two at a time to look into every room, calling in a loud, angry voice for his absent wife.

By the time he re-emerged neighbours were standing at their front doors, peering apprehensively at the wild-eyed man with his flying coat; wondering what could have happened to send him into such a frenzy. They watched as he strode across the road to bang loudly on the door of number twenty-nine with his clenched fist, still shouting his wife's name.

Addie was alone. Jack had gone down to the shops on his bike to collect the weekly grocery order from the Co-op. When she opened the door and Alex pushed his way past her she uttered a frightened little squeak and fell back in alarm.

He strode through the house, throwing doors open to look into all the rooms, then he turned to glare at her. 'Where are they?' he demanded. 'Where is my son?'

Clasping her hands together, Addie shook her head. 'She – they aren't here, Mr Keynan.'

'Where are they then – *where*? Tell me, woman.' Eyes blazing, he advanced towards her and she stepped back, wincing in alarm at the expression on his face, convinced that he was about to attack her.

'They – they aren't here – *really*,' she stammered breathlessly. 'On the days Amy's recording Mark goes to Rosemary's.'

'Rosemary? Rosemary who?' His face dark with anger, Alex grabbed Addie's wrist and twisted it painfully. 'What has that bitch done with the child? *Tell* me, woman. It's my son we're talking about, for Christ's sake.'

'She – it's Mrs Carter,' Addie said, her teeth chattering with fear.

'*Where*? Where does she live? Come on – come *on*.'

'N-number eight M-meadow Walk.'

Rubbing her bruised wrist, Addie watched as he ran down the path and jumped into his car. What on earth was the matter with the man? she asked herself. Fighting drunk at four o'clock in the afternoon. He'd absolutely reeked of drink. It was disgusting. Who did he think he was, bursting into people's homes, shouting and manhandling her like that? And what would he do to poor little Amy when he found her? She wondered if she should call the police. But they never interfered in domestic matters, did they? Should she ring Rosemary Carter? Jack would tell her not to get involved, and maybe he was right. She chewed her lip apprehensively. All the same . . .

Amy's heart was light as she sipped her cup of tea. Through the window she could see Mark playing happily in the sandpit with Rosemary's other three charges in the sunny back garden. Spring was well and truly here now. The trees were bursting with new leaf and blossom and the birds were singing. Life was good again. It had a pattern and a purpose.

'I don't know when I've had a happier little boy,' Rosemary was saying. 'He really enjoys being with the other children and he's so good at sharing the toys.' She laughed. 'Except that teddy of his, of course. He never lets that out of his sight. But then they all have a favourite toy, don't they? By the time he goes to school he'll be quite used to mixing with other children.' She smiled at Amy. 'We all listen to you in the mornings, you know. I get the children their elevenses and we all sit down to hear Mark's mummy on the wireless. You should see his little face light up when he hears your voice.'

Amy laughed. 'Thank you. It's nice to know that someone is out there listening.'

'Oh, I'm sure you have a huge audience,' Rosemary assured her. 'Everyone I've spoken to says how much they enjoy "This Year, Next Year".' She looked out of the window. 'But here I am, chattering on when you'll be wanting to take Mark home and give him his tea.'

'I do like to spend some time with him before bed when I've been away all day.'

'Of course you do. I'll get him for you.'

Mark's eyes lit up when he saw his mummy waiting to take him home. He chattered to her as she fastened his coat, telling her in his baby way what he'd been doing all day, and what Teddy had been doing too.

They'd just stepped through the gate when a car stopped two doors down the road. When it began to reverse at speed, Amy pulled the child out of the way to avoid the back wheels as they mounted the pavement.

From where she stood at the front door, Rosemary watched with horror as a man leapt from the car and snatched Mark from Amy's arms, bundling the terrified child into the back of the car. Then, as Amy made to join him, he grabbed her roughly by the collar of her coat and pushed her into the front passenger seat. A moment later, before a shocked Rosemary could do anything, the car roared off at speed, leaving her watching helplessly from her doorway.

Rigid with terror, Amy hardly dared to look as they careered into the main road without stopping, narrowly missing a passing car and tipping a cyclist onto the pavement.

'Alex, for God's sake, be *careful*! What's the matter with you?' Gritting her teeth, she held tightly to the sides of her seat as the car wove perilously in and out of the traffic. 'Why are you here, Alex? What's wrong?'

'*What's wrong?*' he mimicked. 'You might well ask.'

She glanced at him, alarmed by his strange grey-green pallor. There were beads of sweat on his forehead and his lips were drawn back from his teeth in a menacing travesty of a smile. Alone in the back seat, Mark was being thrown about like a shuttlecock by Alex's erratic driving. He was wailing loudly with fear and calling out for her. Amy turned in her seat and tried in vain to comfort him.

'It's all right, darling. We'll soon be home.' But the baby's wails drowned her soothing. She turned to Alex. 'Please stop,' she pleaded. 'You've been drinking. You don't know what you're doing.'

'I know what I'm doing all right.' He threw her a look of pure hatred, so ferocious that it made her recoil. 'Of course I've been drinking, you bitch – driven to it by you. Why didn't you tell me you'd taken a job? You can have no idea what you sound like in that rubbishy thing. Like some guttersnipe hamming it up in a village hall. How do you think I felt, sitting in some tatty transport café, hearing my wife making a fool of herself? And knowing that half the bloody country knew about it before I did. That must have given you the best laugh of all.'

She bit her lip. So that was it. 'I'm sorry, Alex. I should have told you. And I would have. It was just that . . .'

'That you knew I'd put a stop to it – right?' He turned to glare at her with bloodshot eyes. 'Well, if you want to make a fool of yourself, do it. I don't give a damn any more. You're a selfish little cow and you always were. But I won't have you farming my son out on some idiot stranger. I told you what would happen if you ever did that again, and by God I mean to see that it does.'

'Alex, *don't*. It's not like you think. You can't imagine how lonely I've been – how frustrated, alone in that house with you away all the time. It's wonderful to be working again. It's not doing Mark any harm . . . *Oh* . . .' She gasped as he swung the car across the road directly into the path of an oncoming lorry. The lorry's brakes screeched and the driver leaned out of his cab to hurl abuse at Alex. There was a thud, followed by a scream as Mark fell from the back seat onto the floor.

'*Alex!* For God's sake, stop. You've hurt Mark now.'

The little boy was wailing with pain and bewilderment at what was happening to him. But the child's cries only served to anger Alex even more. As the car lurched forward again he rounded on Amy.

'*I've* hurt him? That's rich. It's you who's hurt him. If he's crying

385

it's because of what *you've* done to him – to Chloe's child. He's all I have left of her, but what do you care? Dumping him like a parcel of rubbish, anywhere that suits you. You've done it on purpose, haven't you? You've done it to get back at me – at *us* – me and Chloe. But you shan't have our child. *We won't let you.* Do you hear?'

Cold with fear, Amy stared at him. What was he talking about? His eyes were wild, the pupils dilated. He was completely out of control – living in some fantasy of his own making. Did he even know what he was saying? Had the drink fuddled him so much that he'd lost his mind? How could she reason with him in this state?

They were speeding through the tree-lined streets of the estate now. Children were playing outside after school. A ball ran into the road and a little girl stepped out from between parked cars to retrieve it. Amy screamed, clenching her fists and closing her eyes, waiting for the inevitable horror. But the child jumped back in time and somehow the accident was miraculously avoided. Next time – oh God, next time they wouldn't be as lucky.

She turned and pleaded with him, her voice thick with tears. 'Please. Oh, *please*, Alex. You must stop and listen to me. We can talk this out quietly at home. I can make you see, if only you'll calm down. Please – *please* stop before you kill someone. If not for me then for Mark. He's hurt. Can't you hear him?'

They had turned into Willow Drive now and suddenly Alex stood on the brakes. The tyres shrieked and the car shuddered to a halt, throwing Amy forward so violently that her forehead met the windscreen with a dizzying thud.

'*Get out*,' he snapped. 'Go on, get out – *now*, before I throw you out.'

Her head still spinning with the pain, she opened the door and got out of the car on trembling legs, almost weeping with relief. Thank God he'd listened to reason at last. She reached for the handle of the rear door to get Mark but before she could open it Alex slammed the car into gear and revved the engine. With a roar the car leapt forward, gathering speed as it roared down the road.

In a blind panic, she ran after it, her arms outstretched, oblivious to the blood trickling down her face from the cut on her forehead. In vain she screamed for him to stop. She could see Mark standing on the back seat, looking out of the rear window as the car sped away. His little face contorted with terror, he held out his arms to her as the distance between them lengthened. As it rounded the corner and disappeared Amy staggered to a stop. Her legs gave way beneath her and she sank to her knees on the road, tears coursing down her cheeks.

386

'Mark. Oh, Mark – my baby. Oh God – *God*, what shall I do?'

Shocked neighbours, who had watched the incident helplessly from their front windows, ran out to help, but it was Addie who was first at her side. She helped the almost hysterical girl to her feet and wrapped her arms tightly around her.

'There, there, luvvie. It'll be all right, you'll see. You come home with me. Jack's already ringing the police. They'll catch him, never you fear.'

She hugged the sobbing girl close, reproaching herself. She'd always known something like this would happen some day. Why hadn't she tried to help – to warn her? If anything happened to that kiddie now she'd never forgive herself.

Chapter Twenty

'I've put her to bed in the spare room.'

Jack looked up at his wife as she came into the room. 'I doubt if she'll sleep.'

'She will. I made her some Ovaltine and I dissolved one of my sleeping tablets in it.'

Jack shook his head. 'You shouldn't have done that. Suppose the police come and want to speak to her?'

'The girl needs rest more than anything else at the moment. She's worn out.' Addie sank into her armchair with a sigh. 'And let's face it, it isn't likely to be good news, is it? The way that maniac was driving.' Her face crumpled. 'Oh, Jack, I'll never forget seeing her running down the road, screaming for the baby, blood running down her face – I thought my heart would stop. If only I'd had the sense to do something earlier. When he came here throwing his weight about I could see he was drunk. I might have been able to stop him. That poor girl.'

'Come on now, love. Don't take on like that. There's no sense in blaming yourself,' Jack said. 'It's a good thing I never forget car numbers. The police'll soon get onto him with what I was able to tell them, never you fear.'

'But the kiddie – little Mark. Thrown about in the back of that car like a pea on a drum, poor little mite.' She sighed. 'I always knew that marriage was all wrong. Didn't I always say so? May and September. It never works. That girl needs her mother at a time like this.'

Jack nodded. 'D'you know where you can get hold of her?'

'I asked her. She never said so, but I got the feeling she'd like to see her mum. It's only natural. But she said she wasn't sure where she lived any more. Seems they had a falling out some years ago and haven't been in touch since. She did give me the name of a friend

388

who might know, though. A Mrs Freer.'

'Some relation?' Jack asked.

'I don't know. She called her – now what was it?' Addie frowned. 'Ro-sheen, or some such queer name. It's an address in Notting Hill. Do you think I should phone?'

Jack nodded. 'I do, love. Sooner the girl has someone of her own with her, the better.'

Maryan was sitting at the table in her flat, carefully composing a letter to Amy. On the table before her the envelope lay, addressed, as Rachel had suggested, care of the BBC. As she had promised, she'd listened to the radio serial that morning and was convinced beyond a doubt that Rachel had been right; the voice was Amy's. But in spite of her desire to get in touch with her again, the letter was proving hard to write.

There was so much she wanted to say, that was the trouble. How did one put into a letter the regrets of a lifetime, and the reasons for them? Also, she had to keep reminding herself that it wasn't a girl she was writing to. At Amy's age three years made the difference between girlhood and womanhood. And Amy had become a wife and a mother since they last set eyes on each other. She didn't want to make her feel obliged to see her again. Yet at the same time she didn't want to appear diffident. There had been too much of that in the past.

She wanted, more than anything in the world, to see Amy again. She had no illusions. She knew there was no hope of making up all they had lost as mother and daughter. But at least they could try to make a fresh start – as equals – two grown women with a blood link. She was sure they could make it work, if only Amy was as willing as she was to try.

But how did she put all this down on paper? She read through what she had written, then, with an impatient gesture, she tore the top sheet off the pad and screwed it into a ball, tossing it into the already overflowing basket. The written words sounded so trite – false, almost. Why was it so hard to put on paper things that seemed so simple in your heart?

She was starting again when the telephone rang. With a sigh, she put down the pen and went to answer it.

'Maryan – it's Roisan.'

'Roisan. How are you?'

'Listen, dear, I have news.'

'So do I. I think I know where to find Amy. I was just . . .'

'Mine isn't good news, I'm afraid,' Roisan interrupted. 'And I'm

389

afraid it concerns Amy.'

Maryan's legs trembled beneath her. 'What is it?'

'I would have come over instead of ringing.' Roisan sounded strained. 'I hate having to tell you on the phone like this, but it was the quickest way. I think – I know you'll want to go to her as soon as you can.'

'She's hurt? In hospital?'

'No, *no*. It's nothing like that. Listen, Maryan. It seems that Amy's husband has abducted their child – driven off with him in the car. I don't know the full details, but there appears to have been some kind of disagreement. The worst aspect of the situation is that he was very drunk as well as angry at the time.'

'My God. When was this?'

'This afternoon. About three hours ago. The police are out looking for him now.'

Maryan sank onto a chair, her knuckles white as she gripped the receiver. 'Oh dear God, poor Amy. Just tell me where she is. I'll go at once.'

'It's Mill Hill. She's being comforted by a neighbour – a Mrs Shaw, at twenty-nine Willow Drive . . . Maryan . . .'

'Yes?'

'You remember last time we spoke I told you I had something to tell you? Well, it was this: there were three letters from Amy, addressed to you at Simons Mews. I found them in Fay's handbag when she was taken ill. One was a card to tell you about the baby's birth.'

So she *had* written. Maryan bit her lip hard. Amy had written and Fay had opened the letters and then deliberately kept them back. That was how she knew so much. And when she received no replies – what must Amy have thought?

'Maryan – are you still there?' Roisan sounded anxious.

'Yes. I'm still here.' Maryan took a deep breath to steady her emotions. 'Thank you for letting me know, Roisan. I'll get a taxi and go at once.'

'You'll let me know if there's anything I can do, won't you? And keep me informed about what happens?'

'Of course I will. Thanks again for letting me know. Goodbye, Roisan.'

When Amy opened her eyes and saw her mother sitting beside the bed she thought at first that she was still dreaming. She closed her eyes, then opened them again.

'Mum?' She framed the word tentatively.

390

'Yes, it's me, love. Your friend Mrs Shaw rang Roisan and she got in touch with me.'

Slowly the reason she was here in Addie Shaw's spare room filtered back into Amy's mind. Filled with sudden alarm she sat up. 'What time is it? What's happened? Have the police found Mark?'

'No, love. Not yet. It's eleven o'clock. Mr and Mrs Shaw have gone to bed.' Maryan put her arms round Amy. It seemed so right and natural to hold her own child. And Amy didn't stiffen in her arms or turn from her. Instead she returned the embrace gratefully, pressing her face into her mother's shoulder.

'Oh, Mum. They *will* find him, won't they? Alex wouldn't hurt him. Not on purpose. I know he wouldn't.'

'Of course they'll find him, love. Everything will be all right. You'll see.'

For a long moment the two women held each other, each drawing comfort from the other. Then Amy drew back to look into her mother's face.

'I did write to you, Mum – after I left home and again when I was married – when Mark was born. Didn't you get my letters?'

Maryan shook her head. 'No, love. Fay Donlan didn't send them on. It was only recently that Roisan found them. It's a long story. One that needn't worry you now. I'm here with you. That's all that matters. We must concentrate on getting that baby back, then we'll talk.'

But Amy shook her head. 'No. I want to talk now. I daren't let myself think – about Mark and Alex – about what might happen. Don't let me think about it, Mum.' She looked at her mother. 'You've been on my mind such a lot lately. I wanted you to get in touch again. I thought that if you heard me on the radio you might . . .'

'I *did* hear you. At least, it was Sam and Rachel Leigh who heard you first and told me. They were so excited. They want to find you too, Amy.'

Amy looked puzzled. 'They do? But why?'

'Rachel has accepted that you're Marcus's daughter now.' Maryan sighed. 'I chose the wrong time to tell them. Rachel was still deeply shocked by Marcus's death. Sam always believed you were his granddaughter, though. He never lost touch, you know. He always made sure we were both all right. It was he who paid your school fees.'

'Oh, Mum. If only you'd told me. I imagined – well, you know what I imagined.'

'I know, love. I've made so many mistakes. Too many.' She took

391

Amy's hand. 'I want so much to make it all up to you, if you'll let me.'

'I wish we'd talked more,' Amy said. 'All those years in the war, when I was at Rhensham. We hardly knew each other. Your work seemed to mean more to you than I did. Then when I found out that Marcus Leigh was my father I was so confused. And when you didn't talk to me about it I thought it was because you didn't understand – or even care how I felt.' She shook her head. 'Since I married Alex I've seen things differently. Since Mark was born and I've spent so much time alone, I've understood what a struggle you must have had and what you must have gone through.'

Maryan nodded. 'Yes, it was a struggle in those early days, trying to keep the four of us together – you and Tom, your grandma and me. Tom felt it so badly, me being the breadwinner. He felt so useless and I did nothing to help him feel better. I regret that. He was a good man, taking on another man's child, and he loved you every bit as much as a true father would, Amy. Every bit.'

'I know, Mum. I remember that.'

'My worst mistake was in thinking I could cover up what I did – pretend it hadn't happened. Two wrongs can never *ever* make a right.' Maryan sighed. 'It was just that you and Tom were so close. After he was killed I couldn't bring myself to tell you he wasn't your real father.'

'Did he – Marcus, know about me?' Amy asked.

Maryan smiled gently. 'I never told him – or anyone else till that night at the Leighs'. But I've found since that he'd guessed. Too late for both of us, he guessed.'

Amy was silent for a moment. 'At least you didn't force him to marry you,' she said softly. 'That might have turned out worse. It's what I did to Alex. That was *my* worst mistake. 'It's terrible to be married to the wrong man, especially when you love him. And now I know how it feels to – to lose your child.' Her voice faltered and Maryan drew her close again.

'You mustn't say that. You haven't lost him.' *And, please God, you're not going to*, she added silently. Inwardly she was asking herself impatiently what the police could possibly be doing all this time – and why they hadn't found Alex Keynan's car when Jack Shaw had given them the colour, make and registration number. How much more could they need? Unless – unless . . . She closed her eyes, shutting out the unthinkable possibility. Somehow they were going to have to get through the night – somehow she must help Amy pass the dark hours still to come in any way she could.

'We've got some catching up to do, you and me,' she said

392

cheerfully. 'Such a lot has happened to me. Some good and some bad. I hardly know where to start. I want to hear about your last three years too. Shall I start, or will you?'

Amy needed little encouragement to talk. She told her mother about her brief stage career and the powerful attraction Alex Keynan had held for her, first as mentor, then as lover; the fiery passion so quickly roused, only to be extinguished by Alex's inability to love her. She told her about his first tragic marriage and how he had never recovered from it; the shattering disillusionment and loneliness marriage had brought them both and, overriding all, the sense of guilt she felt for causing Alex's decline into bitterness and alcoholism.

'He wasn't ready to share his life with anyone else, Mum,' she said. 'And I don't think he ever will be. I was too young and naive to realise it at the time. Even when he told me I wouldn't believe him. I was so sure I could take her place – make it all up to him. But I was wrong – so *wrong*. I think he must be going through some kind of breakdown. I'm afraid it's been coming on for some time. And the awful thing is that I caused it.'

'No, Amy. I'm sure you did your best to bring him happiness,' Maryan said. 'You mustn't blame yourself. Tell me about the happier things – about Mark – your baby.'

Amy went on to talk about Mark and what a joy he was, then about her renewed friendship with Mike and how getting the part in the radio serial had helped to restore her self-confidence. Talking seemed to relieve some of her tension and when she had finished she lay back against the pillow again, looking more relaxed.

'You tell me your news now,' she invited. 'Where did you go after Mrs Donlan took your job and moved into the flat?'

Maryan started at the beginning, filling in the years they'd been apart. When she'd finished Amy smiled. 'You've done well, Mum, haven't you? You've come such a long way since we lived in Crimea Terrace. I wish . . .'

She trailed off, looking uncertain and Maryan said: 'Yes, what do you wish?'

'I wish you'd tell me about Marcus Leigh. I hardly remember him and I want to know so much – what he was really like; how you fell in love; his bravery in the war and how he died. I've wished so often that I knew more about the man who was my father.'

Maryan was reminded sharply of the words Marcus had written to her in his letter. His last words: *Speak to her of me sometimes*. She began haltingly, but once into her story the words poured forth. She talked until her mouth and throat were dry and her eyes stung with fatigue and the unshed tears of the past years. It was so long since she had talked about Marcus – or even thought about him as anything but a sweet and distant memory. And as she unfolded his story to Amy something seemed to happen. Just for a while it was almost as though he was alive again, sitting there beside her, smiling his approval. It gave her a sense of peace that she hadn't known for a long time.

It was only when the first pale rays of early morning sun began to lighten the room that she realised how long she had been talking. She looked at Amy and saw that she was sleeping. One minute she had been listening intently – the next she was fast asleep; all the anxiety and fear smoothed from her face.

Creeping silently out into the landing Maryan went into the bathroom, splashed her face with cool water and ran a comb through her hair. Then she went downstairs to the kitchen.

Addie was already up. Clad in her dressing gown, her grey hair tightly wound in curlers, she was filling the kettle at the sink. She turned when Maryan came in and raised an enquiring eyebrow.

'How is she?'

'Sleeping. We talked for most of the night. I think it did her good to get things off her chest.'

'Doesn't sound as though you got much rest,' Addie remarked. 'Got to admit I hardly closed an eye myself.' She spooned tea into the pot. 'Still, nice cup of tea, eh? That'll soon put us to rights.'

It was while they were drinking it at the kitchen table that the front doorbell rang. The two women exchanged a startled, apprehensive glance.

'Better go,' Addie said jumping to her feet. 'Don't want the whole house roused, do we?'

A young policeman stood on the doorstep. Behind him hovered a WPC. Both looked uneasy. From where she stood behind Addie in the hall, Maryan saw the young constable remove his helmet and finger his collar nervously.

'Mrs Keynan?' he said, looking from one to the other. 'Mrs Amy Keynan?'

'You've got news?' Addie asked.

Maryan stepped forward. 'I'm her mother,' she said. 'She's sleeping at the moment. If there's any news – bad news, perhaps you'd better tell me first.'

Addie led them both into the living room where the young policeman stood in the middle of the carpet, shifting his weight from one foot to the other.

'You've found them?' Addie prompted. 'The car – Mr Keynan and the baby?'

'We've – found a car.' The policeman cleared his throat. 'We have reason to believe it may be the car in question, but . . .'

'But my hubby gave you the number,' Addie interrupted. 'And the colour and make. You must surely know whether it's his or not.'

'This car was totally burned out when we found it, I'm afraid,' he said. 'Apparently it had hit a tree and burst into flames on impact. It was on a quiet country road about ten miles north of Chelmsford. There were no houses within a couple of miles, so no one had seen or heard anything. A farm worker found it on his way to work. We think it must have happened late last night.'

'And the driver? The – the occupants?' Maryan's mouth was suddenly so dry that she could hardly get the words out. She saw the policeman's Adam's apple bob up and down as he swallowed hard.

'The driver's – er – body was found at the wheel, I'm sorry to say, madam. The doors of the car had burst open and there were some items scattered nearby. One was a briefcase. It was badly charred but some of the contents were readable. Mr Keynan's name was on some of the papers.'

'Oh, my dear Lord.' Addie sat down with a bump and clasped her hand to her mouth.

'And – the baby?' Maryan whispered, her face ashen.

'There was no sign of it – *him*,' the policeman said. 'But with a very small child it's hardly . . .' Unable to finish the sentence he trailed off, looking at his feet. Nudged by his woman colleague, he went on: 'There was another item found near the car, though. Perhaps you might be able to identify it.'

The WPC stepped forward. Unzipping her shoulder bag, she produced a small, half-burned teddy bear. Maryan looked at Addie who nodded, then began to sob noisily.

'*That's Mark's.*' They all turned to see Amy standing in the doorway. White-faced, she stepped into the room and held out her hand. 'That is my son's. He never goes – never went anywhere without it. May I have it, please?'

Dry-eyed, she took the charred toy from the policewoman's hands.

Maryan hurried across the room to her. 'Amy – love . . .' But before her hands reached out to catch her Amy had slipped silently to the floor.

It was late afternoon when the police car turned into Willow Drive and stopped outside number twenty-two. In the back the elderly couple peered out of the window.

'Yes, this is the house, George,' the woman sated. 'Don't you remember? We came here to visit Alex's parents in '41. I wonder if they're still alive? They were getting on in years then if I remember rightly.'

George Downes nodded. The journey had been long and his arthritis was playing up from sitting all that time. 'Yes, yes, I'm sure you're right,' he said tetchily. 'Shall we go in and get this business over with? I'm sure the inspector and his assistant here are anxious to get back to the station.'

The policeman driving the car winked at his female colleague and turned to them with a smile. 'Thanks for the promotion, but it's sergeant, sir, not inspector. And we're not in any hurry at the moment so you can take your time.'

He got out of the car and helped the couple out, first the man, who leaned heavily on his stick, then the elderly lady, who stood on the pavement looking at him apprehensively.

'What about the – er?'

'WPC Jennings had better wait here, I think, madam. It would be better to explain things first,' the sergeant advised.

It was Maryan who opened the door. She'd persuaded Amy to go up and rest and she found the interruption irritating. 'Yes?' She glanced towards the stairs. 'Do you think you could come into the living room? And could you keep your voices down, please? My daughter's terribly distressed and I've just got her off to sleep.'

The policeman stepped inside and removed his hat respectfully. 'I take it your daughter is Mrs Amy Keynan?'

'That's right.'

'This lady and gentleman are Mr and Mrs Downes,' he said. 'They have something of importance to tell you.'

Maryan closed the door and invited them to sit down. Kate Downes began: 'Our daughter, Chloe, was Alex Keynan's first wife,' she explained. 'She was killed in the blitz, poor lamb, shortly after they married in 1941. Alex was badly cut up about losing her. He didn't seem to care much about anything or anybody afterwards and we lost touch with him after a while. It must be all of ten years since we saw him last – until he turned up on our doorstep right out of the blue late yesterday evening.'

Maryan's interest was instantly aroused. 'You *saw* him – yesterday?'

'Yes. We still live in the village in Essex where Chloe was born, you see. We don't get many visitors nowadays and it was really extraordinary, his turning up like that. He'd changed quite a lot and just at first I couldn't think who he was.' She shook her head. 'Not that he gave me time. He just rang the bell and when I opened the door he pushed this sleeping child into my arms. "This is Chloe's son," he said. "I want you to take care of him for me." Then he was gone – just like that. Well, it gave me a terrible turn, him saying a thing like that. And of course we knew right away there must be something badly wrong. Alex looked so strange. Tired and sort of wild-eyed. I was about to ask him in, but before I got the chance he'd jumped into his car and driven off as though the hounds of hell were after him.'

George Downes took up the story. 'The child woke up in a distressed state. When my wife undressed him we saw that he had a few bruises too. We didn't know what to do for the best. My wife fed and comforted him as best she could and after she'd put him to bed we talked it over and decided that our best course would be to notify the police and take him to the local hospital.'

'It was then that we heard the dreadful news about poor Alex,' his wife put in. 'The accident must have happened when he was on his way back to London. Thank God he left the child with us.'

Maryan was on her feet. 'Where is the baby? Is he still in hospital?'

'No. He's fine, madam,' the policeman reassured her. 'He's been thoroughly checked over by a doctor and apart from one or two bruises he's none the worse. He's in the car with a WPC at this moment. Mr and Mrs Downes insisted on coming to see him safely home with his mother – them being slightly connected, as it were.'

Maryan shook hands with them both. 'Thank you so much for what you've done,' she said. 'It was very good of you to make the journey. You have no idea what this is going to mean to my daughter. It's like the answer to a prayer.'

Kate Downes smiled. 'I'm so grateful that Alex thought of us,' she said. 'Even if his mind was confused into believing the baby was Chloe's, at least his concern was to make sure the child was safe.' She smiled wistfully at Maryan. 'You're very lucky, my dear. He's a dear little boy. I only wish he was our grandchild.'

Mark seemed none the worse for his ordeal. When the police-woman put him into Maryan's arms he struggled impatiently to the floor, clearly happy to be home again. He made straight for his toy box and was soon playing happily as though nothing had happened.

After saying goodbye to her visitors, Maryan sat down and looked at her grandson for the first time. Thank God he was safe. He was a beautiful child, so much like Amy at the same age that she felt her throat tighten. Her grandson. And Marcus's. How he would have loved him. What did the future hold for him? she asked herself, watching him play. Riches and happiness, success and love? Love above everything, please God, she prayed silently. All the rest is empty without it.

She held out her arms to the little boy. 'Mark – come to Grandma,' she invited, marvelling at how natural the name sounded on her lips.

He stood looking shyly at her for a moment, studying her face solemnly as though weighing her up. Than he dropped the toy he was holding and toddled towards her, a big grin on his baby face. Laughing, Maryan scooped him into her arms and hugged him close, tears of thankfulness slipping down her cheeks.

'Oh, your mummy is going to be *so* pleased to see you,' she said, nuzzling his soft little neck. 'Shall we go and wake her? Shall we go and give your mummy the biggest, *best* surprise she's ever had?'

He smiled. 'Mummy,' he said eagerly. 'Want to see Mummy.'

At the inquest, held to determine the reason for Alex's tragic end, the verdict was 'accidental death'. Maryan was relieved and grateful. If there had been the slightest suspicion that he had taken his own life Amy would probably have blamed herself for the rest of her life. It would have clouded her future and prevented her from going forward. Now, once over the trauma of it all, she would be free to pick up the pieces and make a new start.

Once the funeral was over Maryan persuaded Amy to close up the house in Mill Hill and return with her to Hackney, but for the first few weeks the girl went about her life as though in a kind of daze. She hardly let Mark out of her sight, panicking if they were parted even for a minute. Maryan would often wake in the night to hear her getting up to go into his room, just to reassure herself that he was still there. In spite of her mother's attempts to get her interested in the world outside she remained indoors, engrossing herself in her small son to the exclusion of all else.

Maryan found Mike Taylor a godsend. He was an almost daily visitor, bringing Amy small gifts of fruit or flowers; sometimes a book he thought she would enjoy. And perhaps best of all, he brought news from outside – from the world she seemed to have turned her back on – snippets of news and gossip about his work and colleagues, many of whom Amy knew; things to surprise her and make her smile and look up with the first sparks of interest. Gradually, as the weeks passed she began to come round to the idea of returning to work. The producers of 'This Year, Next Year' had been kind and considerate. She had been written out of the story temporarily to allow her time to recover from her tragedy, and Maryan was afraid that if she kept them waiting too long she might lose the job she had prized so much. But thanks to Mike's patience and good sense she eventually agreed to return. Once the decision was made her energy and enthusiasm began to return and she immersed herself totally in her part again.

Soon she was studying her scripts as meticulously as ever and making the two trips to the BBC each week to rehearse and record. Everyone remarked on how brave she was to throw herself so wholeheartedly into her work, but Maryan understood that the work Amy loved gave her a sense of normality – reassured her that she was still a person in her own right with a positive pattern to her life.

On the days when Amy went to the West End to work, Maryan brought her own work from Feldman's home, so that she could care for Mark. He was a contented child and truth to tell she enjoyed having the opportunity to care for him. There had been precious little time to enjoy Amy when she was little.

On the days that Sam came up to Hackney he often brought Rachel with him. The elderly couple were totally bewitched by their small great-grandson, and loved to spend as much time with him as they could. Rachel's health even seemed to improve with her new interest. Maryan was astonished at the way the years fell away from her as her relationship with the little boy developed and grew stronger.

Mike was Amy's constant companion and support. He was attentive and infinitely patient; never expecting too much of her; making sure that she ate properly on her working days, and did not tire herself too much. Whenever his own work allowed he would drive her home after work, and gradually, as time went by, he persuaded her to go out with him in the evenings, at first for short drives in the car and perhaps a quiet drink, then to the theatre or cinema. Finally one evening, to Maryan's delight, he managed to coax her into dressing up and going out for dinner.

He took her to the restaurant down by the river in Richmond where they'd dined to celebrate the first episode of 'This Year, Next Year'. It was a mild evening in early November and the restaurant was quiet and intimate. Maryan had persuaded Amy to buy a new dress for the occasion, and she had chosen a soft wool skirt in garnet red with a white lace blouse. Mike thought she had never looked more beautiful. The past months had brought a new maturity to her. Her face had lost some of its youthful softness. There were shadows under her cheekbones and soft smudges still beneath her eyes. But for Mike they seemed to give her a new beauty, a quiet dignity which, although born of her traumatic ordeal, gave her a new enigmatic quality that he found irresistible.

As they sipped their pre-dinner drinks he reached for her hand. 'Amy – in all this time you haven't talked to me about how you really feel, about – what happened. Maybe you should. If you want to get things off your chest, you know I'm always ready to listen, don't you?'

She smiled at him. 'I know, Mike. You've been wonderful, and so has Mum. I could never have got through it without the two of you. But I've talked as much as I want to. Nothing can ever undo what happened to poor Alex. In a strange way I think it was somehow inevitable. It was what he wanted. He was so unhappy.'

He nodded. 'Just as long as you don't still feel that you were the cause of it all. Or that you have to spend your life in eternal limbo because of it.'

She shook her head. 'I don't feel that any more. I know I have to put it behind me now and make a new life, for Mark's sake as much as mine.'

He looked at her for a long moment. 'That brings me to what I want to say. Amy – I once asked you to leave Alex and marry me. I've felt my own particular guilt over that. But it doesn't make me want you any the less.' He looked into her eyes. 'Maybe it isn't the right moment. Maybe there's no such thing as the right moment, I don't know. But will you at least think about it? I want you to know that however long I have to wait I'll never change my mind. I'll always love you and want you.'

She curled her fingers round his and squeezed them tightly. 'I told you once, Mike, that I'll always love you. Without you this whole nightmare would have been intolerable.' She lowered her eyes. 'But maybe we should both take time to think it through. You'd be taking on a package, you know. Not just a wife but a stepson too.'

'Do you think I haven't thought of that? You know I love Mark. I'll do my best to be a good father to him.'

'But you wouldn't be his *real* father, Mike.' She looked up at him honestly. 'I'd have to make that a condition. I was kept in the dark about my own real father. I remember what I felt when I found out the truth. I've promised myself that I'll never let that happen to Mark. Alex taught me so much. If only what I felt for him hadn't got in the way he would have taught me much more – about my craft. He was a brilliant director, you know. I'll always want Mark to know about that side of him and be proud.' She looked up at him. 'Do you think you could come to terms with that?'

'Of course. I agree, absolutely.' He looked into her eyes. 'So . . . ?'

She shook her head. 'I don't know, Mike. It's still a bit too soon. Is it unfair to ask you to have a little more patience with me? I married too hastily before and it ended in tragedy.' She held up her hand as he made to speak. 'Oh, I know this is different. We've known each other most of our lives, and I do love you – truly. But I need a little more time – just to be certain. For your sake as well as mine.'

Swallowing his disappointment, he smiled, leaning across to kiss her lightly. 'Take as long as you need, darling. When you decide I'll still be here, waiting.' His eyes sparkled with a hint of mischief. 'I'm making one condition of my own, though.'

'Yes?'

'When and if you decide you want to marry me, *you* propose to *me*.'

She laughed. 'All right, it's a deal.' She held both of his hands. 'I'll make you a solemn promise, Mike. There'll only ever be one man I can marry and that's you. There will never be anyone else I could love or trust more.' Her eyes glowed softly as they looked into his. 'You are my first love, my last love and my very best friend.' She raised her glass. 'So – just for now, shall we drink to that, Mike? To us – first, last and always.'

Mike smiled and whispered, 'To us – first, last and always.' And as they sipped their wine they each made a silent pledge of their own.

On Amy's twenty-first birthday the following February, Sam and Rachel gave her a dinner party at Whitegates. At the end of the meal Sam proposed a toast to her, wishing her long life and happiness, and when Amy got to her feet everyone looked at her, faces upturned, as they waited expectantly for her response.

'First, I'd like to thank you all for being here this evening,' she began. 'And especially my grandparents for giving me this lovely dinner party. I owe very special thanks to Mum for her help and support over the past months – and to Mike too . . .' She looked across the table at him, fingering her glass nervously. 'Mike for whom I now have a very special question.'

The guests were silent as they waited for what was to come, but already Mike's eyes were beginning to sparkle in anticipation. Amy went on: 'A few weeks ago Mike did me the honour of asking me to marry him. I told him I needed time to think. I promised him I'd tell him when I'd come to a decision. Well, now I have and I want you all to be witnesses to what I'm about to say to him.' Looking

401

directly at Mike, she said, 'Michael Taylor, will you marry me, please?'

Instantly he was on his feet, his arms around her, to the delight of the onlookers who laughed and clapped. Maryan surreptitiously brushed a tear from her cheek. It was what she had prayed for. The perfect happy ending.

The wedding took place in April at a small ceremony in the village church at Rhensham. It was what Amy wanted and Maryan had been eager to fall in with her wishes. Rhensham was the place where she had known the most happiness. It was where she had grown up; where she and Mike had met as children. And now neither of them blamed that on anything but the war.

The church looked beautiful, decorated with spring flowers, and Amy looked radiantly happy in a cream dress and picture hat. Marjorie Taylor had offered Mitcham Lodge for the reception and she and Maryan shared the preparations equally.

Although it was a quiet wedding no one had been left out. The entire cast of 'This Year, Next Year' was there, plus Mike's colleagues from the newsroom. Celia came down from York to be Amy's only bridesmaid, bringing her fiancé with her. Sam and Rachel; Vincent and Roisan, and the Shaws came. Even Gina flew over from Paris to join Maryan in celebrating her daughter's wedding.

After the telegrams had been read, the toasts proposed and the cake cut, Maryan slipped out into the garden to be by herself for a while. Finding the little seat under the willow tree, she sat down to assess the past year and the future. On Amy's twenty-first birthday Sam and Rachel had presented her with a cheque for the money Rachel had invested for her from Marcus's estate. And Sam had announced that they had willed Feldman Fashions to their great-grandson, Mark.

Over the past few months, due to her success in the daily serial, Amy had been offered other parts in radio drama and Mike's career looked set to flourish too. He was getting regular news assignments and there was talk of promoting him to television, where his good looks and pleasing personality would be ideally suited. It seemed that the future was rosy for her little family. She was reminded sharply of her marriage to Tom Jessop back in the early thirties. The world had changed so much in the past two decades. Pray God there would be no poverty to sour love for Amy and Mike as it had soured theirs; that there would be no wars to tear them apart and rip away their roots. They deserved an assured future, after they had all fought for it so long and hard and bitterly.

402

But what of her own future? Where did she go from here?

Maryan looked into the water of the little pool pensively. Vinnie and she had seen each other from time to time over the past months. His divorce had come through recently and he had driven out to Hackney to ask her to marry him. Her refusal had shaken him badly.

'I won't pretend I haven't thought about it, Vinnie,' she told him. 'But I've made up my mind that marriage isn't for me. Sam is going to need help with Feldman's. A lot of help. He isn't as young as he was and Rachel's health is poor. She needs him with her. Now that I know that Feldman's will pass to Mark some day, I want to make sure that when he's ready to take over it's still flourishing.'

He looked at her and the hurt disappointment in his dark eyes tore at her heart. 'Of course, I understand that,' he said. 'I'm not asking you to come back and work with Roisan and me, much as I would like that. I just want us to be together, Maryan; to be married. I've always wanted that – more than anything in the world. You know I have.'

'*Have* you?' Maryan looked into his eyes. She couldn't find it in her heart to tell him that she no longer felt able to trust his love and his promises; that she thought him weak for taking back a wife who used and almost ruined him. She loved him still, it was true; loved him too much to risk the heartbreak of being let down again.

'Why won't you marry me, Maryan?' he asked. '*Why*, now that I'm free and we've waited so long?'

'I'm trying to fulfil the family obligations that I should have fulfilled long ago,' she told him truthfully. 'I have so much to make up to Amy. I may not be able to give as much of myself to the marriage as I'd want to.'

He took her hand. 'I'll take whatever there is,' he said. 'I'd rather that than lose you.'

'You won't lose me,' she told him with a smile. 'I'll always be there. We've been friends for too long not to go on seeing each other.'

But somehow it hadn't worked out like that. Since her refusal there had been a barrier between them. She hadn't meant to make him feel rejected, but he was clearly hurt and upset. She hated the feeling of estrangement, but she wasn't sure what she could do about it.

'So this is where you are.' She looked up to see Sam looking down at her. He lowered himself onto the seat beside her. 'I saw you creep away from the festivities and I wondered if you were all right.'

She smiled and tucked her hand into his arm. 'Bless you, Sam. I'm fine. I just wanted some fresh air and time to think.'

'About – what?' He cocked an enquiring eyebrow at her. 'Maryan, is there something you want to talk about? You know I'm always ready to listen.'

'I know you are, Sam. No. It's nothing you can help with.'

'I thought you might have something to tell me,' he prompted.

She looked at him in surprise. 'Tell you?'

He gave her hand a little squeeze. 'My dear, I know something has been troubling you lately and I think I might have guessed what it is. Do you want to go back to work for Vincent Donlan?'

Her eyebrows rose. 'No. Whatever makes you think that?'

He lifted his shoulders expressively. 'I'm not blind, my dear. Vincent is free to marry now. You'll be making plans. And a man's wife should work at his side if she works at all.'

'I'm not going to marry Vinnie,' she said quietly. 'So it doesn't arise.'

'He hasn't asked you?'

'Oh, he's asked me. It's just that I've decided not to.'

'I see.' For a moment he was silent. Then . . . 'You can tell a nosey old man to mind his own business if you like, but – do you want to tell me the reason?'

Maryan sighed. 'It's complicated. There are so many, Sam. We fell in love while he was still married but separated. That was wrong, I know. But although his wife had let him down, left him for another man, he took her back without question, without thinking of what it did to me. Oh, yes, I know that he's Catholic, and divorce is against his religion. But he had lapsed, Sam. He didn't even go to church regularly any more.'

'And you feel that made him – what, weak – unreliable?' He looked at her. 'You're afraid he might let you down – hurt you again?' He took her hand and held it tightly in his. 'My dear, I believe we've known one another long enough for me to give you the benefit of my years – yes?' He looked into her face and she nodded. 'Our religion frowns on divorce too. This is a matter of culture rather than actual religion. It's ingrained – in the roots. Marriage is for ever, a commitment. To hold to that isn't weakness. Being loyal to a wife who is bad takes strength, sacrifice and a great deal of fortitude. Vincent must have suffered so much, losing you. Must you punish him still?'

'There's Amy and Mark to think of too,' she said. 'I want to be a proper mother to Amy. I want to protect Mark's inheritance and make sure that Feldman's is a flourishing business for him when he's ready to take over.'

'And for this you would sacrifice the rest of your life?' Sam shook his head. 'My dear, you're still young. Young enough even to have another child, if that is what you wish. Don't live your life for those who are to come. Live it for yourself. For *now*. Amy is married to a good man who loves her. She'll be fine. And for all we know Mark might want to do something entirely different when he's a man. And if he does, then we must let him. We must do what we can – be there to support and to love. We can give them the benefit of our experience, but we can't live their lives for them. I learned that lesson long ago.'

For a moment they were silent, both of them thinking of Marcus. Then she looked at him tentatively. 'So – you think I should marry Vinnie?'

He smiled gently. 'I think that this time you should do what your heart tells you,' he said. 'You've been through so much, Maryan. You've loved and lost, kept your true feelings hidden from everyone and put yourself last. You've tried so hard to please and serve everyone else all your life, and you haven't always been rewarded as you should. Now it's time to please yourself.' He bent to plant a kiss on her cheek. 'Follow your heart, my dear. Take the happiness you deserve – with my blessing.'

When they went back into the house everyone had gathered in the hall, waiting for the newlyweds, who were about to leave for their honeymoon.

When they appeared at the top of the stairs Amy's eyes shone with happiness and Maryan felt her heart swell as she looked at her daughter, lovely in her lemon suit and the little straw boater trimmed with daisies. Mike looked so proud and happy at her side too. Catching her mother's eye, Amy tossed her posy to the waiting guests and Maryan caught it, blushing at the laughter of the other guests around her.

As they were about to get into their car out on the drive, Amy put her arms around Maryan and hugged her.

'Thanks for everything, Mum. I don't know what I'd have done without you this past year. And you and Auntie Marjorie have given us a wedding we'll always remember. I'm so happy.' Pressing her lips close to her mother's ear she whispered, '*I love you.*'

As the car drove away and the others turned back into the house, laughing and chatting, Maryan stood alone at the gate, watching the car until it was out of sight. Amy had said, *I love you.* Could she possibly know how much that meant to her? It was the first time she'd ever heard her say it. And she knew it came from her heart.

She felt an arm encircle her shoulders and turned to see Vinnie smiling down at her.

'Sam Leigh has just given me a mysterious message,' he said. 'He said you wanted to see me. When I asked him why, he said he had an idea that you'd come to an important decision.'

She smiled. 'Dear Sam. I believe he can see inside my mind sometimes.'

'So it's true?' He looked into her eyes hopefully. 'You do have something to tell me?'

'Yes.' She smiled up at him. 'I think I might just have made the most important decision of my life.' Reaching up, she drew his head down to hers, and as their lips met and his arms closed around her she knew that she had no need to tell him what it was.

You have been reading a novel published by Piatkus Books. We hope you have enjoyed it and that you would like to read more of our titles. Please ask for them in your local library or bookshop.

If you would like to be put on our mailing list to receive details of new publications, please send a large stamped addressed envelope (UK only) to:

Piatkus Books: 5 Windmill Street
London W1P 1HF

PIATKUS

The sign of a good book